BODIES, BADDIES AND A CF

A BLISS BAY VILLAGE M
BOOK 1

Sherri Bryan

CONTENTS

DEDICATION

To my wonderful Dad,
Who fought so hard to stay.

CHAPTER ONE

In the village of Bliss Bay, there was trouble afoot.

Murder, to be precise.

At the Laugh Till You Cry Comedy Club, Detective Sergeant Harvey Decker pulled on a forensic suit and rocked back and forth on the balls of his size-eleven feet.

"It wouldn't surprise me to learn there's a whole list of people who held a grudge against Andy. I heard he had trouble with a few customers over the years, not to mention all the villagers who were against him when he bought this place."

The wind howled and gusted as horizontal rain lashed the windowpanes. Far away, thunder rumbled above the grey clouds as the crime scene photographer snapped his last shot. For the Scene of Crime Officers, who moved in to hunt for any forensic evidence left behind by the killer, it was just another day at the office.

"Well, someone obviously isn't very fond of him, or he wouldn't be slumped over a table with a foot-long pole sticking out of his chest." Detective Inspector Sam Cambridge blew out a measured sigh. He took a step forward from his vantage point and looked at the deceased through narrowed lids. "It looks like a stake someone would use to support a sapling or shrub. Or something beans would grow up, maybe. Definitely something you'd use in a garden, I'd say."

"I'm impressed, boss." Harvey grinned. "I didn't know you knew so much about the great outdoors."

Sam shot his sergeant an incredulous glance, his eyebrows arching over a steely-blue glare. "If you think someone's garden qualifies as the great outdoors, lad, you need to get out in the world a bit more," he said, with a shake of his head. "And, for your information, I happen to enjoy a bit of gardening when I get the time. Not that I often *get* the time, mind you."

Harvey leaned closer to the body and peered at what appeared to be particles of bright yellow powder on its cheek. "What do you suppose that is?"

"No idea," said Sam, "but no doubt we'll find out when forensics have finished doing what they need to." He scratched his jaw, shaded by stubble because he hadn't had time to shave before leaving the house, his gaze coming to rest on the recently departed.

Five years previously, ex-prison officer, Andy Cochran had caused uproar in the village when he'd bought the derelict Bliss Bay fire station and turned it into a live comedy venue.

Situated on the outskirts of the village, it was far enough away from any residential area not to be a nuisance to anyone, but many of the villagers had vehemently opposed it nevertheless.

Had one of them taken a grudge too far?

Sam stared out of the window at the rain bouncing off the pavements and adjusted the hood of the ill-fitting forensic suit that hung off his wiry frame.

The word 'murder' didn't belong in the same sentence as 'Bliss Bay'.

Village crime was usually of a petty nature. Village crime didn't usually upset the balance of the community, or give the residents undue cause for concern.

Andy, however, was the victim of a crime that would most certainly cause undue concern amongst the locals once word got out.

From the first day of opening, he'd quickly gained a reputation for having little patience with customers who didn't follow his rules – *No Spitting, No Throwing Glasses, No Fighting, No Arguing With the Staff* – and had taken great pleasure in forcibly ejecting anyone who thought they were above them. As far as Andy was concerned, his club was no place for troublemakers.

It was fair to say that, over the years, he'd most likely acquired more than a handful of enemies from careers past, and most recent.

"Who found him?" Sam called across to Fred Denby, the village police constable who'd been the first to attend the scene, and was standing guard at the entrance to the club.

"Mary Tang, boss. She cleans in the morning and works behind the bar three evenings a week. She had a terrible shock when she came in at five-past seven this morning."

"Yes, I can imagine. Did she say anything that might help us find out who did this?"

The constable scratched the end of his bulbous nose with his pen and flicked back in his notebook. "Well, I don't know how useful it'll be, but she mentioned that his gold earring was missing. It had a microphone hanging off it, apparently."

"A microphone?"

PC Denby cleared his throat. "She said, 'I saw Andy at around ten-past twelve, just before he closed up. I was the last person to leave the club. When I got here this morning and saw him, I screamed the place down. When I got closer, I could see it was too late to help him so I called the police right away. While I was waiting, I noticed that he wasn't wearing his earring – it was a gold hoop with a microphone charm hanging off it. We all clubbed together and bought it for his birthday. It was perfect for him because we used to call him Mr Mike – he'd get on the mike and warm up the crowd before the comedians came on to do their turns, you see. He always wore it. That's why I noticed it was missing.'" PC Denby snapped his notebook shut. "That's all, boss. She was too upset to say much more."

"Was the door open when she arrived?"

"No, it was closed, but not locked. Apart from Mary, Andy had the only other set of keys and they're still attached to his belt."

Sam Cambridge looked over to the body again. "Get statements from all the staff and find out from someone if Andy Cochran had a partner or any family we need to break the news to. I have a feeling this is going to be a very long day."

CHAPTER TWO
Two months later
Megan Fallon pushed on her glasses and shook out the letter in front of her.

"'I love you, Megan, but you've lost your spark. The hours you work have put so much pressure on you – and on us – and too much work and no play... Well, you know what they say.

"'I'm tired of you being away at conferences, staying late at the office, bringing work home at weekends, and stressing out because you can't get the department budget to balance – it's not fair on me.

"'And as for that useless boss of yours, why you insist on staying up until all hours writing her presentations so she can look good and take all the credit, heaven only knows. The trouble with you is you've always been too soft, and too scared to say 'no'. It's about time you stopped letting people walk all over you. All that extra work you take on is the reason you're always so tired when you get home.

"'Anyway, I think it's fair to say that any sizzle we might have had fizzled out long ago. It's not fair to expect either of us to carry on in a relationship with no passion and spontaneity, so I think it's best if we call it a day.

"'I know that people will be quick to tell you why they think I left, so I want you to hear the real reason from me. While you were away, I popped into *The Snippety Snip* for a haircut and got talking to Mario. You know he's been so lonely since he lost his wife, and I've been lonely, too, with just my memoirs for company. We chatted for so long, we carried on our conversation over coffee after he finished work. By the end of the evening, it was as if we'd known each other for years – we just clicked. He's such a free spirit – being in his company makes me feel like I don't have a care in the world.

"'I want you to know there's no romance with Mario, just companionship, and a wonderful friendship. When he read the first draft of *Finding Hugh*, it was as though he really 'got' me – do you know what I mean? I'm so sorry to hurt you, but Mario's made me realise how much more there is to life than just being a househusband in London for the rest of my days. We'll be leaving for Italy at the end of the week to go to his house in Tuscany – he's invited a group of us over for the summer. Tuscany! I'm pinching myself!

"'By now, you've probably realised that I've moved all my stuff out, and I won't be coming back to the house – I think it will be too painful for both of us. I hope we can stay friends, though?

"'Take care, Megan. I hope you'll take some time to have a serious think about what you want from life, otherwise you're going to be alone for a very long time. You need to stop being scared of your own shadow and start standing up for yourself. The sooner you do, and the sooner you realise there's more to life than work, the happier you'll be.

"'Anyway, must dash, heaps to do. Much love, Hugh. xx PS – The engagement ring is yours, so please do with it whatever you see fit.'"

Megan tossed her dark hair over her shoulder, and the letter she'd read across the breakfast bar to her sister, Lizzie. "'You've lost your spark'. Ugh. Can you believe the nerve of the guy?" She pulled off her glasses, letting them dangle by the cord around her neck. "When he wanted to give up his job so he could write his flippin' memoirs, did I complain? No, I didn't. I *wanted* him to follow his dream, so I encouraged him and worked my backside into the ground to provide for us – it's no wonder my spark went AWOL. And I never *once* heard him complain about the money I was earning so he could spend all day writing and emptying the fridge."

Brown eyes flashing, she paced the kitchen tiles with a slice of garlic bread in her hand, ripping into the crust with her teeth and sending crumbs scattering to the floor.

"And then he leaves me this letter to find when I come home after I've lost my job, and he's run off with my hairdresser. *My* hairdresser. The man I used to tell all my secrets to. The irony of it."

Lizzie twirled spaghetti around her fork. "I wish I could be more sympathetic, but I think it's the best thing that could have happened. Hugh was never right for you, he was far too selfish. Pleasant enough, but everything always had to be about him. Thank God this happened before you got married. You've already got one divorce under your belt – probably best to keep it at that. And it's a good thing this is your house. At least you won't have to go through all the hassle of dividing everything between you." She sucked in a runaway strand of pasta and dabbed a serviette to her lips before pouring two glasses of wine.

"And how *dare* he say I let people walk all over me," Megan continued, her indignation and her voice reaching new heights. "He makes me sound like a pushover."

Lizzie pushed the cork back into the wine bottle and chose her words carefully. "Well, you do let people take advantage of you a bit. You were supposed to be an event organiser but you're so good-natured, you got roped into organising the entire office, just so that lazy-as-sin boss of yours could spend all day sitting on her bum and looking good while you were running around like a maniac. You've got to admit, Hugh was right about that, if nothing else. You always say 'yes' to everything and end up with far too much on your plate. Sometimes, 'no' can be a very useful little word, y'know."

Megan opened her mouth, then shut it again. Lizzie was right. Hugh was right. She'd become a downtrodden, all-work-and-no-play, bore. And what had she to show for it? No job and no fiancé. Although, as consolation, she had a pretty nice payoff for all her hard work.

"And I know it's easy for me to say," Lizzie continued, "but I hope you're not going to waste your whole summer moping because you're going to miss him."

Megan popped the last piece of garlic bread into her mouth and drummed her fingernails on the kitchen counter. "Of *course* I'm going to miss him!" Picking up her glass, she ran a finger around the rim. "No one can do highlights like Mario."

Lizzie chuckled and tucked a blonde tress behind her ear. "That's the spirit! I'm glad you haven't lost your sense of humour."

Megan flopped down onto a stool. "Huh, don't believe I haven't come close. I've had better weeks. First Evie goes off on her gap year to the other side of the world, then I lose my job, and then I find out my fiancé would rather be with Mario than Megan. Talk about bad timing." She took a deep breath, blinked back the deluge of tears that threatened to spill, and gulped her wine. "Anyway, I've done enough feeling sorry for myself. I'm almost forty, for goodness' sake, not a love-struck teenager. I've cried all the tears I'm going to cry. No more."

Lizzie squeezed her hand. "I know I only live half an hour away but I'm sorry I couldn't get here before tonight. There was no way I could leave before school finished – we were so crazy busy organising end-of-term activities for the kids. And I couldn't leave before Shaun went off to summer camp. Poor guy, he's going to need a holiday when he gets back after spending ten days camping with a bunch of eight-year olds. And poor you, having to go through everything without me."

"Ah, don't worry about it," said Megan. "I wouldn't have been the best company if you *had* been here. You know what I feel really bad about, though? Now I've had some time to think things over, I think I'm going to miss the job more than I'm going to miss Hugh. We both knew things hadn't been right between us for ages but we were avoiding talking about it. If I'm honest, it wasn't really a surprise that he ended it. But the job. I *loved* that job."

Lizzie slid off her stool and put her plate in the sink. "Well, you'll get a better job. One you love even more than the last. One that'll

give you more time to enjoy life. Don't worry –
everything's going to be fine."

"I know... I know it is," said Megan. "It's
just going to take some getting used to. I got
complacent and I shouldn't have. I thought
Hugh and the job were permanent fixtures but
now they've both gone, it's a bit scary. It's
ridiculous to feel so vulnerable at my age, but
you know how long it took me to get over what
happened with Laurence. What I should have
done was stay in Bliss Bay and deal with it, not
run away like a wuss."

"I don't think anyone would blame you
for not wanting to hang around after what
happened with your rat of an ex-husband,"
said Lizzie, an eyebrow raised in stern,
schoolmistress fashion. "And as for that witch
of a wife of his, well, the less said about Kelly,
the better."

"Hmm, you're probably right," said
Megan, "but I still wish I hadn't been so quick
to leave. The way things were left with Kelly
still bothers me. I should have stayed and had
it out with her. If I had, I'm sure I wouldn't feel
so nauseous every time I think about going
back to Bliss Bay which, incidentally, I
promised Mum and Dad I'd do soon. Maybe
I'll find a job first and then go down to see
them." She leaned her elbows on the counter,
resting her chin on clasped hands.

"Look," said Lizzie. "There's no rush to do anything, is there? You've got a nice redundancy package, so take a breath, and some time to think about what you really want to do. Don't go rushing into a job for the sake of it. This is the time to think about *you*. To get your confidence up and your life back on track. Trust me, Meg, once you get *you* sorted out, the rest will fall into place. And don't be so hard on yourself because you're feeling vulnerable. We all do, sometimes." She planted a kiss on her sister's cheek. "Now, come on, let's have a toast to the future."

Megan smiled as they touched their glasses together but as she climbed the stairs to bed later that evening, she couldn't stop the churning in the pit of her stomach. She was a thirty-nine year old, unemployed, divorced, single parent. Not that being divorced, single, or a parent were problems, but the thought of job-hunting against competition half her age filled her with absolute dread.

She took off her makeup and looked at the face staring back at her; a little tired, a few fine lines where she'd rather there were none, and pale shadows under her eyes due to a run of sleepless nights but, all in all, not too bad for almost forty.

I might lack assertiveness and youth, but I've got a ton of experience. Surely that still has to count for something these days?

Throwing back the duvet, she laid her cheek on the cool cotton pillowcase. As her eyelids dropped, her phone bleeped, alerting her to an incoming Skype call.

"Hey, Mum, just checking in. How're you doing?"

Evie's face went in and out of focus as the screen froze and the picture broke up.

"Oh, I'm fine, darling. Everything's fine. It's so good to see you. How's life down-under?"

"O.M.G, it's *awesome*! You must try to get over here some time now you're single. Speaking of which, I hope you're not wasting any tears over that moron. He's so not worth it."

"No, sweetie, I'm not. I promise. Your Aunty Lizzie's finished school now so she's staying for a while, and we've set the world to rights this evening, so all's well. Anyway, what are you up to?"

"Well, it's eleven in the morning and we're getting ready to go skiing. Not sure where, exactly, but the mountains are a-ma-zing. Oh my gosh, Mum, even though it's winter, this place is soooo beautiful. You'd adore it here. Oh, hang on a second. Look, I've got to go, okay, but I'll speak to you soon."

"Okay, sweetie, but listen, you don't have to keep checking in to see if I'm alright," said Megan. "All I want is for you to enjoy yourself and stop worrying about me. Okay?"

"Okay. Gotta run. Give Aunty Lizzie a hug from me. Love you loads, Mum."

"Love you more, sweetheart. Take care. And have fun. And be careful. Oh, and don't forget to turn your toes in if you want to slow down," said Megan, the smile fixed on her face until the screen froze again and the connection dropped out. *Or, better still, forget the skiing, make yourself a hot chocolate and curl up in front of a blazing fire with a good book instead.* The thought of Evie hurtling down a mountainside at warp speed made her feel breathless. And not in a good way.

She had a little sniffle and blew her nose before settling down again, her eyes falling on the diamond solitaire she'd taken off the week before and left in a trinket dish on the bedside table. She'd been wondering what to do with it and, all at once, she knew.

I'm going to sell it and send the money to Evie. I can't think of a better use for it. In fact, I'll do it tomorrow.

She snuggled down, happy with her decision, and with a smile on her lips, closed her eyes. Her last thought before drifting off to sleep was, *All I need to do now is get on with the rest of my life. Maybe a change of scenery and something fun and exciting. Yes, a little excitement's just what I need.*

CHAPTER THREE

"Megan. *Megan*! Wake up! Mum's on the phone."

Megan opened a bleary eye to see Lizzie's freckled face inches from hers and was out of bed in a second.

"What? What's happened? Is Dad okay?"

"Dad's fine." Lizzie couldn't keep the smile from her lips. "But you need to speak to Mum." She thrust her phone into Megan's hands and dropped, cross-legged, onto the bed. "I'm staying here. I can't wait to see your face when you hear what she's got to tell you."

"Mum?" Megan's voice was wary. "What's going on?"

"Oh, darling, I'm sorry to call so early but your father and I were so excited, we couldn't wait to tell you the news."

"News? What kind of news is so exciting that it can't wait until after..." she squinted at her alarm clock, "ten-to seven on a Thursday morning?" She rubbed her eyes and yawned, her mouth suddenly snapping shut. "Oh my God! You're not expecting, are you? I was only reading an article the other day about the surge in older mothers."

Claudia Fallon clicked her tongue. "Megan, be sensible. As wonderful as that would be, I'm going to be sixty-four next month and even if I could, there's no way these hips could manage another child. No, of course I'm not expecting." Her voice became muffled as she put her hand over the mouthpiece and Megan could hear that she was calling her husband to the phone. "I'm going to put your dad on the line. *I* told Lizzie, so it's only fair that *he* tells you."

Megan heard her dad's voice, as deep and reassuring as it had been for as long as she could remember.

"Hello, love. Sorry to drag you out of bed." Nick Fallon's apology was sincere. "I assume that's where you were at this ungodly hour of the morning?"

"Never mind the time, Dad, will you please just tell me what's going on?"

"Ah, yes. Well, your mother and I... well, we've decided to renew our marriage vows."

"*What*?" Megan immediately burst into tears. "Dad, that's wonderful!"

"Oh, love, I'm sorry, I didn't mean to upset you."

"No, no, you haven't. In fact, it's the best news I've had in ages." Megan grabbed Lizzie's hand and sat next to her on the bed. "When? Where? Ohmigosh, I've got a hundred questions!"

"Weellll." Nick drew out the word. "That's part of what we wanted to speak to you about. We've been talking about doing it for ages, you see, but we only decided for sure yesterday afternoon."

"I can't tell you how exciting this is," said Megan. "It's going to be amazing. Is it going to be before Evie gets back?"

"What, before next July? Um, yes. Yes, it is."

Megan massaged her temple. "Shall I fly her home?"

"Good grief, no," said Nick. "Let her enjoy herself. She's only just left – I'm sure the last thing she'll want to do is come all the way back to see two old fogeys renew their wedding vows. No, tell her by all means, but don't put any pressure on her. If she wants to come back that's another matter but, otherwise, we can show her the photos."

"Hmm, I suppose." Megan made a mental note to check flight prices from New Zealand. "So, are you going to arrange it for when you get back from your cruise? Or have you not decided on a date yet?"

"Er, yes, we have." Nick cleared his throat. "It's the 16th of August."

Megan took a moment to process the information. "August? What? As in next month?"

"Yes, love, *this* August."

"But that's just over three weeks away!" Megan squeaked. "I'm *so* excited!"

"I know it's short notice," said Nick, "but we thought that as we've had the cruise booked for months, why not renew our vows before we go and, that way, it'll be like a honeymoon? We didn't have much of a honeymoon when we got married, y'see. We couldn't afford one so we went to stay with your Grandma for a week. Not the most romantic time, I seem to recall. It rained every day, the house stunk of boiled offal the entire time, and she kept walking into the bedroom, unannounced, with cups of cocoa." He chuckled. "Anyway, we thought we'd treat ourselves this time round."

"Well, I think it's a great idea," said Megan. "You can... Hang on, if you and Mum only decided yesterday afternoon that you're going to renew your vows, how have you managed to get everything organised so quickly?"

"Well, ahem, it's like this, you see," said Nick, his voice sheepish. "We haven't actually organised *anything* yet because we thought *you* might like to do it for us. We don't want a big do – just a small get-together at home with a few friends, so it's not as though you'd have to book a church, or even anyone from the church to officiate. There are no legal implications for a vow renewal, so we can choose whomever we'd like to carry out the

ceremony. We thought we'd ask Des. Hello...
Hello... You still there, Megan?"

Megan found her tongue. "Des? *Uncle
Des?* Dad, have you lost your marbles?"

Her most harrowing recollection of her
wayward uncle came from her wedding. It had
been her dream day: the man she loved,
friends and family by her side, a beautiful
dress and a fabulous venue. When it had
started to snow, her final wish for her winter
December wedding had come true.

What she hadn't wished for, though,
was her Uncle Des getting blotto.

So blotto, he'd strip naked and slide
down the sweeping banister of the elegant art-
deco hotel and crash onto the piano in the
lobby, where one-hundred and twenty guests
were enjoying canapés and a Champagne
reception.

She winced as she recalled the hotel's
ancient resident pianist having to be revived
with smelling salts and much wafting of
wedding hats, her ivory-tinkling cut short
halfway through her rendition of *The Way You
Look Tonight.*

That, in itself, had been bad enough, but
the banister had been decorated with garlands
of poinsettias, white roses and holly.

Though many years had passed since
that day, and some memories had faded, the
one which remained crystal clear – despite

having tried to erase it from her mind countless times – was of Des being carted off to the Accident and Emergency department, wrapped in a tablecloth, and belting his way through the entire soundtrack of *West Side Story*. As her mother had said at the time, "You know, sweetheart, there are some things you just wish you could un-see."

In spite of Megan's resistance to the idea of Des officiating at the ceremony, Nick continued with his charm offensive,

"Oh, come on, love. Des doesn't touch a drop of alcohol since he had that diabetes scare a couple of years ago; he literally stopped drinking overnight. And Sylvie's had him keeping fit and eating healthy. Honestly, it's great to see him back to how he used to be. He's playing his harmonica after I don't know how long, and he's even started baking again. There's a lot to be said for sobriety, you know. Really, Megan, you need to give him a chance.

"Anyway, what with you losing your job and all that business with Hugh, your Mum and I thought you organising the ceremony was the ideal solution. It'll help keep your mind off what happened and you can earn a bit of money at the same time. I know it's small fry compared to those big corporate events you're used to but if you'd like to do it, you can help us, and we can help you."

"Well, I'm not taking any money from you," said Megan, a slight huff to her voice. "I might be unemployed, Pops, but I've still got my pride you know."

Nick sighed. "Listen, I'm not going to debate it with you over the phone. Why don't you and Lizzie come down and we can talk about it? Honestly, love, we're not *just* asking you because of your situation, we're asking you because there isn't anyone else we'd rather organise this for us. We would never have mentioned it if you'd still been working – you simply wouldn't have had the time – but if you *could* do it, it will make it even more special. Come and see us, and we'll have a chat about it. Will you do that?"

"Well, I'll have to, won't I?" said Megan. "I've only got three weeks to get everything organised."

"So you'll do it then?" Nick's sigh of relief filled her ear like the sound of the sea through a conch shell.

Megan laughed. "Oh, come on, Dad – of course I'll do it! I'd be honoured to."

"That's fantastic, love! In that case, can you and Lizzie come down for the weekend? She's staying with you for a while, isn't she? Get here when you can and stay for as long as you need to arrange things. Or longer, if you like. We'll talk about it when we see you."

The joviality left Nick's voice and he spoke again with a solemn tone. "What about Laurence and Kelly, though? Are you going to be okay coming back here with them being so close by?"

At the mention of her ex-husband and his wife, Megan hid her true feelings and snorted with disdain. "Of course I am. Don't even give them a second thought. Anyway, it's not like I haven't seen Laurence since I left Bliss Bay – I've had to because of Evie – I just haven't seen him recently. Really, Dad, don't worry about it."

"You're sure?"

"Positive."

"Okay. We don't want things to be awkward for you but you probably won't even cross paths. We see Kelly every now and then because she works at the bank, but we hardly ever see Laurence, and they only live twenty minutes away. Anyway, I'd better go, love, we've got a busy day and we want to get out early."

"Okay, bye Dad. We'll see you soon. Yes, love you too."

Megan ended the call and stared at her sister. They clung onto each other and bounced on the bed, squealing with delight. "This is going to be bloody *brilliant!*"

"And talk about fate," said Lizzie. "The perfect job just fell right into your lap!" She yawned and stretched. "Oh my, all this excitement has worn me out. I'm going back to bed for an hour or two. I'll see you later."

Megan nodded. "Yeah, see you later."

Far too excited to go back to sleep, she grabbed the pen and large notebook that went everywhere with her, and propped herself up against her pillows.

As her organiser mentality kicked in, her mind ticked over and she scribbled endless notes on a rough timeline, working backwards from the big day to make sure that everything would be ready in time.

When she'd done as much as she could, she put down her pen and massaged the knots in her neck. As she ran downstairs, she felt happier than she had in ages. Her mood had lifted as soon as she'd picked up her pen and started to make plans. When she was working, she felt confident and in control. So in control, that even the prospect of seeing her ex-husband didn't bother her too much.

Seeing his wife was a different matter altogether, though...

When Megan was nine, she was chosen as Bliss Bay's Carnival Queen.

Most of the village had been thrilled for her.

However, when news of the decision reached her classmate, Kelly DeVille, a full-blown, foot-stamping meltdown in the village hall had ensued. In Kelly's eyes, *she* was the only person worthy of that title.

As the procession had snaked its way through the village, with Megan smiling and waving from the principal float, her blood had run cold when she spotted Kelly in the crowd, glaring at her with hate-filled eyes and an expression that left Megan in no doubt of her dark and vengeful mood.

For the rest of that summer, Kelly went out of her way to make Megan's life as miserable as possible, bullying and taunting her until she was reluctant to leave the safe haven of home without Lizzie or her parents.

The resentment intensified in following years, the rift between them becoming a canyon as one-time friend Kelly grew meaner, never missing an opportunity to bring Megan down with a snide remark or physical force.

Megan still bore the scar on her chin from the afternoon they'd found themselves sheltering in the same café during a summer downpour. Kelly had stuck out her foot, tripping Megan, who'd crashed face-first into the jukebox and sliced open her chin after inadvertently using it to select song number B43.

The pain was overshadowed by the embarrassment of her skirt ending up around her waist, and being hauled to her feet by

Laurence Ford, captain of the Bliss Bay over-18s cricket team, and resident Romeo.

No one was more surprised than Megan when, despite her parents' misgivings, she and Laurence fell madly in love and married a year later, their daughter, Evie, following a year after that.

Unfortunately, despite his marriage vows to be a faithful husband, Laurence's roving eye never stopped swivelling in its socket, eventually settling on Kelly DeVille. He blamed getting married to Megan at such a young age as the reason for needing to sow his wild oats elsewhere.

As soon as she found out about his infidelity, Megan packed her bags, picked up her daughter, and left Bliss Bay. She would never forget Laurence's words when she told him she was leaving. "It's probably for the best, sweetheart... I thought marriage would be more fun than this."

Over the years she'd been back and forth, taking Evie to see her grandparents, and for visits with Laurence during school holidays, but the prospect of returning now, on her own, made her want to throw up.

She'd only ever told Lizzie that every time she returned to Bliss Bay, her stomach was in a permanent state of knots for fear of coming face-to-face with her childhood nemesis. The thought of a possible confrontation made her stomach flip-flop and her anxiety levels shoot skyward. She didn't have the temperament, the resolve, nor the confidence, to deal with Kelly's spiteful grudge.

She shuddered and took a deep calming breath before flopping onto a stool at the breakfast bar. *This is ridiculous. I refuse to spend every minute I'm in Bliss Bay looking over my shoulder. Once the ceremony's out of the way, I'm just going to get on with things without worrying about whether I'm going to bump into Kelly. If I do, I'll just have to deal with it. We're adults now, for goodness' sake. What's the worst that could happen?*

She shuddered again.

Not wanting to spend a second longer thinking negative, happiness-sucking thoughts, she thanked her good fortune and filled the coffee machine instead. She was going to need numerous jugs of the caffeine-laced brew to sustain her while she transcribed her scribbled notes into something more legible.

Things were definitely looking up.

CHAPTER FOUR

"Mum sounded like she was about to hyperventilate when I spoke to her last night and I was only calling to tell her what time to expect us," said Megan, as she came off the motorway and headed for Bliss Bay.

"Well, you know how excited she gets when we go home." Lizzie leaned forward and fiddled with the radio of the ancient red mini. "Especially you. I see them all the time but you haven't had a long visit for ages." She gave an exasperated sigh. "I give up. Every time I try to tune this flippin' radio to another station, all I get is static. I can't believe you've still got this car – it must be over twenty years old. I'm amazed it hasn't been relegated to the scrap heap."

"Yes, I know," said Megan, patiently, "but I can't get rid of him, can I? You *know* when Evie was little, she used to say Vinnie instead of mini. She named him, and he's part of her history. It would break my heart to sell him."

Lizzie rolled her eyes. "It's not a 'him', Meg, it's a car. A really *old* car. Don't you think it'd be nice to use some of your redundancy money to treat yourself? Just think, you could even join the 21st century and buy a car with a radio you don't have to wind up before you can listen to it."

"Haha, very funny. I'm not about to blow a big chunk of money on a car I don't need when there's absolutely nothing wrong with this one. It's been in the garage for years so there's no rust on it, and it was purring like a kitten after the first blast with the jump leads. I'll admit, it's a bit like going back in time after driving a company car for so long, but I love this little mini. And, for your information, I never have any trouble getting the radio to work." Megan touched her fingers to the dial and Elton John crooning a ballad immediately blared from the speakers. "See. Vinnie the Mini never lets me down."

They zoomed along the narrow south Devon lanes, whizzing past patchwork fields, bluebell-clad banks, and random bursts of colour from the wild flowers that pushed their way through the hedgerows.

"You know Mum's going to make a fuss, don't you?" said Lizzie. "When she called, she was pumping me for information, wanting to know how you're holding up. It breaks her heart to think of you on your own, especially after what happened with Laurence. I mean, she still hasn't come to terms with him doing the dirty on you, and that was seventeen years ago. Given the chance, she'd throttle him as soon as look at him. And I swear, if she ever gets her hands on Hugh, he'll be singing soprano for the rest of his life."

"Yeah, I know she's worried," said Megan, with a frown. "When I called to tell her Hugh and I had split, she squawked so much she almost laid an egg. She probably thinks that now I don't have a husband, a boyfriend *or* a job, I'm going to turn into a lonely, shrivelled old hag, with only my daughter and my kindly sister for company."

Lizzie chuckled. "You know, it wouldn't surprise me if Aunty Sylvie tries to fix you up with someone. Remember when you were fifteen, and your date for the end-of-term disco got conjunctivitis at the last minute and couldn't go?"

Megan raised a brow. "How could I forget? Aunty Sylvie got straight on the phone to her Bliss Bay Women's Association pals and, twenty minutes later, the paperboy from the village shop turned up in a pair of jeans halfway down his backside, a sweatshirt the size of a tent, and a back to front baseball cap."

Lizzie giggled. "And when Dad answered the door, the guy just said 'Yo', and gave him a peace sign. What was his name?"

"Barry." said Megan.

"That's it!" Lizzie snorted. "I seem to remember he had about as much charisma as a lump of coal."

"Well, I hope Aunty Sylvie keeps her matchmaking nose out of it. The last thing I need is a man in my life," said Megan, firmly.

"What I *need* is to get back to work. I'm definitely not ready for another relationship – quite the opposite, in fact. I need to get used to being single again. In any case, I'm not going to have any time for men – I'm going to be too busy. It'll be nice to see everyone again, though. Well, *most* people."

Lizzie put a reassuring hand on Megan's arm. "Don't let Kelly get to you, will you? Hopefully, she and Laurence will be so wrapped up in each other, they won't even notice you're back."

Megan's smile waned. "Don't worry, I intend to give both of them as wide a berth as possible. Anyway, all that bad feeling was years ago. I'm sure she won't even give me a second glance if we happen to cross paths." She swallowed, her mouth suddenly dry. "Either way, I don't even want to think about them. I just want to make sure I give Mum and Dad the best day they've ever had, relax for a few weeks, and get my head around what I'm going to do now I've joined the ranks of the unemployed."

"Good for you," said Lizzie. "Any ideas?"

"Something life-changing," replied Megan with a flourish and a grin. "Don't ask me what, though, 'cos I've no idea. I just know I want to put my redundancy money to good use." She slowed the car as the lanes narrowed further, and she and Lizzie craned their necks for the first glimpse of Bliss Bay in the distance.

"We've made really good time," said Lizzie. "It's only taken us a little over four hours."

Megan nodded. "I know it's a pain to drive through the night, but at least we've had a clear run, rather than getting stuck in loads of traffic. You know what it's like in the school holidays – if we'd left it much later, it would have been bumper to bumper all the way."

"Shall we stop for breakfast?" said Lizzie. "At that little place that does the French toast with mushrooms, crispy bacon and grilled tomatoes?"

"I was just thinking the same thing. My stomach's rumbling." Megan took a right turn to the village of Honeymeade, and followed the signs to Joe's Diner. "I fancy a proper fry-up – eggs, bacon, sausages, tomatoes – the full works."

She pulled up behind a solitary open-topped car parked in a bay just a little way down from the diner, its driver lolling sideways in his seat. "He's obviously got the same idea as us," she said. "Looks like he's fallen asleep, though."

Lizzie looked at her watch. "Five-past six. I think it opens at half-past.

"I'm going to stretch my legs," said Megan. "I'll see if the opening hours are on the door." She lifted her arms up over her head and did a couple of bends to loosen up. As she approached the diner, she briefly glimpsed the driver of the other car from the corner of her eye, but ignored him and looked at the notice on the shutter over the door. "Opening hours, 6.30 am to 6.30 pm," she murmured.

A van pulled up behind her car and a man she recognised as Joe, the diner owner, got out.

"Morning, both," he said, his smile reaching from one ear to the other. "If you give me two minutes to get opened up and put the coffee machine on, you can come in and have a cuppa." He looked up the road at the man in his car. "How long's he been here?" he whispered.

Megan and Lizzie shrugged. "No idea. He was here when we arrived. Looks like he's fallen asleep."

"Wouldn't surprise me," said Joe, unloading bags of shopping from the back of his van.

"Are you going to wake him up?" asked Megan.

"Not likely," said Joe. "He can stay asleep until we shut, for all I care. He's a miserable sod. Right, let's get this place open for business."

ooooooo

"Have you decided what you're having yet?" asked Lizzie, when the short-order cook arrived for work, fifteen minutes later.

"Yep, I'm definitely having the full English breakfast," said Megan, scanning the menu once more to make sure she hadn't changed her mind. "I'll go and place the order before anyone else comes in and orders before us. Won't be a sec."

As she approached the counter and saw Joe's face, she knew something was wrong. The cook was talking to him in hushed tones, as white as a sheet and pointing to something outside. The cup Joe was holding slipped from his fingers and smashed on the floor.

Megan's instinct told her not to get involved. She took two steps back with the intention of going back to her seat but when Joe came out from behind the counter and asked if either of them knew any first-aid, Lizzie nodded and rose out of her seat.

"I do. Why? What's up?"

Joe shook his head as he rushed outside. "I don't know, but we might need you. Quickly!"

"What's he talking about?" asked Lizzie, following him. "What's going on out there? Come on, I'm not going on my own." She caught Megan's sleeve and pulled her outside to where Joe and the cook were standing beside the open-topped car.

Megan stole a peek at the sleeping man and her hands flew to her eyes as Lizzie felt for a pulse and shook her head.

"This guy's not asleep... He's dead."

ooooooo

A police constable removed the road block to allow DI Sam Cambridge to drive through.

As he stepped into his forensic suit, he surveyed the grim scene and popped an indigestion tablet out of its plastic bubble, grinding it between his teeth in the hope it would get to work on soothing his acid reflux sooner rather than later. Standing back to allow the Scene of Crime Officers to do their work, he looked over the body of the man in the car.

"Who is he?" he asked DS Harvey Decker. "Do we know?"

"According to his driving licence, the victim's a local resident by the name of Victor Canning, boss. Seventy-four years old."

"Nasty looking wound." Sam gave a cursory nod to the ligature around the deceased's neck. "Anyone see anything?"

Harvey shook his head. "Two women arrived just after six but they thought he was asleep – they could only see him from behind. They're inside if you want a word with them. It wasn't until the cook arrived for work and walked right past the car that anyone realised something was wrong."

"Anything else?"

"Yes. There's yellow powder on his cheek. I'm guessing forensics will find out its pollen, same as they did in Andy Cochran's case, but we'll have to wait and see."

Sam threw back his head and swore silently. "So, what do we know about the victim?"

"Well, Joe – the guy who owns the diner – knew him pretty well. He used to be his first customer every morning and, since he retired, most lunchtimes, too. He'd been coming here for years – even before Joe's time when his dad used to run the diner. And, apparently, he wasn't well-liked, not even back then. Joe said he's not surprised someone's done him in."

"Did he say why?"

"Because he was an objectionable git, not to put too fine a point on it," said Harvey. "According to Joe, Victor Canning was the kind of person who'd force you into moving out of the neighbourhood you'd loved for years if he moved in next door – quite an intimidating character, by all accounts. And he'd often try to leave the diner without paying and was rude to the other customers. He sounds like a real charmer."

Sam shook his head. "He was just sitting in his car. In all my years on the job,

I've never seen what appears to be an unprovoked attack on an elderly man. Maybe he pushed someone too far this time? Did he have a wife, or a partner, do you know?"

"Never married, apparently, and no living family that we know of."

Sam scratched the back of his neck. "Well, I suppose it's possible someone could have bumped him off for being a pain in the backside, but it seems pretty drastic measures to me. Did the guy in the diner say anything else?"

"Only that this is the first time he's ever seen Mr Canning without a bow tie in all the years he's known him."

"A bow tie?"

"Yep. He wore one all the time. People around here used to call him Mr Dickie Bow. He was wearing a yellow one this morning, apparently."

Sam gave Harvey a quizzical look. "How do we know it was yellow if it's missing?"

"Ah, sorry, boss, I forgot to say that Joe saw Mr Canning at around five-thirty this morning when he was on his way to the supermarket. He was turning out of the road as Mr Canning was turning in. He often used to get here early and sit outside in his car until the diner opened. Anyway, that's when Joe saw the bow tie."

Sam called over to the police constable who'd been the first on the scene. "Nothing's been removed from the car, has it?"

"No, Sir. That's exactly as it was when I got here. Why's that?"

"You didn't see a bow tie?"

"No, but I know he used to wear one. He was well-known around here and he always had one on."

Sam cast his eyes over the body again and rubbed at the spot where his glasses pinched the bridge of his nose.

The most serious crime to have occurred in the village of Honeymeade was the theft of a sack of Christmas cards from the village post office. Until recently, murder was unheard of, but this was the second such crime to have been committed in the county in as many months.

Sam glanced over at the car again, its occupant still slumped in his seat.

In the summer, the main industry of the villages in the area was tourism.

The last thing they needed with the holiday season approaching was a killer on the loose.

CHAPTER FIVE

Kismet Cottage, in the village of Bliss Bay, was the Fallon family home.

The last house in a row of ten, it overlooked the village green which, capricious English weather permitting, played host to cricket matches, church fêtes, and Women's Association fundraisers throughout the year. If the rains came down during an event – as they often did – proceedings were swiftly moved into the village hall on the edge of the green, next to which stood the beautiful old St. Mildred's church and cemetery.

Years ago, Nick and Claudia Fallon had bought the cottage at a knockdown price as a home in which to raise their young family. Unable to afford a house with the view they'd always wanted, they'd seen the potential in the cottage and had used most of their savings to extend upwards, the result being that every room on the upper level now enjoyed far-reaching views across the glorious countryside, and the bay that gave the village its name.

As Megan pulled up outside, her dad appeared from around the side of the cottage, his hazel eyes twinkling in his tanned face and a tattered straw boater perched atop his grey curls at the most carefree of angles. He waved a weather-chapped hand above his head, a broad smile creasing his face at the sight of his two daughters.

"Just act normal," whispered Lizzie, out of the corner of her mouth.

The sisters had agreed not to tell their parents about the murder until later, nor that the reason they were two hours late was because they'd been answering endless questions from the police.

"Mum's going to freak out if the first thing we tell her is that we've just seen a dead body."

"Hello, my lovelies." Nick Fallon held out his arms and crushed Megan and Lizzie in the hug he reserved especially for his children. Regardless of their age, neither of them had ever escaped it. "I forgot to ask when you called why you were running late. Did you get stuck in that traffic jam? They've been reporting it on the news since early this morning. They didn't say what's happened but it must be something serious. Is that why you were delayed?"

"Er, kind of," said Lizzie.

"Anyway, never mind about that, you're here now." Nick took off his gardening hat and fanned his face.

"Where's mum?" asked Megan, linking an arm through his.

Lizzie crinkled her nose. "And what's that smell?"

Nick wiggled an eyebrow and gave a rueful smile. "Essential oils. It's your mother's new thing. She's cleansing the house of negative energy. Last time I saw her, she was on her way upstairs spraying everything in sight." He held up a hand. "Don't ask. Why don't you go up? She's dying to see you."

As Megan and Lizzie reached the steep staircase, their old childhood game came back to them immediately.

"First one to make the stairs creak is a numpty," said Lizzie. "I'll go first."

During one particularly rainy school summer holiday, the game was such an obsession that even their parents, aunt, uncle, and visiting friends became infatuated with climbing the staircase from the bottom to the top, learning to avoid every creak and groan on the way. If you failed, you got a point against you and had to go back to the bottom and start again. By the end of the summer, every member of the family was able to scale the stairs at speed, from bottom to top, and back again, without eliciting so much as a squeak from the old boards.

Despite the years that had passed, Megan and Lizzie both climbed the stairs soundlessly, each remembering exactly where not to step.

They followed the herbal aroma and found their mother spraying a fine mist into every corner of Megan's old bedroom.

"Darkness and negativity be gone from our home. Light, love and peace are welcome." She carefully avoided a money spider that lowered itself on a single strand of silken web from the ceiling onto the window sill. "As are you, my little eight-legged friend."

"Hi, Mum." Megan and Lizzie dropped their bags and were caught in their mother's arms seconds later.

What with just having seen a dead body, and not having been in one of her mum's hugs for so long, Megan found she didn't want to let her go. She squeezed her eyes shut to stop the tears from spilling out, and breathed in the scent of the perfume her mum had worn forever.

"Oh, my girls! My darling girls! It's so wonderful to see you. And it's so good to have you home for a while, Meggie. It feels like an age since I last saw you." Claudia Fallon brushed away a happy tear that plopped onto her cheek. "How was the journey? Did you get stuck in that traffic jam? Poor loves, you must be shattered?" As usual, when she was excited, she rattled off questions without waiting for answers. "Let me get rid of this spray bottle and we'll have a proper catch-up."

"What's with the oils?" Megan wiped her eyes and flung open the window to take a gulp of fresh air.

"I've been cleansing the space all over the house to make room for more peace and healing energy – you could do with a bit of both, darling." Claudia resprayed the corners of the room, and gave the space directly above Megan's head a double spritz. "We had a talk at the Women's Association last week by a holistic practitioner – it was absolutely fascinating – and, after she'd finished, she told us about all kinds of natural remedies for all sorts of things. She made up this special blend just for me. Anyway, never mind that. Hurry up and come downstairs and we'll have some breakfast. You didn't stop for anything on the way, did you?"

"We were going to," said Lizzie. "But then we lost our appetites."

"Well, they'll come back as soon as you smell bacon cooking," said Claudia. "I'll go and put some under the grill with some sausages, and you can decide what else you want when you come down. Anyway, don't dawdle, we've got tons to talk about." She gave each of her daughters a loving pinch on the cheek before scurrying from the room, spraying the air as she went.

"We'll have even more to talk about after we tell them what happened this morning," Lizzie muttered.

Megan leaned against the window frame and let her eyes wander. She gazed at the tranquil bay, hugged by the shore and sheltered by the granite crags that soared up to the cloudless sky, the hills that seemed to go on forever, and the coastal paths that meandered down to the beach. She closed her eyes and memories of the happy times she'd spent at the cottage came flooding back.

Why don't I have the guts to come home more often?

"You know, those oils must be working their magic already," she said, as her shoulders dropped. "Even after seeing that poor guy earlier, I feel more relaxed than I have for weeks. And would you look at this view? I forget how beautiful it is."

"Yes, it's gorgeous." Lizzie's efficient voice jolted Megan out of her reminiscing. "But you can look at it another time." She dragged her suitcase into the next-door bedroom. "Come on, hurry up and sort yourself out and then we can tell mum and dad why we were late getting here. The sooner we tell them about it, the sooner we never have to talk about it again."

oooooooo

Nick flicked through the TV channels as he munched on a piece of toast and marmalade.

"Well, they're still not saying anything about a murder on the news. Just that it's a serious incident. Where did you say it was, again?"

"Outside that place we stop at sometimes – Joe's Diner, it's called," said Megan. "In Honeymeade."

Claudia tossed her head. "Well, I don't know about you, but this conversation's giving me the jitters. First of all, Andy from the comedy club was murdered a couple of months ago, and now this. What on earth is going on? I just thank God that the two of you arrived *after* the murderer had left. What might have happened if you hadn't doesn't bear thinking about. Now, if it's all the same with everyone else, can we please talk about something else."

"Suits me," said Megan. "How about we talk about the reason Lizzie and I are here in the first place?"

ooooooo

After an afternoon of making plans for her parents' vow renewal ceremony, and an hour dozing in the sun, Megan felt much less fraught about the morning's events.

"I mean, it's not like we knew the guy," Lizzie said, matter-of-factly, as she rinsed a colander of salad leaves in readiness for dinner. "Of course his death is going to be awful for *someone*, but it doesn't have to be for us. Don't go getting all maudlin about it, will you? You won't enjoy being here if you do."

"No, I won't." Megan sometimes wished she could be a bit more like Lizzie. She was the pragmatic one. The one who could detach herself from situations to find logic when Megan couldn't see the wood for the trees. Lizzie was the impassive one when Megan had a tendency to become horribly over-emotional.

She hoped it would be as easy as her sister made it sound to forget all about the man she'd seen earlier with a wire pulled tight around his neck, but she had her doubts. She shivered and picked a slice of cucumber from the salad bowl.

"Megan, shell those prawns we got from the fishmonger this morning, would you?" Claudia appeared in the kitchen, her curls damp from the shower and sticking to her forehead. "Thanks, love. Your dad wants to wrap them in bacon and cook them on the barbecue with lemons from the garden."

She rolled her eyes. "You know how obsessed he is with that barbecue. If he could barbecue cornflakes, he would." She made herself comfortable at the kitchen table and began to cut a plateful of ripe figs in half. "Anyway, as we spent all afternoon talking about me and your dad, I think it's time we talked about what's going on with *you* now." She held up a hand. "Yes, I know you probably don't want to discuss it with us but I don't want to spend our entire cruise worrying about it, so you'll have to I'm afraid."

Megan sighed. "I'm fine now, Mum. I was a bit upset when it all happened but I'm fine now. Please don't worry about me. I'm thirty-nine, you know – I can take care of myself." By the look on her mother's face, Megan's attempts to allay her concerns appeared to be falling on deaf ears. She blew out a smaller sigh and slid a prawn from its grey jacket.

Claudia raised an eyebrow so high, it went into hiding under her fringe. "'*Don't worry?*' I'm your mother, darling – I'd worry if you were *seventy*-nine. When you have children, it comes with the territory, as you well know." She pressed a button on the mini CD player on the counter and Harry Connick Jr. blared out of the speakers.

"Oh, if we're having music, stick a Babs Streisand in there, will you love?" Nick called from outside where he was firing up the coals and jigging about on the spot.

"So." Claudia turned the volume down and reached across the table to squeeze Megan's hand. "What are you going to do? Honestly, you were all settled, and then that stupid company of yours had to move to Switzerland—"

"Sweden."

"Wherever. My point is that you were settled there, and now you have to deal with all this upheaval. And don't even get me *started* on Hugh." Claudia pursed her lips. "Anyway, Megan Fallon, stop interrupting and explain to your father and I how you're going to pay your mortgage without a job when you get back home? It's not *just* you who needs a roof over your head, you know, there's Evie to consider, too."

"Yes, I know, Mum. Look, I promise I'm not going to fritter away my redundancy money, and I promise I'm going to get another job as soon as I can. I love that you care – really I do – but please *try* not to worry about me. Honestly, everything's going to be just—" Megan stopped mid-sentence to point a prawn at the handsome silver tabby with the amber eyes and deformed ear that had made itself comfortable on the kitchen doormat, and was proceeding to wash its paws. "Er, whose cat is that?"

"What? Oh, that's Cat. He must have smelled the prawns," said Claudia casually, as she pulled on a hairband to hold back her mahogany curls. "Since Mrs Kozlowski from down the road passed away, he spends half his day here. She fed him for years but, when the food stopped, he eventually found his way to us. He's awfully tame for a street cat." She clicked her tongue and the cat immediately trotted towards her.

Lizzie looked up from rolling potato wedges in salt and oil and regarded him sceptically. "Don't you believe it, Mum. You'll never tame a street cat. You want to be careful – he could take your eye out with one of those claws."

"Don't be silly, darling." Claudia gave a husky chuckle and dismissed the very notion with a wave of her hand before bending to pick up the tabby. "Cat's not like that. Although he did frighten the living daylights out of Sandra Grayling the other day. She's just been made Treasurer at the WA, you know. Anyway, she can't abide cats – thinks they're evil freaks of nature. Cat was waiting for me outside the village hall after a meeting last week and Sandra took one look at him and went berserk, so Cat hissed and took a swipe at her. Honestly, I've never seen a grown woman make such a fuss – he didn't even touch her. I'm sure he can sense when people don't like him, you know."

Claudia put Cat on her lap and he immediately sprawled out on his back and began to purr like a well-oiled, petrol-powered lawnmower. "See the way he lets me tickle him? He must know I don't mean him any harm." She cooed and stroked his raggedy ear. "I think he must have been in a fight at some point – looks like something had a good chew on this. Bless him, poor little fella. You know, we really should think of another name for him. Something a little more original than 'Cat'." She looked from one daughter to the other. "Perhaps you could have a think about it while you're here?"

Megan gave a distracted nod. "Anyway, Mum." She tore her eyes away from Cat's razor sharp claws, extended to their full, treacherous length as he kneaded the air with every scratch of his tummy. "Everything's under control, okay? So can we please stop talking about my finances?"

Claudia viewed her through narrowed eyes before giving her the benefit of the doubt. "Oh, I suppose so, but don't think I've forgotten about it. This subject is still up for discussion again before your father and I go away. Okay?"

"Okay." Megan let out a sigh of relief. "For now, though, can we please just eat?"

ooooooo

A family dinner, with conversation and plenty of laughter, almost caused Megan to forget that her parents' big day was a job.

She made a few more notes before flicking the cover of her notebook shut, and pushing her pen into the spiral binder. "Well, I think that's enough to get me started. I'll go out tomorrow and organise the flowers and the entertainment."

"Do you want me to come with you?" asked Lizzie, her head buried in the depths of the fridge.

"No, it's okay. I'm usually better off on my own when I'm working. What are you looking for, by the way?"

"The Greek yogurt for the figs. There are only two cartons of cream in here."

"Oh, blast!" Claudia sighed with exasperation. "Don't tell me I picked up the wrong thing." She grabbed her purse from the counter and glanced at the kitchen clock. "I'll run down to the shop. It stays open till half-eight, so I've got time."

Megan sprang to her feet. "No, you won't, Mum – *I* will. In any case, I could do with stretching my legs before dessert. And it'll give me an excuse to say hi to Olivia and Rob, if they're there. Do we need anything else?"

"No, just the yogurt. And don't say anything to Olivia about the ceremony – I'll tell her tomorrow."

"Okay. See you in a bit."

CHAPTER SIX

The sun still held its gentle warmth as it dipped, casting vast pink and orange swathes across the lilac sky.

Dog walkers monopolised the village green, along with members of the local book club, settled on the exposed roots of the village's giant, centuries-old oak tree, as they analysed and critiqued their 'Book of the Month'.

As she set off on the short stroll, Megan waved to a neighbour who was enjoying a pint outside *The Duck Inn*, the old village pub on the opposite side of the green.

A young couple with a frisky spaniel bid her good evening as they passed by, as did an elderly man sitting at a bus stop.

I forget how lovely it is that everyone says hello, she thought, comparing the friendliness of the locals to the reserve of her city neighbours back home.

The village shop was the first she came to, set back slightly from street, its small forecourt ablaze with colour from the summer blooms that spilled over the rims of numerous earthenware flowerpots. Its frontage was almost completely covered in ivy, save for the windows and doors around which someone had been careful to trim back the glossy green leaves to form perfect frames.

Megan's lips curved in delight when she saw that the old wooden swing seat with its striped canopy still had pride of place outside. She recalled how, as kids, she and Lizzie used to swing back and forth on it after a day on the beach, sharing secrets and eating ice cream, before racing each other back home.

A man reclined on it now, hands behind his head as he swung slowly back and forth, stretched out along the entire striped cushion. His tanned feet were crossed at the ankles and a wide-brimmed canvas hat covered his face. Megan crept past him into the shop and a bell jangled.

A diminutive woman with a snub nose dusted with freckles greeted her. "Feel free to browse or buy," she said, without looking up. Her ponytail, the colour of terracotta, swung from side to side as she cleaned down the countertop, and her cheeks shone like rosy apples. "Give me a shout if you need any help," she added.

Born in Bliss Bay, Olivia and her family had left the village when she was ten, not returning for a visit until almost forty years later. When a holiday romance with Rob Brennan, the village shop owners' son, had developed into something more permanent, Olivia and Rob had taken over the running of the shop when Rob's parents retired.

"Evening, Livvy."

"Megan! Oh my goodness!" Olivia squealed. "Your mum said you were coming back – she was so excited when she came in yesterday." She dragged her palms down the front of her apron. "Get over here and give me a hug. How long are you here for?"

"I'm not sure. A while, I think."

"A while?" Olivia raised an eyebrow. "Well, that's new. I can't remember the last time you had more than a weekend away from that job of yours. Your mum tells me you might as well be running the place, the amount of hours you put in."

Megan went in search of the yogurt. "Yeah, well, you know. I thought it was time for a break." She wasn't in the mood to tell Olivia about her employment status, and she certainly wasn't about to get into what had happened with Hugh.

"It was so long ago that you were last here, and you were in and out so quickly, we didn't have a chance to get together," said Olivia. "We must arrange something before you leave."

Megan put the yogurt on the counter and handed over a £10 note. "Yes, we'll have to sort something out. You know, I love that the swing chair's still outside. I must have told you before that Lizzie and I used to spend ages on it when we were kids."

"Well, not that exact chair," said Olivia. "The seat and canopy have been changed at least three times in the eight years I've been here. We'd never get rid of it, though." She glanced outside and grinned. "As you can see, it's a very popular rest-stop."

Megan smiled and nodded. "How's Rob?" she asked, picking up her change.

Olivia beamed. "Oh, he's adorable. He's just popped out to do a home delivery but you'll be bound to catch him sooner or later. There's a couple who cover the two days we don't work but otherwise, we're always here."

"Okay. I'm sure I'll be seeing a lot of you over the next few weeks, so I'll catch up with him then."

"Right-o, I'll tell him you popped in. Just a minute, before you go." Olivia opened the display cabinet on the counter and took out a large slab of homemade bread pudding. "Here," she said, wrapping it in waxed paper. "A little welcome back present. Made it myself – it'll be lovely with a cup of coffee. Maybe a little ice cream, if you really want to indulge."

"Oh, Livvy, that's so sweet of you. Thank you." Megan breathed in the delicious scent of the highly spiced pudding and gave Olivia another squeeze. "Well, I'd better get going. It's been really good seeing you."

Olivia nodded. "Likewise," she said, turning her attention to another customer.

Megan slipped out of the shop, stopping for a moment beside the swing chair. It was motionless now, but still occupied by the man with the bare feet. If it had been free, she would have tried it out, for old time's sake.

Never mind, plenty of time, she thought as she set off.

"Give me a push, will you?"

She stopped and turned. The man's face was still hidden.

"Are you talking to me?"

A chuckle issued from behind the hat. "Well, I don't see anyone else around. Do you?"

His voice was slow and deep, his accent American, or maybe Canadian. Megan wasn't familiar enough with either to know which.

"How did you know I was here?" Megan peered at his hat.

"Ah, well, I used my x-ray eye superpowers." He chuckled again. "And I can see your feet." His voice told Megan he was smiling beneath the hat. "Anyway, don't be a mean girl—give me a push."

Megan surveyed the man's long body, clad in a loose white tee-shirt and faded jeans cut off at the knee. Mesmerised by his lumberjack forearms, and despite her usual reluctance to have anything to do with strange men, she felt a sudden surge of benevolence. Walking back to the swing, she gave it a gentle push, sending it on its back and forth cycle once more.

"Much obliged." The man stuck up a thumb before putting his hands behind his head again and changing the cross of his ankles, revealing a scar on the top of his right foot, all the more noticeable because it hadn't tanned like the rest of his skin.

"You're welcome," said Megan, as she went on her way. *Honestly, after all the lectures I've given Evie about not talking to weirdos.*

She was no more than a few steps from the cottage when she sensed she was being watched. The driver of a low-slung red sports car parked outside *The Duck Inn* had his eyes fixed on her. She held up a hand and squinted through her fingers against the setting sun, her stomach churning as she recognised the man behind the wheel as her ex-husband, Laurence. He drove around the green and slowed the car to a crawl alongside the kerb beside her, planting his sunglasses in his thick thatch of blond hair.

"Laurence." Megan acknowledged him with a nod, and the briefest of smiles.

"Hello, Megan. I spoke to Evie yesterday. She mentioned you were coming back." He pulled the car off the road and got out to lean against it, his thumbs hooked over his trouser pockets. "I was in *The Duck*, having a coffee with a client, and I saw you go out so I thought I'd hang around for a while." His sleepy-looking eyes swept over her from head to toe. "It was worth the wait – you're looking very well," he said, and gave her a lascivious wink.

Megan shook her head. *Unbelievable.* Biting back an insult, she continued on to the cottage and up the path to the front door. As she fumbled for her keys, she heard his footsteps drawing closer. Her breath quickened and she turned to face him. "If you come one step closer, Laurence, I swear, I'll—" Her hand found the mini canister of breath freshener at the bottom of her bag. "I'll pepper spray you." *Pepper spray?* She groaned inwardly at her choice of threat.

He looked shocked for a second, then threw back his head and laughed. "No, you won't! Even if you had some in your bag, which I seriously doubt, pepper spray's illegal. And you're such a goody two-shoes, Megan, I doubt you've *ever* broken the law." He made no attempt to come any further, just stared at her.

He hadn't changed much at all, she observed. He was still annoyingly good-looking, still lean, still moved without urgency, still had the same thick blond hair that grew horizontally out of his head rather than vertically and, worst of all, he was still a letch. A letch who was about to get a knee in the nether regions if he came any closer. Finding her key, Megan shoved it into the lock.

"Don't make assumptions about me, Laurence – you don't know me any more. Now get lost and leave me alone."

He lifted an eyebrow. "Well, well, well. I remember when you wouldn't say boo to a goose, but you're quite the feisty one these days, aren't you? I'd never have guessed from our meetings over the years."

It took all Megan's control to keep the tremble from her voice as she looked him straight in the eye. "That's because I've done everything humanly possible to keep them brief. Now, if you don't mind, I was in the middle of a meal with my family."

Laurence held up a hand. "Please, don't let me keep you," he said, peering into the bag she was holding and wagging a finger. "Full-fat Greek yogurt. And, if I'm not mistaken, that smells like Olivia's bread pudding. Very naughty. You know what they say, 'A moment on the lips, a lifetime on the hips'. Although, I must say, your hips were always very easy on the eye." He grinned and raked his fingernails up and down a groomed sideburn.

"God, you're disgusting!" Megan spluttered. "In case you'd forgotten, *we're* divorced, and *you're* married to a different wife now, remember?"

"Yeah, but Kelly's not here. Her mum had a double hip replacement so she's staying with her till she's on her feet again, and I'm all on my lonesome. Poor me." Laurence pulled a sad face. "Anyway, there's no need to blow a gasket. I was only trying to be friendly. Perhaps we could get together for a chat while you're here? Maybe over a drink?"

Megan composed herself and spoke through clenched teeth. "Unless it's about Evie, I have nothing to say to you."

"Ah, yes, Evie." Laurence's smile softened. "We did a great job of bringing her up, didn't we? She's a fabulous kid."

Megan's eyes widened. "*We* did a great job? I don't recall *you* being around for most of her upbringing."

"That's because *you* took her away from Bliss Bay," Laurence snapped back. He scratched his blond thatch, sighed, and cocked his head. "Look, don't be snarky, love. It doesn't suit you." His lips curled into a smirk. "Mind you, I'd be snarky if I lost my job, and my fiancée did a runner in the same week." He tried to hide a chuckle by pretending to cough behind his hand. "Evie told me what happened."

Megan bit the inside of her cheeks and took a deep breath as she wondered, for the umpteenth time, what in the world had attracted her to him in the first place. "I'm *not* snarky. And don't call me 'love'. You gave up that right when you waltzed out of our marriage – which, I recall, was why I left Bliss Bay in the first place." She turned on her heel. "Have a nice life."

He grabbed her arm. "Oh, come on, Megan. There's no need to be so hostile."

To her horror, Megan felt a rush of hot tears prick her eyelids. There was no way she was going to give him the satisfaction of knowing he could still get her riled. Her voice shook as her pulse rate quickened. "Take your hand off me. If you don't let go of me, Laurence, I swear, I'll kick you so hard in the—"

A rustling from the depths of the old apple tree in the front garden was followed by the blur of a silver tabby cat launching itself onto Laurence's back. Clinging onto his shoulders with razor sharp claws, it swiped at his flailing hands with a lethal paw.

"Aaaarrgghh! OW! Get off me, you bloody cat! *Get off!*" Laurence shook himself in an attempt to remove Cat, but the tabby was going nowhere. "Aaarrgghh! Oww! *Help*! Don't just stand there, woman!" he pleaded. "*Do something!*"

Against her better judgement, Megan prised the angry feline from Laurence's back and held him in her arms, upon which he turned into a perfectly docile kitty.

"He's obviously a very good judge of character," she said, drily.

So furious, the veins in his neck bulged over his shirt collar, Laurence was raging. "You'd better keep that damned moggy indoors because if I ever see it again, it'll be sorry." He brushed at his shoulders, cursing under his breath as he felt the pulled threads of his shirt.

Megan took great delight in using a phrase she hardly ever used and, leaving him standing on the path, shut the door in her ex-husband's face.

She wasn't an antagonistic person by nature, so it irritated her greatly that even though their meetings had been few and short since she'd left Bliss Bay seventeen years before, Laurence still knew exactly what to do and say to bring out the very worst in her. She'd only been in his company for a few minutes and she could already feel the hostility sweeping over her in waves.

She leaned against the front door, adrenaline pumping, and gave Cat a grateful hug as she waited for her breathing to slow. "Don't worry, he'll never hurt you," she whispered in his ear. "I won't let him." When she heard the low rumble of an engine, she peeped through the letterbox to see Laurence speeding away, and heaved a huge sigh as she put the tabby down and strolled into the kitchen.

"At last! We thought you'd gone to Greece to make the flippin' yogurt," grumbled Lizzie.

"Sorry I took so long. I got talking to Olivia, and then I had an unexpected encounter." She shivered as she opened a carton, realising her hands were clammy and her forehead was beaded with sweat.

Nick frowned. "What kind of unexpected encounter?"

"Oh, nothing to worry about. I bumped into Laurence." Not wanting to make any more of what had happened, Megan ignored the concerned stares from around the table. "He was in *The Duck* with a client and he saw me going to the shop. He just came over to say hello. And, before anyone asks, yes, he's still a pillock, yes, everything's fine and no, I'd rather not talk about him. Suffice to say, I think Cat made sure he won't come back again in a hurry."

Her heartbeat returned to its normal rate as, back in the company of her family, she began to relax. Over a dessert of juicy figs draped in creamy yogurt and honey, the conversation continued about anything and everything.

As she sat back in her chair and listened to her parents' and Lizzie's chatter across the kitchen table, Megan knew that a break at Kismet Cottage was just what she needed.

CHAPTER SEVEN

The following morning, Megan watched the sun rise on a busy day ahead.

"We might not be here when you get back," said Claudia, as she topped a slice of toast with mashed banana and honey. "Now that you've got everything in hand, we're popping in to see your Uncle Des and Aunty Sylvie to give them the good news, and then we're dropping in on a few friends to let them know. The sooner they know to keep the date free, the better. And, just so you know, I'm going to ask Des and Sylvie round for dinner. It's about time you saw them again."

Megan nodded. "Okay, I'll see you later." Grabbing her bag, she blew a kiss and set off the village.

What should have taken no more than five minutes took almost forty-five, she stopped so many times to chat to neighbours on the way. Bliss Bay was that kind of place – no one was ever in so much of a hurry that they didn't have time to stop and chat, or invite you in for a cup of tea.

As Megan went on her way, she munched on a large breakfast flapjack that Dora Pickles at number three had thrust into her hand over the garden gate. Dora had always been one of Megan's favourite neighbours growing up; she'd always had a cake or a biscuit for her and Lizzie, and it seemed that nothing had changed.

As she approached the shop, she saw an old man sitting on the swing chair, head down as he whittled away at a piece of wood, the black Labrador at his feet resting its grey-haired muzzle on its paws. Even though she couldn't see his face, Megan recognised him immediately.

The vast majority of Bliss Bay residents lived on what was commonly known as the 'home side' of the village; the quieter side where most of the cottages and houses were situated. Across the bay, small village hotels, bed and breakfasts, pubs, restaurants, and tourist shops were found on the 'holiday side' of the village.

Although many preferred to walk or drive from one side of the horseshoe-shaped bay to the other, for decades, Bill Spencer's family had operated a service for those who preferred to make the trip by small ferry boat.

"Hello, Bill." Megan removed her large sunglasses and Bill's leathery face broke into a toothy smile. He held out his hand, its swollen joints telling her that the arthritis he'd always suffered with still blighted him. She hugged him, breathing in the smell of his favourite chewing tobacco, and the sea, which hung on him like a heavy overcoat.

"Meggie! Well I'll be! 'S'good t'see yeh again. Yeh got the babby with yeh?"

Megan grinned and crouched to make a fuss of the old Labrador. "No, I came down with Lizzie. The "babby" has gone to New Zealand for a year. And she's twenty now."

Bill's eyes widened. "Twenty? Time flies. Anyway, 'ow are yeh, young 'un?" He patted the seat beside him. "Come on, take the weight off yer feet. Y'ere fer the summer?"

"I'm not sure how long I'm staying. How're things with you and Rita"

Bill raised a bony shoulder. "Not bad. Ups 'n downs, yeh know, but mostly ups, I'm glad t'say. Rita's still on at me t'give up the ferry so someone younger can run it but I can't bear t'think about it. It's not easy, young 'un – I've known that ferry all me life. Reckon they'll 'ave to jus' push me over the side when they don't need me no more." He laughed a wheezy laugh and looked at his old pocket watch. "I'd best be off. I've never missed a nine o'clock start yet, and I don't 'spect I will t'day. By the way, d'yeh remember my nephew, Jack?"

Megan chuckled. "Jelly-Legs-Jack?"

She could hardly forget the boy who'd spent so many of his childhood summers in Bliss Bay, helping Bill on the ferry.

When he was a baby, his parents had left England following his American father's posting back to a US airforce base, but a subsequent posting had seen the family return to the UK when Jack was eleven years old. It was then that his visits to Bliss Bay began, when he and his mum would spend the long summer school holiday with his mum's brother, Uncle Bill, and his wife, Rita.

Among the locals, Jack stuck out like a sore thumb. Not only because of his accent, but because of his nervous stutter and a voice that ranged from falsetto to bass for what seemed like an eternity. Unusually short for a boy of his age, he was incredibly clumsy, bumping into and falling over things with alarming regularity.

He'd once lost his balance in spectacular fashion when the ferry had unexpectedly pitched and he'd fallen onto a large box on Megan's lap. Unfortunately, the box contained a heavily iced chocolate and cream cake that she and Lizzie were bringing back from the artisan bakery as a birthday surprise for their mother. In the ensuing chaos, Jack slipped on the cream which had escaped from the box and caught his foot on a bench seat, acquiring a deep cut that needed to be stitched.

"Of course I remember Jack," she said, with a grin. "How could I ever forget him? Why do you ask, anyway?"

"'E came over t'visit a couple of months ago t'spend a few weeks with us – God 'elp us.

Yeh remember 'e went back t'the States when 'e was sixteen? Well, 'e's been back an' forth ever since. Got 'imself a job an' eventually settled in Berkshire a few years back. We don't see 'im very often but 'e turns up on our doorstep every now an' then, like a bad penny."

His smile and the twinkle in his eye told Megan that Bill was only speaking in jest. He'd always adored his nephew.

She fleetingly recalled the man she'd seen on the swing seat outside the shop, but dismissed him from her mind. There was no way that could have been Jelly-Legs-Jack. Not with a body and a voice like that.

"It must be nice for you and Rita to have him around. I remember Lizzie and I sticking up for him when the local boys used to make fun of his accent. Do you remember how they used to tease him when he helped you on the ferry?"

"Aye, I do. There's a fair few of our friends from across the water livin' 'ere now, though. Not surprisin' really, 'merica's got strong links t'this part o' the country so it's not such a rarity t'ear the accent these days."

"No, that's true." Megan closed her eyes and turned her face to the sun, enjoying the warmth of the morning rays on her skin. "Well, I'll keep an eye out and say hello when I see him."

"'Spose y'eard 'bout the murder couple months back? Andy Cochran?"

Megan nodded. "Dad told us. It's horrible isn't it? I didn't really know him – he was a couple of years above me at school."

"'E was a character," said Bill. "The police still 'aven't found out 'oo did it." He scowled and looked lost in his thoughts. "Don't suppose yeh thinkin' of buyin' a place in Bliss Bay, are yeh?" he said, changing the subject. "'Cos if y'are, now's the time. Yeh know 'bout the new development, I 'spose?"

"We started talking about it last night but Lizzie and I were falling asleep in the armchairs so we never heard the end of the story. What's going on?"

Bill sucked on his teeth. "Y'know the old secondary school on the hill? Well, it's bein' bulldozed so developers can build one o' them big hypermarkets on the land. Huge, it's goin' t'be. People are already tryin' t'sell up before the 'ouse prices drop." He gave a disapproving sniff and handed her the newspaper he'd been sitting on. "'Ere, read this."

Megan scanned the first paragraph of the article.

HYPERMARKET DEAL CLOSE TO COMPLETION

Plans to build a two-storey hypermarket on the site of the original Bliss Bay secondary school were given a boost

*when planning permission was granted for
50,000 square feet of buildings to include a
supermarket and department store, a post
office, fashion outlets, a pharmacy, cafeterias,
bars and restaurants.*

"A lot of folk are thinkin' o' movin' on,"
said Bill, "so there'll be plenty o' places up for
grabs, I shouldn't wonder. At rock bottom
prices too, prob'ly. I keep tellin' Jack t'nab one
while they're goin' cheap."

"But why are people moving away?"
Megan handed back the newspaper. "Why
would house prices drop? Won't a
hypermarket be good for the area? You know,
to bring people to the village? Those big stores
are fantastic. You can get everything under one
roof. They're so convenient."

Bill snorted. "That's the 'ole point – we
don't *need* convenience round 'ere, young 'un.
We don't *want* Bliss Bay being overrun with
cars, pollutin' the air an' increasin' the traffic.
An' give a thought t'all the local businesses.
Most of 'em 'ave been 'ere since before yeh
were born, but what're they goin' t'do when no
one needs 'em no more? What'll become of 'em
when people start takin' the *convenient* option,
eh?"

"Oh, right. Yes, I see what you mean."
Megan scratched her nose. "Well, can't the
residents object to the planning permission?"

"Huh. Yeh think they 'aven't tried? There's been meetings opposin' the plans every week for months. 'Tween us, I reckon it's a lost cause. An' they won't stop at Bliss Bay, mark my words. They'll move through the 'ole county like a swarm o' locusts, knockin' down our 'eritage an' puttin' concrete eyesores in its place." Bill sighed heavily and folded up his penknife. "Make the most of it while yeh can, young 'un. The times they are a changin' an' it looks like it's our turn."

ooooooo

After Bill's prediction, Megan was pleased to see that the village high street, at least, had changed little, apart from a recent lick of whitewash which ensured that the buildings looked even more vibrant than she remembered.

There was a spring in her step as she continued on her way along the high street cobblestones to The Cobbles Café and Flower Shop. She pushed open the door to the flower shop and the sound of birdsong from a speaker filled the air, twittering over the chatter that came from every table in the small, and very popular, adjoining café.

"Be with you in a sec." A familiar voice drifted up from behind an enormous bouquet. "Blossom! Come and help this customer, please."

Megan headed for the wedding display. She was glad her parents had agreed to start telling friends of their plans. Not having to keep it a secret from anyone would make organising the ceremony so much easier.

A pale-skinned girl with dark ringlets framing her thin face appeared from the back of the shop. She smiled like she'd been told she had to, rather than because she wanted to.

She'd changed a lot since Megan had last seen her but her striking green eyes left her in no doubt as to who she was.

"Can I help?" she asked, her lack of enthusiasm implying that she rather hoped Megan would say no.

"Yes please." A blank expression met Megan's smile. "Do you have any brochures that show examples of your wedding bouquets and posies?"

The girl looked relieved that Megan's request wasn't too taxing and took a brochure from the top drawer of a tall dresser. "Here you are. All the wedding stuff's near the back – after the christening gifts and before the funeral wreaths."

"Right, thanks. And can I speak to you about floral displays? I'd like to order some for an event on the 16th of August."

"Oh, you'd better speak to Mum about that," said the girl, jerking her thumb towards the counter. "I'm just helping out during the summer holiday. She'll be free soon."

The woman behind the counter finished what she was doing and handed the vast bunch of Calla lilies to a waiting customer.

"There you go, Natalie. They should last for a couple of weeks if you follow the care instructions I've written on the card – maybe a few days longer, if you're lucky."

"Oh, they're gorgeous. You're *so* creative, Petal." The glamorous customer flicked her post-box-red ponytail over her shoulder. "I can't resist fresh flowers and these are going to look amazing in our dining room. You never know, they might even put a smile on Adrian's face. He's been *such* a miserable sod since he got injured."

"Well, you can't blame him, can you?" said Petal. "Poor Adrian, it must be difficult not knowing if he'll ever be able to do what he really loves again."

Natalie opened her mouth to answer but her phone rang and she retreated to take the call in private. As Petal brushed leaves and stems from the counter, Megan sidled over and cleared her throat.

"Are you free now, or am I going to have to wait *all* morning to speak to you?"

Petal turned with a frown, which disappeared the moment she laid eyes on her old friend. "You're back!" Her jade-green eyes widened as she rushed around the counter and flung her arms around Megan's neck. "I couldn't see you from behind that bouquet!" She stepped back and looked Megan up and down. "Your mum said you were coming back when she popped in yesterday but I didn't know she meant today. Oh, what a shame Lionel's not here – he's usually in the café but he's got man-flu, so he's tucked up in bed."

She ruffled her jet black curls and beckoned the young girl who'd returned to the back of the shop. "Blossom! Come out here and say hello to Megan before she disappears again for goodness knows how long."

The young girl plodded towards them with a heavy tread and limited enthusiasm. "I thought you looked familiar," she grunted, barely taking her eyes from the phone in her hand.

Petal resisted the urge to roll her eyes. "I don't think you saw Blossom the last couple of times you visited, did you, Megan? She's changed a bit since then – turned sixteen in March." She patted her daughter on the shoulder. "Blossom, try to look a little more lively, will you, love? We don't want to scare people away. She's our Sales Prevention Officer," she said to Megan, with a wink. "The complete opposite to her big sister, Daisy. You know, I don't know what in the world happens to her when she steps through that door into the shop, but somewhere outside is a personality with her name on it. Let me know if you find it, will you?"

Megan smiled. "Well, she was very helpful when I came in. And I always thought Blossom was such a lovely name."

Petal stroked her daughter's cheek. "I don't know who she takes after. Lionel, Daisy and I are all livewires but unless she's with her friends, Blossom's as quiet as a church mouse. Always got her nose in a magazine or an e-reader at home. When she's not on that phone, of course."

"Well, thank goodness!" said Megan, as Blossom huffed an embarrassed teenage sigh at being the topic of conversation. "There are a lot worse things she could be doing. I remember Evie was shy at that age."

"Oh, my gosh! Evie! Of course," said Petal. "How is she?"

"She's really well. She's gone off to New Zealand for a year." Megan felt a sudden lump in her throat. "I haven't quite got used to her being away for so long, though, so we'd better change the subject or I'll start blubbing."

Blossom cast her a decidedly uncomfortable sideward glance and disappeared to the back of the shop again.

"Right then, what can I do for you?" said Petal, taking the hint.

"Well, you'll hear all about it from Mum over the next few days, but she and Dad are renewing their wedding vows. She asked me to tell you that your invite'll be in the post on Monday."

"No way!" Petal squealed and clapped her hands. "You know, I *knew* she was keeping something from me when she popped in yesterday. Cheeky minx – wait till I see her!"

Megan laughed. "I'm organising the ceremony for them and I hoped you'd be able to help us out with the flowers? It's on Sunday the 16th of August."

"It'll be a pleasure." Petal reached under the counter and produced a large diary, flicking the pages forward. "We're usually closed on Sundays but I'll make an exception on this occasion and come in and do the flowers first thing. If you can hang on for a while, once Natalie's gone, we can sit down in the café with a cuppa and go through the details, if that suits?"

"Perfect!" said Megan. "They don't want a lot of flowers – the ceremony is going to be at home, you see."

Petal called over to the young woman working in the café. "Amisha, if a table for two becomes free, can you save it for me, please? And just shout if you need a hand and Blossom will come and help." She gave Megan a long look and another hug. "I'm so glad you're staying for a while. How come you managed to get the time off work?"

"It's a long story," said Megan. "I'll tell you about it when there aren't so many people around." She scratched her head. "I'm sorry I haven't kept in touch. I've been pretty useless on that front."

"Don't be ridiculous," said Petal. "Things happen. I know your job is super-busy but, in any case, I totally understood why you wanted a clean break from Bliss Bay after what happened. To be perfectly honest, the way Laurence and Kelly were flaunting themselves around the village after you left, I almost followed you. That guy is such a loser. And as for Kelly. Just don't ever leave me alone with her in the same room or I swear I'll be doing time."

"Speaking of Laurence," said Megan, with a chuckle as she recalled the events of the previous evening. "He stopped by yesterday and he was being a complete pain, so Cat flew out of the apple tree onto his back and scratched his shoulders to pieces. Honestly, his timing was perfect. It couldn't have happened to a nicer guy. Mum must have told you about Cat? He's the stray that started hanging around a few weeks ago."

"Yeah, I've seen him a few times," said Petal. "He's made himself right at home at Kismet Cottage, hasn't he? Your mum said he comes and goes when he wants, has all his meals there, and then stretches out on the stairs and falls asleep. I think he knows he's onto a good thing – your mum spoils him rotten."

"Er, I'm sorry to butt in," the glamorous customer said to Megan, having finished her call, "but I couldn't help overhearing your conversation. You're not a party planner are you?" She stuck out her hand. "I'm Natalie Castle, by the way."

Megan shook her head, and Natalie's hand. "Megan Fallon. And, no, I'm not. Not for anyone else, anyway. I'm just doing this for my parents."

Natalie pouted. "Oh, that's a shame. Ever since my husband got injured, he's been sitting at home, bored out of his brains, with a face like a wet weekend, so I'd love to throw a party to cheer him up. My assistant used to organise everything for us but she left to have a baby, and I'm absolutely useless at stuff like that."

"Natalie's husband's Adrian Castle," said Petal. "The footballer. He started his career at Bliss Bay United but now he plays for Witchester City. They got promoted to League One last season."

"Well, he *was* a footballer," said Natalie, her expression glum. "He was injured last year and he's still not right. He's had one operation after another but so far they haven't been able to fix him. His last op was a couple of months ago and if he doesn't heal properly this time, we're not sure if he'll be able to play again."

"Sorry to hear that," said Megan. She'd long known of Bliss Bay's footballing hero, but wouldn't recognise Adrian Castle if she tripped over him. "I assume it's a leg injury?"

"He broke his ankle. He hasn't played full-time for almost eight months. He can walk, but it won't stand up to a game of football yet." Natalie shrugged. "I suppose getting injured's one of the risks you take when you're running around with twenty-one other men on the field – the testosterone must be flying. I'm not surprised some of them get a little over-excited when they go in for a tackle. Which is what happened, unfortunately. It took me a long time to come to terms with the fact he might not play again, but it's taking Adrian forever."

"What's he going to do if he can't play again, do you know?" asked Petal.

"Not sure. Coach, maybe, but he's not in the right frame of mind to think about it yet – he's still feeling sorry for himself. We've known each other since 2006, and I thought we knew everything there was to know about each other, but I've never seen him this fed up before. I thought *I* knew how to sulk but I've got nothing on him."

Natalie gave a mock scream and grabbed two handfuls of hair extensions. "If he doesn't change his mood pretty soon, I'll have torn this lot out by the time he eventually goes back to work. Anyway, if you have second thoughts and fancy earning a little money while you're here, give me a call. Cash in hand, of course." She dug around in her cavernous handbag and pulled out a white, embossed contact card which she handed to Megan.

"Castle Manor, Coniston Road." Megan read the address. "That's a coincidence. I'm going there next."

"Really? Do you mind if I'm nosy and ask who you're going to see?"

"Timothy and Diana Starr. They're booked for my parents' party."

Natalie kinked a tattooed eyebrow. "'Classical Kin'?"

Megan nodded. "That's right. Do you know them?"

"They live next door at number 39. Nice people, but a bit intense." Natalie picked up her bouquet. "Word of warning – if you appear the *slightest* bit interested in anything they say about music, you're likely to be lured into a lecture on the best performance of Holst's Planets, or why Beethoven had such an impact on the world, so don't say you haven't been warned."

Megan grinned. "Actually, I've known them for years."

"Oh." Natalie's cheeks turned pink. "Sorry. No offence." She glanced at her watch. "Right, I'd better get going. The in-laws are coming round in half an hour to show off their new car. Can I give you a lift?"

"It's okay," said Megan, "I need to talk to Petal first, but thanks all the same."

Natalie nodded before sashaying from the shop, her hips and shoulders swaying with an elegance matched by the exotic perfume that scented the air in her wake.

"Bye all, see you soon."

CHAPTER EIGHT

In comparison to the handsome properties surrounding it, number 39, Coniston Road was a modest town house with no fancy cars in the drive, and no evidence of the trappings of wealth and success that some of the other residents were eager to show off.

The only indication that a family of musicians lived there was a guitar-shaped, frosted glass panel in the front door, and the first bars of *The Hallelujah Chorus* that blared out when Megan pressed the bell.

The door was opened presently by Timothy Starr; a slight, middle-aged man with a receding hairline and a mass of wrinkles that bunched up around inquisitive blue eyes when he smiled. He took Megan's hand in his two and shook it enthusiastically.

"Megan, my dear. It's good to see you again," he wheezed, his voice hoarse. He put up a hand and took an inhaler from his trouser pocket, drawing on it deeply, and coughing until his eyes watered. "Sorry about that. Asthma, *and* the dreaded laryngitis – a singer's nemesis." He stepped aside and waved her in. "Come in, come in. Diana's been looking forward to seeing you ever since you called yesterday."

"Nice to see you, too, Mr. Starr."

Timothy wagged a finger. "I'm not your music teacher any more, and you aren't my student. Please, call me Timothy."

"Hmm, that might be a bit weird," said Megan, "but I'll try." She cocked her head to the sound of an operatic voice warbling up and down the scales. "Is that Mrs Starr?"

"If you mean Diana, yes, that's her. Just follow the caterwauling and you'll find her." Timothy gave a mischievous chuckle and propelled Megan into the living room. "Diana, look who's here."

A petite woman in a black tee-shirt and black Capri jeans cinched in at the waist with a wide belt stood in front of a music stand. She ran her fingers through the white streak at the front of her auburn hair, and extended her arms in greeting.

"Megan!" She kissed the air on either side of her cheeks. "It's so lovely to see you," she said, dabbing at her eyes with a lace-edged handkerchief. "Please, sit down and Timmy will fetch us something to drink. Ginger tea with a spoon of honey for me, please, darling, and for you, Megan?"

"Oh, just water please. Thanks." She cleared a space on the couch and sunk into a cushion.

Diana sat opposite, her legs crossed at their delicate ankles. "Are you still singing?" she asked, and dabbed at her eyes again.

Megan shook her head. "Not if I can help it. Singing was never really my thing. I only took lessons because Petal did. We were a bit like sheep in those days – if one of us did something, the other one did it, too."

The smile dropped from Diana's lips. "Oh, that's a shame – you're missing out, my dear. Song brings such joy to people's lives. Anyway, you'd like us to perform at your parents' vow renewal ceremony on August the 16th. That's what you said on the telephone yesterday evening, isn't it?" She blew her nose as she looked down at the appointments diary on her lap.

"That's right. There'll be other music too – we've got some of their favourite CDs for the dancing later – but you know they've been fans of yours for years so they'd love for you to play before and during the ceremony."

Diana acknowledged the praise with a little bow. "We do love our fans. They're *so* supportive. We owe everything to them, you know." She sniffed and rubbed the pad of her index finger against the corner of her eye.

"Are you alright?" said Megan, with a frown. "Have I called at a bad time?"

"Oh, no, not at all." Diana held her handkerchief to her eyes for a moment. "We just found out this morning that an old acquaintance of ours passed away. Not a friend, as such, but it was still a shock. I'm just being silly. Take no notice of me."

She blew her nose again and took the cup of ginger tea from the tray Timothy brought in. Looking a little happier, she said, "You know, I do believe that just telling someone has made me feel a bit brighter." She sent Megan a grateful smile. "Unfortunately, Timmy and our son, Bailey, aren't the best people to have around when you need a shoulder to cry on." She smiled again as she reached for her husband's hand, and he bent to catch her in a hug.

"Sorry, love. It didn't even occur to me that you'd want to talk about it," said Timothy. "We hadn't seen him to talk to for so many years, I didn't think it would affect you the way it has." He gave a hacking cough and reached for his inhaler again. "And you know me," he said, with an awkward grin. "I've never been very good at picking up on other people's emotions."

Diana touched a hand to his cheek. "Don't worry. It doesn't matter now. And don't forget to drink that honey and lemon while it's hot." She planted a kiss on the end of his nose and wiped her eyes again before turning back to Megan. "Now, didn't you say on the telephone that your mother's particularly keen to have some pieces played on the harp and the cor anglais?"

Megan nodded. "Actually, if it's not too much trouble, do you think it'd be possible to hear what the cor anglais sounds like? I didn't even know what one was until Dad told me it was another name for an English horn, but I'm sure I've never heard one before."

"Of course. It's in the music room. Timmy and I aren't very good on it but Bailey's excellent. He'll be twenty in a few months, you know, and he can play any instrument by ear. I'm sure he'd be delighted to give you a quick demo – any excuse to show off." Diana lowered her voice. "By the way, please don't mention in front of him that I've been upset. He didn't know our friend but he's very sensitive and he'd only worry about me."

The sound of the front door being opened and slammed was followed by an excited squeal in the entrance hall.

"Diana! Timothy! You'll *never* guess what's going on next door at 'common as muck mansion'."

A burly, brassy-blonde laden with shopping bags and sporting a freshly coiled perm and a startled expression threw Megan an enquiring look. "Oh, sorry, I didn't know you had company."

Diana's cheeks flushed with embarrassment. "Belinda, this is Megan Fallon. We're performing at a party she's arranging. Megan, this is Belinda Towers, our cleaner. And I should point out that her opinion of Castle Manor is hers alone, not ours. Anyway, what's going on?"

"Well, I was talking to Eleanor outside," said Belinda, "and she told me that when she was on her way out this morning, that chap who's staying with Adrian and Natalie—"

"You mean Tony Weller?" interrupted Diana.

Belinda nodded. "Well, he was taking delivery of a huge parcel. Almost as big as a small car, Eleanor said it was." She put down the shopping and pulled a lime-green apron over her head.

"And that's of interest to us, because?" said Timothy.

"Because it was an amplifier," said Belinda, her eyes wide and her black mascaraed lashes circling them like spider's legs. "Tony's going to be performing at a nightclub in London soon, so he'll be rehearsing his set for the next few weeks. I thought you'd want to know."

"Oh, for heaven's sake!" Diana threw up her hands and went to look out of the window. "It's bad enough that he plays that dreadful music at all, never mind that we're going to have to listen to him rehearsing for weeks on end. Although why he needs to rehearse when all he does is play records, I have no idea. I mean, what's to rehearse?

Surely all you have to do is put a record on, take it off and repeat as necessary. He's a DJ," she explained to Megan.

Right on cue, a deep booming bass thump filled the air, the volume increasing until Megan felt her ears were going to pop. Then it stopped as suddenly as it had started. "Wow. That *is* loud. You don't have to put up with that often, do you?"

Timothy gave a strained smile. "More often than we should, I'm afraid and once he starts, it can go on for hours. Can you imagine how difficult it is for *us* to rehearse with that racket going on in the background?" He rolled the pads of his fingers against his temples. "Ironically, he's actually a very nice man to talk to – we often chat if we see each other. He gave me some wonderful exercises to help get rid of the tension in my neck and shoulders, and for my lower-back pain – he's very into health and fitness, you see. Same with Natalie and Adrian – they're decent enough people. Adrian even taught Bailey to drive. They're all perfectly reasonable most of the time. That's what makes this situation so awkward."

"Have you made a complaint?"

"I know we should," said Diana, "but I can't bear any kind of confrontation, and I fear a confrontation is how it would end up if we were to complain. Stress is not conducive to producing our kind of music – it's so negative.

Anyway, I'd much prefer to leave any complaining to someone else."

"And is anyone else likely to complain?" asked Megan. "What about the care home on the other side of Castle Manor?"

Diana pinched the bridge of her nose and shook her head. "The residents don't appear to be troubled by the noise because they have triple glazed windows and most of them are hard of hearing, but the neighbours on the other side of us are very keen to put an end to it. If there are any ongoing disturbances, I'm sure they'll involve the police."

"You mean Eleanor and Oscar Cooper?"

"Yes, that's right. I forgot you know them, don't you?" said Diana, fiddling absentmindedly with an earring.

"Well, I used to have a Saturday job in Eleanor's hairdressing salon when I was fifteen," said Megan. "I've seen them around since then, but not recently."

Belinda cleared her throat. Having geared up into full-on gossip mode, she was impatient to resume her story. "If you'd just let me finish, I was about to tell you that Eleanor said she *is* going to complain about the noise."

"Oh, thank goodness. What's a relief," said Diana, exhaling a long breath. "Did she say when?"

Belinda shook her head. "She just said she'll be straight down to the police station if it becomes unreasonable. It'll push Oscar over the edge again if he has to put up with music blaring out until the early hours."

"Oh, that's right," said Megan, "I remember Mum telling me that Oscar's not been well."

"Hmpf. "Not been well" is an understatement," said Belinda. "He's been in a terrible state since he lost his job last year, but that's hardly surprising. I mean, if *you'd* recommended an investment to your clients, and then watched their life savings go down the toilet when it didn't perform, I expect you'd be in a bad way, too. It must be a financial advisor's worst nightmare. Those clients had been with him for years. He'd worked so hard to build up a good reputation – Honest Oscar, people used to call him – and then it was gone in seconds."

"Mum said the people who'd been affected put in claims for compensation, though," said Megan. "So they'll get some of their money back, won't they? I mean, it's still awful but at least they won't have lost everything."

"That didn't help Oscar, though," said Belinda, patting a palm on her permed curls. "He couldn't handle the guilt and had a breakdown the week after it happened. He's much better now than he was, but he can't tolerate loud noises – they give him panic attacks. He associates them with being back at his office, which is where he was when everything went wrong. He spent years surrounded by people shouting, phones ringing, everyone talking at once, and the radio blaring out, and now he shakes in his shoes if he hears a dog barking. It's ever so sad."

She sighed. "I've got a real soft spot for Oscar. It was him who gave me a job when I first came to Bliss Bay a few years ago. I was working part-time in the garden centre and we got chatting when he came in for some mulch. Told me his wife was looking for someone to help with the housework and, as they say, the rest is history. And then Eleanor gave Diana my phone number, and here I am."

Diana raised an eyebrow. "Belinda, I'm sure Megan isn't interested in the minute details," she said, laying a gentle hand on Megan's arm. "Anyway, as I was saying, shall we go up to the music room? Bailey's already up there. Come on, you lead the way, Timmy. Just go at your own pace, darling, there's no rush."

At the top of three flights of stairs, Timothy drew on his inhaler again and pushed open the door to the music studio. The exquisite sound of a classical piece being played on a cello drifted out.

"Bailey, we have a visitor. You probably don't remember Megan, do you?"

Megan stepped into a room filled with musical instruments of every description. A young man with a studious expression glanced up from a piano stool. Slim, like his father, his eyes were wide behind his John Lennon-style glasses and he pushed back the vibrant white-blond hair that flopped over his forehead and his equally-striking eyebrows. He put the cello and bow to one side, his serious face breaking into an open grin as he shook his head.

"I'm sorry. I could lie and say I remember you, but I don't."

"Don't worry about it," said Megan. "It was a long time ago that we saw each other. That was beautiful, by the way. What a talent. I can't even play *Three Blind Mice* on the recorder. I'm completely tone deaf."

Bailey gave her a shy smile and removed his glasses to clean the lenses on his tee-shirt.

"Bailey's very disciplined," said Timothy, his chest puffed out with pride. "He goes to a tutor five evenings a week for extra practice – including weekends and holidays. We've even drawn up a timetable for him to work on during the summer break."

"I'm impressed," said Megan. "That's very dedicated. That can't leave much time for going out with your friends, though?"

Bailey opened his mouth to reply but Diana answered for him.

"He sees enough of his friends at college during term time. And he's not one for going out to bars and clubs," she said, sharply. "There'll be plenty of time for that when he's older. For the moment, it's important that he puts all his efforts into his music. He simply can't afford to have any distractions. All his time needs to be devoted to his studies. Early nights and plenty of sleep are just what Bailey needs to set him up for a good day's practice, and he won't get those by going out with friends." Her tone softened. "You may think that's harsh, but we're hoping he'll be awarded a scholarship to The Academy of Musical Excellence. We're keeping everything crossed that he's accepted."

"Oh, he'll be accepted, don't worry about that," said Timothy. "He doesn't need luck, they'll take him on merit." He put an arm around his son's shoulder. "He'll be offered a place as soon as they hear him play – nothing's going to stop him from getting in."

"By the way, Bailey," said Diana, soothingly, "there's no need to stress about it but we've just found out that Tony from next door had a rather large amplifier delivered this morning. Your father and I are hoping it doesn't prove to be too much of a disturbance for you – you know how loud their music can be."

Bailey channelled a sigh of irritation through flared nostrils. "Yeah, I heard it. You know, it's ironic that we deliberately put the studio at the top of the house so *our* music doesn't bother the neighbours, yet we get disturbed by *theirs* all the time." He stuffed his hands into the pockets of his shorts. "It's *so* inconsiderate. I don't see why we have to put up with it. I wish you'd let me go round there to speak to Tony, Mum. Or even Adrian. I'm sure they'd be cool about it. They probably don't even know they're bothering us."

"I don't think there'll be any need for that," said Diana, with a pained expression. "We have it on good authority that Eleanor's going to complain – once she gets a bee in her bonnet, she usually gets results pretty quickly. In the meantime, try not to get stressed about it. Alright?" She clapped her hands. "Now, Megan would like to hear a piece on the cor anglais. You can do that for us, can't you, darling?"

As Bailey took the instrument from its case and began to assemble it, Timothy and Diana showed Megan the view from the small window, across the park to the village green in the distance, and beyond.

Looking to the left, she could see some of Castle Manor's pristine garden over its high fence. A huge Buddleia bush, heavy with full blooms, shaded a summer house at the end of the garden, and Natalie walked up and down as she talked on her phone, stopping to lean against a life-sized stone statue.

Looking to the right, Megan's eye was drawn to a large greenhouse, surrounded by dandelions, wild flowers and long grass in Eleanor and Oscar Cooper's unkempt garden.

"You ready?" Bailey asked as he flexed his fingers and vibrated his lips.

Megan smiled and nodded. "Ready when you are."

ooooooo

As Megan left the Starrs' house, a middle-aged couple were fawning over a gleaming Porsche on the drive of Castle Manor, the home of Natalie and her footballer husband, Adrian.

"I never dreamed we'd be able to get a car like this after what happened," said the blonde woman, tossing her stylishly coiffured hair over a tanned shoulder. "Even though it's second-hand, it's lovely, isn't it?"

"I told you I'd buy us a Porsche outright one day, didn't I?" said the stocky man with the buzz cut. He punched a banana-bunch fist into a plate-sized palm, his face turning bright red from the collar up. "Although, if it hadn't been for Oscar bloody Cooper, it would have been brand new."

Megan kept her head down and carried on walking, but a voice called her name.

"Hey, Megan!" Natalie waved and beckoned her over. "I'm so glad I've seen you again – can you spare a couple of minutes? This is Adrian's mum and dad, Mark and Christine." She lowered her voice. "Christine, this is Megan, the one I was telling you about who might be able to help with 'Operation Party Party'."

"Oh, I see." Christine hooked her designer handbag over her shoulder and took Megan's hand in a limp grasp. "Our Adrian means the world to Mark and me," she whispered. "He's been so fed-up recently, a good old knees-up's just what he needs to put the smile back on his face."

Natalie took a furtive look over her shoulder. "He'll probably pretend he hates it, but I've decided I'm going to throw a surprise party for him after all. I don't trust myself to do it all on my own, though, so Christine's going to help me. I was thinking that, if we start now, and actually have a plan, we should have enough time to pull it together, don't you think?"

Megan nodded. "Of course. Just make a list of everything you want, and then a list of everything you'll need to do to make it happen, and when it needs to be done by. I usually start at the day of the event and then work backwards. It'll be great, I'm sure."

Natalie shot her a relieved smile. "Brilliant! That's what I was hoping you'd say. Isn't that great, Christine?"

Her mother-in-law nodded. "I'm sure we'll be able to manage it."

"Christine, what have I always told you?" said Mark. "We may be working-class, but there's *nothing* the Castle family can't manage." He puffed out his barrel chest and, in contrast to his wife, almost broke Megan's fingers with his handshake before smoothing the front of his Witchester City football shirt and giving Natalie a hug. "We'd better be off. And make sure that boy of mine keeps up with his physio. The sooner he's able to get back to work – whether it be playing or coaching – the better he'll feel. And you be sure you keep telling him he doesn't have to be scoring goals to be a champion in our eyes."

"I will," said Natalie, as she waved them off. "Drive carefully. And congratulations on the car."

Mark tooted the horn and put his foot on the accelerator before driving off with a screech of rubber on tarmac. Megan imagined the residents of the street bristling behind their net curtains. She doubted many people did wheel spins in Coniston Road.

"Honestly, Mark and Christine seem to think it's perfectly acceptable that Adrian might not be able to play top-level football any more," said Natalie, with a pout. "It's alright for them, *I'm* the one who's married to him. He'll have to take a drop in salary if he has to coach... *I* might even have to get a job. It doesn't bear thinking about." She shuddered and shook the troubled expression from her face.

"Anyway, I've already got the music sorted," she said, continuing with her party plans. "Tony, one of Ade's friends, is a professional DJ. You might have heard of him if you're into the club scene? His stage name's Mirror Man, on account of the sunglasses with mirrored lenses he always wears.

"His career's just starting to *really* take off. He's got a gig in London in a few weeks and, if it goes well, he's been told there's the most incredible gig waiting for him in one of the top clubs in Ibiza. I think he's going to make megabucks – it's amazing how much money DJs make, you know. I haven't actually told him about the party yet but I know he'll be up for it. He and Adrian have been holed up for most of the afternoon with some sound equipment that was delivered this morning, so I'll tell him about it later."

"Tony spends a lot of time here, I take it?" said Megan.

Natalie pulled a face. "You could say that. He was evicted from his flat about eighteen months ago, so he moved in with us while he was looking for another place. It was only supposed to be temporary but he doesn't seem to be in any rush to move out. Every time I mention it to Adrian, it ends up in an argument so I've given up. Mind you, it's worked out quite well recently because he's one of the few people who can put a smile back on Adrian's face when he's fed up." She looked towards the house to make sure no one was listening.

"If he gets the gig in Ibiza, he won't be here much longer, though, and Adrian's going to miss him like mad. Between you and me, I think he secretly likes being the person who always bails Tony out if he needs help. Mind you, as much as he's going to miss him, I think he's a bit jealous that Tony's career looks like it's just about to take off while his is in the balance." She lowered her voice. "Tony's not my cup of tea but he makes Adrian happy, and keeps him out of my hair while he's so miserable, so that suits me fine.

"Anyway, getting back to the party, I can get hold of a caterer to organise the food and drink but the one thing I wanted to ask you about is the cake. In amongst all your contacts, I wondered if there was anyone who makes really amazing themed cakes? I want a huge one in the design of a football pitch with marzipan models of Adrian and the team holding the FA Cup in the air. He captained them to the win, you see, so it'd be good if I could give someone a photograph and they could recreate it in cake form. I'm sure it'd put a smile on his face if they could." She looked up to the sky. "Please God."

"You're in luck," said Megan. "Not only do I know someone who makes fantastic themed cakes, but I've got her card in my bag. Have a chat with her and she'll give you a quote. She's quite pricey but her work is excellent."

Natalie flapped a hand. "Money's no object – well, not as long as I order the cake before we're destitute," she said, pulling a face and grinning. "I hope we won't have to move to a less exclusive area, though. I couldn't bear it if it came to that."

Megan rummaged through her handbag. "She has three shops and I'm pretty sure one of them is only a couple of miles from here. Oh, I don't have her card. Sorry, it must be in my laptop case, but I can call you with the number when I get home, if you like?"

"Actually, I'd quite like to get in touch with her right away," said Natalie. "I'm impatient like that – once I decide I want to do something, I don't like to hang around. How about I give you a lift home and I can get the number now? Then I can call her while I'm out of the house. It'll be easier than calling from here – trying to keep anything secret while Adrian's at home is impossible."

Megan nodded. "Okay, although it's not that far to walk."

Natalie stuck out a foot, clad in a four and a half inch stiletto-heeled shoe. "In these? You must be kidding. Right, come in for a minute. I'll get my keys and tell Adrian I'm popping out for a bit.

She led Megan through to the living room. "In fact, wait here and I'll see if he'll come and say hello. He could do with talking to someone other than me, his physiotherapist, and Tony. Make yourself comfortable. I won't be long."

Megan looked around the living room, struck by the numerous photos of Adrian that decorated the walls and every surface. Photos of him punching the air after scoring a winning goal; in a celebratory huddle with his teammates; shaking hands with the Prime Minister after he'd captained his team to their first FA Cup win; with one of the young royals at a Buckingham Palace garden party; and at his wedding to Natalie, surrounded by their ten pageboys and ten bridesmaids.

She was still looking at the photos as she lowered herself into a leather armchair and put her handbag beside her. Not paying attention, she completely missed the seat and her bag fell onto the rug, spilling its contents everywhere. As she scrabbled around on her hands and knees to retrieve her things, she caught sight of two small photo frames on a low table in the corner, almost hidden behind some larger frames containing yet more pictures of Adrian.

Crawling over to look at them, she saw that one was of a group of women, all in pale green uniforms with dark piping around the collar and cuffs. *Nurses, maybe?* Megan looked more closely at the photograph – particularly at the woman on the edge of the group who looked very familiar. "Well, I'll be..."

At least two stone heavier, with a noticeably bigger nose and a considerably smaller chest, Megan recognised the woman as Natalie, her pale hair pulled off her face in a bun, and her front teeth protruding slightly over her bottom lip.

She turned her gaze to the other photograph – the 'after' version of the picture next to it. It was of Natalie again, this time with a friend outside a cinema in London's Leicester Square, the marquee above the door advertising the UK premiere of *Pride and Prejudice* on September the 16th, 2005.

Slimmer, with eye-popping scarlet hair, perfectly straight, gleaming white veneers, a chiselled nose and a curvaceous figure encased in a fitted shift dress, Natalie looked like a younger, more glamorous version of the woman in the other photograph.

Guess you can look however you want when you've got the money to pay for it, thought Megan, and scurried back to the armchair when she heard Natalie's voice outside the room.

"Megan, this is Adrian. I apologise in advance for his mood – it's bloody awful." Natalie moved her fringe from her brow with a recently-painted burgundy nail and rested a hand on her ample hip. "I told him just because *he's* lost his sense of fun, doesn't mean we *all* have to sit around with faces like a pug chewing a thistle."

Megan stood to greet him. Blond, broad, and taller than he looked in his photos, Adrian almost filled the doorway before limping towards her, helped along by a pair of crutches. "Megan Fallon – nice to meet you." She nodded to his leg. "Sorry to hear about your injury. It looks painful."

Adrian grimaced. "I'm better than I was. And I'll be even better next week when the physio gives me the OK to walk without these damn things." He scowled before giving Megan an apologetic half-smile. "Sorry, I don't mean to be rude but I'm going a little stir crazy – being stuck at home is driving me up the wall.

The sooner I can get back to work, the better. Even if it isn't playing football."

Natalie clicked her tongue in exasperation. "I *do* wish you'd stop saying that."

The sound of whistling drifted into the room, followed by the arrival of a man in a kilt and flip flops, a pair of large sunglasses with blue mirrored lenses covering his eyes. His bare torso was covered in tattoos and his bald head was decorated by a channel of short fluorescent-green hair which ran from his forehead to the nape of his neck.

"Y'alright, doll?" he said, lifting his chin in Megan's direction. "Ade, you gotta come listen to this bass. It's sweet. I'm gonna get myself a beer, you want one?"

Natalie raised an eyebrow and hung her handbag over the crook of her elbow. "C'mon, Megan." She jerked her head towards the door. "I think that's our cue to leave."

CHAPTER NINE

"Right, Natalie, let's see if I can find this card for you. Come on in." Megan tossed her handbag onto the hall stand and called up the stairs. "Hellooo! Anyone home? I thought my parents and my sister might be back," she said, "but obviously not."

"This is a lovely house," said Natalie. "Very homely. Have your parents lived here long?"

Megan nodded as she hunted through her laptop case for The Baking Lady's business card. "Ever since we were kids."

"My mum and dad would have killed for a nice place in a nice neighbourhood when they were young, but they didn't have two pennies to rub together," said Natalie, her face suddenly clouded by a serious expression. "They've got one now, though." She smiled. "It's nice that I've been able to help them out since I've been married to Adrian."

"Aha!" Megan held up an elegantly-designed business card. "Here you are – The Baking Lady. She's very good, so definitely worth a call. I hope she can help you out."

Natalie tucked the card into her handbag. "Thanks. I'll give her a call from the car before I get home. Right, I'd better be off. I'll see myself out."

"It's okay, I'll walk out with you."

"Is that your cat?" Natalie asked, as she teetered down the garden path in her heels.

"Kind of." Ever since Cat had made a pincushion out of Laurence's back, Megan had felt an affinity with the temperamental tabby. She threw him an affectionate look as she stopped to make a fuss of him, and he swivelled an eyeball to look up at her from his recumbent position as she tickled his tummy. "He's a fabulous guard-cat, but he's quite friendly if you want to stroke him."

"Actually, I'm not really keen on cats." Natalie eyed Cat with suspicion before a sudden change of heart. "Although he does look quite friendly," she said, taking a couple of cautious steps towards him.

"You don't have to stroke him if you don't want to," said Megan. "I'm sure he won't take offence."

Crouching down, Natalie leaned forward and reached out a tentative hand to stroke Cat on the back of his neck. "Here, kitty, kitty, kitty."

It all happened so quickly, it caught them unawares.

Cat flipped himself over onto all fours, feet firmly planted and back arched, fur on end and lips curled back in a venomous hiss. He gave an agitated yowl before taking a swipe at Natalie's hand, leaving her wrist with four angry-looking scratches. She jumped back, toppling off her heels and fell flat on her backside.

"*Cat*! What are you playing at!" Megan ran to Natalie's aid, putting herself between her and the furious tabby.

"Bloody hell! He's gone berserk!" Natalie scrabbled to her feet, tears welling in her eyes. She stared at Cat, her eyes following him as he fixed her with a stare, the end of his upright tail twitching from side to side, like a cobra preparing to strike.

"I have no idea what sets him off." A bemused Megan shook her head. "He just doesn't take kindly to some people. Come on, we'd better get that cleaned up."

As she dragged Natalie back into the house, the dishevelled footballer's wife glared at Cat, and he glared back.

ooooooo

"Oh good grief! Was she hurt?"

Claudia Fallon's eyebrows shot up in alarm after hearing about Cat's latest hissy fit. "The last thing we need is an insurance claim from a footballer's wife that our cat ruined her manicure, or punctured one of her fake boobs," she said, closing the oven door on a sizeable dish of lasagne.

Megan giggled. "She's fine, Mum. And I don't think she'll cause a fuss. For a start, it was *her* fault. She leaned right over Cat so she probably scared him. I'm not surprised he went for her. In any case, she wouldn't be able to make a claim if she wanted to because he's not really our cat, is he? Don't worry, after I'd cleaned up her hand, she drove home as right as rain, and I imagine she'll want to give Cat a wide berth so I doubt we'll ever see her again."

"Well, let's hope not," said Claudia. "The last thing we need is a malevolent cat on our hands."

oooooo

Aunt Sylvie pinched each of Megan's cheeks between a thumb and index finger and jiggled them about. "Oh, love. It's been far too long," she said, planting a lipstick imprint on Megan's cheek which she proceeded to wipe off with a lick of spit on a tissue she produced from up her sleeve. "It's about time you came back for a visit – we've missed you." She pulled her niece into a hug that forced the air from her lungs, and gave her a couple of hearty slaps on the back.

When Aunty Sylvie loved you, you knew about it.

Stepping over the doorstep, she offered a powdered cheek for a kiss. "Here, take this, will you." She shook out her curls – like Claudia's, but threaded with silver – and shoved her cycling helmet into Megan's arms. "Where's your mum?" Without waiting for an answer, she went into the living room.

"Evenin', Megan." Uncle Des set down his cycling helmet and gave her a wide smile and a hug. "It's good to see you again." He stood back to take a long look at her. "Hello, what's this?" He put a hand up to her ear and pulled out a pound coin.

She laughed with delight to see his old trick, her reluctant heart filling with affection for the uncle who'd been such a huge part of her childhood.

"I've brought dessert." Dropping a kiss on her forehead, Des handed her a large box tied with a bow. "Freshly baked, they are." He crossed his arms over his chest and squinted through one eye. "There's something different about you since I saw you last."

"Well, it's been a few years."

Des snapped his fingers. "I know what it is. You've had some of those headlight thingies, haven't you?"

Megan chuckled. "You mean highlights. Yes, I have."

"Thought so."

She put her nose close to the box Des had given her and inhaled. The aroma took her right back to summers spent with her aunt and uncle, sitting on the back step with a handful of Uncle Des's lavender Madeleines she'd carried from the kitchen in her skirt.

At Sylvie and Des's, Sylvie had always been the one to tackle any odd jobs, while Des had acquired the knack of effortlessly turning out the most delicious, lightest, cakes, biscuits and pies. To say he had the touch of an angel when it came to baking was no exaggeration.

When he'd joined a wine club and become a little too fond of the red variety, though, the baking had stopped. It was good to see it had started again.

"You look really well, Uncle Des."

"I *feel* really well, love. I may be sixty-five but I feel like a new man. It's like I've been given a second chance at life and I'm grabbing it with both hands."

With his full head of tousled salt and pepper hair, and his once-bloodshot green eyes having regained their roguish twinkle in his crumpled face, it warmed Megan's heart to see her uncle on such good form.

"I'm doing everything I can to make sure I'll be around for a few more years yet. I've been exercising, keeping my brain active, taking up new hobbies, that sort of thing." He scratched his left ear and a high-pitched whistle rang out.

"What's that noise?" said Megan, with a start.

"Oh, blast! It's this bloomin' hearing aid!" said Des, his voice blaring out. "I got it the day before yesterday and I can't get the settings right. One minute I can't hear a thing, next minute I'm blowing my eardrums out.

And in between, there's this infernal whistling the audiologist tells me is called 'feedback'. It's a damn nuisance."

"Stop yelling, Des, for heaven's sake!" Sylvie called from the living room. "And can't you do something about that whistling? Honestly, it's like spending the evening with a steam engine."

Des fiddled with his ear and the whistling stopped. "Ah, that's better. Sorry to shout, but when I can't hear properly, I don't know I'm doing it, see?" He coughed and looked at the floor. "By the way, Megan," he said, quietly, "while I've got you on your own, I know it's been a long time coming but I owe you an apology. My behaviour at your wedding was inexcusable – I don't know what I was thinking." He raised his gaze and his lips curved in a bashful smile. "I'm sorry."

Taken aback, and touched by the apology, Megan waved a dismissive hand. "I'd forgotten all about it," she fibbed, "but thank you."

Des gave her hand a brief squeeze, then sniffed the air as he made his way into the living room. "Now, if my nose isn't mistaken, that's lasagne baking in the oven, isn't it? My favourite."

Megan smiled as she opened the fridge for the salad dressing and saw the apple juice that Des favoured these days. For too long, drink had robbed her of the mischievous, loving, harmonica-playing uncle who used to spend hours playing silly games with her and Lizzie when they were kids, but he was back now, and she was over the moon to see him again.

She set the kitchen table and poured the apple juice into an ice-filled jug before calling through the serving hatch.

"Dinner's ready!"

oooooooo

"You know, how on earth that Kelly DeVille woman has managed to keep Laurence from straying for all these years is beyond me," said Sylvie as she pulled her chair closer to the table and tucked a serviette into her collar. "She must have some extraordinary bedroom tricks up her sleeve."

As Claudia choked on a glass of water and Nick, Megan and Lizzie chuckled at Sylvie's blunt delivery, Des stared at his wife in amazement. "And you think *I* choose unsuitable dinner conversation topics? Perhaps we could talk about something else?" He jerked his head in Megan's direction.

"Sorry, love." Sylvie reached across the table and patted her niece's hand. "Sometimes I don't realise I'm thinking aloud. I was just looking at you and wondering why on earth Laurence thought that woman was a better bet than you. She's so awful, I can't think what he sees in her. Anyway, Lizzie was telling us earlier about what happened on your way down yesterday," she said, dumping a large portion of lasagne onto Des's plate. "Did you see the early evening news?"

"No, why?"

"We caught it just before we came out – there was a report on it about the chap who was strangled in his car. His name was Vincent Cannon."

"No, it wasn't," said Des, helping himself to a jacket potato. "It was Victor Cann*ing*."

"Oh, whatever," said Sylvie. "He'd lived in Honeymeade all his life, it said. Poor chap – what a way to go."

Des scowled as he cut into his potato with savage strokes of his knife. "For Pete's sake, what kind of person strangles an old man in his car? I'll tell you who – a bloody coward, that's who."

"Well, he wasn't *that* old, Des," said Sylvie. "Seventy-four, the news report said. Isn't that middle-aged by today's standards? If I tell myself that, I've still got half my life ahead of me." She winked at her nieces across the table.

"I wonder if the murders are connected?" said Nick. "This one, and Andy Cochran from the comedy club a couple of months ago."

"Why would they be connected?" asked Megan.

"Well, there's never been a murder in Bliss Bay, or any of the surrounding villages, and suddenly there are two," said Nick. "It just makes me wonder if there's a connection."

"Well, I hope they get a move on and catch whoever's responsible sooner rather than later," said Sylvie, "and lock him up for a very long time."

"Might not be a 'him'," said Lizzie, heaping salad onto her plate. "Plenty of women have bumped people off over the years."

"Of course," said Des, "the police don't catch *everything*, you know. Sometimes things slip through the net because witnesses forget to tell them something, or get confused about what they've seen or heard." He leaned across the table, a knowing look on his face. "Working on wrong information can be the difference between finding the clue that helps solve the case, or not."

"Well thank you for that, Chief Inspector Harper," said Sylvie, with an eye roll. "Pass the potatoes, please."

"Here, you know what we should do?" said Des, jabbing his fork in Megan and Lizzie's direction. "We should take a drive out to that diner where that chap was found, and have a word with the owner. I bet he's remembered a few things since yesterday that went right out of his mind at the time. Shock can do that to you, you know. Makes you forget all kinds of things."

Sylvie shot him a look. "Yes, because that would be a fabulous way for the girls to while away a few hours, wouldn't it? Desmond, I do wish you wouldn't get these madcap ideas – I'm sure the police know what they're doing."

"Yeah, count me out," said Lizzie. "I can think of a thousand other things I'd rather do while I'm here."

"Erm, can we talk about something else, please?" said Claudia. "We've got a happy event to look forward to and I don't know about you, but talking about dead people takes the edge off it a bit for me."

"Good idea," said Sylvie. "You know, you could put a hundred people in a room and sooner or later, the conversation would get around to bad news stories. It's human nature, the fascination with the macabre. Funny, isn't it?"

"About as funny as haemorrhoids on a bike ride," muttered Des, as he tried to work the salt and pepper mills.

"I suppose you'll be too busy to go to the residents meeting next Wednesday, Nick?" asked Sylvie, changing the subject, and mopping cheese sauce off her plate with a bread roll. "Shame, 'cos we need as much support as we can get if we're going to have any chance of putting a stop to that hypermarket debacle."

"No, I'll be going," said Nick. "Claudia's going, too. It's too important not to. We've got to do whatever we can to stop that hypermarket being built. Between you and me, I've got a horrible feeling that all our efforts are going to come to nothing, but we've got to try."

"I can't believe they're going to knock the old school down," said Claudia, pushing her plate away and loosening the drawstring on her yoga pants. "It breaks my heart to think of the old clock and bell tower being smashed to bits because someone who doesn't even know the community has decided that Bliss Bay needs to keep up with the times."

"It's called progress, Claudia." Des belched, not so discreetly, behind his serviette. "Under different circumstances, I wouldn't disagree with it, but when it threatens our way of life, well, that's another matter. Anyway, there's no point in getting all worked up about it because it won't get us anywhere. All we can do is stand up for what we believe in and hope for the best."

ooooooo

Dinner over, Megan and Des loaded the dishwasher as the others had a lively debate about the state of the education system.

"Well, your sister's obviously not interested, but what d'*you* think about going to talk to the chap from the diner?" Des whispered. "The sooner the better, if you ask me. What about Monday?"

Megan rinsed off the dinner plates as she considered Des's proposition. It had taken less than a minute for her beloved uncle to fall back into favour with her, but she wasn't sure she wanted to take him up on his offer to become an amateur detective duo. In fact, just the thought of it made her chest feel tight.

"I'm sorry. I'd rather not, if you don't mind. I'd just like to forget about it."

"Des nodded. "Alright. If that's what you want," he said, stacking the plates in the dishwasher rack. "Although we wouldn't be doing anything illegal or dangerous, if that's what you're worried about. We'd just be asking a few questions, that's all." He took the plate Megan handed him. "It would be a terrible shame if Evie came back to Bliss Bay, to find it had become the murder capital of the UK, just because we didn't do our bit to help catch a killer. Ah, well, not to worry." He sighed and gave Megan a sly look from out of the corner of his eye.

She glared at him. That wasn't fair. Evie was her weak spot, and Des knew it. But then she remembered the vow she'd made before she'd come back to Bliss Bay. The promise she'd made to herself to explore the world outside her comfort zone in search of fun and excitement.

She started the dishwasher and looked up at Des before chuckling at his persuasive argument. Rather than jump in headfirst, perhaps a little dip of her toe in the waters of the unknown wouldn't be so bad? Of course, if she was really lucky, the killer would be caught soon, and she and Des wouldn't have to go anywhere.

"Okay, you've convinced me," she heard herself say. "Monday it is."

ooooooo

"Where was the body?" asked Des, as they pulled up across the road from Joe's Diner.

"Just there, in that parking bay." Megan shuddered at the memory as she got out of the car. "The guy looked like he was asleep." She peered through the window of the diner. "Looks like they're quite busy – we might have to wait a while to speak to someone."

"I've seen the coppers do this a thousand times on the TV," said Des. "Just leave the talking to me

The man Megan recognised as Joe looked up as they walked in. "Hi. I'll be with you in a sec."

As they hovered by the counter, Des scratched his ear, setting off the whistle from his hearing aid.

"Damn it!" He fiddled with the control and the whistling stopped.

"Sorry about that," said Joe, "what can I get you?"

"We're here about the dead man," bellowed Des, his voice rising above the hubbub of chatter as he continued to fiddle with the earpiece.

As every head snapped round, the diner fell silent, except for the whoosh of a steam pipe in a jug of milk, gurgling as it turned it to creamy foam, and the piercing *eeeeeeeeeeeee* issuing from Des's left ear.

Megan tapped him on the shoulder. "I think you've turned the volume down too much."

"What say?" he hollered, a hand cupped behind his lughole.

Megan jabbed a finger at his ear. "*The volume. Turn it up!*"

"Oh." Des fiddled with the switch again and the whistling stopped. "Sorry 'bout that," he said, his voice returning to its normal level. "Was I shouting?"

Megan raised a brow. "A bit." The chatter from the tables behind resumed and she turned to Joe. "Have you got a couple of minutes? We just want to have a quick chat."

He nodded. "If you're quick. "He stared at Megan through narrowed eyes. "I know you, don't I?"

She nodded. "I was here the other morning with my sister."

He snapped a finger and thumb. "I knew I recognised you. Sorry, my mind's been a blur since then. It's a wonder I've remembered anything."

"Told you shock does funny things to your memory," said Des, nudging Megan in the ribs.

"Lucky you came today," said Joe. "We've only just opened up again. The police had the whole area cordoned off until last night – it's been crawling with forensics." He topped up a coffee cup with milk and took it to a nearby table. "Who are you, by the way?"

"Just a couple of concerned Bliss Bay residents," said Des. "You might have heard we had a murder of our own a couple of months ago, so we wondered if you could tell us anything that might help to shed some light on whether there's a connection between the two, or if they're totally separate. We just want the killer, or killers, off the streets."

Joe shrugged. "I'm not sure I can tell you anything that'll be of any use but I can tell you what I told the police, if you like."

"Anything you can tell us will be a help," said Des. "The victim, for example. Did you know him well?"

Megan did a double-take and bit the inside of her cheeks when her uncle whipped out a notebook and pen from his inside pocket.

"Only as a customer," said Joe. "Victor Canning wasn't the kind of person I'd choose as a friend, if you know what I mean."

"I see," said Des. "And was he married, divorced, widowed?"

Joe shook his head. "None of the above. Although there was a woman he spoke about sometimes. He said she was the love of his life and if he couldn't be with her, he didn't want to be with anyone."

"Did he say who she was?"

"No, and we never asked. It was best not to ask too much – sometimes he got nasty if he thought you were prying."

Des flipped over a page in his book. "And do you know anyone who might have wanted him dead?"

Joe scoffed. "How about everyone he met? He wasn't well-liked. He really wasn't a very nice man."

"Didn't he have friends?" asked Des? "People he used to come in with?"

Joe shook his head as he emptied freshly ground coffee beans into a filter. "No one. He said something a few weeks ago, though, that we thought was strange, didn't he Moira?" He turned to the woman behind the counter who was loading up a tray with mugs and two large earthenware pots of tea for a group of builders who were tucking into their breakfasts.

"Yeah, he said he'd been offered the opportunity of a lifetime." Moira blinked repeatedly and blew her fringe out of her eyes. "He was very smug about it – said he couldn't wait to be working again among people who appreciated him. I've no idea what he was talking about, though, because he'd been retired for years, and I didn't ask. Like Joe said, sometimes it was better not to." She lifted the heavy tray from the counter. "Mind your backs, please, I'm coming through."

A bell rang in the kitchen.

"Gotta go, that's a food order," said Joe. "Sorry I can't tell you much."

"On the contrary," said Des, snapping his notebook shut. "You've been very helpful."

"Thanks for your time," said Megan, as she pulled the door shut behind her.

"Well, *you* didn't say much," said Des, as they crossed the road to the car.

Megan raised her eyebrows. "Well, I didn't see any need, Detective Harper. You had everything well under control. All you needed was a crumpled raincoat and a half-smoked cigar."

As they were getting into the car, the diner door swung open and Joe ran over to them. "I just remembered – the police were making a big deal about Victor's bow tie. When I saw him earlier that morning, he'd been wearing one but when he was found in his car, it had gone."

Des took out his notebook again. "Was wearing bow tie first thing, but missing when found in car," he said as he wrote the words. "Thanks. You've been very helpful. If we need to speak to you again, we'll be in touch."

oooooo

"'If we need to speak to you again, we'll be in touch'?" repeated Megan, as she crunched Vinnie the Mini into first gear and drove off. "I think that's getting a little bit *too* much into character."

Des gave a triumphant cackle and rubbed his hands together. "That was brilliant! I haven't had so much fun in ages! And what's the problem? I wasn't doing any harm, was I? I was only asking questions and making a few notes. I told him we were concerned Bliss Bay residents, didn't I? It's not as though I was impersonating a police officer."

Megan gave him a wry smile as she headed home. "I suppose not."

"*And*, we found out some really useful stuff. The bow tie, for example – where could that have gone?" He drummed his fingers against his knee. "Of course, you know what would be *really* useful? If we could find out some more about Andy Cochran's murder. Then we'd be able to compare the two to see if there were any similarities." He wound down the window and breathed in the fresh air. "I suppose you've got a lot left to organise for your mum and dad's ceremony?"

"A fair bit. Why?"

"Oh, no reason," said Des, casually, his elbow leaning on the window frame.

"You want to go to the comedy club now, don't you?" said Megan, with a sigh. "To have a nose around?"

Des turned in his seat. "D'you think we could?" he said, excitedly. "I know it's closed down but there are some offices nearby. There must have been police coming and going for days after the murder, so someone there must be able to tell us something. What d'you think?"

Megan hesitated. She wanted the killer behind bars as much as anyone. And, as Des said, they weren't doing any harm, or breaking any laws. Organising her parents' ceremony was going to take *some* of her time, but it wouldn't take it all. And, surprisingly, she was quite enjoying herself.

"Okay, but not until after the ceremony? How about next Thursday. Will that do?"

Des beamed and took his pencil and a sharpener from his pocket.

"That'll do nicely."

ooooooo

DI Sam Cambridge looked over the forensics report before flipping the file shut.

"Harvey!" he called out for his Sergeant.

"Yes, boss?"

"I got back the forensics report on Victor Canning's death this morning."

"Anything enlightening?"

"The angle of the ligature, and the wound, indicate that he was strangled by someone standing outside the car rather than someone inside it. The roof was down, so the killer would have had very easy access."

"Is that it?"

"No. The pollen that was on Mr Canning's face is a match to the pollen found on Andy Cochran, so it looks like our comedy club killer has struck again."

"I take it forensics are still trying to locate the pollen's source?"

"Yes. All they know so far is that it definitely didn't come from any of the flowers in the vicinity where either of the deceased were found."

"Anything else, boss?"

"Actually, there is. There was a lot of unidentified DNA at the first crime scene. Not that that's surprising in itself – there's often unidentified DNA at crime scenes – but what's interesting is that one of the samples found there, is a match to one found at the *second* crime scene. Of course, we can't say for sure that it definitely belongs to the perpetrator, but I'd say it's a pretty safe bet."

"Well, it's the best lead we've had so far," said Harvey. "All we have to do now is find out who it belongs to."

Sam took a peppermint from the packet on his desk and cocked an eyebrow. "If only it were that easy. A club that had hundreds of people passing through its doors every week, and an open-topped car are hardly isolated crime scenes. I dread to think how long it'll take to get a DNA match." He crunched his peppermint. "But it's a step in the right direction. Now all we need is a few more, and they'll lead us right to the killer."

CHAPTER TEN

With preparations for the ceremony well under way, Megan barely had time to breathe. It seemed that every minute was filled with something to organise, and the days flew by.

On the morning of the ceremony, she jumped out of bed at quarter-past six and flung open the curtains, praying that bad weather hadn't made its way to Bliss Bay during the night.

She let out a sigh of relief to see the sun already shining in a blue sky flecked with wispy clouds. Pulling on jeans and a tee-shirt, she shoved her feet into a pair of slippers.

"Morning Cat." She jumped over the tabby as he was waking up in his favourite spot – halfway up the stairs. Pointing her phone at him, she snapped him with the camera as he yawned and stretched across the whole width of the step.

"That's picture number one for my album, kitty."

Cat opened an eye and gave her a look that seemed to say, "Do you mind?"

Although a local photographer was booked to take pictures to commemorate the day, Megan wanted some informal snaps to make into an album to give her parents when they got back from their cruise.

The sun had yet to gain much heat, and she shivered in the cold air as she snapped a picture of the garden, quiet and still on a perfect morning, with a light mist hanging over the lawn.

"Right, coffee." Megan took one step onto the tiled kitchen floor and her feet almost went from under her. Grabbing the corner of the worktop, she steadied herself. Her slippers, soaking wet from the dew on the grass, had turned the tiles into a skating rink. She swore under her breath and kicked the slippers off as she headed for the coffee maker to get a jug of her favourite brew on the go.

She'd wake the rest of the family at seven but, until then, she wanted to enjoy what she knew would be the last few minutes of peace and quiet she'd get until the ceremony was over.

And, if she had anything to do with it, the subject of murder was well and truly off the agenda for today.

oooooooo

With Sylvie and Lizzie helping Claudia get ready, and Nick, Des and Shaun mingling with the guests, Megan was checking, double-checking and re-checking that everything was in place.

In a shady corner of the garden, Classical Kin were getting ready to play their first set of the afternoon.

"Everything okay?" she asked Timothy. "Are you on schedule to start soon?"

Timothy coughed, stuck a thumb in the air and replaced the cap of his hip flask. "Everything's perfect. Bailey and I are raring to go, and I'm having a swig of honey and lemon to lubricate the old throat." He drew deeply on his inhaler. "Diana's just popped to the bathroom, then we'll be ready to start. Ah, here she comes."

Diana took her place at the harp and flexed her fingers.

"Ready, darling?" asked Timothy.

"Ready as I'll ever be," she replied, and counted them in to their first piece.

ooooooo

"Well, if we're not ready now, we'll never be ready," said Megan, snapping a photo of Petal, Lionel, Blossom and Daisy as they arrived.

"I'm sure everything's going to go like clockwork," said Petal. "Why don't you listen to the music and chill out a bit?" She nodded towards the corner of the garden. "They're very good, aren't they? I mean, I'm not sure I'd buy their records – I'm more of a heavy metal girl myself – but they're perfect for this."

"Yeah, they're not bad, are they?" said Megan, snapping a few more pictures. "I'm not really into classical music but this is lovely."

"Hey! We're here!"

Megan turned to see Olivia and Rob from the village shop. "You made it! Thanks for coming. Can I get a quick photo? I know you've only just walked in but if I don't do it now, I might forget to ask later."

"Course you can! How's this?" Olivia grabbed Rob and pulled him towards the camera. "Say cheeeese!" she said, holding up the skirt of her blue silk dress. "Will that do?"

Megan looked at the picture on her phone. "Perfect! You look fabulous!"

"I love your dress," said Petal. "What a gorgeous colour."

"Yes, it's lovely, isn't it? It's exactly the same colour as the stones in my bracelet, so I guess it must be sapphire blue." Olivia held up her wrist and the gems twinkled in the sunlight. "It's nice to have a chance to wear it. It's usually stuck in a box on my dressing table."

She leaned forward and cupped a hand beside her mouth. "And don't tell anyone, but I got the dress from the Hearts and Minds charity shop. I've got your Daisy to thank for finding it for me – she's a fantastic shop manager. Or should I say, personal shopper. As soon as she held it up, I knew it was the dress for me. You'd never believe it only cost £10.00, would you?" Her eyes fixed on a waiter, handing out glasses from a tray. "Ooh, Champagne! I'll be back in a minute. Anyone care to join me in a glass of bubbly? Sorry, Blossom, not you. You can have a soft drink." Olivia made herself scarce, followed by the others.

As Megan did another check of the room, a light tap on her shoulder preceded a low rumble of a voice.

"The invitation said 'Smart Casual'. This is the only suit I brought with me that looked like it might fit the brief. I hope it's okay?"

She turned and raised her gaze eight inches to find herself looking into the pale grey eyes of a man whose serious face broke into an easy smile with a dimple in each cheek. His dark hair skimmed the collar of his charcoal-grey linen suit, and he ran a hand across his rugged, clean-shaven jawline as he waited for answer.

"You're perfect." *Gaaaah!* "I mean, you *look* perfect – the suit, obviously. For the occasion. The suit's perfect for the occasion. Fits the brief perfectly. You look very nice." *Just stop talking, Megan, for God's sake.* She returned the smile before looking down at her clipboard to hide her blushes. "I'm sorry, could you give me your name, please? I'm checking off the guests as they arrive so I know when we can get started."

"So you don't remember me?" He sounded amused.

Megan studied his face. She didn't recognise him at all, but if she'd met him before, there was absolutely no way she'd have forgotten. His voice rang a bell, though.

"I'm really sorry, I don't remember you, but you do sound familiar. You say we know each other?"

"Yeah, we know each other," he replied. "From way back, originally, but more recently from the other day when you gave me a push on the chair outside the village shop."

Megan snapped a finger a thumb. "That's it! I *knew* I recognised the voice." She looked at him again. "But I haven't spent much time in Bliss Bay for quite a few years, so I don't think you could know me from way back. You sure you're not confusing me with someone else?"

He crossed his arms. "Well, if you don't remember me, I guess that must mean I'm forgiven, at last."

Completely confused, she shook her head. "Forgiven? Forgiven for what?"

"For flattening your mom's birthday cake into a pancake all those years ago, of course."

Megan's mouth fell open. "*Jack*? You're Jelly-Legs-Jack Windsor? You're kidding! Your uncle said you were back but the last time I saw you, you looked – and sounded – so different. *Really* different. And now, you look so... so, um, tall. I mean, there are quite a few Americans living in Bliss Bay now but even if there weren't, I would never have guessed that was you the other day. She looked him up and down again. "I just can't believe it."

Jack smiled. "Well, I promise you, it's me." He pulled up his right trouser leg to reveal a long scar on his leather-loafer-clad foot. "I got that when I fell over on the boat that day. If I remember rightly, you lent me your sweater to stem the flow of blood until we got to shore."

Megan nodded. "You're right. I did. Well, I'm glad to see you've managed to stay in one piece since then. You were so clumsy."

He chuckled and scratched his head. "Still am a bit. Never did find my sea legs, either – it definitely does *not* run in the family. Which reminds me, Aunt Rita wasn't feeling too well this morning so I've come along as my uncle's plus-one – he felt a little uncomfortable about showing up on his own. I hope that's okay?"

"Of course it is. I hope it's nothing serious? With your aunt, I mean."

Jack shook his head. "Just a cold, but the last thing she wanted to do was pass anything to your mum and dad before they go off on vacation, so she thought it best to stay away."

"Well, give her my love when you see her. And it's great to have you here. I hope you'll enjoy the afternoon."

"Oh, I'm sure I will. It'll give me a chance to talk to some of the people I haven't managed to catch up with since I've been back. I've been hanging out with Lionel and Rob the last couple of months but it's still kind of weird being back among people I've known for years, but don't actually know very well anymore. Does that make sense?"

"It makes perfect sense," said Megan, with an emphatic nod. "I feel exactly the same." She glanced at her watch. "Look, I'm sorry, I'd love to stop and chat but I've got a ton of things to check on. Perhaps we can catch up later?"

"Sure. You go do what you gotta do. It's good to see you again."

"Yeah, it's good to see you too."

As she walked away, Megan was surprised to realise that it really was.

oooooo

As Megan and Lizzie wiped the tears from their cheeks, Megan wondered why she'd ever doubted Des's suitability to officiate at the ceremony.

He'd gauged the mood exactly right, with sentiment, loving tributes and humour in all the right places at all the right times.

When her dad thanked him in his speech, no one cheered louder than Megan as she raised her glass of Champagne to Des, and he raised his glass of apple juice in response.

As Nick and Claudia started off the dancing, Lizzie joined Megan by the edge of the dance floor.

"You did good, sis," she said, giving her a hug.

"Aaw, thank you." Megan hugged her back. "I'm so relieved it all went okay. You know, I couldn't tell you how many events I've organised but this was more nerve-wracking than all of them put together."

She giggled at Jack, dancing opposite Sylvie in the middle of the dance floor to some old disco music, narrowly avoiding the other guests with his flailing arms and legs which seemed to have a mind of their own. He hadn't been joking when he said he was still clumsy.

Megan looked at her mum and dad, and hooked her arm through Lizzie's. She was going to miss them terribly when they all left the next day.

"You okay?"

Megan nodded. "I was just thinking about what it'll be like after tomorrow. It's going to be quiet around here."

Lizzie raised an eyebrow. "Doubtful. Not with Uncle Des, his nose for crime and his trusty notebook living just around the corner.

Anyway, stop thinking about what it'll be like when we've all gone while we're still here, and come and have a dance!"

ooooooo

A police constable stood outside the gates of 37, Coniston Road, opposite which a crowd of people had gathered.

"What's going on in there? Has something happened to Adrian?" An anxious middle-aged man and his equally anxious son clutched their Witchester City football scarves as they waited for news.

"I can't say, I'm afraid," the police officer said. "But I'm sure there'll be an update soon. Afternoon, DI Cambridge." The constable removed the cordon to allow Sam to pass through and make a beeline for Harvey, who wasted no time in bringing him up to speed.

"Right, boss. The deceased is a gentleman named Tony Weller – cause of death appears to be blunt force trauma to the head. He was a friend of Adrian Castle's and he'd been staying here for a while."

"A burglary gone wrong, perhaps?" said Sam. "An area like this is ripe pickings."

Harvey shrugged. "Could be, although there's no evidence of anyone attempting to have gained entry to the actual house. It seems they just forced the lock on the side gate, killed Mr Weller, and legged it. I suppose there could have been a scuffle which resulted in his death, and scared off the intruder – or intruders – but there are no self-defence wounds on the body, so that looks unlikely at the moment. In any case, the wound is on the back of his head so it appears he wasn't in a combative position when he was hit. Whatever happened, Natalie Castle raised the alarm at approximately twenty-past three this afternoon, just after she first came downstairs and saw Mr Weller from the kitchen window."

"Twenty-past three was the first time she came downstairs?"

"When Adrian's not working, they sleep late on a Sunday. They didn't wake up until then."

"What caused the injury?"

"There's a bloodstained stone dish on the ground next to the deceased. It's part of a decorative statue – I'd say it was probably a birdbath."

"Anything that links this to the other murders?" Sam crunched on an indigestion tablet and rubbed a weary eye with the heel of his hand.

"There are grains of yellow powder on his cheek. I'll bet they're the same as the other two."

"And you say entry was gained via the side gate?"

"Yes, boss. It was forced open."

Sam strode halfway up the garden, to where a body lay beside the fishpond. A life-sized statue of a water nymph looked over the scene, the stone bird bath which had once been held aloft in its right hand now lying on the ground beside Tony Weller.

"Is there any CCTV footage?"

"There are cameras inside and out, but I haven't seen the tapes yet. Mrs Castle said she doubts there'll be anything useful on them, though, because they only switched the cameras and the alarm on when they went to bed, and the first thing Mr Weller did when he came down every morning was switch them off, along with the security lights. According to Mrs Castle, he thought the cameras were too intrusive, so he persuaded her and Mr Castle that it wasn't necessary to have them on during the day."

"Did he now?" Sam glanced at the security features around the perimeter of the house and its grounds.

"What're you thinking, boss?"

"Well, you'd have thought that the lights and security cameras all over the place, and the big red alarm boxes on the walls, would have been enough of a deterrent to stop someone breaking in, wouldn't you? I mean, that's kind of the point of having them. Come on, I want to take a look at the CCTV footage to see what was captured before the cameras were switched off. We can take a more thorough look around outside later."

They found the Castles in the living room, Natalie attempting to comfort Adrian as she handed him wads of tissues to mop his tears.

"How did this happen?" Adrian was saying, over and over, to no one in particular.

"Ahem. Mr and Mrs Castle, I'm DI Cambridge." Sam nodded a greeting. "I'm sorry for your loss. And I'm sorry to disturb you at such a difficult time but DS Decker and I would like to view the CCTV tape if possible? I understand you're upset but the sooner we can see it, the better our chances of catching whoever did this."

Natalie blew her nose. "It's alright, Adrian, you stay here. I'll show the detectives the tape in the kitchen." She rose from the couch and led the detectives from the room. "Although I'm not sure you'll see anything that'll help. I already told you that we only switched on the CCTV before we went to bed, and Tony switched it off again as soon as he got up. Unless we all went out, we never had it on during the day while Tony was here because he didn't like being 'under surveillance', as he put it." She rolled her eyes and pushed the kitchen door shut.

"Did anyone else know that Mr Weller switched off the security systems every morning?" asked Sam.

Natalie shrugged. "I've no idea. Why d'you ask?"

"Because the house is so well protected, it's odd that someone would risk activating the lights, setting off the alarm, or getting caught on camera. Don't you think?"

"'Spose so. I hadn't thought of that. You'd be better off asking Adrian, though. He's more likely to know than me." She rewound the footage to see Tony that morning, coming into the kitchen before switching off the security systems, a pair of black-framed mirrored sunglasses wrapped around his eyes.

"Stop the tape," said Sam. "Are you sure that footage is from this morning?"

"Of course I am. Look, it says so here." Natalie pointed to the bottom of the monitor screen to the date and time stamp. *Sunday 05:26:04*

"Then why was he wearing sunglasses in the house? The sun's not even out at that time."

"Because Tony *always* wore sunglasses with mirrored lenses. They were his trademark – that's why his stage name was Mirror Man – but he didn't just wear them for work, he wore them *all* the time, day and night, inside and out."

"So, if he wore them all the time, where are they now?" asked Harvey.

Natalie shrugged. "Don't ask me, but they must have fallen off or they'd still be on his face. Have you checked the fishpond? There's not a lot of water in it just now because the lining's been changed and Gerald – that's our gardener – is testing it to make sure it doesn't leak. Anyway, you'll easily be able to see Tony's glasses if they're in there."

Sam fixed Natalie with a pointed stare. "I can assure you, Mrs Castle, there's nothing in the pond except a couple of inches of water and some leaves. And, as we know from the CCTV that Mr Weller was wearing the glasses this morning, I have to wonder where they are now?"

Natalie returned his stare. "How should I know? I didn't even go near him. It was Adrian who went out and he wouldn't have touched them. If the sunglasses aren't there, one of your lot must have taken them."

Sam and Harvey exchanged glances.

"Well, regardless of their whereabouts for the time being," said Sam, "we'll need to take a look at previous CCTV recordings, and we'll also need to speak to your neighbours, and your husband."

Natalie nodded. "You're welcome to look at whatever you want. And if you want to speak to Adrian, can you give him an hour or so to get himself together? I'd better get back to him."

Sam waited until Natalie was out of earshot. "I reckon those sunglasses have found their way to the same place as Andy Cochran's earring and Victor Canning's bow tie." He scratched his craggy jaw. "Although, something's puzzling me. Whoever killed Andy took the weapon with them, so we have to assume they went to the comedy club with the intention of killing him. Same with Victor Canning; the wire that was used to strangle him was taken to the crime scene by the killer." He looked out of the kitchen window at the team of officers scouring the garden for clues. "If the same person killed Tony Weller, why would they change their MO by turning up without a weapon?"

ooooooo

"No, I don't know what happened to Tony's sunglasses and no, I don't know if he told anyone he turned off the security systems in the morning," Adrian snapped. "I was his friend, not his keeper."

"Do you know the names of any of his acquaintances?" asked Sam. "People he might have spoken to about living here?"

"We can probably give you a list," said Natalie, stroking Adrian's hand. "Can you give us a while to think about it? I can call you with it later, or tomorrow?" Her brow creased. "We can't think straight just now – we need some time to get our heads around what's happened."

Slumped on the couch beside her, Adrian glowered and said nothing.

oooooooo

"They were very good, weren't they?" said Nick as he, Claudia, Megan and Des waved goodbye to the trio of musicians.

"Catchy name, isn't it?" said Claudia. "Classical Kin."

"Classical *Din*, more like," grumbled Des. "You know I can't stand all that arty-farty music. Sometimes, being able to turn my hearing aid off is a blessing – it made them marginally more bearable that I only had to listen with one ear. Incidentally, did anyone tell Diana Starr this was a celebration? She looked like she was sucking a lemon for most of the afternoon."

"Yeah, well, I'm not sure how much she appreciated you joining in with *Ave Maria* on your harmonica." Megan glanced at her uncle from the corner of her eye.

"I was only trying to get involved," he said, with an impish grin. "Now I don't drink, I need to find other things to keep my hands occupied, see? Hello, what's going on?" Des craned his neck as two police cars sped past, lights flashing and sirens wailing. "That's an unusual sight in Bliss Bay."

"Well, whatever it is, it's nothing to do with us," said Megan, putting her arm through his. "Come on, let's go and get you another non-alcoholic cocktail."

ooooooo

Much later that evening, when all the guests had left, and a tearful Evie had made an emotional Skype call from New Zealand to congratulate her grandparents, Megan, Lizzie, and Shaun tackled the clearing up.

"You know, it's amazing what people leave behind," Shaun called over the banister as he ran down the stairs, avoiding the creaky boards as Lizzie had taught him, and holding up a blue satin sling-back shoe. "I mean, how can someone not realise they're missing a shoe?"

"Ah, I think it might be Olivia's," said Megan. "I remember her taking them off on the dancefloor. She was very merry when they left so she probably didn't even realise she didn't have it with her. I'll drop it in at the shop tomorrow."

"And what about this?" Lizzie held up a handful of sheet music she'd found on the dresser. "Shall I get rid of it?"

"Oh no, give it to me and I'll take it back to the Starrs' place in the morning. I bet they don't even know they've left it here."

Claudia and Nick appeared from the kitchen where they'd been chatting with Des and Sylvie. "Right, we're going up in a bit," said Claudia. "We've got an early start, so we don't want to be too late to bed. We want to talk to you first, though." She pulled Megan down next to her on the couch.

"Thank you for agreeing to arrange this for us, sweetheart – we couldn't have wished for a better day. It's been fabulous."

Megan beamed as Claudia gave her a hug. "Well, that's all that matters – I'm chuffed to bits that you enjoyed it." She looked at her mum's face, suddenly serious. "What's wrong?"

"Listen, love," said Claudia. "Your dad and I, and Sylvie and Des, have been talking. I know you were thinking of staying on for a while, and you know you're welcome for as long as you like. Likewise, if you want to go home, don't feel obliged to stay, because Des and Sylvie will keep an eye on Cat, and water the plants. The thing is, with two murders so close to home, we're not comfortable about you being here on your own so we want to get an alarm fitted. We'll leave the money but you'll have to organise it. Will you do that?"

Megan took Claudia's hand. "Honestly, Mum, you don't need to go spending money on an alarm on my account. Really, I'll be fine. Des and Sylvie are only a few minutes away. I can always call them if I need to."

Claudia fell back on the couch and heaved a sigh of exasperation. "And how do you think *they're* going to protect you from a crazed murderer? If you haven't already been chopped into little pieces by the time it takes them fifteen minutes to cycle over here, what are they going to do then? Run over the killer with their bicycles? Make a citizen's arrest? Pelt them with Madeleines?" She turned to Sylvie and Des. "No offence. Look, Megan, we're leaving the money for an alarm, and that's final. I just want you to promise me two things. That you'll arrange for it to be fitted, and that you'll stay at Des and Sylvie's until it is."

Megan hesitated.

As much as she loved her aunt and uncle, she knew that staying with them for longer than a couple of days had the potential to drive them all bonkers. They were all too set in their ways to have other people around for too long.

She also happened to know that their guest bedroom was home to the smallest single bed known to man. She knew, because when Evie had stayed at Des and Sylvie's during one half-term weekend, her feet had hung off the end of it. She'd been twelve at the time.

She knew how much it would reassure her parents, though, so she nodded with as

much enthusiasm as she could muster.
"Course I will. If it's okay with you two?"

"It's more than okay, love," said a
delighted Sylvie, as she pulled on her coat. "It's
wonderful! It'll be just like old times. I'll make
up the bed in the spare room as soon as I get
home. Come on Des, let's leave these good
people in peace." She hugged everyone and
wished Claudia and Nick a safe trip, before
fastening the strap of her cycling helmet under
her chin and rubbing a tube of Cherry Kisses
balm across her lips.

"By the way, Megan, did you know that
Bill and Rita's nephew is staying with them for
a while? That nice American boy who was here
today – you remember him, don't you?
Anyway, in case you'd forgotten, Bill and Rita
live across the road from us. " She gave Claudia
an obvious wink as she returned the lip balm
to her handbag before snapping the clasp shut.

"I saw that, Aunty Sylv," said Megan.
"And I don't need you two trying to fix me up
with anyone again, thank you. I'm perfectly
capable of organising my own social life. I'm
sure Jack's very nice but I'm not interested.
Not in that way, anyway."

"*Not interested?*" said Sylvie, with a
look of disbelief. "Well, you must have been
the only woman here today who wasn't. Apart
from your mother and I, of course," she added,
hastily. "I thought we were going to have to roll

the woman from next door's tongue back into her mouth before someone stepped on it, it was hanging out so far."

"Was it really?" said Megan, with a distinct lack of interest. "Well, I was too busy to notice."

Nick chuckled as he hugged his daughters. "Right, we're off to bed. See you all in the morning. And, Des and Sylv, we'll see *you* when we get back in December."

CHAPTER ELEVEN

It was a bleary-eyed Megan who met Lizzie and Shaun downstairs at five o'clock to wave off Nick and Claudia's taxi.

What with knowing she had to get up early, and seeing Evie upset, she'd barely slept a wink. She filled the coffee machine and took a mug from the cupboard. "You want one?"

Lizzie yawned and slipped onto a chair at the kitchen table. "Might as well. We were going to go back to bed but I suppose it makes sense to stay up and leave earlier. Hopefully, we'll beat the Monday morning traffic if we do."

Megan set two more mugs on the counter, let Cat out and switched on the small TV in time for the local news while she waited for the coffee to brew. As she stretched, her mouth froze, mid-yawn.

"The body of a man discovered at the home of Witchester City midfielder, Adrian Castle, has been identified as local resident, Tony Weller," said the news reader.

"Mr Weller, who was thirty-four and a guest at Mr Castle's home, was found unresponsive in the back garden of the property yesterday afternoon, at approximately twenty-past three. Sources report that Mr Weller suffered a head injury, but whether or not that was the cause of death has yet to be confirmed.

"When questioned by our reporter, Detective Inspector Sam Cambridge refused to speculate about whether this incident is linked to two recent murders.

"The first victim was Andy Cochran, who was killed in Bliss Bay's Laugh Till You Cry Comedy Club on the 23rd of May, and the second was Victor Canning, who was murdered in the neighbouring village of Honeymeade on the 24th of July.

"DI Cambridge did tell us, however, that Mr Weller's death is being treated as suspicious. We'll bring you more on this story as we have it.

"In other news, plans to build a hypermarket on the site of the old Bliss Bay secondary school..."

Megan pointed at the TV, her mouth agape. "That guy! He's the one I was telling you about. You know? The DJ."

"The guy who was annoying all the neighbours with his loud music?" Lizzie filled the mugs with coffee.

"Yeah, that's him. I can't believe it," said Megan, rubbing at a furrow between her brows. "One minute he's rehearsing for a gig without a care in the world and the next..." She shuddered. "It doesn't bear thinking about."

"Look, are you sure you're going to be okay here on your own?" said Shaun. "That's three people now who've been done in by some nutter. Even with an alarm, are you sure you want to stay here all alone?"

Megan's face paled. "Well, I hadn't thought about it until you just said *that*."

"And now *I'm* worried," said Lizzie. "Look, alarm or not, why don't you just go back to your place? Des and Sylvie will look after the flippin' cat. Or you could take him with you and then bring him back once mum and dad get home."

"I couldn't take the cat with me," said Megan. "He'd be forever trying to find his way back here. What if something happened to him? I'd never forgive myself. No, I can't do that." She chewed her lip. She'd run away from Bliss Bay once before. She didn't want to do it again. And, in any case, billions of people *didn't* get murdered every day. Why should she? She took a slow deep breath in and out. It was a simple technique to help reduce anxiety, but it worked.

"Well?" Lizzie gave her an impatient prod on the shoulder.

"Look, it's completely irrational for us all to be feeling so scared," said Megan. "These murders are nothing to do with me. Why are we worrying so much?" She sipped her coffee, until a scratch at the back door told her that Cat was ready for his breakfast. She let him in and picked him up, burying her face in his fur. As anxious as she was, he soothed her. She didn't know why, but he did. And he made her feel safe. She'd seen him in full fight mode and he'd been pretty impressive.

Her decision was made.

"I came here for a break, and that's what I'm going to have. I'll have an alarm and the best guard-cat in Bliss Bay to keep me safe so, for the time being, I'm staying put."

ooooooo

"We're going to a christening in Bude next weekend," said Lizzie, as she hauled her suitcase downstairs behind Shaun. "So we'll drop in on Friday and see you on the way through." She pulled Megan into a double-armed hug, her blue eyes tearful. "Promise me you'll keep all the doors and windows locked *all* the time."

"Liz, it's the middle of August. I promise I'll be careful but I'm not locking myself in, or you'll come back on Friday to find me lightly poached."

"Alright then." Lizzie begrudgingly agreed. "But you have to be extra, extra-vigilant, okay? Promise?"

"Okay, I promise," said Megan. "Now, if you want to miss the traffic, you'd better get going. Drive carefully and call me to let me know you've got home safe."

ooooooo

Having arranged for someone from the alarm company to call round at lunchtime to give her a quote, Megan pulled the front door shut behind her and stepped out into the morning sunshine.

"See you later, Cat." She stroked the silver tabby's mangled ear and left him sitting on the garden wall, washing his paws.

Her parents had left their nice shiny car for her to use, but she sidestepped it in favour of Vinnie the Mini. Dull in comparison, and a little battered, Vinnie's virtues were that he could nip in and out of traffic, and fit into parking spaces other cars drove past.

Arriving at Coniston Road, Megan had to park right at the end, in view of the fact that almost the entire length of the usually quiet road was filled with cars.

As she got closer to the Starrs' home, she saw a TV crew and a huddle of reporters on the opposite side of the road to Castle Manor, and two police officers standing guard outside the gates.

"I'm visiting Mr and Mrs Starr at number 39," she told one of them before being waved on.

She could see the reporters' curious stares, and guessed they were wondering if she was anyone important to the investigation, and whether it was worth their while to stop her and ask questions. She was glad they decided not to.

As she rang the doorbell, she found herself wishing she'd waited a day or so before calling round. *Too late now*, she thought, as a figure appeared behind the frosted-glass guitar panel on the door.

Megan was shocked to see that Timothy Starr looked like he'd aged ten years since the day before. His eyes were dull and sunken in deep hollows, his cheeks sagging and pale.

"Megan. What a surprise," he said, his voice flat and devoid of expression.

She handed over the sheet music. "I won't keep you – I can see it's not a good time – but you left this at our place yesterday. I didn't know if you'd need it so I thought I'd better bring it back."

Timothy looked blankly at the papers. "Oh, right, thanks. Look, I won't ask you in, if you don't mind. I assume you've heard about Tony from next door? The police have been asking questions since yesterday and Diana's got one of her migraines." He rubbed the ridge at his brow. "She's finding his death very hard to take, particularly as it comes so soon after the acquaintance of ours she told you about the other day."

"Of course. I don't want to intrude, I only came round to give you your music back, although I wasn't sure I was going to get past the bank of reporters unscathed. They're out in force, aren't they?"

Timothy gave her a look of distaste. "What do you expect? This spate of murders is the biggest thing to ever happen around here – especially this one." He gave a nod in the direction of Castle Manor. "A murder in a celebrity's home is a heaven-sent story for a reporter."

"We don't know it's a murder for sure, though, do we? The news report just said the death was being treated as suspicious."

Timothy shot Megan an incredulous look. "Well, Tony was in the garden, on his own, and someone bashed him over the head. That's hardly accidental, is it?"

"Hmm, I suppose not. Have you spoken to Natalie or Adrian since it happened?"

"Briefly. We knew something terrible had gone on as soon as we got back from your place yesterday to find all hell breaking loose. We thought something had happened to one of them, until Natalie called to let us know about Tony."

Megan mulled over the situation. Although she hadn't gone with the intention of asking questions, now she was here, she realised she wanted to know as much as possible. If she was going to stay at Kismet Cottage on her own, she wanted details of anything she should be on the lookout for. *Forewarned is forearmed, and all that*, she thought. "So, do the police know anything more about what actually happened? Like how someone got into the garden in the first place?"

Timothy rubbed a hand across his weary face. "The intruder forced the side gate."

"Well, hopefully, it won't take the police too long to find out who's responsible," said Megan. "Castle Manor's like Fort Knox with all those lights and security cameras outside."

Timothy gave a humourless laugh and leaned against the doorframe. "Yes, and it has an alarm system too but, unfortunately, everything was switched off."

"What? Why?"

"Natalie said Tony didn't like the CCTV, so he always switched it off when he got up. The alarm and the lights, too. They have all those security measures, yet they didn't save him. It's ironic, isn't it? The police are going to have to do some proper old-fashioned detective work to solve this one," said Timothy, his expression grim. "I can't tell you how unnerving it is to know that someone's been murdered next door to where you live. It was bad enough when that chap at the comedy club was killed but this one's a little *too* close to home. I'm not surprised Diana's got one of her headaches."

"I suppose it must have happened yesterday after you left to come to our place?"

said Megan. "The news report said he was found in the afternoon."

Timothy shook his head. "He was *found* in the afternoon, but Natalie said the paramedics told her he'd been dead for a few hours. They think he was probably attacked soon after he went outside yesterday morning. He liked to see the sunrise, you see – used to say it was the best time of day to exercise."

He sighed. "Anyway, whoever killed him probably wasn't expecting anyone to be awake at that time on a Sunday morning, let alone outside in the garden." He took his inhaler from his pocket and puffed it into his mouth. "Sorry, what was I saying?"

"You were saying that the paramedics said Tony was killed in the morning," said Megan, with a puzzled expression. "So, if that was the case, why wasn't he found until the middle of the afternoon?"

Timothy scratched the back of his head. "Ah. Well, that'll be because Natalie and Adrian didn't get up until then. She was in a dreadful state when she came round to tell us about it – she said she and Adrian can't come to terms with the fact that they slept right through what happened. They wear earplugs if they've have a late night, you see, so they didn't hear a thing." He lowered his voice. "And, take it from me, Saturday night *was* a late night. I can't remember the last time I looked at my alarm clock but I know Tony was still playing music at three in the morning."

"They must be feeling terrible," said Megan.

"Natalie said they're going to stay with Adrian's parents later today. He doesn't want to stay at Castle Manor after what's happened."

A weak voice called out from inside the house.

"Coming, love." Timothy's lips curved in a smile that didn't quite make it to his sad eyes. "Sorry, Megan, I'd better go. Thanks for bringing these back."

ooooooo

As she made her way back to the car, Megan passed the property belonging to the Starr's other neighbours. As she glanced up the driveway, a willowy woman with waist-length fair hair appeared from inside the house and walked down the driveway towards her, carrying two rubbish sacks.

Recognising her as Eleanor Cooper, Megan was about to say hello when the woman turned on her with a mouthful of abuse.

"Why don't you clear off?" she shouted as she put her rubbish in the waste bin and slammed down the lid. "Sticking your nose in where it's not wanted. Damn newspaper hacks, twisting everyone's words and printing what you like. Go on, get lost!"

Before Megan could reply, Belinda, the gossipy cleaner she'd met at the Starrs' house, appeared and shook a feather duster outside the front door. "That's not a reporter, Eleanor, it's the woman who organised the party Classical Kin played at yesterday. The woman I was telling you about, remember? The one you said used to work in your salon."

Eleanor squinted down the drive. "Megan? Oh my goodness, I'm sorry! I haven't got my contacts in yet – I didn't recognise you. Come over here and give me a hug. It's so nice to see you. Or not see you, should I say." She laughed, and put her arms around Megan's shoulders. "Honestly, it's been nothing but a constant stream of reporters ringing the doorbell and calling the house since yesterday afternoon. Can you believe we've had to take the phone off the hook? We've had so many calls from reporters digging for dirt on Adrian, Natalie or Tony, it's disgusting. That poor man's been murdered and all they're interested in is whether they can uncover a scandal."

Megan shook her head. "That's awful. And it's such a worry, too, knowing that whoever did this is still out there."

"Maybe not *just* this," said Belinda. "Whoever it is could have murdered those other people, too. A crazed killer, right here in Bliss Bay. "Who'd have thought?"

"Actually, I'd rather *not* think about it," said Eleanor, massaging her neck. She lowered her voice to a whisper. "Between you and me, I told the police they needed to talk to that hussy, Caroline Gibbs. I wouldn't be surprised if she's right up to her neck in this. If anyone wanted Tony dead, it's her. Did you know he used to turn off the security systems every morning so, conveniently, there's no CCTV footage which might help the police?"

Megan nodded. "Timothy mentioned it. Who's Caroline Gibbs?"

"She was Natalie's assistant. She worked at Castle Manor for long enough, so I bet she'd have known Tony's routine."

"Oh, is she the girl who left to have a baby?" Megan asked, but didn't get an answer. The crowd of reporters suddenly rushed off down the road, their tape recorders and microphones at the ready, and Eleanor ran to the end of the drive. Seconds later, they reappeared in a huddle around a tall, heavy-set man whose long strides brought him quickly to the house, leaving the reporters outside on the pavement.

"I told you, I can't hear a thing with these on and even if I could, I wouldn't answer any of your questions. Now, please, leave me alone." Oscar Cooper pulled off the headphones he was wearing and stormed past Megan, ignoring her as he headed for the open front door, stooping slightly to avoid banging his head on the frame. Eleanor followed him immediately.

"Poor Oscar," said Belinda. "He usually goes out walking at the crack of dawn but he hung back today in the hope those reporters would clear off, but they didn't. In the end, he just went for it and ignored them. Eleanor thinks they followed him for a while but he walks so fast, they probably gave up and came back here to wait for him. You know, he has to wear those headphones when he goes walking to block out any loud noises. It's such a shame. Apparently, before he got ill, he and Eleanor used to have the most fabulous dinner parties. It was before my time but I understand that all the neighbours were invited – even Natalie and Adrian. You know, Oscar used to—"

A curtain in the front room of the house moved to one side and Oscar's glaring face appeared at the window.

"Oops, I'd better go. It wouldn't do for him to get uptight – he can be a bit unpredictable. It takes ages for Eleanor to calm him down when he gets really upset. See you around," said Belinda, and scuttled back inside.

As Megan went on her way, she wondered how easy it would be to pacify a man who was over six feet tall, and broad with it, when he got really upset.

ooooooo

After dinner at Des and Sylvie's, Megan washed the dishes and handed them to Des to dry.

"By the way, the guy's coming to fit the alarm tomorrow morning, so I'll go back to Kismet after breakfast. He said it should only take a couple of hours."

"Oh." Sylvie's face dropped. "I hoped you'd be staying a bit longer. I know you've probably got things to do during the day, but I had all kinds of things planned for the evenings. Cards games, Monopoly, looking through the photo albums. I thought we might even get in a bike ride after dinner. We've got one of my old ones in the garage – you could borrow it, if you like."

"Well, we *can* go for bike rides," said Megan. "I'll only be a few minutes away, won't I? You can come and visit whenever you like, and I'll be popping in to see you all the time. You can even come and stay with *me*, if you want to. There's plenty of room at mum and dad's."

"I know that," said Sylvie. "I was just hoping to have you here for a while, that's all. In *our* home. We used to have so much fun when you were little and you and Lizzie would come and stay for a week every summer. Do you remember?"

As she scrubbed baked-on chicken skin off a roasting tin, Megan stole a sideways glance at her aunt and felt a pang of guilt. The truth was, she hadn't wanted to stay any longer than necessary so when the engineer had asked when she wanted the alarm fitted, her answer had been, 'as soon as possible'.

When she'd been a child, she'd always looked forward to time spent with her favourite aunt and uncle. There was always something to do. They'd all set up camp in the countryside, or spend the days exploring rock pools on the beach.

When the rain came down, they'd stay inside, as warm as toast. They'd play hide and seek, or make collages from bits of macaroni and dried beans for Sylvie to stick on her corkboard, and help Des bake his signature lavender Madeleines.

She recalled the concerts she and Lizzie would put on, singing at the top of their voices to Des's harmonica accompaniment.

She remembered reading countless books as she lazed in the hammock strung between the two lilac trees in the garden, and lying on the warm grass next to Des's deckchair, listening to the stories he'd conjure up from his imagination, and fighting sleep because she couldn't bear to miss the endings.

Those days had been exciting and idyllic.

Now, though, the house felt claustrophobic and after a while, it seemed as though the walls were closing in. The rooms were full of knick-knacks, large, cumbersome display cabinets made from dark wood, mismatched soft furnishings, and small beds. It was what Lizzie called 'a proper old person's house', stuck in the past, with few concessions to modernity. She remembered how Sylvie had resisted having a mobile phone for years, until she'd realised she could play Solitaire on it. Megan doubted she'd ever used it to call anyone.

She glanced at her aunt again and her resolve crumbled. How could it not? She loved her to bits.

"Actually, on second thoughts, I think I *would* like to stay for a couple more days. I'll have to get back by Friday, though, because Lizzie and Shaun are stopping by on their way to a christening. And I'll need to go and feed Cat, of course, but if it's okay with you, I'd love to stay a bit longer."

Sylvie's face lit up with a beaming smile. "Are you sure?"

Megan took her hands out of the sink and shook the suds from them. "I'm positive. In fact, how about a game of Monopoly in the garden with a cup of coffee? Give me a minute to finish this and I'll be out."

As Sylvie scampered off to get the board game, Des, who'd been quietly watching the two women as he dried the dishes, dropped a kiss on Megan's forehead. "That was a very good thing you just did."

Megan shrugged and gave him a crooked smile, then sighed as she remembered that her feet would be hanging off the end of the bed for the next few days.

oooooooo

When she went down for breakfast the following morning, Megan found Sylvie changing a fuse, and Des flicking through a cookbook.

"Morning, love," chirped Sylvie. "Sleep well?"

"Like a log," lied Megan. "I've just had a text from Mum. Apparently, the ship is beautiful and their cabin is to die for. She says it's like a proper honeymoon and they feel like a newly married couple. Aaaw, that's so sweet! I bet they're having the time of their lives. You know, Mum was telling me that she knew Dad was the one for her when—"

"Never mind all that mushy stuff," said Des, wagging a finger at the television. "Quickly! Grab a coffee and pull up a chair. There's something on the news about the murders. Sshhh, here it is now."

"We start the hour with news of a press conference which is to begin shortly,

*being held by the detective in charge of the
investigation into the recent murders in Bliss
Bay and Honeymeade. To bring you more on
that, we're crossing to that live coverage
now."*

The camera panned round to DI
Cambridge, who shuffled a bundle of papers,
and settled some items on the desk, before
turning to the camera and clearing his throat.

"That's one of the guys who questioned
Lizzie and I after that guy was found in his
car," said Megan.

*"Good morning. I'm DI Sam
Cambridge. I'm the Senior Investigating
Officer into the recent murders in Bliss Bay
and Honeymeade.*

*"Firstly, it is with regret that I can now
confirm that Tony Weller, the man who was
found dead at the home of Adrian Castle on
Sunday the 16th of August, **was** the victim of a
murder. Our condolences go out to Mr
Weller's family and friends.*

*"We believe his murder is connected to
two other murders committed in Bliss Bay
and Honeymeade in recent months*

*"The first victim, Andy Cochran, was
killed at the Laugh Till You Cry Comedy Club
in Bliss Bay, by a single stab wound to the
chest. The weapon used was a wooden stake,
like this one. The last reported sighting of him*

alive was at the club at around ten-past midnight on Saturday the 23rd of May.

"The second victim, Victor Canning, died from strangulation with a length of green, plastic-coated garden wire, similar to this. He was killed in his car on the morning of Friday the 24th July outside Joe's Diner in Honeymeade. The last reported sighting of him alive was on the same morning, at around five-thirty.

"The third victim, as I've just mentioned, was Tony Weller, who was killed by a blunt force trauma wound to the back of the head . Mr Weller was last seen alive on the morning of Sunday August the 16th, at around 3.15 am. The murder weapon was recovered at the scene.

"As part of our investigation, we are appealing for the public's help in tracing personal items belonging to the victims which were missing from the crime scenes, and have yet to be found. With the permission of their families, I am showing you recent photographs of Mr Cochran and Mr Weller, which show the items being worn. In these cases, we are keen to trace a gold hoop earring with a microphone charm hanging from it, and a pair of sunglasses with blue mirror lenses and black frames.

"Unfortunately, we have not been able to obtain a photograph of Mr Canning, but a

witness who saw him on the morning of his murder has confirmed that he was wearing a yellow bow tie, which was subsequently found to be missing from the crime scene.

"These missing items are evidence, and form part of our investigation into the murders. As we continue our enquiries, I would like to assure you that we are doing everything we can to find the person, or persons, responsible for the murders, but we need your help.

"To this end, I would ask anyone who has any information regarding any of these items, or their whereabouts, to call our incident room or Crime Busters on the numbers at the bottom of your screen. All calls will be treated in the strictest confidence.

"Likewise, we are appealing for witnesses who may have seen any of the victims prior to their deaths and may be able to pass on vital information. Please do not think that what you have to tell us is too insignificant to be of importance – all information is valid.

"To conclude, I would like to reassure you that the police are doing everything in their power to ensure that the perpetrator, or perpetrators, of these crimes are apprehended as soon as possible. We are waiting for your calls. Thank you."

"What d'you think of that then?" said Des, turning down the volume on the TV.

"I think it's horrific," said Megan. "When Joe from the diner told us Victor Canning's bow tie was missing, I didn't think much of it then, but hearing the Detective Inspector talking about it gives me the shivers. Why would anyone want to take personal items?"

"That's often the way with murderers," said Des. "They take their victims' belongings as trophies."

"And what do *you* know about it?" said Sylvie, her eyes widening. "Honestly, you watch a couple of episodes of Midsomer Murders and you think you know everything. I wish you'd keep your opinions to yourself, sometimes, Des. This is unsettling enough as it is without you scaring us half to death."

She put down her screwdriver and picked up a bunch of bananas from the counter. "Anyway, I'm going out. I've got a still-life watercolour class at the WA." She dangled the bananas in front of Megan's face. "If all goes well, there'll be a picture of these hanging on the wall later in a frame. Keep your fingers crossed for me, won't you?"

She jammed on her cycling helmet and patted her pockets. "Keys, phone, mints, tissues, lip balm, bananas. Right, I'll see you later. And don't get up to any mischief, Des

Harper. I know what you're like if you don't keep yourself occupied."

Des blew her a kiss. "Promise you'll try extra hard with the curve today, Sylv?" he called as the door slammed behind her. He gave Megan a weary smile. "She's been trying to paint a bunch of blasted bananas for four weeks now, but she can't get the 'curve' right, so she keeps bringing them home, and she won't move onto something else until she's got them just right. I used to love bananas but I've baked so much banana bread, banana muffins and banana fritters recently, I'm quite looking forward to the kitchen being a banana-free zone for a while. Which is why I'm about to make a treacle tart. You want to keep me company?"

Megan filled a bowl with Rice Krispies while Des got his ingredients together.

"I'll come with you when you go back to the cottage for the alarm to be fitted," said Des. "To check around the place. You can't be too careful, you know."

"You don't need to do that – it'll be the middle of the day. I'll be fine," said Megan, through a mouthful of puffed rice.

"I'm coming with you, and that's final." Des gave her one of his looks that meant the conversation was over. "And don't talk with your mouth full."

Megan laughed at being scolded like a schoolgirl for the first time in over thirty-five years. "Okay, thank you." She looked around the kitchen. "Look, is there anything I can do to help around the house while I'm here? I mean, I can see I don't need to do any cleaning – the place is spotless – but there must be something else I can do?"

Des measured flour into the scales. "You can water the flowerbeds in the front garden. The watering can's in the green chest in the porch. That alright?"

"Course it is – I'm not a paying guest, you know. Give me five minutes to finish this and jump in the shower, and I'll be down."

ooooooo

As she stepped into the front garden, the first thing Megan saw was Jack Windsor washing his black Mercedes outside Bill and Rita's house across the road.

"Megan? Hey, Megan!" He threw his sponge into a bucket of water and ran over to her. "I thought it was you. Good to see you again. What're you doing here?"

Megan tucked her still-damp hair behind her ears. "Oh. It's a long story. I'm staying here for a few days."

Jack nodded and smiled. "That was a great party, by the way. Olivia danced me into the ground – that woman's got some *moves*!"

"Yes, she was having fun, wasn't she?" Megan chuckled as she filled the watering can from the outside tap. "Glad you enjoyed yourself."

"Yeah, I really did," said Jack, cocking his head and catching her eye. "You busy today?"

"Well, I've got to be back at mum and dad's cottage by half-twelve. We're having an alarm fitted. Why?"

"'Cos I was thinking about taking a drive out later – don't know where, I was just going to point the car and see where it headed. Maybe grab some lunch along the way. I could do with the company if you want to tag along? I thought it'd be nice for us to catch up." Jack held up his hands. "No strings, obviously, just as old friends."

Megan shook her head. "Sorry. I'd love to but I've no idea how long I'll be. The guy said the alarm would only take a couple of hours to fit but you know how these things can drag on. Maybe another time?"

"Oh. Okay. No biggie. It was pretty short notice, I guess."

"Morning, Jack." Des appeared, wiping his hands on a towel as he stepped outside. "Did I hear you inviting Megan out for a drive?"

"Morning, Des. And, yes, you sure did."

"Well, if you want to go, Megan," said Des, "you should go. I'll stay at the cottage until the alarm's fitted."

Megan shook her head as she refilled the watering can. "Thanks, but I wouldn't ask you to do that."

"Well, you wouldn't be asking me, would you? I offered." Des turned and went back into the house. "You can get on and make your plans now. Be back in time for dinner, though," he called over his shoulder. "Sylvie's cooking a ham. And there'll be plenty, Jack, so consider yourself invited."

Megan grinned at her old friend. "Looks like you've got yourself some company."

CHAPTER TWELVE

"This is delicious," said Megan.

She and Jack sat on a stone wall beside a small food truck, eating fish and chips out of paper that they both said were the best they'd ever tasted.

They'd driven just four miles out of Bliss Bay when the aromas of freshly cooked fish and chips, spritzed with vinegar and lemon juice, had been enough to lure them to the small truck which was doing a roaring trade from the side of a hill.

Appreciative diners sat alongside them on the wall, or lolled on the grass, as they took in the magnificent views, with nothing to disturb the peace except the occasional crunch of teeth biting into crispy, light-as-a-feather batter, the sound of the sea, and the cry of the odd gull as it flew overhead.

Jack screwed his food wrapper into a ball and executed a perfect slam-dunk into a nearby waste bin. "I know these guys are only selling one thing but sometimes it's better not to have too much choice. You know what I mean? They only sell fish and chips, but they sure do it well. Very smart business move."

"Speaking of too much choice," said Megan, "you've heard about the plans to knock down the old school and build a hypermarket, I suppose?"

Jack took off his sunglasses and rolled his eyes. "Only about a hundred times every evening when my Uncle Bill gets home," he said, with a deep chuckle. "He's furious about it."

"I know," said Megan. "He asked me if I was thinking of buying a place down here because the property prices have dropped so much."

"And are you?" asked Jack.

"No way," said Megan, with a firm shake of her head. "I couldn't live here again. Not all the time, anyway. What about you?"

Jack shrugged a shoulder. "Sometimes I think it'd be nice to have a place here, but I don't know. I'm pretty settled back home. Never say never, but I think what Uncle Bill says is right – one of those big stores will make a huge difference to Bliss Bay, and not a good one. As villages go, Bliss Bay's a little bigger than average, but it's still a village. I'm not sure I'd want to live here if a hypermarket was built right in the middle of it – it'd change the whole vibe of the place."

"Yeah, it'd be awful." Megan frowned as she popped the last chip into her mouth. She stole a glance at Jack out of the corner of her eye. "Can I ask you a personal question?"

"Sure."

"Do you have someone back home? I'm only asking because I'm nosy," she added quickly, "not for any other reason. You just said you were settled. I wondered if that meant you have a wife. Or a girlfriend. Or maybe a boyfriend – you never know these days." She giggled at Jack's amused expression. "Sorry, I told you I was nosy. Tell me to mind my own business if you want. I've told you all about me but I hardly know anything about you."

He smiled. "It's okay. And, no, there's no wife, no significant other, and no kids. I came close to tying the knot once, but she got cold feet."

"Oh. I'm sorry."

Jack shrugged. "Don't be. It was just one of those things – and probably for the best. I worked in advertising, and she decided I was always too wrapped up in work to ever give 100% to a marriage."

"Huh, that sounds familiar," said Megan. "That's why my fiancé broke up with me. Said I'd lost my spark." She felt glad she could talk about it now without wanting to throw up or burst into tears.

Jack shook his head. "Well, your fi-an-cé didn't know what he was talking about. From where I'm sitting, that spark's burning as bright as it ever did." He grinned and bumped his fist gently against her arm. "And I'm sorry your ex-husband turned out to be such a jerk. That guy is a deadbeat of the highest order – always was, always will be." He took Megan's

screwed-up food wrapper from her hand and
threw it with a flick of his wrist, the ball falling
in a perfect arc and landing in the waste bin.
"Anyway, this conversation's getting *waaay*
too deep." He slid his sunglasses back over his
eyes. "Did you catch the news report this
morning? About the murders?"

Megan nodded. "Talk about sobering."

"So, what's your theory?"

"I wish I had one. Although I was
talking to someone yesterday who said she'd
told the police to speak to someone called
Caroline Gibbs. She seemed pretty sure she
was involved in Tony Weller's death, but I
don't know why. She used to work for Natalie
Castle, apparently."

"Ah, well, that's where I might be able
to enlighten you a little," said Jack, shuffling
round on the wall to face her. "Caroline Gibbs
was Natalie's personal assistant until she gave
up the job last year to have a baby, and the
rumours are that Adrian Castle is the baby's
father."

"*What?* Wow." Megan frowned. "But
what's that got to do with Tony Weller's
murder?"

"Well, according to village gossip,
Caroline's been in love with Adrian for years,
and she was jealous of his friendship with
Tony so she wanted him out of the way."

"How do you know all this stuff when you've been away for so long?" said Megan, shaking her head.

"Because I've been back a couple months, remember? I've had a head start on you. *And* I've been hanging out with Lionel and Rob. I tell you, what those guys don't know 'ain't worth knowing. You wouldn't believe the things I've learned since I've been here."

"I don't get it," said Megan. "If what you've told me is true, and Caroline really *did* want Tony out of the way so she could get closer to Adrian, what was she intending to do about Natalie? And speaking of Natalie, I wonder if *she* knows about the rumours?"

"No idea," said Jack. "The general opinion is that she was either completely oblivious to what was going on under her nose, or she knew about it but chose to ignore it. Apparently, when Caroline worked for her, she used to hang around long after she'd finished work for the day – her car was often parked outside until late. *And*, when Natalie went away to a family wedding early last year, guess who spent all weekend at Castle Manor?"

"Really? Well, that *is* interesting." Megan slid off the wall and paced back and forth. "So, let's assume that Natalie knew Adrian was the father of Caroline's baby. And she also knew that Caroline was jealous of

Adrian's friendship with Tony. Maybe *Natalie* killed Tony, and intends to put Caroline in the frame for it? She'd be getting back at both of them, then, wouldn't she? You know, a woman scorned, and all that."

"Could be."

"Although," said Megan, tapping her finger on her lips, "according to Petal, Natalie and Adrian are the epitome of love's young dream. They adore each other."

"Well, if there's any truth to the latest rumour from the mill, that might not be the case for much longer," said Jack. "Apparently, Adrian's just about had enough of Natalie spending money like it grows on trees. As I understand, she thinks nothing of blowing a few grand on a Saturday afternoon's shopping." He held up his hands. "I'm just telling you what Rob and Lionel told me, but I wouldn't read too much into it, if I were you. It's probably nothing more than Chinese whispers – you know how village gossip gets blown out of proportion. Rumours are often based on a little truth and a lot of speculation. In fact, I don't even know why I'm making it my business. I'm not usually one of life's gossipers but you just kinda get sucked in after a while."

Megan turned to face him, her hands resting on the wall. "You know what I can't figure out? The killer forced the lock on the side gate to get into the garden."

"What's to figure out?" said Jack. "That sounds like pretty normal intruder behaviour to me."

"Yes, but if Tony was already in the garden, why didn't he hear them? The news report said he had a wound on the back of his head. If he'd heard someone breaking in, why would he have had his back to them? I just don't get it. I can't imagine forcing a lock is something you can do quietly, is it?"

"Well, I'm no expert," said Jack, "but I broke in to my girlfriend's place after she locked herself out one time and it made a heck of a noise."

"See? That's what I mean. I don't understand." Megan sighed and looked at her watch. "Come on, d'you fancy driving a bit further? We've got loads of time. It's nice to just drive and forget about everything else that's going on for a while."

"Is that why you've had an alarm fitted at your parents' place?" asked Jack, as they walked to the car. "Because of the murders?"

Megan nodded. "Mum and dad weren't happy about me staying on my own without one. Doesn't matter how old we get, we're always kids to our parents. I thought they were over-reacting but, between you and me, I'm glad to have it now."

"Better safe than sorry," said Jack.

Megan grinned. "Yeah, you're right, although I'm sure I'll never need it."

ooooooo

"Hey! You did it!" As they sat down to dinner, Megan pointed to the painting of a bunch of bananas propped up on the shelf. She leaned over and gave her aunt a hug. "You must be over the moon!"

"Not as much as I am," said Des. "If I *never* see another flippin' banana, it'll be too soon. Anyway, Megan, love, the alarm works a treat. We'll have to go back to your mum and dad's place some time so I can run through the instructions with you, but it's straightforward enough. Just remember to switch it on every night before you go to bed and no one will be able to get in without waking up the whole village."

"Did you have a good day, you two?" Aunt Sylvie flashed Megan a knowing smile.

"Yes, we did, thanks," said Megan, ignoring her aunt's obvious attempt to fish for gossip where there was none.

Sylvie didn't give up. "What did you get up to?"

"We had a bite to eat and a chat. That's all," said Megan, as she filled the glasses with wine, and apple juice for Des. "We ate fish and chips on the side of a hill and chatted about the hypermarket and the murders."

Sylvie pulled a face. "Charming conversation for a first date, I must say."

"It *wasn't* a first date," said Megan, with an eye roll. "It was lunch with an old friend. Wasn't it Jack?"

"Yep, that's about the measure of it," he said, helping himself to a thick slice of ham.

"And did you come up with any new theories about the murders?" asked Des.

"Not really," said Megan, not wanting to go over everything again during dinner. "Although when I saw Eleanor Cooper yesterday, she said she thinks she knows who may be involved in Tony Weller's murder."

"Not Caroline Gibbs, by any chance?" said Sylvie.

Megan's eyes widened. "How did you know?"

"I've lived in this village a long time, Megan," said Sylvie. "I might not know everyone but I hear all the rumours, same as you do."

"What rumours?" said Des, as he mixed butter into his mashed potatoes.

"That Caroline Gibbs is doing the horizontal rumba with Adrian Castle and wanted Tony Weller out of the way."

"Oh, *that* rumour. I thought we were talking about something new."

"And is it just a rumour?" asked Megan. "Or is there something to it?"

"I don't know," said Sylvie, "but, if there's any truth to it, and I was Natalie Castle, I'd be pretty fed up that I'd given Caroline a job and she'd repaid me by jumping into bed with my husband."

"Now there's a motive for murder, right there!" said Des, pointing at Megan with his fork. "Natalie wanted to get her own back at Caroline and Adrian, so she killed her husband's best friend and now she's planning to put her love rival in the frame for the murder."

"That's *exactly* what I said!" said Megan.

"Ah, well, great minds, as they say." Des winked and poured a green river of parsley sauce into a moat of mashed potato.

Megan munched thoughtfully on a mouthful of ham. "Anyway, Eleanor said she'd told the police her suspicions about Caroline, and they were going to speak to her."

"Of course, it's all just speculation and rumour," said Jack. "No one knows *who* murdered Tony Weller, or those other guys, so I guess we're just gonna have to leave this one to the police."

"Well, I hope we don't have to leave it too long," said Megan. "I wish there was something we could do to help."

"Tell you what," said Des, "I know Gerald, the gardener at Castle Manor. He hasn't been able to work there for a while – it's been off limits while forensics have been gathering evidence – but I can call and ask if he'd be happy to have a chat with us, if you like? He knows the Castles very well, and he knows Castle Manor inside out, so he may be able to tell us something useful."

"What good will going to see Gerald do?" said Sylvie. "He won't know anything, you old fool. You just said he hasn't been allowed to work at Castle Manor since the murder."

"Yes, I know that, my little battle-axe," said Des, "but he can tell us if he's heard anything on the grapevine, can't he?" He turned to Megan. "You fancy meeting up with him to see if he can shed any light on the mystery? I'll ask if we can pop round to see him, shall I?"

"That's a brilliant idea." Megan chased parsley sauce around her plate with the ham on her fork. "I mean, I'm not doing anything else just now, so we might as well do a bit of snooping around to see what we can find out."

"Give me two minutes," said Des, as he went off to make a call.

"Don't get your hopes up too much," said Jack. "I'm not sure you'll get any new information from the gardener guy. He'll have already told the police everything he knows."

"Probably, but I reckon it's still worth talking to him."

"Jack's right, love," said Sylvie. "The police know what they're doing. You should just let them get on with it."

"Right," said Des, as he sat back down at the table. "Gerald said the police are going to let him know this week when he can go back to work at Castle Manor. As soon as they've finished gathering all the evidence they need, they'll give him the all clear. If he can, he's going to go back there on Saturday and when I told him about our conversation, he said we could go and have a chat with there. If you want to, that is."

"We can go to Castle Manor?" said Megan. "Really? And that'll be okay?"

"As long as we stay in the garden, Gerald's sure it won't be a problem. He said he sometimes takes his son and his grandkids with him and Natalie and Adrian are okay with it, so he's certain they won't mind if we go along," said Des. "Not that they're there, mind you, because they're still staying with Adrian's parents. Anyway, Gerald's going to let me know for sure nearer the time."

"That's great," said Megan. "Thanks for asking him."

"And you won't forget we're going to the comedy club on Thursday, will you?" Des reminded her.

"The comedy club?" Jack gave him a quizzical look.

"Yes. We're going to see if we can find out anything about Andy Cochran's murder," said Des. "See if anyone can tell us anything that might help figure out who's behind all this. Just doing our bit to help the community."

Sylvie rolled her eyes. "Are you sure you don't mind your uncle shadowing you around like a boxer, love? All you have to do is say the word and he'll leave you in peace. *Won't* you, Des?"

"No, honestly, Aunty Sylv – as long as it's okay with you, it's fine with me," said Megan. "I should probably start looking for another job soon, but I'm having a few days off first."

Sylvie cut four generous portions of warm treacle tart and topped each of them with a scoop of clotted cream.

Des rubbed his hands together with glee. "Y'know, since Sylv's had me eating healthy, we've cut our dairy intake by half so to have proper Devonshire cream is a real treat." He turned to his wife. "What's the special occasion?"

"Well, if you're going to start using your brain for sleuthing," said Sylvie, with a wry smile, "you won't want to do it on an empty stomach, will you?"

ooooooo

At the end of the evening, Jack and Megan exchanged a hug.

"Thanks for keeping me company today," said Jack. "It was fun."

"Likewise." Megan smiled. "We'll have to do it again sometime."

"We sure will." Jake hesitated, a fleeting frown creasing his brow. "You'll be careful, won't you? The police have got this – they might not appreciate you and Des poking around in their business."

"Of course I'll be careful. We're only asking a few questions, not chasing criminals through the streets."

Jack grinned. "Okay, okay. G'night. I'll see you around."

Megan went back inside to tackle the dirty dishes with a bit of elbow grease and a pan scourer; there was nothing so modern as a dishwasher at Des and Sylvie's.

She tuned out from their banter in the background and tried to put all thoughts of murder from her mind. Instead, she thought how good it had been to spend the day with a man who was attractive, funny, intelligent and kind.

Sylvie kept telling her he was 'perfect relationship material', but all she was interested in was friendship and some fun, with no strings, no pressure, no expectations, and definitely no romance.

And, for that, Jelly-Legs-Jack Windsor was the perfect partner.

CHAPTER THIRTEEN

"So, he'd been dead for hours by the time he was found?" said Petal.

"That's what Timothy Starr told me the other day. Natalie and Adrian were having a lie-in, so they didn't get up until after three." Megan leaned on the counter in the flower shop, sipping a caramel latte and munching on a butterscotch cupcake.

"Honestly, this whole business is a nightmare, isn't it?" Petal jabbed sprigs of gypsophilia into the bouquet she was working on. "It's awful to think that while most of us were enjoying a lazy Sunday lie-in, that poor guy was getting his head bashed in."

Tying florist's wire and ribbon around a bunch of scarlet roses, she wrapped it in red foil and called out to a customer in the café who was engrossed on his laptop. "Mr Filbert, your bouquet's ready. I hope these'll help to make up for forgetting your anniversary. The care instructions are on the card inside. Yes, you have a good day, too." She waited until he'd left the shop before continuing her conversation with Megan.

"Blossom's been to a few of his gigs. Mirror Man, he was called, did you know? She said he's amazing – sorry, *was* amazing." She puffed out a long sigh. "Oh, Megan, I hope the police find this creep soon. It gives me the shivers to know there's some nutcase out there on the loose. I mean, how are we supposed to keep our kids safe?"

Petal shoved flower stems into a rubbish bag and barely smiled at two customers who came into the shop. "Sorry if I'm a bit grouchy," she said to Megan, "but these murders have put me right on edge. I've lost count of the number of times I've snapped at Lionel, and Blossom and I had a screaming argument this morning. A dance troupe from her school are playing an open-air concert this evening in the market square, and I told her she couldn't go unless I go with her, which didn't go down well. I can understand she doesn't want me tagging along but I told her, it's my way, or no way. If Lionel was free, I'd ask him to come with me but he's got plans tonight. Anyway, that's why Blossom's not here today – she was in such a stinking mood, I thought it would be better if we spent a few hours apart."

"Is she at home?"

"No, she's gone to work with Daisy. Maybe a day working at the charity shop with her big sister will help her see sense." Petal raked her fingers through her dark curls. "I just don't understand why she can't see why I'm so worried. I know I'm coming down hard on her but it's only because I'm so petrified that if she steps out of the house alone, it'll be the last time I ever see her."

"I understand you're concerned, because if Evie was here, I'd feel exactly the same," said Megan, resting a hand on her friend's shoulder, "but you can't keep Blossom locked in until the murderer's found. It's the summer holidays – of course she wants to go out and have fun with her friends. Look, what time's the concert?"

"Six till half-seven. Why?"

"Well, how about if you and I go with her? We can walk down to the square together, she can go off and be with her friends, we can all watch the concert, and then we can all walk back together. How's that?"

Petal's face brightened considerably. "You'd do that?"

Megan rolled her eyes a full 360 degrees. "Of course I would, you dodo! That's what friends are for. Just as long as I'm back in time for Aunty Sylvie's nine o' clock game of Monopoly. So, what time shall I call round for you?"

oooooooo

"What about here?"

"Suits me. Anywhere I can put this flippin' cool box down. It weighs a ton."

Megan and Petal set down their deckchairs on a spot a few rows back from the stage in the busy market square.

"They're my friends over there, Mum. See the girl with the lilac hair?" Blossom had cheered up since that morning, the argument between her and Petal forgotten.

"Good. You'll be close enough so you can get to us if you need us, but far enough away so we don't ruin your street cred. Now, we'll stay here until the concert's finished, alright? Come and get a cold drink, or something to eat, if you want. We've got quiche, sandwiches, chicken legs and salad. And bring your friends with you. We don't bite. And don't go sneaking off anywhere when you think I'm not looking, because I see everything. I'm your mum – I've got eyes in the back of my head. All mums have them, isn't that right, Megan?"

"Yep. We get them right after the baby pops out," said Megan, with a wink.

Blossom grinned and fished a tube of roll-on lip gloss out of her pocket. "You two are bonkers. I'll see you later."

As they settled down to wait for the concert to start, Megan glanced around the crowd. "Looks like all the other parents are as concerned as you are. There are more adults here than kids."

"Good," said Petal. "And so there should be until that maniac's behind bars. Anyway, thank goodness for a little light relief. What with people getting done in at every turn, and a truculent teenager to boot, it's nice to have a few hours of escapism." She lowered herself into her deckchair and let out a satisfied sigh. "Did I mention that Lionel's out with Jack this evening?"

Megan shook her head as she looked around the crowd. "You told me he was out, but you didn't say he was with Jack."

"And Jack didn't tell you?"

"No. Why should he?"

"Just thought he might have mentioned it, that's all." Petal produced two plastic stem glasses and a bottle from the cool box. "He stopped at the café early this morning on his way back from a run and told Lionel he had a really good day with you yesterday."

"Oh," said Megan. "Yes, we did have a good day. But that's *all* it was – just a day out with a friend. Don't go getting any ideas, okay?"

"Alright, Miss Touchy. I was only asking. Right, you want a glass of fizz? It's only elderflower cordial – I thought I'd bring something Blossom and her friends could drink, too – but I always think a few bubbles makes an occasion a bit more special. D'you know what I mean?" She gasped. "Oh Lordy! Of all the people I did *not* expect to see."

"What? Who?" Megan lumbered round in her deckchair.

The chatter among the crowd lulled as Natalie Castle made her way towards the market square, her red hair scraped into a messy ponytail and her face without its usual make-up.

Petal went to her immediately and steered her in Megan's direction.

"Oh, Natalie, You must be feeling awful. Come on, come and sit with us."

Natalie gave her a relieved smile. "Thanks. I was starting to feel a bit conspicuous. I knew everyone would stare but now that I'm here, I feel a bit like a laboratory experiment under a microscope. Adrian's brother's popped round to see him so I grabbed the chance to get out for a while. Don't get me wrong, his parents are lovely, and you know I love Adrian to bits, but these past few days have been so intense, I really needed a break."

"I'm not surprised," said Petal. "I can't imagine how stressed you must have been."

Natalie grimaced. "It's been awful. I feel like all the pressure's on me to be strong for Adrian but he's in such a state, I'm not sure if he's ever going to get over it. It's bad enough that Tony was murdered, but what makes it even worse is that Adrian can't get it out of his head that he may have been calling for help while we were sleeping. We can't hear a thing when we've got our earplugs in." She gulped back the tears.

Petal gave Natalie's hand a squeeze and pushed her gently into her deckchair. "You poor thing. Come on, sit down, have a good cry and let it all out. You'll feel better for it. Tony had been living with you for a long time – you're bound to be upset about what's happened."

Natalie shook her head. "Oh no, I'm not upset because of Tony, I'm upset because Adrian's in such a mess and it unsettles me to see him like this." She chewed anxiously on a false nail. "Don't get me wrong, I wouldn't have wished anything terrible on Tony, but he's not why I'm upset – he really wasn't one of my favourite people."

"Feel free to tell me to mind my own business," said Megan, "but do you mind if I ask why?"

Natalie blew her nose. "It sounds petty now, but Tony was such a freeloader. In all the time he was staying with us, he never once made a cup of tea, or cooked a meal or even loaded the dishwasher – he just helped himself to whatever he wanted without so much as a please or thank you. It would have been nice if he'd offered to take us out for a meal or a drink, or bought a takeaway, or done something around the house every now and then. He stayed with us rent-free, and he got paid good money when he did a gig, so it's not like he was broke. Not all the time, anyway." She sighed. "Sorry. I shouldn't speak ill of the dead, should I?"

Petal shook her head. "No apology necessary – not to us, anyway. You can't help how you feel, can you?"

"S'pose not." Natalie stared blankly ahead and took a tomato from the plastic tub Megan held out, squashing it distractedly between her finger and thumb. "You know, it's ironic that we had the side gate made extra-high so no one could climb over it, and then someone forces the lock. It was a strong lock, too, so it can't have been easy."

"And you say you didn't hear anything at all?" asked Megan, wiping tomato juice from her eyelid.

Natalie shook her head. "Not a thing. And the police spoke to the neighbours and none of them heard or saw anything, either. Not that any of them were awake that early, mind you. I suppose that's why whoever it was decided that was the best time to break in. Of course, all the security we have didn't help Tony. I told you before, didn't I, Petal, how he used to switch everything off?"

"Yeah, you did. Do the police have any suspects in mind, do you know?"

"Not to my knowledge, although they asked Adrian and I if we'd give a DNA sample. I'm sure they don't think we had anything to do with it, it's just so they can eliminate us from their enquiries. Mind you, they were quite keen to speak to Gerald – our gardener –

but he won't be able to tell them anything I haven't already."

"Is he a suspect?" asked Megan.

"Good grief, no! He's about a hundred years old. I shouldn't think he had anything to do with it."

"And you've no idea why someone would have wanted to kill Tony?"

Natalie shook her head. "He was no angel, but he was harmless. I thought what happened to him was random, but the police think it could be linked to the other murders."

"Well, even if they didn't think it was linked, it doesn't sound very random to me," said Petal. "Not to go to all that trouble to break-in. There must be hundreds of houses in the village that are easier to break into. Sounds like someone wanted him dead."

Natalie nodded and twirled a lock of hair around her finger. "Yeah, but who? To my knowledge, he never upset anyone so much that they'd want to kill him. Even the neighbours got on with him, and that's saying something 'cos they're a whining bunch. Eleanor Cooper was forever complaining about his music, and I could tell that Diana Starr had a bee in her bonnet about it, too. Not that she ever had the guts to say anything to Tony about it, mind you."

Her phone gave a shrill ring. "Hi. Yes, I'm okay. I just needed to get out for a while –

get some air. Oh. Alright, yes, I'll come home now. See you in a bit." She ended the call with a sigh. "Adrian wants me to go back. He's started worrying that something's going to happen to me whenever I'm not with him. I'll be glad when he goes back to work next week – I really hope he feels up to it." She gathered up her things. "Anyway, thanks again. I'll see you soon."

As they watched Natalie teeter off on her heels, Petal turned to Megan. "Well, *she's* definitely not a member of the Tony Weller fan club, is she?"

ooooooo

On a breezy Thursday afternoon, Megan and Des stood on the pavement outside the Laugh Till You Cry Comedy Club.

"Shame it had to close down," said Des. "I heard a lot of customers stayed away after Andy's death but I thought they might have got over the bad patch."

Megan cupped her hands around her eyes and peered through a dusty windowpane. "I wouldn't be surprised if it's a long time before someone else takes over. I'm sure loads of people are put off by the fact that someone was murdered here. Doesn't really fit with the comedy theme, does it?" She bent down to pick up an old drinks mat that was sticking out from under the door, bearing the picture of a rotund, red-cheeked man, clutching his sides, and large tears spurting from his eyes. "Looks like this is all that's left of the club."

A young woman appeared from the office block next door and shook out a rug. "Sorry," she said, when Megan covered her mouth and spluttered. "I wasn't expecting anyone to be out here. You're not waiting for the club to open, are you? 'Cos, if you are, you'll be standing there for a long time. The staff who were left tried to keep it going for a few weeks, but there was no way they could – not with Andy gone. He was the life and soul of that club so it would never have been the same without him."

"Actually, we were wondering if there was anyone around who could tell us something about Andy's murder," said Des. "I don't suppose you know what happened, do you?"

The woman shrugged. "Only that he was killed one night after closing. Someone stuck a wooden stake in his chest."

Des started scribbling in his notebook. "It said in the newspaper that an employee found him?"

"Yeah, it was Mary – Mary Tang – but she was too upset to talk about it at the time. Even if the club had taken off again, she said she could never have worked there after what happened, so she moved on." The woman gave the rug another shake. "If you want to talk to her, though, I heard she started working at The Duck Inn on the village green last week. Do you know it?"

"I know it very well," said Megan. "Thanks for your help."

oooooo

Tucked away in the corner of the village green, almost opposite Kismet Cottage, was The Duck Inn.

A popular stop for locals, and sought out by tourists who wanted to have their picture taken outside Bliss Bay's oldest pub, The Duck Inn was well-known for two things: its vast selection of real ales, and the traditional English afternoon tea it served every day.

As was often the case during good weather, customers spilled out onto the green, the vast, exposed roots of the village oak tree providing seating once all the wooden benches were filled.

"Excuse me." Megan said to the man who was refilling a fridge with beer bottles. "Is Mary Tang working today?"

He nodded and called over his shoulder to the kitchen. "Mary! Someone here to see you."

A buxom woman with olive skin and glossy black hair that swung around her shoulders appeared, swigging from a water bottle. She grabbed a serviette from the counter and dabbed her forehead. "Phew, it's hot in there." She smiled. "Did you want to book a table?"

Megan shook her head. "Actually, we wondered if you have five minutes to spare?"

Mary's forehead furrowed. "What's this about?"

"It's about what happened at the comedy club," said Des, lowering his voice. "We hoped you'd be able to help us out with a few details."

"As long as you don't mind talking about it, that is," said Megan, hastily, before Des came over all Chief Inspector again and started a full-on witness interrogation.

"You're not the police, are you?" asked Mary, casting Des a suspicious look.

"No, but we live in Bliss Bay." He looked at her through narrowed eyes. "Let's just say we have a common interest in seeing whoever killed your friend put behind bars, and we'd like to do whatever we can to help see that they are."

Mary looked thoughtful, then nodded. She turned to the man filling the beer fridge. "Kevin, is it okay if I take a break for five minutes?"

She led Megan and Des to a table in a far corner. "So, what do you want to know?"

"What happened, if you feel okay to tell us about it," said Megan. "I know it must have been upsetting, so please say if you'd rather not."

Mary shrugged. "I've been over it with the police so many times, I'm numb to it now." She tipped the bottle to her lips and drank the last of her water. "I got to the club that morning at a little after seven. I used to work behind the bar in the evening, but I also opened up and did the cleaning three mornings a week. As soon as I saw Andy, I knew he was dead – he was slumped over a table with a wooden stick poking out of his chest. I freaked out and ran over to him but I knew it was too late to save him."

She gulped and took a breath. "I called the police and while I was waiting for them to arrive, I noticed he wasn't wearing his earring. You probably saw that detective talking about it on the news?"

"The gold hoop with the microphone charm?" said Megan.

Mary nodded. "It was a birthday present to Andy from all of us. He used to get on the mike and warm up the crowd before the entertainment started, you see. We thought it was perfect for him, and he wore it all the time."

"Were there any signs of a struggle?" asked Megan.

"None at all. Quite the opposite, in fact. It seemed he'd been drinking with someone after he'd closed up."

"And how do you know that?"

"Because the police asked me to check the register to see if any drinks had been paid for after the club closed, and it showed that five double brandies with orange liqueur, and a bottle of sparkling water had been rung in between twenty-past twelve and quarter-past two in the morning. Brandy and orange is what Andy used to drink so whoever was drinking the water must have bought them for him because Andy never paid for his own drinks."

"Good grief!" said Des. "It's no wonder there were no signs of a struggle. After that much booze in less than two hours, I should think Andy's killer was able to dispatch him without any resistance at all."

Mary nodded. "You're probably right. Andy was a big guy, and if someone came for him – which they did on a few occasions – he'd always retaliate. The fact that he didn't, probably meant that he couldn't. I suppose that much drink dulled his reactions."

Des screwed up his face. "I should think it did. Take it from me, I should know."

"You've no idea *who* he'd been drinking with, I suppose?" said Megan.

Mary shook her head. "No idea. And whoever it was took their bottle with them, because there were no empty sparkling water bottles in the recycling bin."

"So there was nothing for the police to take fingerprints from?" said Des.

"No. And we found out a few days later that there were none on the murder weapon, either. We gave the police a list of customers we could remember had been in that night so they could speak to them, but I guess that didn't help seeing as they still haven't made an arrest."

"Did Andy often stay behind after hours?" asked Megan.

"Occasionally. Sometimes he got chatting to customers, and they'd stay behind for a couple of drinks, but not very often. I don't recall seeing him talking to anyone in particular that night, but we were so busy, I wasn't really paying attention to what he was doing... I wish I had now." Mary's eyes misted over and she squeezed them shut. "Anyway, whoever killed him was either someone he let in after he'd closed and was about to cash up, or someone who stayed behind after closing time."

"Had the takings been stolen?" asked Megan.

Mary shook her head. "No. They were all there, right down to the last penny. Oh, and I've just remembered, there was some kind of yellow stuff on Andy's cheek. It looked like yellow dust."

A group of late-afternoon drinkers ambled in. "I'd better get back to work." Mary's serious expression was replaced by a smiling face for her customers as she went off to serve them.

"If Andy let someone in for an after-hours drinking session it must have been someone he knew," said Des, flicking back through his notes as they made their way out. "Or at least, someone he felt comfortable enough to sit and drink with."

"And, as there were no prints on the murder weapon, the killer must have been wearing gloves," said Megan. "You'd think that was odd, wouldn't you? Someone wearing gloves at night, while they were drinking in a club?"

"Not necessarily in the middle of the night in May," said Des. "I wouldn't look twice at someone who was wrapped up in a hat and scarf, either. It can be bloomin' cold at that time of year. I know we get some good weather at times, but it's hardly the tropics, love."

"Hmm, I suppose so. I wonder what the yellow dust could have been?"

"Yes, I wonder." Des scratched his chin, deep in thought, and put his notebook back in his pocket.

"Before we head back to your place," said Megan, "will you show me how to set the alarm again?" She headed across the village green to Kismet Cottage. "I'm not sure I got it the first time."

"Course I will," said Des, as he stopped by the garden wall to say hello to Cat. "Once you've set it a couple of times, it'll be second nature. And you know how useless I am with anything technical, so if *I* can understand how it works, you definitely will. Honestly, it's a piece of cake."

He stepped into the cottage and picked up the instruction leaflet from the hall stand. "Now, let's see..."

CHAPTER FOURTEEN

"Shaun's had to take the car into the garage." Lizzie sounded harassed when she called Megan with an update on her weekend travel plans. "Something to do with the clutch, so we'll be late setting off, and late getting to you. It's such a pain – I was hoping we could all have dinner together. You don't have to wait up for us, though, okay?"

"Don't worry about it," said Megan. "And I'll see how I feel. If I need matchsticks to keep my eyes open, I'll go to bed, otherwise I'll wait up till you get here."

"Alright, but I'll make breakfast in the morning. Deal?"

"Sounds perfect."

"You'll have to let me know what to do with the alarm, though, or it'll go off and wake up the whole street," said Lizzie.

Megan dropped her voice. "To be honest, I got a bit confused when Uncle Des was explaining it to me, so I'm not sure. He's already showed me twice so I don't want to ask him again. I'll have another look at the instructions when I get back home, and Skype you. That way, I can show you what to do."

"Okey-dokey," said Lizzie. "I'll see you later."

ooooooo

Megan scratched her head. "Well, I'm sure that's what Uncle Des told me to do. He

came back here with me and ran through it all
again. I don't know why I can't get it to work."

At the other end of a Skype call, Lizzie
was equally perplexed. "Have you read the
instruction leaflet?"

"Yes, but it's just gobbledegook to me."

"Look, Shaun will know what to do –
he's good with stuff like that. Why don't you
leave the alarm off, just until we get there? If
you leave the instruction leaflet on the kitchen
table, I'll ask him to take a look and set the
alarm before we go to bed, and then he can
show you how to do it before we leave in the
morning. It's not as though it'll be off all night
– just a few hours. I reckon we'll be there
between one and two. Anyway, I'd better go.
See you soon."

"Yeah, see you later." Megan stretched
her arms to the ceiling and yawned. She'd been
looking forward to a good night's sleep, in a
full-sized bed, since Monday. "I'd better get
you your dinner before I doze off," she said to
Cat, who opened an eye that followed her from
the couch to the kitchen.

With Cat fed, and lacking inspiration for
her own dinner, Megan opened a family-sized
carton of raspberry yoghurt which she
proceeded to finish, standing up and looking
out of the living room window at a game of
bowls that was being played on the village
green.

As Lizzie and Shaun weren't due until much later, she rethought her plans for the evening and decided to have a very early night. It was still light after she'd soaked in a deep bubble bath but she was so tired, she didn't envisage having any problems falling off to sleep.

Double-checking that all the doors and windows were locked, she changed Cat's litter tray and left him halfway up the stairs – his preferred place to sleep if he was staying in for the night.

"See you in the morning, kitty. Don't freak out when Lizzie and Shaun come in, will you?"

Megan was a little perturbed about not setting the alarm, but seeing as there'd never been one at Kismet Cottage in all the years her family had lived there, she didn't suppose one more night without one would matter. In any case, she was too tired to care.

She climbed into bed and pulled the duvet up to her ears, drifting off to sleep almost immediately. She was dreaming of wallowing in a bathtub filled with raspberry yoghurt when suddenly, somewhere in her subconscious, she heard a creak on the stairs.

Must be Lizzie and Shaun.

Then another creak, and another.

It took a while to register but, once it had, she was wide awake.

It wasn't Lizzie and Shaun.

Someone else was in the house.

Someone who didn't know that the Fallon family were *very* particular about the way they climbed the stairs.

She froze, not knowing what to do. She reached to the bedside table for her phone, realising she'd left it in the pocket of her jeans which were hung haphazardly over the chair in the corner of the room.

Flinging off the duvet, she crept across the rug, looking around for something to defend herself with. Not wanting to switch on the light, she made out the silhouettes of an old thigh-master and a teddy bear in the light cast by the moon coming through the chink in the curtains. Finding her phone, she was about to call 999 when an almighty wail pierced the silence. An almighty wail that was followed by muffled cries and the sound of footsteps becoming distant as the intruder ran down the stairs and out of the house.

She switched on the light and flung open the bedroom door to see Cat where she'd left him – halfway up the stairs – and looking most aggrieved that his night's sleep had been interrupted. He stretched and yawned before settling down again, but not before he'd opened an amber eye and given her a look which clearly said, 'Don't even *think* about disturbing me again.'

Heart racing, Megan ran downstairs and pushed the open front door shut before her legs gave way and she slid down it and called the police.

oooooo

"Yes, I know I *should* have set the alarm, but it's new and I couldn't work it out. My sister's boyfriend's going to show me how to do it when they arrive," Megan explained to a very grumpy PC Fred Denby, who'd left his warm bed to attend the call.

"Looks like they used a crowbar," he said, examining the front door. "And you say you don't think anything's been stolen?"

"Not that I can see, said Megan. "Nothing's even been disturbed. I don't think whoever it was was here for long enough to take anything – thanks to Cat."

Meeeeoooowww.

PC Denby stopped his questioning to glance at Cat before turning a page in his notebook. "And you didn't see, or hear, the intruder?"

"No, I just heard them on the stairs – they creak, you see. And then Cat yelped and, after that, there was the most almighty racket – muffled shouts and lots of wailing – so I reckon Cat must have scared them off." She bent to tickle the tabby and he purred with delight.

"You think the cat might have attacked the intruder?"

Megan shrugged. "It's possible, especially if they tripped over him in the dark. He often sleeps halfway up the stairs, you see."

"I'd like to see if we can get a swab from his claws," said the constable.

Megan raised a brow. "Good luck with that," she muttered.

PC Denby pursed his lips. "And you have no idea who the intruder might have been, or why they would have wanted to break in?"

"No idea at all. I would have thought the main motive for break-ins was robbery, but as nothing's been touched, that obviously wasn't the case." She shivered. "You don't think it's connected to the murders, do you?"

Fred yawned and scratched the inside of his ear with the end of his pen. "I doubt it, Miss Fallon. I'm more inclined to think it was an opportunist. I understand your worries that the intruder was on their way upstairs to do you harm but, believe it or not, burglars often start at the top of the house because that's usually where the most valuable stuff is. I'll have a word with my Sergeant about your concerns, though, and we'll see what he says. In the meantime, I can give you the number of a 24-hour locksmith. Is there anyone you can ask to come and stay with you until we've finished here and the door is fixed?"

Meeeooowwwww. Cat extended a leg and stretched his neck before rolling onto his back.

PC Denby threw him another disinterested glance, this time doing a double-take. He walked over to where Cat lay and crouched down beside him.

"My sister and her boyfriend should be arriving any time now," said Megan. "I'll call her in a minute to see how far away she is. Er, I wouldn't get too close to him, if I were you. He can be a bit unpredictable with strangers." She watched as Cat eyed the policeman and swatted at him with a flexed paw.

"His ear," said PC Denby. "Do you know how it got to be like that?"

"What, all raggedy?" Megan shook her head. "No idea. It's been like that ever since my family have known him, I think. Why?"

The police officer ignored her question. "And he's a stray? He doesn't belong to anyone?"

"No," said Megan, "although I suppose we've kind of adopted him. He's a street cat. One of the neighbours used to feed him but when she passed away, he started coming here for his grub. Why are you so interested?"

"I'd rather not say at the moment, but if my hunch is correct, there's only one person I know who can verify it." PC Denby looked at his watch. "Excuse me a moment, I need to make a call. He's not going to believe this."

oooooooo

Fifteen minutes later, Megan opened the door to see Detective Inspector Sam Cambridge standing on the doorstep.

"Good evening, Miss Fallon, we meet again. Well, this is quite the coincidence, isn't it? As soon as PC Denby gave me your address, I recognised it from the statement you gave in Honeymeade. It's very memorable. Can I come in?"

"What? Oh, yes, of course. Come in." Megan covered a yawn with her hand. "What are you doing here? It's a break-in, not a murder. Not that I'm not glad to see you, of course – the more police the better, as far as I'm concerned. In fact, I don't suppose you could arrange to have a car posted outside till the morning, could you?" Aware that she was rambling, Megan stopped talking and took a breath. "Sorry to babble. It must be the adrenaline."

"My colleague tells me there's something here that may be connected to an old unsolved case I worked on," said Sam.

Megan stifled another yawn and stepped aside to let him pass.

PC Denby pointed to Cat, who was stretched out on the rug. "There he is, boss."

Sam circled Cat, observing him from above before crouching down and studying him more closely, just as PC Denby had done.

"Er, would either of you like to tell me what's going on?" asked Megan. "I called because there was an intruder in the house, not because I wanted you to examine the cat."

Sam's knees creaked as he stood up. He crossed his arms and strolled across the room and back again. "PC Denby and I go back a long way, so he knew this would be of interest to me. Years ago, when I was a Sergeant, PC Denby and I were officers in another force. After I moved to this county to work for the CID, PC Denby put in for a transfer soon afterwards and moved to Bliss Bay, but we left behind one unsolved case, and it's always bothered me that we didn't get a result."

"And what's that got to do with Cat?" asked Megan, with an increasingly bemused expression.

"It was the case of an elderly woman whose silver tabby kitten was stolen – over a decade ago, it was. It went missing from her front garden while she went inside to answer the phone and it caused a lot of excitement in the community because she offered such a generous reward for its return."

"That's awful," said Megan. "Why would someone steal her cat?"

"Because the cat was a pedigree, Mrs Curtis was wealthy, and she lavished gifts on it like you wouldn't believe," said Sam. "That little kitty used to wear a custom designed collar decorated with sapphires – twenty of them, set on black velvet – with a spherical sapphire hanging from the front. We couldn't believe it when we saw the photograph we were given for identification purposes, could we Fred?

"Anyway, unfortunately, Mrs Curtis wasted no time in telling everyone about her cat's new collar, which is why we think he was taken. If she'd kept it to herself, I'm sure the sapphires would have passed as fake. I mean, who would ever think that someone would spend thousands of pounds on a cat collar? Shame, really, if she'd said nothing, no one would ever have given little Tabastion a second glance."

"Tabastion?" Megan raised a brow.

"That's his name," said Sam. "A cross between Tabby and Bastion. The old lady liked the idea that her little tabby kitten would eventually grow into a strong protector, so she thought it was fitting. She'd originally planned to show him in competitions, but when he got into a scrap with a neighbour's tomcat and got his ear all chewed up, it put paid to his future as a show cat."

"Oh no! Poor little thing." Megan felt a wave of affection for the cantankerous tabby. "That must have been a really one-sided fight."

"Huh, don't you believe it," said Sam. "He might only have been a kitten but, apparently, he didn't take very kindly to having his ear munched on so he gave as good as he got."

"Weren't there any suspects?"

"We interviewed plenty of people. All the neighbours, the guys from the supermarket who used to deliver Mrs Curtis's shopping, and the care-home staff who used to visit her, but we didn't find a thing. It was as though he'd just vanished off the face of the earth." Sam bent to tickle Tabastion on the tummy. "Pity Mrs Curtis never got to see him like this."

"Well, perhaps she'd like to have him back?" As she said the words, Megan felt a pang of remorse. She'd grown attached to Cat and the thought of him leaving was surprisingly painful.

DI Cambridge shook his head. "As wonderful as that would be, she passed away not long after he went missing, but I know she'd have been very happy to know that he's been so well looked after for the past few years. Obviously, whoever nabbed him took the sapphires and then got rid of him."

Megan frowned. "Honestly, some people. That's just cruel." She patted her lap and Cat padded over and jumped onto it. "But how did he end up in Bliss Bay?"

Sam shrugged. "No idea. I wouldn't think he walked here on his own so I would guess that whoever stole him dumped him here, or close to here. Mind you, it's not unheard of to hear of cats walking long distances."

"Yes, but that's usually only if they're lost and trying to get back home, isn't it?" said Megan. "Not because they wake up one morning and feel like embarking on a half-marathon." She stared at the cat on her lap as he lounged on his back, legs akimbo. "You really think Cat is Tabastion?"

"Having seen his markings, those amber eyes, and his ear, I'm absolutely sure of it," said Sam. "I looked at his picture for hours a day, and days on end, so it's engrained in my memory. That's no street cat. That's a pedigree from a grand champion lineage."

ooooooo

"I *knew* it! I bloody well *knew* it!" Lizzie dashed past the police car outside Kismet Cottage and flung her arms around Megan's neck, tears streaming down her cheeks. "I knew if you stayed here, something terrible would happen. I'm so sorry I told you not to turn the alarm on."

"Don't be daft, it's not your fault. I couldn't have turned it on if I'd wanted to – I didn't know how, remember? And nothing's happened, I'm fine," soothed Megan, "but I'm so glad to see you. Someone broke in, but the detective said he doesn't think it's connected to the murders. That's what you said, isn't it, DI Cambridge?"

Sam nodded. "This bears all the hallmarks of a burglary, so I really do think that's what it is, as opposed to anything more sinister. That's not to say you shouldn't be vigilant, mind you. Maybe a deadbolt lock wouldn't be a bad idea." He rapped his knuckles against the old front door. "Looks like whoever broke in took a crowbar to this without too much trouble." He raised both eyebrows. "And start setting the alarm."

"Just a minute," said Lizzie, suddenly recognising Sam. "Wasn't it you we spoke to in Honeymeade after that guy was found in his car?"

Sam nodded. "Hello again, Miss Fallon."

"Why is there a Detective Inspector here?" Lizzie looked from Sam to Megan in alarm. "Has someone been hurt?"

"I'll tell you later," said Megan. "It's a long story, but nothing to worry about." She turned to Sam. "Anyway, yes, I'll start setting the alarm from now on. And I'll get the door sorted out tomorrow."

"My boyfriend's going to show Megan how to set the alarm until she can do it in her sleep," said Lizzie, wiping her eyes.

"Good idea." Sam gave them a brief smile. "Well, I'd better get going. Nice to see both of you, but in the nicest possible way, I hope our paths don't cross again."

oooooooo

"So he knew all about Cat's family history but he had no idea who the intruder was? Some detective he is," said Lizzie, rolling her eyes as she hugged a mug of hot chocolate.

"His name's Tabastion now, not Cat. And, no, DI Cambridge didn't know who broke in, but they didn't leave any clues behind so it's hardly surprising. All he had to go on was what I told him, which wasn't much. PC Denby said he thought it was most likely an opportunist who knew that Mum and Dad were away, but didn't know I was staying here. They might have had second thoughts about breaking in if I'd left Vinnie on the drive, but I parked on the street so you could get your car on.

"Whoever it was must have had the shock of their life, thanks to Tabastion. They obviously expected to find the place empty, not a cranky cat waiting to claw their eyes out," said Megan, scratching the tabby under the chin and eliciting a deep, rumbling purr. "Anyway, apart from the door, nothing's damaged, nothing's been taken and no one was hurt. Thank goodness."

The whining of a drill went through their ears.

"That won't go down very well with the neighbours at this time of the morning," said Megan, anxiously, as Shaun carried out a temporary repair.

"Tough," said Lizzie. "We can't leave the front door open all night. I'm sure they'll understand once they find out what happened."

"Right," said Shaun. "I'll have to unscrew everything in the morning so we can get out, but that'll keep things secure until tomorrow."

Megan gave the door a rattle, reassured to find it fixed solid in its frame. "You're a sweetheart," she said. "Thank you."

"No problem." Shaun put down the drill and looked at his watch. "And I don't know about you, Lizzie, but I need to get my head down, or I'll never get up in the morning. See you tomorrow, Megan."

oooooooo

Just like old times, Lizzie and Megan snuggled under the duvet in Megan's bed to chat about the events of the day.

"I hope Cat stuck his claws right into whoever broke in," said Lizzie. "Or better still, his teeth. He's better than a guard dog any day."

Megan nodded, a distracted expression on her face.

"You okay?" said Lizzie. "I know it must have been a real shock but no one's going to get past Shaun's repair, so you don't have to worry."

Megan chewed at a hangnail, deep in thought. "Lizzie."

"Yeah."

"You're going to think I'm nuts when I tell you what I'm thinking, but I haven't been able to get it out of my head since DI Cambridge mentioned it."

"Mentioned what?"

"At Mum and Dad's ceremony, Olivia was wearing the most amazing sapphire bracelet. It was gorgeous."

"Yeah, I saw it. So what?"

"Well, what if she's the person who stole Tabastion? And then had his collar made into jewellery?"

"Olivia? Are you mad?" Lizzie shook her head. "No way. I just can't see it – she wouldn't do something like that. And, anyway, you said Tabastion was stolen from another county, didn't you?"

"Yes, but some people live all over the place before they settle down. And Olivia first came here eight years ago. What if she stole

Cat before she came to Bliss Bay and then dumped him?"

"Hmm, I see your point," said Lizzie, with a yawn, "but I still don't think she had anything to do with it. She just doesn't strike me as a cat-napper. Tell the police about your suspicions if you want to, though."

Megan frowned. "I'm not sure what to do. You're probably right but it's a coincidence, don't you think?"

"Yeah, but I think that's all it is." Lizzie shook her head as she got out of the bed. "I can see where you're coming from but I really think you're meowing up the wrong tree with Olivia." She yawned again. "Night, sis."

CHAPTER FIFTEEN

"Are you sure you're going to be okay?" said Lizzie, after a late breakfast.

"I'm going to be fine." Despite her mild anxiety, Megan stuck up a thumb and put on a smile. "I've got an alarm I know how to set, thanks to Shaun; an amazing warrior cat; someone's on their way to fix the door; and Uncle Des is on his way round. How much safer could a girl be?"

"Well, if you're sure, we'd better get going," said Lizzie, reluctantly.

Megan gave her sister a hug. "Drive carefully – the wind's really getting up. I'll speak to you soon."

ooooooo

"But I showed you twice how to set the alarm," said Des, his arms folded and a foot tapping. "You should have said you didn't understand."

"Well, I thought I did until I tried to explain it to Lizzie," said Megan, rolling her dark hair into a bun and sticking a pen through it to hold it up. "Anyway, I know now. And the police don't think the break-in is connected to the murders, so I feel a lot calmer about it." She pushed her shoulder against the newly fixed door a few times. "And nothing's going to get through this in a hurry."

Des gave a little snort and shook his head. "Come on. Let's go and see Gerald."

ooooooo

Des leaned forward and studied the sky. "Looks like rain."

"I hope not. It's bad enough driving in this wind," said Megan, as she fought to keep the little mini on the right side of the road, her knuckles white from gripping the steering wheel so tight.

By the time they got to Castle Manor, the wind had dropped and the sun had made a late appearance through the low cloud.

"Gerald told us to go straight through to the garden," said Des. "Dear, oh dear, someone's made a right mess of this, haven't they?" He pointed to the broken lock in the sturdy wooden gate.

They found Gerald wheeling a barrow full of leaves and broken branches to the compost heap. Contrary to how Megan imagined him to be, and Natalie Castle's description that Gerald McGuire was 'about a hundred years old', he looked to be in his sixties, and was tall and upright with broad shoulders and strong arms. He pushed and emptied the heavy barrow with ease before wheeling it back to where Des and Megan stood.

"Nice to meet you," he said, with a nod, and wiped his hand down the front of his shirt before shaking Megan's hand with a firm grasp.

"Likewise," said Megan, smiling at the man with a twinkle in his brown eyes, and a gap where his two front teeth had once resided.

"Someone did a good job on that gate, didn't they?" said Des.

Gerald nodded. "The police have given me the okay to get it repaired, so that's the next job on my list." He looked at the sky. "That wind's made a right mess of things. Brought down the branches on half the trees, it has. This is the fourth barrow I've cleared. And there's rain on the way by the look of those clouds, maybe even a storm."

"Can we help you clear up?" asked Megan.

Gerald waved a soil-stained hand. "No, I'll be done in five minutes. Why don't you have a nose around, meantime? You might see something useful – Des tells me you're doing a little detective work of your own?"

"Just trying to find out what we can to help speed things along," said Megan.

"Don't suppose you know where the body was found, do you?" asked Des.

"Just where you're standing, apparently. By the fishpond. Whoever killed Tony used the birdbath that statue used to hold in its hand to hit him over the head with." Gerald nodded to the stone water nymph and muttered under his breath. "Don't ask me what kind of world we're living in when a man can't even go about his business without getting murdered." He wheeled the now-empty barrow into the shed. "It's a terrible state of affairs, so it is." He took off his flat cap and wiped his forearm across his forehead. "By the way, d'you like fruit and veg?"

"I love it," said Megan. "Why do you ask?"

"'Cos I've had a bumper crop on my allotment this year – more than family and friends can eat. It'd break my heart to see it go to waste so you'd be doing me a big favour if you'd drop by and help yourself to as much as you can carry. You too, Des. There's nothing like home-grown fruit and veg to see you right."

"That's very decent of you," said Des. "Shall we pop over on Monday, Megan? I could knock up a few pies and quiches for a change, instead of cakes. That okay with you, Gerald?"

Gerald nodded. "Come when you like and take what you want."

As Gerald and Des chatted about the culinary merits of over-ripe fruit, Megan strolled around the garden and looked past the grounds of the house to the neighbouring properties.

A sudden movement drew her eye to a silhouette of a figure at the top window of Oscar and Eleanor Cooper's house, two doors down. She held her hand above her eyes and squinted, but the reflections on the glass prevented her from seeing who it was.

When Des had finished chatting, they both took another look at the side gate, its battered wood splintered and the lock hanging from its housing.

"There's no way someone did that without making any noise," said Megan.

"Agreed," said Des, inspecting the area around the fishpond. He grunted and scratched at his greying thatch of hair. "I can't see any clues, can you?"

"Not really."

After fifteen minutes, Des blew out a frustrated sigh. "I think we've seen enough, don't you?" he said, taking his pen from behind his ear and putting it back in his pocket. "Shall we make a move?"

Megan nodded. "Thanks for letting us come and have a look around, Gerald. We'll see you at the allotment on Monday."

As they turned to leave, she looked up at the Cooper's house to see that the figure was still at the window.

ooooooo

"Are you absolutely sure she wants an electric drill?" asked Megan, with a dubious expression.

"Of course I'm sure." Des rubbed his hands together, a mischievous twinkle in his eye. "She's been dropping hints about it for months but I've been pretending I'm not listening so it'll be a nice surprise when I give it to her."

"If you say so," said Megan, not entirely convinced.

In the village electrical shop, Megan and Des browsed the shelves for a present for Sylvie's birthday.

"Look at this one." Megan picked up a box with a smaller box taped to it. "It comes with a free blowtorch."

"Er, I'm not sure it's a good idea to let Sylv loose with a flame-thrower," said Des, with a frown. "You know how carried away she gets with new tools, and I've grown quite attached to my eyebrows." He squinted over Megan's shoulder. "Isn't that Timothy Starr over there?"

As Megan turned to see Timothy wandering aimlessly through the shop, he looked her way, his fraught expression turning to a smile and he waved and walked towards them.

"I don't suppose either of you know where the curling tongs might be, do you? I thought they'd be in the beauty section but they aren't and there's no one around to ask. Diana was getting ready for a concert we're performing at tonight and her old ones blew a fuse. She's sitting at home waiting for me to bring her a replacement."

"Look in the grooming section." Megan pointed to the other side of the shop. "There probably isn't much of a selection, but there's bound to be something that'll get you out of a fix."

"Ah, that's great, thanks," said Timothy, and made himself scarce.

"Good grief, he doesn't look well, does he?" whispered Des, as he and Megan made their way to the cash desk. "Looks like he could do with a month's sleep."

"Well, it can't be very relaxing living next door to where someone you know has been murdered. I'm not sure I'd be able to sleep at all until the killer was locked up."

They joined the back of a long queue of customers, just as it came to a standstill when the person at the front paid for her £45.99 coffee machine with a bag full of coins.

"Oh, for heaven's sake. Trust there to be a delay," grumbled Timothy, who'd joined the queue behind them. "Just when I'm in a rush."

"You can go in front of us, if you like," said Des, standing aside. "That'll save you a couple of minutes."

"How's Diana?" asked Megan.

"Oh, you know," said Timothy, rubbing his brow. "She's a little better, but Tony's death has hit her very hard, especially as she's still upset about her friend passing away. The fact that she was already stressed, worrying about Bailey's scholarship, hasn't helped, so it's been a difficult time all round."

"Well, I'm glad to know she's a bit better," said Megan. "She told me how upset she was about your friend when I saw her at your place."

Timothy looked to the head of the queue where the customer was still counting out her coins and rubbed his brow again. "I suppose there's no harm in telling you – at least it'll help to pass the time. The chap who died was merely an acquaintance of mine, but he was very fond of Diana when we were younger. More than very fond of her, actually – he was in love with her. That's part of the reason she was so upset; she's felt guilty for years."

"Guilty?" said Des.

Timothy nodded. "He proposed to her on her eighteenth birthday, but she wasn't interested because she'd just started going out with me. It all caused a bit of a scandal back then because Diana had only just left school, and he was twenty-seven. Not such a big age gap these days but back then, it was considered quite risqué." Timothy ran a hand over his bald spot. "Anyway, he was devastated that Diana chose me over him. He never got over it, apparently. We heard on the grapevine that he was heartbroken."

"And did you see him after that?" asked Des.

Timothy nodded. "Every year, although not to speak to. We always play the Honeymeade Christmas concert, you see, and every single year, he'd turn up and sit at the back. I'm pretty sure he only came along to see Diana, but he always left before the end, so we never crossed paths again. Mind you, I doubt he'd have spoken to me, anyway. He ignored me from the day Diana told him she wasn't interested in him. He must have been furious with me for over forty years. What a waste of energy." Timothy shrugged. "Not my problem, though. And between you and me, Victor wasn't a very nice man, so he had no one but himself to blame that he ended up on his own."

Megan's ears pricked up. "Victor?"

Timothy nodded. "Yes. Victor Canning."

"The guy who was murdered in his car in Honeymeade?"

"Yes, that's him." Timothy gave Megan a quizzical look. "Did you know him? You seemed surprised when I said his name."

"Oh, no. No. It's just that, er, it's been on the news quite a lot recently, so it rang a bell, that's all." Megan didn't want to get into the ins and outs of how she and Lizzie had been at the café when Victor's body was discovered.

"Ah, I see," said Timothy. "Anyway, I've lost count of the number of times I've told Diana she shouldn't feel so guilty. She didn't upset Victor intentionally, but she feels responsible that he spent so many years with a broken heart. Oh, thank goodness! The queue's beginning to move at last. Diana's hair's going to be one big frizz ball by the time I get home with these." He chuckled. "Thanks for letting me take your place," he said, with a smile and a nod, once he'd paid for his purchase. "Much appreciated. See you around, no doubt."

Des couldn't hold his tongue for a second longer. As soon as Timothy was out of earshot, he blurted, "Diana must be the woman Victor talked about to the people in that diner! The one he said was the love of his life. Remember?"

"Exactly what I was thinking," said Megan, as they walked back to the car. "Timothy said Victor was twenty-seven when he proposed to Diana, and it said on the news that he was seventy-four when he was killed, so that's forty-seven years he was in love with her. She really *was* the love of his life. Although I'm not sure how knowing that helps us."

"Well, that would be a murder motive for plenty of men," said Des. "Maybe Timothy took exception to Victor lusting after his wife?" He scratched his chin. "Although why would he have waited all this time? He knew Victor lived in Honeymeade, so he could have done away with him at any time over the past forty-seven years if he'd wanted to. Why wait until now? It doesn't make sense."

Megan frowned. "No, it doesn't. That's a pity. I thought we were onto something for a minute." She looked at her watch. "Anyway, come on, I'll take you back to Kismet and you can wrap Sylvie's present and leave it there, if you want. She's such a snoop, she'd bound to find it if you take it home."

oooooo

Sam Cambridge ended a call from forensics, which confirmed that the unknown DNA found at the Andy Cochran and Victor Canning murder scenes had also been found on Tony Weller's body.

He was cursing to himself when Harvey stuck his head around the door. "You got a minute, boss?"

Sam beckoned him in and told him about the forensic findings. "I could really do with some good news but from the look on your face, Harvey, I don't think you're going to give me any."

Harvey shook his head. "Sorry. There's been an incident involving a young woman. She was walking to her car last night to pick up a takeaway, and a vehicle mounted the pavement and drove straight for her.

Fortunately, she was able to dive into a shop doorway, so apart from a few scratches and being badly shaken-up, she's fine. She's pretty sure it wasn't an accident, because the car was going so fast, and it sped off without checking to see if she was okay."

"I can tell by the tone of your voice that there's a reason for you telling me this rather than leaving it to the local police?"

"The woman is Caroline Gibbs."

"The woman Eleanor Cooper suggested we get in touch with? The one we spoke to last week, who's the subject of all the rumours flying around about Adrian Castle?"

"The very same."

ooooooo

"Are you sure you can't tell us anything about the car or the driver, Miss Gibbs?" Sam leaned forward on the couch, his hands clasped between his knees, his eyes fixed on the young woman. "Anything at all?"

Caroline shook her dark hair over her shoulder and rocked her baby to sleep. "You know, it doesn't matter how stressed I am, as soon as this little one's in my arms, all the tension just drains away." She kissed the baby's downy head. "Anyway, I've already told you everything. And I told that other policeman, too. I was walking to my car when the road lit up behind me. I turned around but

I couldn't see a thing because the headlights were blinding."

"You couldn't see if it was a man or a woman? Or the type or colour of the car?"

"No. I couldn't see the driver but I think the car was a dark colour. I suppose it could have been a drunk driver, rather than someone aiming for me purposely, but I can assure you, I won't be going out that late at night on my own again. I'm not taking any more risks – not with this little one to look after.

"Whether this was intentional or not, it's really spooked me so we're going to stay with my brother and his wife for a few days. They live a couple of hours from here but I've given the other policeman his address in case you need to get in touch with me again. Now, if you don't mind, I need to feed my baby. Can you see yourselves out?"

ooooooo

The howling wind battered the rain against the windowpanes of The Cobbles Café, which was packed with customers sheltering from a summer thunderstorm.

Inside, Megan, Des and Petal huddled around a table, reading the morning's newspaper.

"You don't mind if I sit with you for a bit, do you?" said Petal. "I doubt anyone's going to come out to buy flowers in this weather, and Lionel and Amisha have got everything under control, so I might as well take the weight off my feet." She snuggled between Megan and Des.

"No, of course we don't mind, love," said Des. "We were on our way to see someone but when the rain started coming down, we thought we'd take cover in here till it clears. Looks like everyone had the same idea."

"Haven't you got the car with you?" said Petal.

"Oh yes, we've got the car." Des cleared his throat and cast a glance at Megan from the corner of his eye. "But Vinnie the Mini's not very good at going through deep puddles, so we have to wait until the rain stops." He raised a brow and carried on with the newspaper.

The bell above the café door jangled and Blossom stepped in, soaked to the skin.

"Thank goodness you're back," said Amisha. "We're almost out of milk until we get a delivery later."

"Oh, love! Just look at you!" Petal jumped up. "There's a towel and a change of clothes in the back of the shop. I'll get them and you can dry yourself off before you catch your death of cold."

"These are absolutely ruined, Dad," Blossom complained, as she handed a bag filled with milk cartons to Amisha, and squelched around to the other side of the counter to show Lionel her shoes. "I only got them last weekend."

"They'll dry out, love," said Lionel. "Might take a couple of days but you've got loads of shoes you can wear in the meantime, haven't you?"

"*No*, I mean they're ruined because you're not supposed to wear them in the rain. If I'd known we were going to have a storm, I wouldn't have put them on this morning." Blossom's expression was pained in a way that only a fashion-conscious teenage girl's could be.

"'Not supposed to wear them in the rain'?" echoed Des. "Why not? They're shoes, aren't they? What good's a pair of shoes if you can't wear them in the rain? What're they made of, for goodness' sake? Cardboard? I've never heard anything so ridiculous." He gawped at Blossom's sorry-looking pink suede shoes as she trudged off to where Petal was waiting to envelop her in a large towel.

The bell above the door jangled for a second time and Sylvie got blown in, battling to close a flimsy umbrella.

"Shut the door!" the customers chorused.

Sylvie shook the rain from her curls and sprayed everyone within two feet with water as she hurried to the table, an excited look on her face. "Thank goodness you're here! Can I have a toasted teacake please, Amisha?" She took a serviette from the dispenser on the table and dabbed at her pink cheeks. "I don't know what to tell you first! You'll never guess what's happened," she said, without pausing for breath, and carried on speaking before anyone had a chance to answer.

"You know Caroline Gibbs? The one that... Well, you know the one. When I went past her place this morning, the police were outside so I popped in to see Maude Reilly who lives next door to her to ask what was going on. She said Caroline's mum told her that someone tried to run Caroline over late last night as she was walking to her car. She's terribly shaken-up."

Sylvie took the slice of toast out of Des's hand before taking a large bite and handing it back.

"Is she okay?" asked Petal, reappearing from the back of the shop.

"Well, she's not injured, if that's what you mean," said Sylvie, wiping butter from her chin.

"Did she have the baby with her?" asked Megan.

"No, thank goodness. Her mum moved in with her after the little one was born, so she was with her."

"It could have been an accident," said Petal.

Sylvie shook her head. "Maude said Caroline couldn't see anything, because the headlights dazzled her, but she's almost sure it was intentional because the car was heading straight for her and didn't stop, or even slow down. If it was an accident, surely the driver would have stopped and checked to see that Caroline was okay?"

"What's happened to respect and common decency?" said Des, with a scowl.

"Well, as long as she's alright, that's the main thing." Megan shivered. "She must have been petrified." She recalled Eleanor Cooper's opinion that Caroline was involved up to her neck in Tony's death. "I wonder if the attack was anything to do with the murders?"

"If it is, she should thank her lucky stars she got off so lightly," said Sylvie. "If only the other victims had been so fortunate."

"So what was the other thing, Sylv?" asked Lionel, as he set down a cinnamon teacake in front of her. "You said you didn't know what to tell us first."

Sylvie beckoned him closer with a jerk of her head. "After I'd spoken to Maude, I went to the library to return some books and when I came out, I noticed a kerfuffle across the road in the alley between Peel's Ironmongers and Hiccups Wine Bar." She loaded a knife with butter and spread it thickly onto her teacake before looking at the expectant expressions around the table. "Adrian Castle had Bailey Starr pinned up against the wall."

"What do you mean, he had him 'pinned up against the wall'?" said Lionel.

"Exactly what I say," said Sylvie. "His arm was across Bailey's neck and his face was right up close to his. I don't know what he was saying but it didn't look very friendly."

"Wonder what that was about?" said Megan.

Sylvie shrugged and pushed an escaping currant back into her mouth. "No idea. It had just started raining so I didn't hang around to find out, but it looked like Adrian threw something down the alley and then he pushed Bailey onto the ground. Then Bailey got up and ran off and Adrian limped back to his car."

"Don't suppose you got a chance to see what it was that he threw?" asked Lionel.

"No idea," said Sylvie, picking a currant pip from between her teeth with a fingernail. "I was too busy making myself scarce to notice."

Des shook his head. "It's like a bloomin' war ground round here at the moment. Why can't we all just get along?" He peered out of the window and tapped Megan on the arm. "Right, come on, love. It's stopped raining. Let's make a dash for it. See you later, Sylv."

CHAPTER SIXTEEN

With the storm passed, and the sun once again shining down from a sky as blue as cornflowers, Megan and Des trundled down the twisty country lanes on their way to Gerald's allotment.

"Aah, I love the smell of the land after it's rained," said Des, sticking his head out of the window and taking in great gulps of fresh air. "And speaking of rain, if I was Blossom, I'd be taking those shoes straight back to the shop and demanding a refund. Can't wear them in the rain? I've never heard anything like it."

"I wonder what was going on between Adrian and Bailey?" said Megan. "I've only met Adrian once, so I don't know him well, but Natalie said he's been really grumpy lately. And I don't know Bailey well, either, but he's always seemed really placid. Certainly not the type to go looking for trouble. In fact, certainly not the type to go *anywhere* if his parents have anything to do with it. They're very strict on him."

Des shrugged. "I've no idea, but some people are offended by the slightest thing these days. Maybe Bailey said something Adrian took exception to?" He sat quietly for a minute. "Speaking of Bailey, did it rain the day before yesterday? Early on, I mean."

"No." Megan slowed down to let a rabbit hop across the road. "Why?"

"Because I saw him when I walked down to the village green newsagent's to buy a paper," said Des. "Nice lad, isn't he? I had a long chat with him at your mum and dad's party. Very intelligent young man."

"Yes, he is. He's a sweetie," said Megan, "but what's that got to do with whether it rained or not?"

"Because when I saw him, I noticed that his shoes and the bottom of his jeans were wet. He came into the newsagent's as I was on my way out and he left wet footprints on the floor. Actually, he almost slipped over. If it hadn't been for one of the customers catching his arm, he would have fallen flat on his backside. I forgot all about it until I just thought about Blossom's shoes."

"Maybe he'd been washing his car," said Megan, distracted as she looked out for the turning to Gerald's allotment. "Ah, here we are. Right, let's go and fill our baskets!"

ooooooo

Gerald waved a hand across the expanse of his fruit and veg garden. "Take as much as you want – especially those broad beans, because I'll be cutting them right back at the end of the week. Just help yourself."

With their baskets at the ready, Des and Megan picked what they wanted, before accepting Gerald's offer of a cup of coffee from his flask. He fetched a folding chair from the small shed and wiped off the dust with his sleeve, before setting it down on the grass.

"Here you are, Megan. Take the weight off your feet."

"Thank you. You know, I think I'd quite like an allotment," she said, taking the chipped pottery cup Gerald handed her. "It must be great to have fresh fruit and veg on tap whenever you want it. And it's so peaceful. I'm not surprised you love it here so much."

"That's what the chap who has the allotment next to mine says." Gerald emptied the dregs of his coffee cup onto the mud. "He says the smell and taste of fruit and veg you've grown yourself is the most satisfying thing in the world. He's forever saying 'it's like being at one with nature'. He comes here for the peace and quiet. Sometimes he's here at the crack of dawn, pottering about in his shed."

He peered at a huddle of lopsided tomato canes at the far side of the allotment. "Looks like the wind got to some of those. 'S'cuse me while I secure them before they fall over completely. Oh blast, there's some over there, too. Des, do me a favour, will you? Hold those canes up for a minute until I can tie them together? And Megan, can you get some wire from my potting shed so I can tie them in place? It's on the shelf in front of you as you walk in."

Megan rubbed her sweaty palms down her jacket before pushing at the door's old timbers. She had an intense fear of sheds: they were home to spiders that lurked in corners, and hung from the ceilings, scuttling out of sight when the slightest movement disturbed them. Looking straight ahead, she saw an almost empty reel of yellow plastic-coated wire and grabbed it quickly before rushing out, leaving Spider Central behind her.

"Is this it?" She handed it to Gerald. "There's not much on here. Will that be enough?"

He shook his head. "I've got a new reel at home but I forgot to bring it with me." He raised his chin in the direction of the neighbouring plot. "Have a look in that shed over there, will you? It'll be on one of the shelves."

"But isn't that someone else's shed?" said Megan.

Gerald nodded. "Don't worry, we borrow stuff from each other all the time. Just pull the door open. He doesn't keep anything valuable in there so he never locks it. And can you cut me a length of wire? About two foot long should do it."

Megan gave the door a tentative push. Unlike Gerald's orderly potting shed, this one was like something from the set of a horror movie. Shafts of light filtered through the grimy windows, highlighting the dust that hung in the air. She coughed as it hit the back of her throat, and screwed up her nose against the smell coming from a large barrel of potting compost in the corner. A lone fly buzzing at the window did nothing to dispel the eerie atmosphere, and she heaved a sigh of relief when she spied a large reel of green garden wire on a shelf. She looked around the small dusty space. Now she had the wire, she had no idea what to cut it with. A gardener, she was not.

As if he'd read her mind, Gerald called out. "There should be a pair of wire cutters in the drawer unit under the shelf in the corner."

The drawer was full of odds and ends and Megan reached a reluctant hand to the back and felt around. "This must be them," she muttered, feeling something hard in the bag she pulled out. She peered inside and gasped.

There were no wire cutters in the bag. Instead, there was a pair of sunglasses with black frames and blue mirrored lenses, a yellow bow tie, and a gold hoop earring with a microphone charm.

She looked around the shed in a panic, her eyes coming to rest on a skew-whiff shelf behind the door and the bundle of wooden stakes upon it.

The kind of stakes you pushed into the ground to support trees and shrubs. The kind of stakes which proved lethal when their pointed end was driven into someone's chest. Andy Cochran's, to be precise.

She stared at the reel of green, plastic-coated wire. Was it the type that had been used to strangle Victor Canning in his car? She would bet money it was.

"Gerald, whose shed is this?" she called back to him, her voice shaking.

"Eh? Oh, it's that chap who had a bit of trouble a while back. Oscar. You know, Honest Oscar, the investment chap. Have you cut me that wire yet?"

Des appeared in the doorway. "Have you found the cutters? We need to tie those canes up." He frowned and walked towards her. "You feeling alright, love? You look a bit pale. You seen a spider?"

Megan looked at her uncle's kindly face and shook her head.

"I think we need to call the police."

ooooooo

"And this breaking news just in. Following the discovery of evidence pertaining to the investigation into the deaths of Andy Cochran, Victor Canning and Tony Weller, a man was arrested today on suspicion of murder.

"The evidence was found this afternoon at a rural location and the suspect, a 53 year-old local man, was arrested at his home

shortly afterwards and taken to Bliss Bay police station where he is currently being questioned by detectives.

"The scene of the discovery, along with the home of the suspect, are being searched for further evidence. Detective Inspector Sam Cambridge said earlier, "This is a significant development in the investigation, and one which we are hoping will help to solve these cases and give much-needed closure to the victims' families."

Megan switched off the TV and curled up on the couch. Beside her, Tabastion sprawled across the cushions, a constant, thunderous purr vibrating from his throat.

DI Cambridge had asked her, Des and Gerald not to mention the missing items to anyone. The police would do that when they were ready, he'd said, and they didn't want the information getting out before then.

Of course, Des had blurted it out to Sylvie as soon as they'd walked through the front door with their baskets full of fruit and veg – there was nothing he didn't share with her – but, otherwise, they were keeping quiet.

Even though the police had told Megan they didn't think the break-in at Kismet Cottage was connected to the murders, she was relieved to know that a suspect was in custody, even though Oscar Cooper was the last person she'd have believed was capable of murder.

I guess what happened to him must have affected him much more deeply than anyone realised.

She went into the kitchen to check on the tray of fresh vegetables roasting in the oven. It seemed strange that her life was carrying on as normal when Oscar Cooper's was about to change so horribly.

As she poured herself a coffee, she went over the events of the past few hours.

A murderer had been arrested after taking the lives of three innocent people.

All was well in Bliss Bay once more.

She breathed a sigh of relief and sat back to enjoy her coffee.

CHAPTER SEVENTEEN

The Cobbles Café was always extra-busy on a Tuesday. Market day always brought a deluge of visitors to the village.

This particular morning, however, the hubbub of chatter was even more lively than usual.

"Can you believe it? Who'd have thought it of Oscar?"

"Eleanor must have known, don't you think?"

"Well, I hope they lock him up and throw away the key."

"It's about time things got back to normal around here."

Although the name of the suspect hadn't been divulged in the news report, Oscar's arrest from home the previous evening had been witnessed by a number of villagers, none of whom had wasted any time in spreading the word.

In the flower shop, Petal worked swiftly on a table centrepiece of summer flowers. "I don't know about you," she said to Megan, "but I slept like a baby last night. That's something I haven't done for a while. And Blossom stayed out till ten o'clock – no arguments, no worries. Happy daughter, happy mum. Do you know, she even said to me this morning—"

The jangle of the bell above the café door interrupted her, and Olivia rushed in.

"Hello, Livvy," Petal called out. "What are you doing out of the shop at this time of day? You're not bunking off work, are you, you rebel? " She raised an eyebrow. "And what's with the big hair? Is there an '80s revival going on somewhere I don't know about?"

A flustered Olivia smoothed a palm over her tangled fringe. "Can I have a pot of tea for two when you get a minute, please, Amisha?" She peered out of the window before scurrying over to the flower shop. "Eleanor came into the shop earlier in a terrible state," she whispered. "She was wailing so much she was scaring the customers away, so Rob told me to take a break. I got in the car with her and she drove for miles into the countryside, and back, with the roof down, like a thing possessed.

"As if Oscar having a breakdown and losing his job wasn't bad enough, now they've got all this to deal with." She glanced out of the window again. "She's just tidying up her make-up in the car. Her mascara was a bit streaked by the time we got here. Uh-oh, act natural, here she comes." Olivia scuttled back to the café and sat down at a recently vacated table.

Eleanor walked in, looked around the café, and pulled out a chair next to Olivia. "It's gone very quiet all of a sudden," she said, with her head high and her chin stuck out in defiance, belying the slight wobble in her voice. "And if you're waiting for me to get upset, you're going to be disappointed. I'm sure you all have your opinions, and you're entitled to them, but as most of you know Oscar, I hope you also know there's no way he could have been responsible for any of those murders."

"Well, you *would* say that, wouldn't you?" said Sandra Grayling, the overbearing Treasurer of the Woman's Association, before stuffing a sultana scone into her mouth. "The police must have had their reasons or they wouldn't have arrested him, would they?"

"I think that's a bit unfair, Sandra," said Olivia, jumping to Eleanor's defence. "People are often arrested and then released because the police realise they've got the wrong person."

Sandra scowled, her bushy eyebrows drawing together. "Pah! If you ask me, there's no smoke without fire." She fixed Eleanor with a glare and wagged an accusing finger. "It's karma, that's what it is. For what your husband did to all those poor people who lost their life savings. He's getting a taste of his own medicine now, that's what's happening. What goes around, comes around – and about time, too."

"That's *enough*, Sandra," said Olivia, giving Eleanor's hand a squeeze. "Can't you see how upset she is?"

Eleanor's lip quivered and she gave Olivia a grateful smile.

"What actually happened?" asked Petal, joining them at the table.

"The police just turned up on the doorstep yesterday evening and arrested him," said Eleanor, wringing her hands. "They said some significant evidence had come to light which made him a primary suspect in the murders. They took a load of stuff from the house: our computer, a whole filing cabinet of household paperwork, and both our phones. Don't ask me what they're hoping to find, but if it's something that'll incriminate Oscar, they'll be looking for a long time."

"I wonder what evidence they found to make them think he was involved?" said Petal.

"I've no idea." Eleanor shrugged. "But when they came round to speak to us after Tony Weller was murdered, they were very interested to hear that Oscar goes out walking most days while most of the villagers are still tucked up in bed. If he can, he prefers to walk early in the morning and late at night, because they're the quietest times of day. At any other times, there are too many people around and he can't bear the noise. He was out walking the morning Tony was murdered and the police kept on and on at him about the route he takes, and whether anyone could vouch for where he'd been. Even back then, they were talking to him as though they were trying to catch him out.

"And when one of the detectives asked him if he'd heard anything suspicious that morning, Oscar said he never heard a thing because he always wears those noise-reducing headphones when he goes out. And do you know what the detective had the cheek to say? He said, 'Well, that's very convenient, isn't it?' Honestly, I could have swung for him, the smug git." Eleanor chewed on a nail, her head bowed, and looked up through damp eyelashes.

"Well, for what it's worth, I don't believe Oscar had anything to do with the murders," said Olivia, giving Eleanor a reassuring pat on the shoulder. "And if you need someone to pop round every now and then to keep you company until he comes out – which I'm sure he will – you know where to find me."

"Thanks, Livvy," said Eleanor, with a sniff. "You're a real pal."

"I remember you saying what a comfort the neighbours were when Oscar had his breakdown," said Petal. "Did any of them come over to see you last night after he was arrested?"

Eleanor stared at her hands clasped in her lap. "A few. Maureen and Henry from across the road dropped in and our cleaner, Belinda, was there this morning, buoying me up. And Diana came over yesterday with Timothy and Bailey."

"Well that's good. You've always been friendly with the Starrs, haven't you?"

Eleanor pulled a face. "We used to be, but not so much any more. We talk when we see each other but I just tolerate them these days. Quite frankly, apart from Bailey, I could throttle them. Diana, mainly."

"Oh. You used to be so close. What happened?" asked Petal, and half the customers in the café leaned forward, their ears pricked up. "Did they do something to upset you?"

"Huh, it's what they *didn't* do that's the problem," said Eleanor, pushing her hair from her weary face. "Whenever Tony used to play his music until all hours of the morning, keeping us awake for most of the night and Oscar shaking in his bed, Tim and Diana always left it to me to do all the complaining. Even though it bothered them just as much, they didn't want the hassle of dealing with the police so *I* was the one who always made a fuss.

"It was so selfish of them to leave everything to me – I had enough on my plate already, what with Oscar not being himself. I shall never forgive them for that. I wouldn't be at all surprised if that's why the police are picking on him now – I'm sure they must think we're troublemakers." Eleanor blew her nose on a serviette. "I expect you need to get back to the shop, Olivia?"

Olivia nodded. "I should really. I don't want to leave Rob holding the fort for too much longer on such a busy day."

Eleanor pushed back her chair. "Sorry to offload on everyone. I'm trying to stay positive but I haven't quite got the hang of it yet. And those reporters who keep calling aren't helping." She turned as she got to the door. "If any of you feel you'd like to help, I'd be grateful if you'd tell the police – should they ask – that Oscar would never hurt a fly."

As Eleanor went on her way, and the village gossip grapevine went into overdrive, Megan watched her drive off. She hadn't said a word all the time Eleanor had been talking.

Like Olivia, she was finding it hard to believe that Oscar Cooper was responsible for the murders, despite her findings of the previous day.

He'd always been such a gentle man. A kind man who'd do anything to help anyone out if he could. She'd got to know him years ago when she'd worked in Eleanor's hairdressing salon on Saturdays. He would bring in ice-creams or cakes for all the girls in the afternoons, and keep the customers entertained with his jokes and banter. She just couldn't believe he was a killer.

And she couldn't help but feel guilty that it was because of her he'd been arrested.

She finished her coffee and said goodbye to Petal.

It was time to pay Des a visit.

ooooooo

"Megan, how much more proof do you want?" said Des, removing a tray of cranberry muffins from the oven. "All the missing belongings from the murder victims were in Oscar's potting shed, *and* it looks like that's where two of the murder weapons came from."

"I know, I know." Megan sneaked a muffin from the tray and nibbled at a warm cranberry. "I know all the evidence points to him but it just doesn't feel right. I can't explain it."

"We're all having a hard time accepting that Oscar Cooper's a serial killer, love, not just you," said Des. "The saddest thing about all this is that he must have been struggling to come to terms with what happened much more than anyone knew. The stress must have turned him a bit loopy. Terrible, really"

Sylvie appeared with a hammer in one hand and a chisel in the other, her eyes covered by a pair of work goggles. "Uh-oh, you two are looking awfully serious."

"Hello, Aunty Sylv." Megan gave her aunt a hug. "We were just talking about Oscar Cooper."

"Well, in that case, I'll leave you to it," said Sylvie. "I'm going to crack on with my wood carving, and I've got Dora Pickles coming round in half an hour with her cross-stitch, so we'll be keeping ourselves entertained. Help yourself to coffee, won't you?" she said, as she disappeared into the garden.

"Let's get a cuppa and go and sit in the front room while we wait for these to cool down, shall we?" said Des. He eyed the half-eaten muffin in Megan's hand and shook his head. "You know you'll get gut ache if you eat warm cake?"

Megan ignored him and kicked off her shoes before flopping into an armchair. "I know it *seems* obvious that Oscar's the murderer but that's exactly why I think he might not be. It's all very convenient, don't you think? The wooden stakes and the garden wire being right there in plain sight, for anyone to see? I mean, why would Oscar keep them so visible if he'd used them to kill people with?"

"But why *wouldn't* he keep them in plain sight?" said Des. "He probably used them all the time on the allotment. He just never expected anyone to see them and link him to the murders. After what he's been through, who would have suspected him enough to even *look* in his potting shed? The poor man was incapable of stepping outside his front door for weeks after his troubles, so I doubt anyone had him down as a crazed murderer."

"Hmm, I suppose so." Megan sipped her coffee. "It's just that, after hearing what Eleanor said, I'm not convinced the police have got the right guy in custody."

"Well, if it isn't Oscar, someone's done a pretty good job of making it look like it is. But who?" Des fetched his notebook. "The obvious place to start has to be someone who had a grudge against him, and I'm not sure I've got enough pages in this book to list all those names."

"One of his ex-clients, you mean?" Megan shook her head. "You really think one of them could have set him up for the murder of three people, just to get their own back because the investment he recommended went bad? That's taking a grudge a little too far, don't you think?"

"Not when you consider that some of them lost every penny of their savings," said Des, fixing Megan with a stern expression.

"Oh, Yes, I suppose that'd be enough to drive some people to murder." Megan uncurled herself from the armchair and stretched her legs. "It just seems like pretty drastic measures to settle a grudge."

"Well, you know what they say," said Des. "The motive for all murders is either love, lust, lucre, or loathing."

Megan tapped a fingernail against her teeth. "Actually, I've just remembered something. While I was at Adrian and Natalie's recently, I overheard Adrian's dad talking about Oscar, and he wasn't being very complimentary. He'd just bought a second-hand car and he said it would have been a new one if he hadn't lost so much money because of Oscar's bad investment advice. He wasn't happy about it at all."

"No, he wasn't very happy when it happened, either," said Des. "He spent every day for weeks propping up the bar in The Duck, telling anyone who'd listen how he and his wife had escaped bankruptcy by the skin of his teeth because they'd been shrewd enough to only invest *half* their savings. He was so bitter about it, he almost turned my apple juice sour."

"He still is bitter, by the sound of it," said Megan. "I wonder if the police have interviewed him. D'you think I should tell them what I heard?"

Des heaved a great sigh. "He's not the only one of Oscar's clients who felt that way — they *all* did. You can't go accusing him of something on a whim, Megan."

"I'm not accusing him. I just think the police need to investigate every avenue, that's all. I mean, if Mark Castle's angry enough to settle a grudge with murder, he's hardly likely to march round to the police station and volunteer the information, is he?"

"I suppose not." Des scratched his head, leaving a lock of hair sticking upright. "Well, while we're on the subject of the Castle family, what about Adrian as a suspect?"

Megan nodded. "Yes, I wondered about him initially but Natalie said they'd both given the police a DNA sample, remember? That being the case, it can't be him. Anyway, Tony was Adrian's best friend so I doubt he'd have murdered him."

Des nodded. "Oh yes. I forgot about the DNA sample. Although Adrian obviously has a temper, or Sylv wouldn't have seen him throttling the living daylights out of Bailey Starr yesterday. There's definitely something funny going on there, and I'd love to know what."

Megan drained her coffee cup, a pensive expression on her face.

"Oh dear, I know that look," said Des. "What are you planning?"

"I'm going to talk to that detective. Eleanor said it might help Oscar if someone told the police that it's not in his nature to hurt anyone. And I don't believe it is—I think he's innocent." Megan pulled on her shoes and grabbed her bag. "You coming, or staying here to babysit those muffins?"

CHAPTER EIGHTEEN

Bliss Bay police station had never seen so much action.

Due to the usual lack of crime in the village, the tiny station was often closed, its two small holding cells typically used for stationery storage rather than the incarceration of criminals.

In the improbable event of the police being required to attend a misdemeanour, a constable was most likely to be found in the living room of a hospitable member of the community, after being persuaded to join them for a cup of tea and a slice of cake.

Today, though, Megan and Des pushed open the door to see a team of detectives from the central police headquarters, squashed around desks squeezed into the small reception area. They all talked at once with a sense of urgency, to which the folk of Bliss Bay were unaccustomed.

"Excuse me," said Megan, as she approached the front desk, looking around a tower of paperwork that was so tall, it almost hid the police officer behind it.

"Can I help you?" said PC Denby's voice from behind the tower.

"I'd like to speak to DI Cambridge regarding the murder investigations, if he's here, please."

Fred blew out a sigh. "Doesn't everyone? I'll go and see if he's available." He pushed himself up from his chair and peered across the desk. "Well, if it isn't Des Harper," he said, taking Des's hand and shaking it enthusiastically. "Long time, no see. Sing-songs in The Duck aren't the same without you and your harmonica, you know."

"Yes, well, I don't get in there too often these days. Too much else to do since I've given up the booze," said Des distractedly, champing at the bit for an audience with the Detective Inspector.

Unfortunately, Fred Denby had other ideas. "Hang on, and we'll have a catch-up. Anything to get a break from this paperwork," he whispered before glancing Megan's way. "Who shall I tell the DI is calling?" He looked at her through a scrunched-up eye. "Here, you're the lady with the cat, aren't you? Miss Fallon, isn't it?"

Megan smiled. "That's me. You've got a good memory."

PC Denby winked and tweaked the end of his bulbous nose. "S'what they pay me for. Give me a second and I'll pop upstairs and tell the DI you're here. Be back in a bit."

"I'd rather come with you than stay here and 'have a catch-up' with Denby," grumbled Des, jabbing his pencil behind his ear and looking miffed. "I didn't come here to reminisce about old times, I came to see DI Cambridge." He slapped his notebook against the palm of his hand. "Why should *you* get all the fun? You didn't even want to get involved."

"Oh, don't be so grumpy," said Megan. "I won't be long. I'm only going to tell him I don't think Oscar's the person they're looking for. If he'll even talk to me, that is. He'll probably tell someone else to take the details. Anyway, I didn't know you knew PC Denby? It'll be nice for you to have a chinwag."

Fred reappeared, red in the face from having to walk up the staircase and back down again, all in the space of two minutes.

"DI Cambridge will see you now, Miss," he puffed. "Top of the stairs, door on the right. Opposite the window with the long green curtains." He turned to Des as he took his seat behind the desk. "Now then, how's Sylvie? Do you remember when..."

Megan chuckled at Des's ill-concealed look of disgust as he shoved his notebook back into his shirt pocket. "I won't be long."

At the top of the stairs, Sam Cambridge was hanging out of the door. "We meet again." He ushered her into the tiny office and pointed to a plastic chair before settling himself at a makeshift desk squeezed into a space between a water cooler and a giant Aspidistra. "Sorry, we're a bit short on luxuries. So, what can I do for you?"

Megan shuffled to get comfortable. "Well, it's about Oscar Cooper. I'm not sure he's the murderer." As soon as she'd said the words, she realised how stupid they must sound, considering what she'd discovered in Oscar's potting shed the previous day.

Sam looked puzzled. "And why's that? You didn't say you thought he was innocent when you called us yesterday."

"I know, but I've had time to think since then. I knew him when I was younger and he was always so kind. He used to buy ice-creams for all the girls when I worked at Eleanor's hairdressing salon." Megan gave an exasperated sigh when one of Sam's eyebrows arched in amusement. "Look, I know this probably sounds ridiculous to you but I honestly don't think Oscar murdered those people. You don't know him. I mean, *I* don't know him that well any more but I think *someone* would know if he was a killer. Or that he had homicidal tendencies, at the very least.

"And before you say anything, I know people's personalities can change after they've been through a trauma like Oscar has, but I really think you've locked up the wrong person. He's just not the murderous type." She concluded her statement by defiantly crossing her arms.

Sam leaned forward, his hands clasped on the desk. "Well, as I'm sure you'll appreciate, we can't release him just because he bought you an ice-cream every now and then. I'm interested to know, though, if you have any ideas as to whom the guilty party is. If you're so sure it's not Oscar Cooper, then who?"

Megan shrugged. "I don't know." Now she was sitting in front of Sam, she couldn't bring herself to mention Mark Castle and his grievance against Oscar. Des was right – there was no proof he had anything to do with it. "You must know what happened, though," she said. "I've been told that a lot of people were very upset with Oscar when their investments went south."

"Yes, I'm aware of Mr Cooper's unfortunate experience – we've spent the morning taking statements from a number of his disgruntled clients. Excuse me a moment." Sam picked up his ringing phone. "This is DI Cambridge. Yes. Okay, give me five minutes."

He stood up, giving Megan her cue to leave. "Look, we're not in the business of keeping innocent people locked up. If Oscar Cooper didn't commit those crimes we'll find out but, for the moment, there's no one else in the frame. Now, if you'll excuse me, I need to make a call. Feel free to get in touch if you think of anything else that might help us out, won't you? We're relying on members of the community to—" He cocked his head. "What's that noise?"

"What noise?" said Megan.

"That whining."

Megan shook her head. "I can't hear anything."

Sam wiggled a finger about in his ear. "Anyway, as I was saying, we're relying on members of the community to help us out wherever they can. They're the ones who always have their ears to the ground, so they can help the police tremendously. I always think—" A high-pitched whistling interrupted him. "What the...? Surely you must be able to hear that?"

Megan recognised the noise instantly. "Oh. *That* noise. Yes. Erm, I think it might be—"

Sam flung open the door to the office to find an empty corridor. He was about to shout down the stairs when a pair of blue deck shoes poking out from the bottom of the curtain opposite caught his eye. Pulling it to one side he came face to face with Des, who was fiddling with his hearing aid and completely unfazed to be discovered, as though lurking behind other people's curtains was a perfectly normal pastime.

"—my uncle," said Megan, finishing her sentence.

Des beamed at Sam and stuck out his hand to the bemused detective. "Hello there. Harper's the name, Des Harper. Saw you on the news the other day. Nice to finally meet you in person." He jerked a thumb over his shoulder. "I was just, er, just admiring the view."

They all looked out of the window to see a brick wall and a dead pigeon on the fire escape.

"I thought you were waiting downstairs," said Megan, giggling when Des gave her a bashful smile at being caught out telling fibs to the police.

"Yes, well, Fred got into something with one of the detectives so rather than stand around twiddling my thumbs, I thought I'd come and find you. Have you finished? Or can I help?" he said, hopefully, his fingers twitching to open the notebook that was sticking out of his shirt pocket.

"No, we're all done." Megan grabbed him by his sleeve and escorted him down the staircase. "Thanks for your time, DI Cambridge," she called over her shoulder. "I'll be in touch if I think of anything else.

oooooooo

"Well, that was a waste of time, wasn't it?" said Des, after Megan relayed the details of her conversation. "I thought the whole point of going to see him was so you could tell him about your suspicions. I knew I should have come up with you."

Megan waited for Vinnie to stop spluttering before easing him out of the parking space. "Well, I *was* going to tell him but once I was there, it didn't seem right. I kept thinking of what you said about not being so hasty to implicate someone without any proof, so I didn't want to mention Mark Castle by name. Mind you, DI Cambridge said they'd already taken statements from a number of Oscar's 'disgruntled clients' so they've probably already spoken to him. I did tell him I didn't think Oscar was guilty, though, which he thought was a bit strange, under the circumstances."

As she headed back through the village to drop Des home, they passed a group of villagers with placards, making their way along the main street to the sound of passing drivers tooting their car horns in solidarity.

"They'll be going up to the old school," said Des, reaching over and pressing the horn to show his support. "There's a group of protestors up there every day, y'know. Sylv and I take them up cakes and flasks of tea when we can."

"Well, I hope all those protests come to something," said Megan. "I'd hate to come back to Bliss Bay one day and see a big ugly hypermarket where that lovely school used to be."

A young man appeared from nowhere and ran across the road in front of her. She slammed on the brakes and wound down the window. "Are you *trying* to get yourself killed, you *idiot*?" she yelled, as the man disappeared into the alley between Peel's Ironmongers and Hiccups Wine Bar. She left out a sigh of relief. "Honestly, if I hadn't been on the ball, I'd have run him over."

"Wasn't that Bailey Starr?" said Des. "I'm sure that's the family car." He pointed to the dark-blue estate parked haphazardly beside the kerb.

Megan stared at the young man, who was crouching down in the alley across the road, strands of white-blond hair poking out from underneath a knitted beanie hat. She pulled in and parked in front of his car, and opened her door.

"Where are you going?"

"Don't you remember what Aunty Sylv said about Adrian having Bailey pinned up against the wall in the alley?"

"Of course I do. I wrote it in my notebook," said Des, tapping his shirt pocket. "It looks like he's looking for something." The penny suddenly dropped and his face lit up. "Probably whatever Adrian threw down the alley!"

"Exactly," said Megan. "Come on, hurry up."

"What are you going to say to him?" hissed Des, as they crossed the road.

Megan shrugged. "Don't know until I get there."

She peered into the alley to see Bailey crouching down, his eyes scanning the floor.

"Bailey? Is that you?" she said. "It's me, Megan Fallon. Fancy seeing you here."

He looked up and she saw the beginnings of a black eye and a cut to his cheekbone.

"Ouch! What happened? You look like you've been in the wars."

A scowl clouded his face as he instinctively put up a hand to hide the wounds. "It's nothing. I walked into a shelf at home."

"Oh. Well, it looks painful." Despite Bailey obviously not being in the mood for conversation, Megan pressed on. "Have you lost something?" she asked, cheerily. "We can help you look for it, can't we, Uncle Des?"

"It's alright, I can manage," snapped Bailey, his vibrant white-blond eyebrows dipping with his scowl.

Ignoring him, Des strolled up the alley, hands behind his back and humming tunelessly.

"I *said*, I can manage," Bailey snarled. "Why don't you get lost?"

Des fixed him with a glare. "I'd thank you not to use that tone with me, young man. This is a public right of way and I have as much right to be here as you. By the way." He stretched his arm up to a window ledge. "Is this what you're after?" He reached up to a gold chain that was hanging off the ledge and let it swing on his finger. "You should have been looking up, not down."

Bailey snatched the chain and put it on, pushing it inside his shirt, before shoving his way past Megan and speeding off in his car.

"What was that you gave him?"

"A gold chain with half a heart hanging from it. It looked like it was engraved with the letters 'LEY', but he snatched it out of my hand so quickly, I couldn't be sure."

"'Half a heart with 'LEY' engraved on it?" Megan scratched at the frown at her brow.

"Yes. One of those heart-shaped pendants that come in two halves that fit together. You know what I mean?"

"Yes, but it's not usually the type of thing you'd have your *own* name engraved on, is it? It's the type of pendant you'd share with a partner; they'd wear the half with your name on it and you'd wear the half with theirs. If the half you saw had 'LEY' engraved on it, though, then I guess someone else is wearing the other half that's engraved with 'BAI'. That's just weird."

"Well, whoever's wearing what, that must have been what Sylvie saw Adrian throw down the alley," said Des, making a note of everything in his book.

"But why would he have done that, I wonder?"

Des raised a shoulder. "Because he was angry, I suppose. He probably saw the chain around Bailey's neck and grabbed it in the heat of the moment."

"I'd love to know what they were arguing about," said Megan. "I know it might not have been anything to do with the murders, but I'd still like to know, just because I'm nosy."

"You know what?" said Des, as they got back into the car. "I've seen a different side to Bailey Starr. I always thought he was such an easy-going lad but he was different today."

"Yeah, he was rude."

"Yes, he was, but there was something else, too," said Des. "He seemed desperate – scared, even. You didn't see his eyes. If you ask me, he's a very troubled young man."

oooooooo

Having dropped Des home, Megan was about to drive off when she saw Jack coming out of his uncle and aunt's house with a suitcase in his hand. She wound down her window. "You going somewhere?"

"I was gonna call you later," he said, hauling the case into the boot of his car and crossing the road to speak to her. "There are a few things I need to do so I'm going away for a while. I'm leaving in an hour or so."

"Oh." Megan felt a pang of disappointment. "I thought you were going to be here for a bit longer. Are you coming back?"

Jack crouched down beside the car. "Maybe, maybe not, but if I don't, I'll keep in touch. It's been great to catch up with you. You take care, okay?" He gave her a brief smile before going back to packing his luggage into his car.

Megan nodded. All of a sudden, she didn't trust herself to speak for fear she'd start to blub.

CHAPTER NINETEEN

"Gone? Gone where?" Petal looked up from the bundle of eucalyptus stems she was trimming.

Megan shrugged and licked the toffee butter icing from a coffee cupcake. "No idea. I thought Lionel might have mentioned it."

"He hasn't said a word." Petal called across the flower shop to the café. "Lionel, did you know Jack's left?"

"Oh, didn't I tell you? Yeah, he said he had some things to do."

"What things?" said Petal. "Where's he gone? Is he coming back?"

Lionel sent his wife an eye-roll as he delivered two currant teacakes and a cheese and ham scone to a table. "I dunno. I didn't ask him. Men are simple souls, you know – we prefer not to interrogate our friends. We're happy just to know the basics."

"Yes, but the basics don't tell us anything, do they?" said Petal, returning her husband's eye-roll with one of her own. She turned back to Megan. "Well, it was nice having him around while it lasted." She covered a huge yawn with the back of her hand. "'Scuse me. After all these years, you'd think I'd be used to getting up early to go to the flower market, wouldn't you? Speaking of which, I saw Eleanor on the way back. She couldn't sleep so she'd been out for a walk."

"How is she?" asked Megan.

"Not great. In fact, if you've got any time to spare, she'd probably be grateful of the company."

Megan licked her fingers. "Okay. I don't have anything planned for today, so I'll pop round to see her. And I'll take her one of these cupcakes – it might cheer her up a little."

ooooooo

"It's so sweet of you to call round." Eleanor grabbed Megan's hands and practically dragged her over the doorstep. "I'm afraid I'm not coping very well on my own. It's all getting a little too much for me."

"Well, it's bound to." Megan handed over the cupcake and patted Eleanor's tense shoulder. "Have you heard anything from the police about what's happening?"

"Nothing. I know I should stay positive, but every hour that goes by without Oscar being released, the more I wonder if he ever will be."

"You mustn't think like that." Megan opened her arms to pull her old Saturday-job boss into a hug.

"No! Don't be nice to me, or I'm likely to burst into tears," said Eleanor, before promptly bursting into tears. "Oh dear. I'm sorry. I just don't know if I'm coming or going at the moment. And all the goodwill people started off with seems to be wearing thin.

Maureen and Henry from across the road were so sweet when Oscar was arrested, but they were in their front garden when I came back from the shops this morning, and they practically trampled each other to death trying to get back into their house so they wouldn't have to speak to me."

"They probably feel awkward," said Megan. "And they don't want to say the wrong thing so they're avoiding talking about it. I'm sure they're not avoiding *you,* though."

"I'm not so sure. You know how people gossip. You heard what Sandra Grayling said in the café – 'there's no smoke without fire'. And I bet she's not the only one who thinks Oscar's guilty." Eleanor pinched her nose between her brows and squeezed her eyes shut. "And I know this is a terrible thing to say, but what if Oscar really *did* kill those people? I just can't get the thought out of my head." Her chest heaved with sobs and tears dropped off the end of her nose. "I mean, what an awful thing to think. I'm his wife, for goodness' sake. If I can't be supportive, who can?"

Megan guided her into the kitchen and sat her down. "Look, you're tired, and worried, and you're having all these crazy thoughts because you don't know what's happening. And I expect the reason the police can't tell you anything is because there's nothing to tell. Which is a good thing, isn't it?" She spied a coffee machine on the counter. "Shall I make us a brew and we can have a chat?"

She busied herself, opening cupboards until she'd found the coffee and the coffee filters, and took two mugs from hooks on the wall.

Eleanor sniffed and blew her nose. "Thank you for the cake. I've barely eaten a thing since Oscar was arrested but this smells so delicious, I think I might be tempted to have it with my coffee."

"I see there are still some reporters out there," said Megan as she settled herself at the table. "Have they stopped bothering you yet?"

"Not really, although I gave them a mouthful yesterday and told them to make themselves scarce, in not so many words. They're just relentless. It was bad enough when Tony Weller was murdered but this is so much worse."

Eleanor broke a piece off the cupcake and ate it in small bites. "Honestly, it's been horrible, and the police haven't helped. I think I said in the café that they've taken most of Oscar's things, and some of mine, didn't I? Well, having had some time to think about it, I can understand why they've taken the laptop and the phones but I don't understand why they've taken Oscar's hibiscus plants."

"His hibiscus plants?"

Eleanor nodded. "He breeds them. You know, to make new varieties. Actually, I shouldn't say 'breeds'. Oscar says the correct term is cross-pollinates. He started doing it a few years ago. And thank God he did, because I'm sure it helped him after all his troubles started – it gave him something to focus on. He'd go to the allotment early in the morning to pick the flowers, then bring them back here to dry them. He'd disappear upstairs to the attic room, and just get on with it. He'd spend hours up there collecting pollen, and whatever else he used to do. He's got a proper little production line set up on a table under the window. Or should I say, he *had* a production line. The police have taken everything away now."

"Aah, I see." Megan nodded as she realised the figure she'd seen at the window from the garden of Castle Manor must have been Oscar tending to his plants. "I wonder why they took them?"

"Don't ask me – I'm just his wife. Why would they tell *me* anything." Eleanor scowled as she popped the last piece of cupcake into her mouth and dusted the crumbs from her fingers. "I just pray that some evidence will come to light that will prove Oscar didn't kill any of those poor people. I keep telling the police that someone's set him up, but they won't believe me."

Megan nodded. "Eleanor, do you remember you started telling me about Caroline Gibbs the other day? You said you'd told the police you thought she had something to do with Tony's murder? Why do you think that?"

"Why? Because it's the common opinion of people in the village that Caroline wanted Tony out of the way so she could get closer to Adrian. Everyone knows that baby is his – she was having a fling with him for over a year. She probably still would be if she could get anywhere near him, but I hear he's so distraught, he's not in a particularly sociable mood at the moment.

"Think about it, Megan. Why else would she have spent so much time there after she finished work? She wasn't staying late to spend time with Natalie, that's for sure. Natalie was only too quick to tell everyone that Caroline was an employee, not a friend."

"Do you think Natalie knows about Adrian and Caroline?"

Eleanor shrugged. "I would think so, but she's taking it very well if she does. I don't think Adrian ever intended for her to find out, but I'm equally sure he didn't intend for Caroline to get pregnant, either. When she did, I think he probably asked her to leave, for Natalie's sake." Her nostrils flared. "Caroline's so shameless, I'm sure it wouldn't have been *her* decision to leave. In fact, she probably dreamed of having the baby right there, at Castle Manor, with Adrian by her side."

Megan recalled Jack telling her similar stories he'd heard from Lionel and Rob, but he'd said he thought the rumours were founded on village gossip with just a smidgeon of truth to them.

"That's my opinion, anyway," Eleanor continued, "and if you ask me, I think it's only a matter of time before Natalie goes the same way as Tony." She tapped the side of her nose. "*If* a certain person has her way."

Megan nodded, thoughtfully. "So, do you think Caroline was responsible for the other murders too?"

Eleanor shook her head. "She's been so preoccupied with scheming to get her grubby little mitts on Adrian, I doubt it. I mean, as much as I'm convinced she was involved in Tony's death, I don't think she killed those other people.

"I'll tell you something, though, Adrian's just as bad as she is for going with her in the first place. Honestly, I don't know why some people bother getting married." She finished her coffee and gave Megan a hopeful smile.

"I'm feeling so much better after our chat," she said, lifting her cup. "You'll stay for another, won't you?"

ooooooo

At Bliss Bay police station, Sam Cambridge mulled over the details in the files on his desk. He leaned back in his chair and cracked his knuckles one by one.

There was incriminating evidence pointing at Oscar from every angle, but there was no conclusive proof that he was responsible for any of the murders.

Although he was still the prime suspect, and the pollen found on the faces of the victims was an exact match to the hibiscus samples seized from Oscar's attic room, not a single trace of his own DNA had been found at any of the crime scenes.

Of course, it was possible that, with care, Oscar could have prevented the transfer of his DNA but even if that *had* been the case, it still left Sam with a major headache.

Who did the unidentified DNA – which had been found at every crime scene – belong to?

He took off his glasses and massaged his temples, the pads of his fingers running down to his neck to prod at a mass of knotted muscles.

Apart from Megan Fallon, no one had come forward with any evidence of any substance, and no one who'd been questioned had given the police the slightest reason to believe they might have been involved in the murders. All their leads had come to a big, fat, dead end.

He heaved a great sigh. Right now, there was no other option. Unless some irrefutable proof against Oscar presented itself, there simply wasn't enough evidence to charge him with anything, and the length of time he could be held without charge was running out.

It infuriated him, but it looked very much like Sam was going to have to release Oscar pending further investigation.

ooooooo

"Oscar's been released?" Megan's mouth fell open as she looked up from the salad vegetables she was washing.

"Yep, but he's got to stay in Bliss Bay. In spite of everything you found in his potting shed, there wasn't enough evidence to charge him." Des put his notebook back in his pocket and looked very pleased with himself. "He's still the main suspect in the investigations but he was released last night."

"Well, Eleanor's going to be over the moon," said Megan. "How did you find out?"

"I saw Fred Denby yesterday evening. After our chat at the police station, I thought I'd pop into The Duck with Sylvie – just for old-time's sake, of course. Bill and I were playing all the old tunes on our harmonicas and Fred was singing at the top of his voice." Des chuckled. "We ended up staying until closing time and, um, I was a bit naughty, I'm afraid."

"Oh no!" said Megan, clutching Des's arm, her eyes wide with alarm. "Please don't tell me you had a drink?"

He rolled his eyes. "Of course not. Well, not apart from apple juice, anyway. No, I mean I was a bit naughty because after a couple of pints, Fred's tongue started to loosen and he told me a few things he shouldn't have. I should have stopped him but I didn't. I felt a bit guilty afterwards but I found out some interesting things. Some quite puzzling things, actually."

"Oh?" Megan gave her uncle her full attention. "What did he say?"

"Well, apart from spilling the beans about Oscar being released, he told me that all the murder victims had traces of pollen on their face. The police have had a heck of a job trying to find out where it came from. They've been testing samples from all over Bliss Bay ever since Andy was killed back in May, but they recently got a match."

"Pollen?" Megan frowned. "Eleanor told me yesterday that Oscar breeds hibiscus plants. She said the police took them away but she didn't understand why."

"Well, that's the reason," said Des. "And don't tell anyone I've told you any of this, or Fred'll get into trouble. You've got to admit, as much as you don't want to believe Oscar's the guilty party, there's a lot of evidence against him. He goes out walking early in the morning, or late at night, which is when all the murders were committed; all the missing personal items were found in his shed; and the pollen came from his hibiscus plants. It seems like an open and shut case."

"So why was he released, then?" asked Megan.

"A-ha," said Des. "Now that's where it starts to get a bit foggy. Y'see, despite all the evidence against him, they haven't found one speck of his DNA at any of the crime scenes. What they have found, though, is the same DNA at all three murders, but they've no idea who it belongs to. I told you it was puzzling, didn't I?"

"So, if they can't place him at any of the murders, someone *must* have set him up," said Megan. "Eleanor's convinced of it."

Des helped himself to a handful of cherry tomatoes. "I wouldn't disagree. The question is, who?"

CHAPTER TWENTY

"Brilliant. Just brilliant," Megan grumbled as, halfway back to Kismet cottage on an afternoon walk, the storm clouds emptied. Her loose shirt, which had been comfortably cool in the sun, suddenly became semi-transparent and horribly embarrassing as it clung to her like a second skin.

She was cursing under her breath when a dark-blue estate car slowed down and pulled to a stop beside her. "I thought it was you," Diana Starr called through the window. "Can I give you a lift home?"

Megan was belted into her seat before Diana finished telling her to 'hop in'. "It was a blue sky when I left home this morning so I didn't think I'd need an umbrella – I should have known better after all the storms we've had recently. Thank you."

"Well, I could hardly have driven by and left you, could I?" said Diana, flicking a switch on the dashboard which sent warm air wafting over Megan's wet feet. "I think Timmy put a box of tissues in the glove compartment last time we used the car. If Bailey hasn't used them all, they'll help you dry off a little."

Megan pulled a handful of tissues from the box. "How are you?"

"I'm better, thank you," said Diana. "I have my moments, but I'm just trying to get on with life and remember that there are far more good things that happen in the world than bad." She smiled and waited for a gap in the traffic to pull out. "By the way, I need to stop at the village shop, but I won't be long."

"You've saved me from the rain," said Megan, dabbing at her hair. Take as long as you like."

"I only need to pick up some honey and a few lemons for Timmy. Over the past few weeks, he's been suffering terribly with his asthma, and the organic honey and lemons they sell in the shop seem to do him the world of good. He's alright at the moment but we're performing at the Women's Association fundraiser next week. He'll need to be in top form for that, so I need to have supplies on hand in case he takes another turn for the worse."

"I've noticed him struggling a little the past few times I've seen him," said Megan, rubbing her hands up and down her arms to get warm. "He seems to have been relying on his inhaler quite a bit."

Diana nodded. "Between you and me, the stress of not knowing if Bailey will get his Academy scholarship isn't helping. On the surface, Timothy's very confident that he will, but I know he's worrying about it and I know how much the stress has affected me, so it must be affecting him. A scholarship is Bailey's only chance, you see. Without one, we simply won't be able to afford the fees."

"Ah, right. Yes, I can see how that would be causing Timothy stress. Has he always had asthma? My sister used to have it but she grew out of it."

"He didn't suffer with it until he was in his mid-forties," said Diana. "His first attack took us completely by surprise – it was so scary. We were driving back from a New Year's party and all of a sudden, he was hunched over the steering wheel struggling to breathe. Thankfully, we weren't far from a hospital so the friends who were in the car with us helped me to get him out of the driving seat, and we took him straight there. He was given oxygen and a whole list of tests until the doctors finally confirmed it was asthma.

"They think a combination of stress and the cold air most likely triggered it, which made sense because I'd been suffering with a few post-natal issues for some time, and he'd been worried about me. Since then, every time he's been stressed, or been out in the cold, he's had an attack. It's strange how something you've never been affected by before can suddenly cause such a reaction."

She sighed. "Actually, I can't help but feel a little responsible for his most recent bout, because it started after he took me to the airport a while ago. I went to Paris in May for my sister's 60th and it was a late-night flight. He was wheezing like an old man for days afterwards."

"Because he'd been out in the cold?"

Diana nodded. "Of course, he has medication to relieve it but that's why he avoids the cold. Even at this time of year, the air can be such a shock to the vocal chords and that's an absolute curse if you're a singer. And when he gets anxious, his chest tightens up and he gets the most dreadful cough and starts spluttering all over the place – I call it his stress cough. You can imagine how all the worry about Bailey's scholarship is affecting him."

"Bailey doesn't suffer with anything like that, does he?"

"No, thank heavens. Although he's not been himself recently, either. He sailed through most of his teenage years without any problems at all but now he's so moody, he won't even talk to us. I have no idea what's wrong with him but I hope we're not going to have a sulky millennial hanging around the house for much longer." Diana pulled up outside the shop. "Won't be a tick – do you want anything?"

Megan shook her head as she continued squeezing the rain from her hair into a tissue, and rattled the car windows with an almighty sneeze.

"Oh, for heaven's sake," said Diana. "Just a minute." She disappeared from view as she opened the boot of the car, delving into it and reappearing with a fleece-lined jacket. "Here, you can borrow this till I see you again. It'll help you stop shivering."

"Oh no, it's okay. I'll be fine once I get out of these wet clothes," said Megan before sneezing again, three times in succession.

Diana shoved the jacket towards her. "Please take it. It's just an old jacket we keep in the car in case of emergencies, but it'll keep you warm."

"Okay, thank you." Megan slipped it over her shoulders and glanced down at the distinctive emblem on the front. "Oh, it's a Witchester City jacket."

"Yes, it used to belong to Adrian but when the club got new ones, he gave it to Bailey. He'd only worn it a few times – it was like new." Diana held a palm upwards. "Oh bother, it's starting to rain again. I'll be back in a bit."

Megan snuggled into the jacket and leaned her head against the car window. She would have loved to ask Eleanor if she knew why Bailey and Adrian might have reason to argue, but felt it would be too intrusive. Maybe if she broached the subject subtly, she'd be able to find something out. If Adrian had given his old football jacket to Bailey, there must be some connection between them, however tenuous.

"Told you I wouldn't be long," said Diana, flinging open the car door. "There was no one else in the shop. That downpour we had earlier must have kept them away." She passed a bag of fragrant lemons over to the back seat and sniffed the air. "Isn't that a gorgeous smell?"

They sat in companionable silence until they neared Kismet Cottage. "Are you feeling a bit warmer now?"

"Much, thank you. Thanks for the loan of the jacket."

"You're welcome. And there's no rush to return it. If I don't see you before, you can give it back to me at the summer fundraiser, if you'll be there."

"Yes, I'll be there." Megan took her opportunity. "Are you sure Bailey won't want it before then? Seeing as it was a gift?"

Diana shook her head. "I told you, we keep it in the boot as our emergency jacket – it's nothing special. The only reason Adrian gave it to Bailey was because he was kind enough to take him on some last-minute driving lessons before his test, and they became quite friendly. Timothy tried his best with the lessons but he and Bailey ended up having so many arguments, it wasn't worth the hassle. Anyway, Adrian gave Bailey the jacket because he was going to get rid of it, not for any other reason. Bailey really won't mind if you borrow it."

"Oh, I see." *That doesn't explain why they were at each other's throats, though,* thought Megan.

"Here we are." Diana pulled up outside Kismet Cottage. "I'll see you soon."

ooooooo

"Lionel asked if I'd like to bake a few things for the café. You know, for them to sell. They'd keep their share, and I'd get a percentage."

At The Cobbles Café, Des poured two mugs of tea from a large pot. "I thought I'd start off with a batch of lavender Madeleines and one of my banana and cranberry cakes. Dora Pickles is always telling me I should broaden my horizons. She said my baking's too good to keep to myself – and she should know, 'cos she eats enough of it." He chuckled, then looked serious. "Of course, that doesn't mean I won't have time for," he looked around furtively before dropping his voice, "*other* things, if you know what I mean."

Megan grinned. "Speaking of 'other things', I saw Diana Starr yesterday." She quickly filled Des in on her conversation. "I thought I might be able to find out what Bailey and Adrian Castle were arguing about but she didn't say anything that gave any clues. I felt quite sorry for her, though. She's obviously worried about Timothy because his asthma's quite bad at the moment, and Bailey's behaviour's been a bit odd."

"You can say that again," said Des. "It's pretty obvious something's troubling him."

They sat in the bay window of the café, looking out across the village high street, still puddled with rain from the previous day's downpour.

"It wouldn't surprise me if the stress of trying to get into the Academy is affecting him – probably more than he's letting on. If it's making Timothy ill, it must be getting to Bailey too." Megan gazed out of the window at a toddler jumping up and down in a puddle. "I can't imagine how much the fees must be if you have to pay." She put down her mug, her eyes fixed on the child.

"What's up?" said Des. "You've got a very strange look in your eyes."

"Do you remember that day you saw Bailey in the newsagent's? When you went to get the Sunday papers? And his shoes and the bottom of his jeans were wet but it hadn't been raining?"

Des nodded. "Yeah, that was a head-scratcher. What about it?"

"Well, the day of mum and dad's ceremony, I took some pictures just after sunrise and the dew on the grass soaked my slippers. They were so wet, I almost went head over heels on the kitchen tiles."

Des frowned. "So you think that's why Bailey's shoes and jeans were wet? Because he'd been out early?" He shook his head. "I was out early, too, but my shoes were perfectly dry."

"Yes, but you probably didn't walk on any grass, did you?" said Megan. "If you walk to the paper shop on the village green from your place, you can walk all the way there on the road and the path. If Bailey's shoes and jeans were wet at that time of the morning, and it hadn't been raining, he must have walked across the green, or the park. Unless he really had been washing his car or been for a paddle, both of which I doubt. Anyway, we know all the murders were committed in the early hours, don't we? And we know that Bailey was definitely out early that particular morning, so what's to say he wasn't out early on other mornings, too?"

Des wagged a finger, suddenly excited. "And do you remember what Sylvie told us about Caroline Gibbs almost being run over? Caroline said she thought it might have been a big dark-coloured car. Well, Bailey drives a big dark-blue car, doesn't he? I mean, I know lots of people drive big dark-blue cars, but it all fits, doesn't it?"

"It's not enough proof to accuse him but I think it's definitely worth digging a little deeper to find out some more," said Megan. "How, though?"

Des scratched his chin. "I could ask Fred, I suppose."

Megan shook her head. "He's already told you more than he should have, albeit accidentally. No, we'll have to see if we can find out another way."

"Should we tell that detective?" asked Des.

"Let's see if we can find out a bit more first," said Megan, remembering DI Cambridge's scepticism the last time she'd shared her thoughts with him.

"Tell you what," said Des. "How about we both give it some thought and talk again tomorrow – around midday? Sylv and I are going up to the old school to join in the protest later this afternoon, and I'll be busy baking for a few hours tomorrow morning."

"Suits me," said Megan. "Petal's coming over tonight, so I'm not free until tomorrow anyway."

"Thing is," said Des, "what reason would Bailey Starr have for killing those three people? Or for trying to kill Caroline Gibbs?"

Megan tapped her finger against the ever-present notebook in Des's shirt pocket.

"Well, that, my dear uncle, is exactly what we need to find out."

oooooooo

Petal cut a wedge of ripe Stilton and squashed it onto a tortilla chip before curling up on the couch next to Tabastion. She kicked off her sandals and wiggled her toes as she scratched the tabby behind the ears, and he flexed his paws in mid-air.

"So, anyway, because Oscar Cooper's been released, we're not letting Blossom out on her own until the police have charged someone with the murders. Lionel and I had a long chat with her and something must have sunk in because she's going along with it without any arguments. Thank goodness – I couldn't handle any more screaming matches."

"That's good," said Megan, as she loaded up a brush with pale pink varnish. "I'm sure that must make for a much more peaceful household."

"You could say that," said Petal, wiping cheese from her top lip. "By the way, I heard something yesterday you might be interested in."

"Did you?" Megan didn't look up as she concentrated on painting the nails of her right hand with her left. "Why didn't you tell me earlier, then?"

"Because I was busy when you came in and I forgot." Petal sprawled out and reached for another piece of cheese. "Lionel's mum called last night – I told you she's moved to Dublin, didn't I? Anyway, she's been on one of those senior's holidays for a month and got back yesterday, so she called for a natter. She couldn't believe it when Lionel told her all about what's been going on here. She used to know one of the murder victims – the old guy."

Megan looked up. "Victor Canning?"

Petal nodded. "She said that, years ago, he and Timothy Starr were love rivals."

"I know! Can you believe it?" said Megan, as she drew the varnish-loaded brush down her nail. "Timothy mentioned it to Uncle Des and I the other day. Apparently, Victor was furious with him for years because he was in love with Diana, but she was in love with Timothy."

"Yeah," said Petal. "And I bet that's why Victor put a block on Timothy's application for a scholarship to the Academy; to get his own back."

Megan looked up again and frowned. "What scholarship?"

"To get into the Academy of Musical Excellence."

"I think you're getting confused," said Megan. "It's Bailey who's trying to get a scholarship."

"Yes, I know that," said Petal, "but years ago, so was Timothy. He was super-talented, apparently, and everyone was convinced he was going to be awarded a scholarship. But he wasn't. It was given to another guy who was nowhere *near* as good as Timothy. Heather said it caused a huge stink at the time."

"But what's that got to do with Victor Canning?" said Megan. "How could he have put a block on Timothy's application?"

"Well, according to Heather, Victor was the youngest person to ever sit on the Academy's Admissions Board, and his opinion on who the scholarships were awarded to, and who they weren't, was very highly regarded. Back then he was a very influential guy, and hugely gifted – some kind of musical genius, apparently."

"So you mean Victor Canning recommended the scholarship be awarded to someone else, just to spite Timothy?" said Megan, blowing on a freshly-varnished nail.

Petal shrugged a shoulder. "That's what people thought, but I suppose the only person who ever knew for sure was Victor. It took Timothy ages to get over it."

"Wow, that's harsh. And what happened after that?"

"Nothing, as far as I know. Timothy and Diana eventually got married and Victor Canning just got on with his life, I guess. It was decades ago."

"How does Heather know all this? Was she friends with Timothy?"

"No, but she was in his music class at school. It was all everyone talked about for months." Petal picked up a newspaper and flicked through to the TV guide. "Ooh, the first episode of that new period drama's on in twenty minutes – the one with the swoon-worthy guy with the long hair and the broody stare. Shall we watch it before I go home?"

Megan replied with a distracted nod. Petal's news had started her brain ticking-over again.

oooooooo

"Victor Canning blocked Timothy Starr's scholarship because Diana chose Timothy over him? Are you sure?"

Des looked sideways at Megan as he bent over a flowerbed in the garden at Kismet Cottage.

"That's what Lionel's mum told Petal. She was in the same music class as Timothy."

"Well, I suppose that could have been motive enough to kill someone *at the time*," said Des, "but like we said before, why would it suddenly become so important to do it after waiting forty-seven years?"

"I've no idea," said Megan. "You're right, it doesn't add up, but I thought it was worth mentioning."

"You've got to pull all these out by the roots," said Des, turning his attention back to the weeding, "or your mum and dad will come back to a jungle." He huffed and puffed as he bent to wrestle a clump of dandelions from the grass.

Megan handed him a glass of lemonade. "I'll definitely tidy it up before I leave but it's the creepy-crawlies that put me off. You know I could never kill anything but that doesn't mean I want to share their habitat." She clicked her tongue. "Look, you've got mud all over your shirt. I was just about to put a wash in – do you want to give me that and you can borrow one of dad's?"

Des gulped the last of his drink and took off his shirt, putting his notebook on the garden table. "I'll go and have a look in your dad's wardrobe."

"While you're up there, could you bring down the jacket that's hanging on my bedroom door, please? It's the one Diana lent me when I saw her the other day. I'd like to wash it before I give it back."

Des disappeared leaving Megan pulling half-heartedly at a few weeds. She ran a hand across the back of her neck, lifting up the hair plastered to it with sweat.

"Is this the one?" said Des, reappearing in one of Nick's shirts.

"That's it," she said. She laid the jacket on the garden table and patted the outside pockets. "Nothing in there, nothing in that one, either." She pulled out a small handful of papers from one of the inside pockets and set them down on the table. She was about to check the other pocket when something caught her eye. Putting on her glasses, she looked at a small square of cardboard; a drinks mat with a picture of a rotund, red-cheeked man, clutching his sides, large tears spurting from his eyes.

"Found something interesting?" asked Des, as he resumed the weeding.

"It's a drinks mat from the comedy club. Like the one we found poking out from under the door when we went over there. D'you remember?" She held it up for Des to see. "I wonder who used to go there? Bailey wasn't allowed out, and I can't see it having been Timothy or Diana's cup of tea. And here's a ticket for the club's car park." She peered at it and gasped. "Oh no! Oh my goodness!"

"What's up?"

"The date on it is Saturday the 23rd of May," said Megan, her voice faltering. "The driver arrived at quarter-past midnight, and left at twenty-five past two in the morning."

Des stopped jabbing at the ground with his trowel. "The 23rd? Isn't that the day Andy Cochran was killed?" He heaved himself up and took the ticket to have a closer look. "We have to take this to the police, love," he said, fanning out the rest of the scraps of paper on the table. "This is proof that... Good grief!"

"What now?" Megan grabbed Des's arm when she saw the colour had drained from his face.

He held up a second slip of paper. Although it was creased, it was still possible to read the print on it.

"Five double brandies, five orange liqueurs, and a sparkling water," Megan read aloud. "And this receipt is also dated the 23rd of May,"

"Is there a time on there?"

She inspected the receipt more closely. "Five-past two in the morning."

"Whose jacket is this?" said Des, his face as stern as Megan had ever seen it.

"Well, officially, it's Bailey's – Diana said that Adrian gave it to him when Witchester City got new ones – but they keep it in the car for emergencies. Since Bailey's had it, the whole family's probably worn it, and goodness knows who else."

"I think we need to take all this stuff to DI Cambridge," said Des.

Megan nodded. "Yes, we do. I want to pop over to The Duck and have a quick word with Mary Tang again first, though." She snapped a photo of the jacket on her phone. "To see if this jogs her memory. Come on."

oooooooo

Mary looked at the photo and shook her head.

"It's hard to say. So many people wear similar jackets, I can't be certain if I've seen it before. Even the emblem on the front wouldn't have made it that distinctive in a dimly-lit club."

"Do you remember any of the customers, then? Please, think hard," said Megan. "This could be really important."

"Of course I remember the customers. I worked at the club for years. We used to give them nicknames. Why?"

Des ignored the question, his pen racing across the page of his notebook. "Do any of them stick out in your memory more than others?

Mary cocked her head. "Hmm. Well, there was Cry Baby, the guy who always liked to sit on the table right in front of the stage. If he didn't get that table, he'd have a complete hissy fit. Andy only put up with him because he spent so much money. Then there was Fancy Pants, the couple who always turned up in fancy dress. Nice, but weird. And there was Platinum, the young guy who always sat at a table right at the back, in the darkest corner of the club. He was always waiting for someone.

Nice guy, but I don't think he ever watched any of the acts – he always seemed too wrapped up in his own little world. He always wore dark glasses and had his hood up. It's a wonder he could see where he was going in here at night." She looked at the jacket again. "I suppose this could have been his, but I'm really not sure."

"Why was he called Platinum?" asked Megan.

"Oh, because of his eyebrows. They were so blond, they looked silver, even in the dark."

Megan gave Des a look and tried to keep the excitement from her voice. "You don't know his real name, I suppose?"

Mary shook her head. "I only knew a few customers by their actual name – I prefer not to get too familiar with people when I'm working behind a bar."

"Do you remember who it was he used to meet?"

"No, sorry. Whoever it was usually sneaked in late and then they'd both leave before the last act finished and the lights went up. They were always very low key. They used to wear jackets with hoods, or hats – they obviously didn't want to be bothered – and they always sat with their backs to the stage." Mary looked over her shoulder to make sure they weren't being eavesdropped on. "You learn not to ask too many questions. If people want to keep themselves to themselves, that's their business. As long as they paid their bills and didn't cause any trouble, they were welcome. I should get back to work."

Des pumped her hand up and down. "Thank you. You've been very helpful. Very helpful indeed."

oooooooo

"I'm going to call the police station," said Megan. "I want to make sure DI Cambridge is there first. I don't want to leave all this evidence with just anyone – I want to give it to him."

"It's probably a bit late to be mentioning this," said Des, as they walked back across the village green, "but try to touch everything as little as possible. Because of fingerprints, I mean. We probably should have thought about that a bit earlier."

He frowned and scratched his chin. "So, we know Bailey Starr was a regular visitor to the comedy club, and I'd say those receipts are pretty conclusive proof he was there the night Andy was killed. I wonder what his motive was?" He shook his head. "That's a very troubled young man – it's little wonder he's been behaving strangely."

As Megan opened the front door, her phone rang. She spoke briefly before ending the call. "That was Aunty Sylvie. She said to ask if you can call Gerald the gardener. He wants to speak to you about something – he said it was urgent."

"Urgent?" said Des. "What could that be about? Maybe his marrows have exploded. They were looking a tad over-ripe when we went over to the allotment." He chuckled. "I suppose I'd better give him a quick call. I'll use the landline, shall I? Won't be a tick."

As Des went off to call Gerald, Megan remembered his advice to touch all the evidence as little as possible, and pulled on a pair of washing-up gloves before folding up the jacket to put it into a bag. As she squashed it flat, she heard a rustling noise. She opened it up again and felt the inside-left pocket. In the excitement earlier, she'd forgotten to check that one. She pulled out a folded envelope and shook it over the table. A letter and a small plastic bag fell out. Pushing her glasses on again, she saw that the inside of the bag was stained bright yellow. She read the letter, shaking her head as the mystery of the murders began to unravel.

"Look at this," she said, when Des put the phone down, and looked up to see him looking equally dumbstruck.

"You won't believe what Gerald's just told me." He sat down and rubbed a hand across his forehead. "He's been talking to one of the chaps from the allotment. He had his appendix out a few months ago and hasn't been around much since so today was the first time he's spoken to Gerald in almost four months.

"He told him he was getting his allotment in order, early one morning, before he went in for his op in May, and he saw someone picking Oscar's hybrid hibiscus flowers, and taking some stuff from his potting shed. And guess what? It wasn't Oscar."

"Did he give Gerald a description?"

Des nodded.

Megan held up the envelope she'd taken from the jacket pocket and showed Des the addressee. "Was it this person?

"Yep. That's who he saw." Des's jaw stiffened. "Oscar's been well and truly set up, hasn't he?"

"He has," said Megan, "and it's about time he was proved innocent."

ooooooo

Sam Cambridge patiently listened to every one of Megan's and Des's theories, and surveyed all the evidence in front of him.

"If forensics can find a match on this jacket to the unidentified DNA found at all the crime scenes, I'll be a very happy man," he said, looking at Megan and Des across the desk.

"Thank you for your efforts on this. I told you before, Miss Fallon, we often rely on feedback from members of the community to help us solve crimes, and I'm sure that what you've both told us, and brought us, is going to be a huge help in solving the recent murders."

He pushed out his chair and stood up to shake their hands.

"Will you be making an arrest soon?" asked Megan.

"If we can get some conclusive proof from what you've brought me," said Sam, "we'll be making an arrest immediately afterwards. It'll take a little while to get the DNA tested but I'll do what I can to get it done as a rush job. In the meantime, keep your fingers crossed."

CHAPTER TWENTY-ONE

The village green buzzed with activity as members of the Bliss Bay Women's Association bustled and organised the late-summer fundraiser.

As usual, Classical Kin had been booked to play, and Timothy, Diana and Bailey were busy tuning their instruments and carrying out a sound check on the portable stage under the shade cast by the boughs of the ancient oak tree.

"Ah, Mr Starr." The overbearing bellow of Sandra Grayling, the WA treasurer, cut through the chatter as she marched across the green in her sensible shoes, a hair grip holding her snow-white fringe at an acute angle across her forehead. "You'll be kicking off the proceedings with The National Anthem, I assume?" She produced a handkerchief the size of a small bedsheet from the pocket of her padded waistcoat and gave her nose a vigorous blow.

"Of course, Mrs Grayling, as we—"

"It's *Miss* Grayling." Sandra interrupted, fixing Timothy with a beady eye.

"Yes. Of course it is," he mumbled, forcing a smile. "As I was saying, we'll be playing The National Anthem, as we always do, and we thought we'd—"

"Spiffing!" Sandra cut him dead and marched on her way, stopping to glare at Des who was grappling with a trestle table in a prime spot on the green. "You'll need to get a move on, Mr Harper," she ordered, tapping the face of her watch. "We'll be starting soon. What is it you're trying to do, exactly?"

Des straightened up and glared at her, digging his fingers into the small of his back. "What does it *look* like I'm trying to do, you silly moo? I'm *trying* to put up this blasted table. And *you* breathing down my neck isn't helping."

With a sharp intake of breath, Sandra turned on her heel and stomped off.

"Bother and blast!" Des's breath came in laboured bursts. "I refuse to be beaten by an inanimate object!"

"Oh, for heaven's sake, you've been struggling with that for almost twenty minutes. Will you just let us do it?" said Sylvie, and she and Megan each took an end of the table. In a matter of seconds, it was open and covered with a white cotton cloth from Sylvie's second-best set of table linen.

Megan glimpsed Des from the corner of her eye, chuckling to herself as he cursed under his breath. It had always amazed her that he was so ham-fisted when faced with manual tasks, yet had such a feather-light touch when it came to baking.

She made a start on displaying the cakes and pies she'd transported from her uncle and aunt's kitchen in the boot of her mini and, before long, the table creaked under the weight of apple, peach, and rhubarb pies, alongside Paradise slices, banana and cranberry muffins, and, of course, Des's signature lavender Madeleines.

He stood back to admire the efforts of a frantic morning's baking, and Sylvie and Megan linked their arms through his.

"You're a wonder, you are, Des Harper," said Sylvie, proudly, and planted a kiss on his cheek. "Just look at all that – you'll be the talk of the WA." She held a hand above her eyes. "Is that Dora over there? Yes, it is. I won't be a sec. I just want to have a quick chat with her before we get started."

As she marched off, Des bent his head close to Megan's. "I wonder how DI Cambridge is getting on? I thought a certain person might have been arrested by now."

Megan raised a shoulder. "Me too. Maybe the jacket didn't match the DNA from the crime scenes after all. Or maybe our theories didn't stack up like we thought they did." She cut up some cake samples and stuck cocktail sticks into them so customers could try before buying. "I really thought we were onto something."

Des gave her a hug. "We did our best, didn't we, love? We couldn't have done any more." He chuckled. "I'm still relishing the look on the DI's face when you put all that evidence on his desk. It was like all his birthdays had come at once."

"Yes, I quite enjoyed that myself, I have to say," said Megan, the grin on her lips turning to laughter when one of Des's magic tricks produced a pound coin from out of her nose.

The sun climbed in the September sky as the crowds descended on the village green and the sound of feedback from a microphone signalled the arrival of Sandra Grayling to the stage.

"Good morning, everyone," said Sandra, tapping heavily on the microphone and managing to make even her welcome to the fundraiser sound bossy. "As you know, this yearly event is all about raising funds for the Bliss Bay Women's Association, as well as various community projects." She waited for a ripple of applause before continuing. "And I hope you'll all bear that in mind as you walk around the stalls and activities. Now, before I leave you to enjoy yourselves, it gives me great pleasure to hand the microphone to our most generous benefactor, Witchester City star and Bliss Bay's favourite son, Adrian Castle, who would like to say a few words."

To a roaring round of applause and cheers, and his mum and dad's whooping from the front of the crowd, Adrian limped to the stage and waved to his adoring fans. "Good morning, everyone. Before I declare the fundraiser open, I'd like to take just a few minutes of your time." His voice distorted and echoed around the green, and he held the microphone further away from his mouth.

"As you all know, I lost a good friend recently. For those of you who knew Tony, I've no doubt you're missing him, too. He was a crazy guy – I never knew what he was going to do next – but that was Tony. If it hadn't been for him, I don't think I'd have recovered as quickly as I did after every operation. It was Tony's encouragement, energy and sense of humour that kept my spirits up and made sure I stayed positive."

He took a deep breath, his voice shaking as he started to speak again. "As we're all together, I thought this was an ideal opportunity to say a big thank you on behalf of Tony's family, and from me. I don't know how I'd have got through the past few weeks without the kindness shown to me by this community. Thank you for your condolences, and your support. They've meant more than you'll ever know." He bowed his head and held a hand to his eyes before sending out a smile to the crowd. "And, with all that said, it gives me great pleasure to declare the fundraiser open, and to introduce Bliss Bay's favourite trio – although they need no introduction – will you please all put your hands together for Classical Kin!"

Timothy, Diana and Bailey waved and took a bow from their places on the makeshift stage under the shade of the oak tree.

As Timothy counted them in to the beginning of The National Anthem, Sam's car pulled up at the edge of the village green and he and Harvey got out and made their way through the crowd.

Des nudged Megan in the ribs. "Look! Megan, look! They're here!"

Megan's stomach lurched and a wave of anxiety flooded over her. She clutched Des's arm. "Here we go."

"Excuse me." Sam held up a hand. "Sorry to interrupt, everyone. I know what an important event this is for the village, so we'll try not to keep you too long." He put down a large holdall he was carrying.

"Er, do you mind?" With her fingers poised to pluck the strings of the harp resting against her shoulder, Diana fixed the detectives with a withering glare. "We're about to start our performance. And, I have no idea what this is about but surely it can wait until we've finished?"

"What do you think you're playing at?" Timothy lowered the flute from his lips. "What's going on?"

Sam gave him a brief smile. "All will be revealed before too long, Mr Starr."

"Honestly," said Diana. "Your timing couldn't be worse, Detective Inspector. Please say whatever it is you've come to say as quickly as possible, and then leave."

"If you'll just bear with me for a while, Mrs Starr," said Sam, handing her a copy of the letter Megan had found in the Witchester City jacket pocket. "I think this might help answer a few questions. It's a copy of the Academy of Musical Excellence's latest newsletter, which was sent to your husband at the beginning of July. Take a look at the main story."

Diana took the paper, adjusted her glasses, and read out loud. *"CANNING RETURNS TO AWARD CENTENARY SCHOLARSHIPS. We are delighted to announce that Victor Canning will be returning to the Academy's Admissions Panel to participate in the forthcoming awarding of scholarships.*

"Mr Canning, who was a revered member of the Admissions Panel from 1968 to when he retired in 2007, was asked to return to mark the Academy's centenary year. He will attend all admission interviews for this year's candidates and will play an integral part in deciding to which students the scholarships are awarded."

Diana took off her glasses. "Timothy, why didn't you tell me about this? And of what interest is it to the Detective Inspector?"

Timothy pulled himself up to his full height. "I didn't tell you about Victor Canning because I didn't see any point. And, as for why DI Cambridge is so interested in an old A.M.E newsletter, I really have no idea." He coughed and wiped his mouth with a handkerchief.

"Is this really necessary, detective?" said Diana. "Whatever you want to talk to us about, can't it wait until after the fundraiser?"

In the background, Timothy continued to cough and splutter.

Diana turned to him and frowned. "What's suddenly started you off with that stress cough? You're never going to be able to play the flute with that. Honestly! We're going to have to swap instruments."

Sam walked slowly around the edge of the stage, the large holdall in his hand, and came to a stop next to Timothy. "I'm afraid we can't wait until after the fundraiser, Mrs Starr. You see, we have some rather important business to attend to here. With your husband."

Timothy's head snapped round, his eyes meeting Sam's steely glare. "What business?" He coughed again, droplets of his saliva flying through the air and landing on Sam's coat.

Sam didn't flinch as he removed his glasses and cleaned the lenses with a handkerchief from his coat pocket. "Would it surprise you to learn, Mr Starr, that DNA found in bodily fluids such as saliva can be matched to DNA found on clothing? Hair, skin cells, that kind of thing. And have you any idea how much DNA a single cough can leave behind at, let's say, a crime scene for example?"

He reached into the holdall and pulled out a large, transparent evidence bag which he held out in front of Timothy. "The evidence on this jacket, for instance, can be invaluable in helping us match DNA found at crime scenes to the DNA of the perpetrators of those crimes. Even criminals who go to great pains to cover their hair with hats and their hands with gloves can leave behind the most telling DNA with a single sneeze or cough."

Timothy peered at the bag, the Witchester City emblem of the jacket Diana had lent Megan clearly visible.

He covered his mouth with his handkerchief and coughed again until he was red in the face.

"Would someone like to tell me what on earth is going on?" said Diana, pouring a cup of hot honey and lemon from a flask, and handing it to her husband.

Timothy glared at Sam, then turned his gaze to his wife, the look of dread shrouding his face turning to resignation. He dabbed at his mouth and pulled Diana into a hug. "Oh, my love, I'm so sorry. I didn't want you to find out like this."

"Find out? Find out what?"

"That it was me. I killed Victor."

Diana pushed him away and frowned. "I don't know what kind of sick joke this is, Timmy, but that isn't even the remotest bit funny."

For a moment, Timothy looked as though he was about to burst into tears, but then he threw his head back and laughed until tears were running down his cheeks. He held his sides and laughed and coughed, Diana and Bailey staring at him in bewilderment.

"Oh my, oh my goodness, I'm sorry. Just let me get my breath." He shook his head. "It's not a joke, Diana. I really did kill him." He laughed again. Actually, it was quite good fun, stalking him to figure out the best time of day to do the deed. I just went to Honeymeade a few times, hung around and asked a few questions. It's amazing what people will tell you when they think you're someone trying to catch up with an old friend. Not that Victor ever *was* a friend, of course, but they weren't to know that. It took me no time at all to find out he went to the diner for breakfast every morning. And on his last visit, I was there waiting for him."

Apart from the whimpering of a baby in a pushchair, there was complete silence from the crowd. Diana stared at her husband, her face a mask of sheer horror.

"Why, Timmy? Oh please God, please tell me you didn't kill him because you thought he was in love with me? I must have told you a thousand times he meant nothing."

Timothy chuckled and rubbed a palm across his bald patch. "Diana, you don't understand do you? You think I was bothered that Victor was in love with you?" He shook his head. "On the contrary, my darling, I couldn't have been happier that you were the love of his life. Every day he lived with the pain of losing you was a bonus, as far as I was concerned. Knowing you chose me when Victor wanted you so badly has been what got me through all these years. Knowing I had what he wanted was enough. I had no plans to kill him until I found out he was going back to the Academy."

"You're making no sense," said Diana, the colour draining from her cheeks.

"When I found out Victor was going back to the Academy to judge the candidates, I had no option other than to kill him," said Timothy. "Don't you see? He would never have recommended Bailey for a scholarship. It would have been a case of history repeating itself."

The newsletter fell from Diana's fingers. "You killed Victor because you thought he'd stop Bailey from being awarded a scholarship? Because of something that happened between the two of you decades ago?"

Timothy put his hands on her shoulders. "I didn't *think* he would, Diana, I *knew* he would – to get back at me. How can you not see that? There was no way I was going to let him deny Bailey the future he deserved – just like he did to me. It's bad enough that one member of the Starr family had their entire career ruined. I wasn't going to let it happen again. Do you really think after what Victor did to me, I was going to let *anything* stand in Bailey's way?"

"Good grief." Diana put the back of a hand to her brow and beckoned Bailey to her side with the other. "Your father's lost his mind, darling."

"I should have got that scholarship, Diana," said Timothy. "But because you chose me over him, he gave it to someone else, just to spite me – we all know that's what happened. *Everyone* said it should have been mine, but he persuaded all the judges on the Admissions Board that it should go to another student. For so long, I've had to wonder what *could* have been.

"And then, when I read that newsletter about Victor coming out of retirement to be an honorary judge, I knew I had to do something. If I didn't, I knew he'd stand in Bailey's way. That man's spite knew no bounds."

Diana's bottom lip trembled. "I can't believe you killed a man so that Bailey could get his scholarship."

Timothy held her gaze and then dropped his eyes to the floor. "Actually, I didn't *just* kill one man so that Bailey could get his scholarship."

A gasp went up from the crowd. Megan and Des gawped at each other, and Bailey put an arm around Diana's shoulders as Timothy continued his confession.

"With Victor out of the way, I thought I'd got rid of everything that would keep Bailey from the career he deserved. But then Tony Weller started again with that infernal row he called music, getting louder and louder, day after day, night after night. I couldn't stand it. I even spoke to him about it, to ask if he could keep the noise down for Bailey's sake, and he laughed in my face. 'Live and let live, bro. If Bailey's got the talent, he'll get his scholarship', is what he said.

"I'd known for a while that I was going to kill him. I just didn't know when. And then, after that final night, when the music didn't end until past three o'clock in the morning, I knew I couldn't wait any longer. Every minute I lay in bed, listening to that racket shaking the walls, was another minute I spent planning exactly how I was going to get rid of him. Killing him was only way to stop it, you see."

"For heaven's sake, Timothy!" wailed Diana. "Eleanor was going to report him – the music would have stopped eventually. Why did you have to kill him? You told me you thought he was a nice man."

Timothy threw her a scornful glare, his blue eyes hard and cruel. "Well, I had to say that, didn't I? To put you all off the scent. He was nothing more than a ridiculous upstart who thought he knew about music. Pah! How he could even *dare* to call the tripe he played 'music', I don't know. And even if Eleanor *had* reported him, if he hadn't got that DJ job in Ibiza, the music would have started again after a while. It always did."

He turned to Bailey. "I hope you can understand why I did what I did, son. Everything he did was affecting your chances of getting into the Academy. His noise was a constant distraction – so much so, you couldn't focus on your studies. I could see how off-putting the disturbances were for you, and I wasn't about to stand by and see your future destroyed."

Bailey dropped his gaze. "I can't even look at you, Dad. I don't understand why you thought any of this was okay."

Timothy shrugged his shoulders and spread his hands. "Killing Tony was the only solution – don't you see? And he made it so easy. It was like it was meant to be. I already knew where he exercised every morning, because I'd seen him from the window of the music room. And I knew he switched off the security systems first thing, because he told me when we spoke about his exercise routine. He said he couldn't relax if they were on. I'd seen the gardener change the water in the birdbath a thousand times, so I knew it would be the perfect murder weapon.

"I quietly let myself into the garden with the key I had for the gate, and crept up behind him. He didn't stand a chance." Timothy smiled. "After I'd done the deed, I locked the gate with the key and then used a screwdriver to force the lock from the outside to make it look like someone had broken in. I knew Adrian and Natalie wouldn't hear anything because Tony had already told me they wore earplugs if they had a late night so they could lie-in without being disturbed."

No one could stop Adrian Castle from launching himself across the stage and swinging a punch at Timothy's chin, knocking him backwards. "I swear, I'd kill you now with my bare hands if I could," he yelled, before Sam and Harvey each took an arm and restrained him.

Amidst the chaos, Diana looked like a startled deer. She flopped down onto a stool and waited until there was calm before turning to her husband again. "Where did you get a key for Adrian and Natalie's gate? And if you let yourself in with a key, and then locked the gate behind you on your way out, why did you force it open again?" She dropped her head into her hands. "I don't understand."

Timothy crouched in front of her and rubbed at the bruise already forming on his chin. "I just said, my darling. I had to make it look like someone had forced the gate to avert suspicion for Tony's murder away from Bailey."

"Bailey?" Diana's hand flew to her throat as her voice grew higher. "What on earth does Bailey have to do with all this?"

For the first time, Timothy looked guilty. He rubbed at his chin again before turning to his son.

"The key. It was Bailey's. I took it from his keyring when he was asleep the morning I killed Tony. I knew it was a key to the gate because Tony had one exactly the same. It was a very long key – not like any of ours – and I saw him use it to open the side gate one morning while I was chatting to him. When I first saw the same key on Bailey's keyring, though, I had no idea why he had it. I just knew it was the same."

He glanced over to his son. "I almost asked you why you had a key, but I knew I wouldn't want to hear the answer. All I knew what that after I'd killed Tony, I had to protect you from anyone thinking you were involved in his murder. I had to, because suspicion would have fallen on you, son. Sooner or later, someone would have found out that you had a key to that gate."

There was a low murmur of chatter as every pair of eyes turned to the young man on the stage.

"But *why* do you have a key, Bailey?" said Diana. "For the love of Mozart and Beethoven, please don't tell me you have anything to do with this?"

Bailey looked Timothy up and down with disgust, then turned to Diana and shook his head. "Well, I haven't killed anyone, Mum, if that's what you mean."

"Well, that's one blessing to come out of all this," said Diana, pulling a handkerchief from her pocket and holding it to her eyes. "But I still don't understand why you have a key?" She looked form her son to her husband. "Will one of you please just tell me?"

"I only recently figured it out for myself, Diana, but why don't you ask Adrian?" said

Timothy, sending the footballer a spiteful glare. "Maybe he'd like to explain."

Adrian returned the glare from where he sat on the side of the stage, Harvey watching over him.

Diana's eyes darted from left to right. "What are you talking about?" She clutched Bailey's arms and shook him. "Bailey!"

"Oh for pity's sake! He's got a key because of *that girl!*" Timothy roared, pointing a finger at Caroline Gibbs who was standing at the front of the crowd, her baby in its pushchair. "He's been seeing her for months. Every time he told us he was going to music practice, he was sneaking out to see that tart. I only wish I could have got rid of her too."

Adrian turned to Diana, his voice shaking with rage. "*I* gave Bailey a key last year. He's a good kid and I felt sorry for him. You never gave him a break and he needed some fun. He met Caroline when she was working for Natalie, and he came round to wait for me when I was giving him driving lessons. They hit it off, and I trusted him, so I gave him a key to let him come and go through the gate whenever he wanted. He asked Natalie and I not to tell anyone about it because he didn't want you to find out. They used to meet in the summerhouse at the end of the garden after Bailey finished college, and sometimes at weekends.

"They stopped meeting there when I got injured, though. I told them I didn't want people coming and going until I got back to form, but I told Bailey to keep the key until then. When Tony was killed, I thought Bailey was involved but I couldn't understand why the lock had been forced, seeing as he could have just let himself in with the key. But now I know."

Adrian shook himself free from the Harvey's hand on his shoulder and turned to Bailey. "I'm sorry I doubted you. I wasn't thinking straight. And I'm sorry about that." He pointed to Bailey's face, still bearing the faint scars of their altercation. "I didn't mean to hurt you but I was so angry that day, I had to find out if you were involved in Tony's death. I think I always knew you had nothing to do with it, though. That's why I didn't tell the police."

"Bailey would never hurt anyone," said Timothy. "He's like you, Diana." He returned the looks of horror from his wife and son with a pleading one. "Please, you have to understand – I only did this for you, son. And for us. We all wanted the scholarship for you so desperately."

Diana pulled Bailey to her. "Yes, we wanted it, Timmy, but not like this. For God's sake, not like this." She turned from her husband and took Bailey's face in her hands, tears running down her cheeks as she steeled herself to break even more bad news to him. "Bailey, darling, I'm so sorry to be the one to tell you this, especially in light of everything we've just learned, but haven't you heard the rumours?" She dropped her voice to a whisper. "Adrian is the father of Caroline's child. She'll never love you like she loves him."

Bailey took a long look at her. "So you believed them, too?" He shook his head. "Caroline isn't in love with Adrian, Mum. She never has been. She's in love with me. And he isn't the father of her child. I am."

The biggest gasp of all went up as Bailey jumped off the stage, hugged Caroline and took the baby from her pushchair. Her little fingers clamped tight on his glasses and he laughed as she pulled them from his face. "This is your grand-daughter," he said, as he climbed back on stage and handed her to Diana. "Meet Carley."

As a stunned Diana cradled her granddaughter in her arms, Bailey walked across the stage to face his father. "Why, Dad?"

"For you," said Timothy, showing no interest in his grandchild. "I did it all for you. For the scholarship. I had to get rid of anything that stood in your way."

"But I wasn't bothered about the scholarship." Bailey ran both hands through his hair. "I just went along with it for you and

Mum. You never *once* asked me what *I* wanted – you just assumed I wanted the same as you, but I don't. I never have. I just want to be with Caroline and Carley."

Timothy clutched at his son's shirt. "No. No, you don't mean that. You don't understand what you're saying. I've sacrificed too much for you to throw everything away. I've killed *three* people for you – three people who were standing in your way. Victor Canning, Tony Weller and Andy Cochran."

"Andy?" Bailey took a step backwards, his mouth gaping in his horrified face. "Why did you kill Andy?"

Timothy ran his fingers down his cheeks, his face twisting in a lopsided grin. "Because I had to. I heard you sneak out of the house one night when you thought your mother and I were asleep, and I followed you all the way to the comedy club. You probably thought you were being clever by not taking the car, didn't you? You must have thought we'd never know you were missing if the car was still on the drive, but I heard you. I knew.

"I waited outside the club until you came out with Caroline. Then I followed you back to her place, and then I came home. I knew I had to put a stop to it. And the easiest way to do that was to put the club out of business." He examined his fingernails. "Which is why Andy Cochran had to die."

He clasped his hands behind his back and paced up and down the stage. "I went to the comedy club after I'd dropped your mum at the airport – remember when she went to Paris in May for your aunt's 60th? Well, on the way back, I went to the club on the pretext of leaving my phone there. Andy had closed up but he let me in to look for it. We got chatting and I bought him a few drinks. If it's any consolation, he was so drunk when I stuck that stake into his chest, I'm sure he didn't feel a thing."

Bailey stared at his father in disbelief. "You killed Andy, just so Caroline and I wouldn't have a place to meet?" He wiped the back of his hand across his eyes. "I can't believe you," he screamed.

"I had to, Bailey!" Timothy flung his arms into the air. "I had to make it as difficult as possible for you to see that girl. She was just another distraction, and a bad influence. You never used to lie to us, son, but you've been lying to your mother and I for months because of her, haven't you?

"When you told us you wanted to start walking from one side of the village to the other every morning, to clear your head before you started practice, did you know I knew you were lying? And then you'd come back home, pretending you'd been walking for the past hour and a half, when the only place you'd been was across the park to Caroline's place. And do you know how I knew? Because I used to watch you from the music studio window.

"Even if I hadn't seen you, I would have known you hadn't walked across the village, because it's paving stones all the way. Unless it had been raining, your jeans would have been dry when you got back. Not wet, like they were, because you'd walked across the park on dew-covered grass."

Bailey's cheeks turned pink.

"Oh, yes, son. I've followed you all over Bliss Bay, so I know all your tricks. That's how I found out about the baby. I drove to Caroline's place one morning, just after you'd set off, and waited down the road. When I saw the way you reacted when you arrived and she opened the door with the baby in her arms, I knew then that it was yours. I just knew it. And I guessed that having a key to Castle Manor must have made it easy for you to cultivate your secret, seedy little relationship for months."

"It *isn't* seedy," said Bailey, through gritted teeth. "And the only reason it was secret was because I knew you'd freak out if you knew we were seeing each other. That's why we couldn't tell anyone. When we couldn't meet at Castle Manor any more, we started meeting at Caroline's place because I could hardly have invited her round to ours, could I?

You don't approve of *any* of my friends. But we found a way because Adrian was good to us in the beginning. And because we love each other."

Timothy threw back his head and laughed. "Love? *Love?* Don't be ridiculous – you're twenty years old. What do *you* know about love?" He jabbed his finger against his chest and paced the stage. "Now me, *I* can tell you about love.

"*Love* is when you risk your own wellbeing for someone. Why do you think I've been so stressed, and my asthma's been so bad recently? I'll tell you why, because being out in the cold at all hours of the day and night while I've been trying to make things right for you, has done my health no good at all.

"*Love* is killing three people so that someone you care for can have the future they deserve." He sneered. "And it would have been four if *she* hadn't jumped out of the way." He jerked his chin in Caroline's direction and the crowd ooooh-ed and aaahh-ed once more. "When I thought I'd done everything to stop you from seeing each other, but you still found a way, there was only one thing left I could do.

"I drove to Caroline's late one Sunday night. I'd been watching her place on and off for weeks, so I knew she always left home to pick up a takeaway around ten-thirty. Luck must have been on her side that night – I nearly hit her when she was walking to her car but she jumped into a shop doorway."

It caught everyone off-guard when Bailey threw himself at Timothy.

"I can't *believe* you would do that!" he cried, lashing out with his fists. "What is *wrong* with you? I'm ashamed to call you my dad. Do you know, I wanted to leave home that night when Caroline called to tell me what had happened, but she stopped me? She said no harm had been done and we should carry on seeing each other in secret. She knew what a hard time you'd give me if I left home. She went to stay with her brother after that – did you know? I didn't see her or Carley for a whole week.

"Now I know what you've done, I won't be taking the scholarship exam. I never wanted to anyway. And I'm going to move in with Caroline. If I have to spend another second in our house with the memory of you breathing down my neck every minute of the day, I'll go mad." Bailey settled his ruffled hair with a sweep of his hand and stomped back across the stage to his mother's side.

"I suppose I deserved that," said Timothy, wiping his shirt sleeve against his bloody nose. "But you'll think differently once you've calmed down. Music is your life. You know it, and I know it."

"Oh my goodness!" said Diana, suddenly. "Oscar! That poor man has been at his wits' end because of all this. And Eleanor, too. They're probably both sitting at home, worrying about how on earth he can possibly have been accused of murdering three men. And all along, *you* were to blame."

"Yes, that was a shame, but it was so easy to set him up," said Timothy. "Do you remember, ages ago, he told us about his ridiculous plant experiments? Well, when I knew I was going to have to do something drastic to ensure Bailey's place at the Academy, I had to be sure there'd be no trail back to me, and Oscar's plants were the perfect decoy." He smirked.

"Of course, at that time, Andy's murder was the only one I'd planned from start to finish. I knew where and when I was going to kill him. I'd deliberately planned it for when you went to Paris, Diana. And Tony, well, I knew I was going to kill him, too, but I hadn't decided when until that last night. And as for Victor, his fate was sealed as soon as I found out he was going back to the Academy."

"But where do Oscar's plants come into all this?" said Diana.

"Ah, well, you see," said Timothy, "the pollen from Oscar's hybrid hibiscus flowers is unique, so I knew there was every chance it would put him in the frame for the murders if some was found at every scene.

"As soon as I knew I was going to kill Andy and Tony, I went to Oscar's allotment early one morning to pick the flowers for the pollen. Luckily, the flowers I took gave me enough pollen to use for Victor's murder, too, when I later found out that he would also have to be dealt with.

"And I took some wooden stakes and garden wire from his potting shed. I'd originally planned to use the stake to kill Andy and the wire to kill Tony, but Victor Canning's death became my priority, so I used the wire on him instead. No matter, the birdbath was an excellent substitute.

"After I'd killed them all, I went back to the allotment to hide the items I'd taken from each of them – I had it all planned. I knew it was only a matter of time before the police would follow the trail back to Oscar. I knew when they searched the shed, and found the hibiscus plants at his house and on his allotment, that he'd be arrested. I'm sorry, Diana, but I couldn't have them coming after me, could I? I've got nothing against Oscar – in fact, I was rather hoping he'd be let off lightly because of what he's already been through."

Diana handed her granddaughter back to Bailey before marching to Timothy and punching him in the stomach. "Exactly,

Timothy! You know what he's *already* been through." Her voice soared to soprano heights. "And all you've done is pile misery on top of misery. You're despicable!"

The crowd gasped again before breaking into agitated chatter.

The snap of handcuffs around Timothy's wrists, and the sound of Diana's hysterics, accompanied the dulcet tones of DI Sam Cambridge reading Timothy Starr his rights.

CHAPTER TWENTY-TWO

"Well, I don't know about you, but that was the most eventful fundraiser I can remember for quite some time," said Des, after Timothy had been marched away and the activities had finally begun.

"I have to say, I wasn't sure who the murderer was for ages," said Megan, "but when I began to think of the dates and times of the murders, and I remembered Diana telling me that Timothy's asthma was aggravated by breathing in cold air, it just started to all come together. His asthma flare-ups seemed to coincide with the murders, which all took place in the early hours when the air was cold.

"You know, when we went to the police station and explained everything to the Detective Inspector, I was convinced he was going to throw us out, but when he saw the receipt from the club for the drinks, and the car park ticket, he knew we were onto something."

"And then, when we read the music academy's newsletter, and saw that Victor Canning had been invited back to judge, we knew that Timothy would be really concerned about it because of what had happened in the past, and because he was so stressed about Bailey getting a scholarship," said Des. "It had us racking our brains, didn't it, love?"

Megan nodded. "It was the DNA match that clinched it, though. That jacket came in handy in more ways than one."

"Here," said Des, "did you see Sandra Grayling's lips when she found out Bailey and Caroline had had a child out of wedlock? They pursed so much it looked like there was a cat's rear end under her nose." He chuckled to himself.

"I feel so sorry for Diana and Bailey," said Sylvie. "There's going to be an empty chair at their table for a long time. Regardless of what Timothy did, he's still part of their family, and they're going to miss him terribly. Makes you feel lucky to have your family around you." She gathered Des and Megan up in a hug.

Des nodded. "I agree, it's not their fault, but it serves Timothy right. What did he expect was going to happen after murdering three people? He should have thought about the consequences before he went off on his killing spree."

As Caroline Gibbs walked past with her daughter in the pushchair, Sylvie tapped her on the arm and smiled. "That's an adorable baby you have."

"Thank you," said Caroline. "Bailey and I love her to bits – she's an absolute joy. And I'm so thrilled we don't have to skulk around any more, although I wish the circumstances were different. I'm taking her to spend the rest of the day with her grandma. I hope Carley will be a comfort to Diana. She's going to need it."

"I don't doubt it," agreed Sylvie. "And, before you go, I owe you an apology."

"An apology?" said Caroline. "What for?"

Sylvie wafted a handkerchief in front of her pink cheeks. "Because I was one of those villagers who believed the rumours about you and Adrian, and I shouldn't have. I'm sorry. I really am."

Caroline's tired face lit up with a smile. "Thank you. I appreciate it. I knew that everyone was talking about Adrian and me, but we couldn't put a stop to the rumours because we didn't want anyone to know that Bailey was Carley's dad. The only people who knew the truth were me, him, Adrian, and Natalie. And Tony knew, too – God bless him. He was a sweetie, that guy."

She touched her fingers to the pendant around her neck; half a gold heart with the letters 'CAR', engraved on it. "We even had to be careful about these. The name Carley is Bailey's and my name combined, you see. When she was born, Bailey and I both wanted to get a pendant with her full name engraved on it but we knew that would give the secret away, so I had half of it on mine, and he had the other half on his. We knew we'd be together one day, so we'll get new ones now,

with her full name on them. It's about time."
She sighed. "Anyway, I'd better get going.
Thanks again."

ooooooo

"I think that's everything." Des brushed
his palms together and put his hands on his
hips after squeezing his fold-up table into the
boot of Megan's car. "You sure you don't mind
giving us a lift home? It's not far for us to walk.
I'm sure I'll be able to carry that table if Sylv
takes all the plates."

"Don't be daft," said Megan. "It'll take
me two minutes. I'm hardly going to let you
struggle, am I? Are you ready to go?"

"Uh-oh," said Des. "Don't look now but
DI Cambridge is back, and he's making a
beeline for you. Wonder what he wants?"

Megan turned to see the wiry-framed
detective approaching, and sighed. "I've got a
good idea."

"Miss Fallon, I'd like a word with you,
before you disappear, if you don't mind." Sam
stood in Megan's path, feet apart and arms
crossed over his chest.

She nodded. She'd guessed this was
coming. Even though she and Des had helped
the police with their enquiries, it wouldn't
surprise her if someone had complained about
them asking questions, and Des taking notes.
Either way, she'd been expecting a telling-off
from the Detective Inspector.

"It's okay." She threw her keys to Des. "You and Sylvie get in the car. I'll be there in a minute."

"You sure?" Reluctant to leave, Des eyed the detective with suspicion.

"I'm sure. Go on. I won't be long." She looked at the grass and steeled herself for a lecture.

"It's my daughter's birthday in November," said Sam.

Megan looked up. "Huh?"

"Zoe. My daughter. She'll be eighteen."

"Er, okay. And you're telling me that, because?"

"Because I heard some very good things about that shindig you threw for your parents," said Sam. "I've become quite friendly with Olivia and Rob from the village shop since I've been here, and they said it was one of the best parties they've ever been to. 'Classy but relaxed', is how they described it. Now, I don't know what your plans are but me and Jillian – that's my wife – would love to give Zoe a really special party, but with the hours we work, organising something ourselves is going to be nigh on impossible."

The beginning of a smile curved Megan's lips. "So you're asking *me* to do it?"

"Well, I don't know what your plans are but if you're planning on staying around until then, would you consider it?" asked Sam. "You can have a think about it, if you like, and let me know. Obviously, we'd pay you whatever the going rate is, providing the going rate's not too exorbitant, that is. Zoe's my princess, but I don't have a king's budget, if you know what I mean."

Megan remembered what Natalie had said the first time she'd met her.

If you feel like branching out and earning a little money while you're here...

She'd never really thought it a possibility in Bliss Bay but why couldn't it be? If she could organise huge corporate events, why shouldn't she be able to organise parties on a smaller scale? She'd already done it once.

She nodded. "Okay, thanks. I'll give it some thought." She looked back at him as she walked to the car. "You caught me totally unawares – that isn't at all what I expected you wanted to talk to me about."

"Oh? And what *did* you expect I wanted to talk to you about?"

Megan laughed as she settled herself in the driver's seat. "Never mind, DI Cambridge," she called out of the window. "Some things are best left unsaid. I'll be in touch."

CHAPTER TWENTY-THREE

Megan strode through the village, all the way to the end of the high street to the Hearts and Minds charity shop. She'd intended to get together with Petal's eldest daughter, Daisy, for lunch ever since she'd come back to Bliss Bay but what with the small matter of a multiple-murderer on the loose, they hadn't got round to arranging a date until now.

She pushed open the gleaming navy-blue door with its polished brass fittings, and a bell bing-bonged to announce her arrival.

A pink-faced woman poked her head out from the stock room. "Won't be a tick," she said. "Please feel free to browse."

As Megan looked through the racks, it occurred to her what a good eye for design Daisy had. She'd done such a good job of dressing the window to make the shop look appealing to passing customers, many of them didn't even realise they were in a charity shop until they saw the price tags. Unlike some shops that sold second-hand clothes, every item was laundered and pressed before being hung on a padded hanger.

The pink-faced woman reappeared. "'Scuse me," she said. "Are you Megan?"

"I am. I've got a lunch date with Daisy."

Pink-face gave her a dubious smile. "Erm, I'm not sure she'll be able to make it.

She's out the back, and she asked if you can go through.

In the stock room, a flustered Daisy Montgomery sat among a mountain of bags filled with other people's unwanted clothes, and looked as though she might burst into tears.

"Megan, I'm so sorry. I should have called you but it went right out of my head. I won't be able to make lunch today. Maybe next week?"

Megan nodded. "Okay, don't worry. Is everything okay?"

Daisy ruffled her jet-black hair and dragged her hands down her face. "The Area Manager's been in to tell us that a woman from head office is coming in on Tuesday morning, so he wants the entire shop tidied up before then." She waved a hand around the stock room. "I mean, look at this place," she said, her voice verging on ultrasonic.

"There must be fifty bags of clothes to sort through. And Andrea and Wendy have got that virus that's going around, so how on earth he thinks it's all going to get sorted, cleaned, ironed, and put on the racks by Tuesday with just me and Mandy working, I don't know." She clasped her hands together. "I don't suppose you'd be able to help me sort through some bags, would you?" Her request was more a plea than a question.

Megan put an arm around Daisy's shoulder. "Of course I'll help. Look, don't panic. Nothing's unsolvable, y'know." She took off her jacket and pulled up a chair. "Right. What do I have to do?"

Daisy heaved a sigh of relief. "Thank you *so* much – you're a lifesaver." She shoved a pile of assorted sacks in Megan's direction. "Right, we need to sort everything into five piles: men's, women's, children's, footwear, and rubbish. I know a lot of the people who donate, and most of the stuff they bring in is good, but some people only bring stuff that's fit to be thrown out because they're too lazy to get rid of it themselves. Oh, you might want to put on a pair of these." She passed over a box of latex gloves. "Just in case some of the clothes are a bit grubby."

"Delightful." Megan screwed up her nose before pulling on a pair of gloves and digging a tentative hand into a bag.

"So, how are you?" said Daisy. "Are you enjoying being back?"

"I am, actually. Much more than I thought I would. Especially now that all that murder business has been resolved, but I'm sure we could have *all* done without that. Ooh, this is lovely." Megan held up an expensive-looking dress in a shimmery, turquoise fabric and looked at the label. "Designer, by the look of it." She put it into a pile and continued sorting through the bag.

"Have you told Evie about the break-in and the murders?" asked Daisy.

Megan shook her head. "No way. The last thing I want is for her to be worrying about what's going on with me. And she *would* worry because she's so protective. Which is lovely, of course, but totally not her job. If her dad wants to tell her what's been going on, that's up to him, but I'm not saying a word."

She pulled a pair of black quilted trousers from the bag and held them out in front of her. "Now, these are *really* nice – unusual, too. If they were two sizes bigger, I'd buy them for myself. Oh, wait, they're torn on the front here." She held them up for Daisy to see. "There's no way that could be mended without it showing. It wouldn't be so noticeable if there was just one tear, but there are four. Never mind. Shall I put them in the rubbish pile?"

They carried on sorting until Daisy's colleague stuck her head around the door four hours later. "Just to let you know, it's five o'clock. I'd stay, but I've got to take my little one to karate. Are you going to carry on and let yourselves out when you've finished, or are you stopping now?"

Daisy rotated her neck and stretched her back. "Definitely stopping now. And, unless you've got other plans, Megan, you're coming home with me and I'm cooking you dinner. It's the least I can do to say thank you for helping us out."

Megan was already pulling off her gloves and pulling on her jacket. "No thanks necessary, but dinner sounds wonderful, thank you." She smiled and linked her arm through Daisy's. "Lead the way, and I'll be right behind you."

ooooooo

At The Duck Inn, Megan and Petal were enjoying a long-overdue Sunday lunch in the autumn sunshine.

"Thanks for giving Daisy a hand in the shop the other day. You've got a fan for life."

"Ah, it was nothing," said Megan. "Anyone would have done the same. I'm just glad it helped her out. She's such a lovely girl, and she reminds me a little of Evie." She blinked a couple of times. "You're very lucky to have her here with you. And Blossom too."

Petal nodded. "I know. They're great kids." She took off her sunglasses and waved her empty ginger ale bottle at a passing member of bar staff. "Can I have another one of these, please?"

Megan leaned back in her chair and closed her eyes. "You should suggest to Lionel that he goes out with his friends more often. This is lovely, you and I spending a full day

together – I never had much time for
socialising before I came back to Bliss Bay."

"Yeah, it's nice, isn't it? I love Sundays."
Petal yawned and stretched her arms above
her head. "Particularly Sundays when someone
else cooks for me."

"Did you say that Blossom and Daisy
have gone to a party?"

"Yeah. Well, they've gone for a pizza.
They've each got a friend in the same family
and one of them has a birthday today. I love it
when they spend time together. Apart from me
not having to worry about them so much, it's
good that they hang out with each other. Even
though there are four years between them,
they've always been close."

"Long may it continue," said Megan. "I
missed out on doing loads of things with Lizzie
because I got married so young. Not that I
begrudge it, mind you, because I wouldn't have
Evie otherwise, but while I was changing
nappies and taking a crash course in
motherhood, most girls my age were having
the time of their lives, doing the things that
teenagers do. You must remember what it was
like? You, Lizzie, and Mum used to come
round and keep an eye on Evie enough times
so I could grab half an hour's sleep here and
there."

"I do," said Petal. "We *had* to help – you wouldn't have got any rest otherwise, would you? I don't recall Laurence being much help."

"Huh. You're right about that. He used to pick Evie up until she started crying, and then he'd put her down and disappear. He even moved into the spare bedroom until she was two so I didn't wake him when I got up to see to her during the night."

Petal clicked her tongue. "Honestly, that guy is such a pig. Thank goodness he's out of your life now. I can't think of a more suitable partner for him than Kelly. They're a perfect match. By the way, have you thought any more about what you're going to do? About staying on here, I mean."

Megan shrugged. "I don't know. I've already been here far longer than I'd planned because I slipped back into village life so easily. I really should be looking for another job but I'm not sure what I want to do. Or where I want to do it. I told you that DI Cambridge asked me if I'd arrange his daughter's birthday party in November, didn't I, so I'm definitely staying until then. After that, who knows?"

She looked out across the village green which was playing host to picnickers, sunbathers and people relaxing with the Sunday newspapers. This was the Bliss Bay she loved.

On the other side of the green, Tabastion jumped onto the wall outside Kismet Cottage, the family home she'd fallen back in love with over the past few weeks. As she watched the silver tabby washing his paws, she felt a small tug at her heart.

She was going to have to make a decision soon.

"Well, it would be fab if you stayed," said Petal. "You know we'd love to have you back permanently." She took the drink the server brought to the table and changed the subject. "Shame about Jack Windsor," she said, refilling her glass.

"Why? What's happened to him?"

"Nothing's happened to him. I just meant it's a shame he left. He was a lovely guy, wasn't he? I thought something might have come of that. You and him, I mean."

"Me and Jack? No way," said Megan, shaking her head. "I've already told you I wasn't interested in him. I mean, he's nice but I remember only too well what he was like when we were young. He was forever bumping into someone, or falling over something, or tripping up, or dropping something. Clumsy doesn't even *begin* to describe him. You must remember, surely?"

She shook her head again, with more conviction. "No, I definitely didn't see a future with Jack Windsor. Friendship, yes, romance, definitely not. He was a nightmare. And, anyway, I'm not looking for a relationship. And even if I was, I doubt he'd have been interested. Huh! Me and Jack! No way."

"Wow! Me thinks the lady doth protest too much." Petal grinned. "I told you, didn't I, that he told Lionel he thought you were fabulous? He said he really enjoyed your company."

Megan felt her cheeks flush. Since the nosedive in her confidence after the divorce, she felt awkward every time someone paid her a compliment. "For goodness' sake. We saw each other a couple of times while he was here. We were just friends. No hand holding, no smooching, and certainly nothing else."

Petal held up a hand. "Okay, okay, you don't have to explain to me, lovie. I'm just saying I think it's a shame he's not around any more. He had a nice way about him, didn't he?" She cocked an ear to the sound of the radio drifting out from inside the pub. "Ooh, shush a minute, it's that quiz I've been listening to for the past few weeks. It's the semi-final today."

The radio DJ's voice crackled over the speaker.

"Susie and Dale from the Copley Bakers, here comes your first question. In which year was the film, Pride and Prejudice, released? Was it 2004, 2005 or 2006? You've

got ten seconds to confer and give me your answer. Time starts now."

A buzzer sounded signalling the end of the ten seconds. "*We think it's 2004,*" said a contestant named Susie.

"No, it isn't," said Megan. "It's 2005."

Petal stared at her. "How on earth did you remember that? I'm rubbish with dates."

"I have absolutely no idea," said Megan, with a puzzled frown. "It just came out. Must have been hiding in my subconscious, but I don't know how it got there."

"*You say 2004, Susie?*" said the DJ. "*Well, let's see if you're right. Is the answer 2004?*"

A loud noise, like someone blowing a raspberry, sounded over the speaker.

"*Ohhh, so sorry, Susie and Dale, the answer is* **2005**. *Pride and Prejudice was released in 2005. Don't worry, though, you have four questions left, so plenty of chances to put right the wrong. Okay, question number two...*"

ooooooo

Back at Kismet Cottage after lunch, Tabastion wandered into the kitchen, stopping to lap from his water bowl before rubbing up against Megan's ankles and padding into the living room.

"Sorry I've been gone so long, puss, but I could see you were doing alright without me."

She chattered away to the tabby as she kicked off her shoes and ran upstairs to change into her pyjamas. "Aaah, that's better." Flinging herself onto the couch, she felt down the side of the cushion for the TV remote. Her large lunch in the sunshine was starting to make her feel sleepy, so she had nothing more taxing than watching TV planned for the rest of the evening. Stretching out, she flicked through the channels, her gaze wandering to Tabastion as he ambled towards her from his bed in the corner of the room.

She pushed herself up on her elbow. "You need a new bell on that collar, Tab. I've never noticed before that it doesn't actually ring – it's more of a clunk."

The cat jumped up on the couch, the bell around his neck barely registering a sound.

"There's no point in a handsome kitty like you having a bell that doesn't jangle," said Megan. "I'll make a note to buy you a new one tomorrow. She took her notebook from the coffee table. "Buy new bell," she said as she wrote a reminder on a clean page.

She stretched out again and carried on looking for something to watch. "Ooh, look, Tab, it's *Pride and Prejudice*. That's a coincidence after that quiz question."

It wasn't until she settled back to enjoy the film that something started to bother her.

It was nothing she could even put her finger on, but it was definitely something. As she tried to figure out what it was, her eyelids dropped and she fell asleep.

Twenty minutes later, her phone beeping woke her up. She scrabbled for it, smiling when she saw it was Evie on Skype.

"Hello darling. How are you?"

"I'm good, Mum. We've just got back from a midnight showing of Little Dorrit – you know how much I love that story – so it's pretty late here, or early, depending on which way you look at it. Anyway, how's things? I don't expect there's much news, is there? Bliss Bay is always so deathly quiet."

"*Deathly* quiet is one way of putting it," said Megan, keen to change the subject. "You know, I just realised that Tabastion's bell doesn't jangle, it just sort of clunks. Look." She held her phone in front of the cat and flicked the bell with her finger.

"Maybe the thingy inside the bell that makes the noise has worn out over the years," said Evie. "You said he's a stray that's been coming around for ages, didn't you?"

Megan nodded. "Hmm, I guess that must be why. I'll get him a new bell tomorrow morning."

"Well, I hope he doesn't sneak up on any poor unsuspecting birds before then," said Evie. "You'll freak out if he brings you a present to the back door. That's what some cats do, y'know. And sometimes they don't even kill their prey, so you might have to deal with something that's only half-dead."

"Yikes, I hadn't thought of that," said Megan. "Although he hasn't stalked anything so far, so hopefully he won't start tonight."

They chatted for a while longer before promising to speak again soon. As Megan stroked Tabastion with her foot, he lifted his head and opened his mouth in a wide yawn, giving her the benefit of a close-up of his needle-sharp teeth.

With Evie's warning ringing in her ears, she dashed upstairs to change back into her shorts. It was unlikely to happen, but now the thought of Tab bringing back dead birds and dropping them on the doormat was in her head, she couldn't stop thinking about it.

She grabbed her purse and ran down to the shop. Fifteen minutes later, she was back with a new collar with a bell that jingled when she gave it a gentle shake.

"It's about time you had a smart, new collar, Tab. You must have had that one from a kitten – I can see how every hole's been used as you've grown. Thank goodness you found your way to Mrs Kozlowski, because she obviously took good care of you."

She unfastened the old collar from his neck. "Wow, that's heavy." She weighed up the collar in the palm of her hand. "What on earth is inside that bell? Rocks?" She tossed it to one side and replaced it with the new one. "There. You look very dapper." She ruffled Tabastion's fur and went to make a cup of coffee before settling down to watch what was left of *Pride and Prejudice*.

In the commercial break, she plumped up her cushions and the old collar she'd tossed to one side fell off the couch. *This bell is ridiculously heavy for a cat bell,* she thought. She took it into the kitchen and hunted in the odds and ends drawer for something with which to prise it open.

"This'll do," she said, finding a box of mini-screwdrivers and putting one inside the bell and wiggling it about to open it. She shook the bell and her jaw dropped when a sparkling blue stone fell out from inside and trundled slowly across the kitchen table before coming to a stop.

Her eyes grew wide. "Wow! Tab! Look what you've been carrying around with you."

Casting her mind back to what DI Cambridge had told her about Tabastion's original collar which had gone missing when he was stolen, she recalled it was black velvet decorated with twenty sapphires, and a large spherical jewel hanging from the front.

The collar she'd just taken off Tab wasn't black velvet, and the twenty sapphires were nowhere to be seen, but this had to be the large spherical sapphire DI Cambridge had told her about.

Who had put it inside Tabastion's bell?

Megan picked up her phone and scrolled through it for Sam Cambridge's number. She dialled, then hung up. The detective had left Bliss Bay after Timothy Starr's arrest, and would be back in his own neighbourhood now.

Drumming her fingers against her knee, she thought about her predicament until a solution came to her.

PC Denby.

DI Cambridge had said he'd been involved in trying to find Tabastion too. She dialled the police station and hoped it would divert to him. It might be Sunday, but this was important.

As Fred Denby answered, Megan hoped he would think so, too.

ooooooo

The first thing Fred Denby had done after hearing Megan's story was call Sam.

As they waited for him to arrive, Megan paced the floor, unable to relax. With her mind racing, a thought occurred to her. Had the intruder who'd broken into the cottage really been interested in robbing the house, or had their only interest been Tabastion. Or rather, what was hanging from his collar?

That being the case, who would have known about it?

She jumped when the doorbell rang. "Sorry to disturb you on a Sunday," she said, stepping aside to let the detective in.

Sam shook his head. "Don't worry about it. If this is going to help solve this case, it's worth it. Where's the sapphire? Evening, Fred."

Megan led him into the kitchen and pointed to the brilliant blue stone in the middle of the table. "I haven't touched it – I thought my fingers might smudge any prints that are already on there."

"Wise move." said Sam.

"It's a corker of a stone, guv," said Fred. "I feel quite privileged to have finally seen one of the missing sapphires after all these years."

"Yes, it's a stunner, isn't it? Must be worth a fortune." Sam examined the stone from every angle before picking it up with a gloved hand and dropping it into an evidence bag.

"You know," said Megan, "you'll probably think I'm over-reacting but I was wondering if the person who broke-in could have been after the sapphire. What d'you think?"

Sam nodded. "Quite possibly. The question is, who would have known where it was? Until you found it today, no one – except the person who put it inside the bell – knew it was there, so if the intruder really *was* after the sapphire, who was it, and what are they doing in Bliss Bay?"

He put the evidence bag containing the sapphire into his jacket pocket. "If you make any more discoveries," he said, with a wry smile, "you can call me direct."

ooooooo

Megan's thoughts were far too preoccupied to watch TV, so she took herself off to bed, where she sat bolt upright, unable to sleep.

She'd told Lizzie, Shaun, Des, Sylvie, and Petal about Tabastion's history, but no one else. Was it possible that any of them could have spoken about it in front of anyone who might have known about the sapphire?

She lay back on her pillow. Seeing as Tabastion had been wandering around the neighbourhood for years without anyone bothering him, why had someone only recently tried to get their hands on his collar? And who was it?

She thought about the sapphire bracelet Olivia had worn to her parents' vow renewal celebration. Could it really have been her who'd stolen Tabastion and his precious collar?

Megan had put the idea from her mind after her conversation with Lizzie, but it was creeping back in again. She tried to keep it out. She didn't want to think that Olivia was a cat napper.

Olivia was the lovely woman from the village shop who gave her goodies. Olivia was her mum's friend.

She sighed and pulled the duvet over her head.

With her thoughts swirling round and round, she eventually fell asleep.

oooooooo

She woke with a start to the buzz of her alarm. All night long, her restless sleep had been filled with dreams of sapphires, silver tabbies, and masked cat snatchers.

She ran downstairs and put on a jug of her favourite coffee as Tabastion purred around her ankles, accompanied by the tinkling of his new bell.

Switching on the TV, she sat at the kitchen table to watch the news. "Same old, same old," she said to the tabby, as made himself comfortable on the floor beside her.

She changed channels when a report about abandoned pets came on. She couldn't bear to see animals in distress. "I hope you know we'll never hurt you, Tab," she said, scratching him between the ears and sipping her coffee with a scowl. "I'd love to know who it was who took you from your first home. I'd like to give them a piece of my mind."

She lifted Tab onto her lap and made a fuss of him. "I wish you understood what I was saying." She smiled as she remembered how Tabastion had propelled himself out of the apple tree, sending Laurence on his way with a few holes in his shirt and a very dented ego. "Although, it seems like you're a pretty good judge of character so you probably *do* understand." She turned her attention back to the TV and her coffee.

A minute passed before her brain started ticking over again. She frowned. *What if Tab really **is** a good judge of character?*

The implications of her words suddenly hit her like a brick, along with the theory which had just popped into her head and was refusing to go away.

She knew nothing about the film *Pride and Prejudice* but, all at once, she knew why the quiz question had triggered the memory that had enabled her to recall the year of its release.

If her recollection was accurate, and her hunch was right, the identity of Tab's abductor and the fate of the twenty missing sapphires could have been right in front of her all along.

She tapped her finger against her chin and thought back to what DI Cambridge had told her about Tab's abduction.

He said he'd gone missing from his owner's front garden and had never been seen in the area again. The motive for his disappearance was thought to have been the theft of his sapphire collar, worth thousands.

At the time, the police thought his abductor had probably let him loose shortly after they'd snatched him. That being the case, was his re-emergence in Bliss Bay because he'd simply found his way to the village by chance, or was it because whoever had stolen him had brought him back to Bliss Bay with them?

Tabastion rolled onto his back and stretched out all four legs. As Megan watched his paws flex and relax, her eyes were drawn to his claws. Four very sharp claws on each foot.

"Of course!" she said, as a thought wheedled its way into her head. "That's it! It has to be!" She peered closely at Tab. It was a long shot but, if nothing else, she'd learned a little about the transfer of DNA from object to object during the murder investigations, and she wasn't about to ignore her instincts.

She swiped through the contact list on her phone until she found the person she wanted to speak to. It was a little early to be making social calls but this was important.

"Hi, Daisy, it's Megan. Sorry to call so early. Yes, fine thanks. Look, this might seem like a strange question but do you remember the quilted trousers I showed you when we were sorting through the clothes at the shop last week? The ones that were ripped? They had four long tears on one of the legs – do you remember? I don't suppose you know who brought them in, do you? I mean, I know I'm probably asking an impossible question but you said you knew a lot of the people who donate to the shop and I wondered if you'd know who brought those trousers in? You *do*? Daisy, you're a diamond. Who was it?"

She ended the call. Her theory was right, she was sure of it now. And, even better, Daisy still had the trousers in a bag, waiting for the recycling truck to collect them.

She dialled another number. This time she was calling DI Cambridge direct, as he'd suggested.

"Oh, hi again. It's Megan Fallon here. About Tabastion... I wondered if you remember whether his owner had a carer? Did she really? In that case, I think I know who took Tabastion, and what happened to the sapphires."

ooooooo

Megan grabbed her bag and set off for the Hearts and Minds charity shop.

DI Cambridge had listened to her theory, asked if she could pick up the trousers, and then wait for him. He had a meeting to get to, but he said he'd come straight over afterwards to collect them, and take a full statement from her.

He'd been rather non-committal when she'd told him her thoughts, but she figured he wouldn't be jumping in his car and driving all the way over if he didn't have at least a little faith that what she'd told him could be true.

She gave Tabastion an extra fuss as he sat in his usual spot on the wall, sphinx-like and silent. "I'll see you later, Tab. With some good news, I hope."

Despite the fact that it was only just five minutes past opening time, the charity shop was already heaving with customers browsing through the racks of clothes.

"Hi Megan." Daisy gave her a hug and handed over a bag containing the ripped trousers. "Dare I ask why you want these?"

"I can't say just yet but if I'm right about something, you'll probably find out soon. And if I'm not, I'll look like a complete idiot and bring them back. I'd better be off. Be seeing you – and thanks again."

She checked her watch. She had at least another couple of hours before DI Cambridge arrived, so she headed for The Cobbles for a coffee and a chat with Petal.

oooooooo

"What are you up to today?" Petal called over to the café where Megan was sharing a table with Dora Pickles.

"Oh, you know, this and that, nothing special," said Megan, sipping through the froth on her caramel coffee. She would have loved to tell Petal what was going on, but she knew she couldn't say anything. Even though she was convinced that what she thought was true, there was no proof.

"And what about you, Dora?" said Petal. "You got any plans for today?"

Dora nodded as she wiped a moustache of foam from her top lip and settled her dentures. "Archie and I are going to book a holiday. We thought it was high time we went abroad, but we've no idea where. We're going to the travel agent's this afternoon to look through some brochures."

"Ooh, you lucky things!" said Petal. "You'll have to come back and let me know where you decide on. You're the second person since Saturday to tell me they're going on holiday."

"Am I?" asked Dora. "Who's the other person?"

"Natalie Castle," said Petal, filling a stand with sacks of compost. "She's back at Castle Manor now but she's got a lot on her plate at the moment, so she's getting away for a couple of weeks."

"Oh," said Megan. "Where's she going?"

"Portugal. Today."

Megan spluttered as her coffee went down the wrong way. "*Today*? When? Do you know?"

"I'm not sure exactly but she said she wanted to leave for the airport quite early. Her flight's not until five but she said she'd rather get there too early than too late. I think she'll probably while away a couple of hours doing some airport shopping."

Megan grabbed her bags, put some money on the table, and downed the remainder of her coffee in one.

"That's for mine and Dora's coffees," she called to Lionel. "It's been lovely chatting, Dora. I'll see you soon. I've got to go, Petal, but I'll probably be in tomorrow."

"Blimey, where's the fire?" said Petal.

Megan grinned. "I'll tell you tomorrow."

ooooooo

She dialled Sam Cambridge's direct line and went straight through to his answerphone. *Damn, he must still be in his meeting.* She tried again and got the same message.

She called the police station, hoping to speak to Fred Denby, but was told he'd gone to help retrieve a resident's cat that had climbed up the old, village green oak tree, and was too scared to come down.

Des. That was it. He'd be able to help.

ooooooo

Megan could hear Des cursing at the top of his voice before Sylvie had even opened the front door.

"What's going on?"

Sylvie rolled her eyes. "He's just broken a tooth on a piece of crusty bread. As you can hear, he's not in the best of moods, but go through and talk to him while I try to get an emergency appointment at the dentist, will you?"

Megan poked her head around the kitchen door. "You alright, Uncle Des?"

"No, I'm bloody well not." Des put a hand to his jaw and scowled. "Damn bread." He glared at her. "What d'you want, anyway?"

Megan quickly explained the situation. "Seeing as I can't get hold of anyone, I wondered if you'd be able to call PC Denby, tell him what I've told you, and ask him to let DI Cambridge know? I'm supposed to be waiting for him at Kismet to give him the trousers, but I didn't know Natalie was going away. If I don't get over there soon and try to delay her, she might leave for the airport."

She looked at her uncle's miserable face. "I didn't know you'd be feeling so rough, though. Do you think you'd be able to try to get hold of him, please? And tell him what I've told you? D'you feel up to it?"

Des took his notepad from his top pocket and prodded it repeatedly with his index finger. "Just write the flippin' numbers down for me, and I'll see if I can speak to someone," he grumbled. "Damn tooth."

CHAPTER TWENTY-FOUR

Megan pressed the button on the intercom outside the gates at Castle Manor. "Oh, hi, it's Megan Fallon here. Sorry to bother you. Have you got a minute?"

A buzzer sounded and she walked through the gates, up the drive to the front door, which was opened before she reached it.

"This is a surprise," said Natalie, standing aside to let her in. She smirked. "I hear I missed quite a treat at the fundraiser? I would have loved to have heard old Timmy confess, but I had better things to do than spend my afternoon at a boring WA event."

Megan followed her as she sashayed into the living room. "Oh my goodness! What's happened?"

Every single picture of Adrian had been removed, leaving the walls and surfaces practically bare.

"What's happened is that Adrian's moved out. He's at his mum and dad's. I've told him I want a divorce."

"Oh. I'm sorry. I had no idea."

Natalie shrugged. "Why would you? It's not common knowledge. In any case, it's his loss. What are you doing here, anyway?"

"What? Oh, I was just passing and I thought I'd pop in and say hello." Megan looked around the room, which seemed to echo with so few photos in it. Her eyes fell on two pink suitcases by the door and she feigned surprise. "Are you going somewhere?"

"Yeah. Portugal. I've got a taxi picking me up at eleven-thirty. I need a change of scene for a while – I've had this place up to here. And Adrian's gone soft in the head since Tony died. I thought he'd be over it by now but goodness only knows how long he's going to be snivelling about it. *And* he went mad when the credit card bill arrived last week. He told me he'd been meaning to speak to me about my spending for a while, but there'd been too much going on. He said I had to cut back – can you believe it? Told me I could only spend £2,000 per month." Natalie's eyes almost rolled back in her head.

"He has absolutely no idea what things cost: manicures, pedicures, hairdressers, clothes, shoes, makeup, lunch with the girls, Champagne, Prosecco. It all adds up, you know. Anyway, I told him to shove it, and he burst into tears. He's a grown man, and he was boo-hooing like a baby – what a total turn-off. When I asked him what was wrong, he said he hadn't been himself since Tony died and he asked me if I could bear with him until he's feeling better. Er, hello? I don't think so. I've already done enough waiting around for him to get back on form.

"The Adrian Castle I fell in love with was fearless and strong, not some wimp. I could deal with him when he was injured, I could deal with his mood swings and his grumbling, and I could even deal with him being upset right after Tony died, but I can't deal with him *still* blubbing like a little kid. No thank you very much. I mean, how long did he expect me to put up with it? It's been ages." She blew out an impatient breath through her nose. "So *I'm* staying here till things are sorted out, and he's with his parents. And, come the day, he'd better make sure I get my share, or he'll be sorry."

She wound a strand of hair around her finger, sat down on the couch and crossed her long legs. "So, what's going on with you?"

Any sympathy Megan had felt disappeared as soon as Natalie spoke about Adrian with such contempt. Her lack of sympathy and empathy for her husband made Megan furious. Coupled with the fact that she was 99% sure Natalie was the person who'd taken Tabastion from a loving home when he was just a kitten, she wasn't in the mood to hold back, even though the sole purpose of her visit was simply to delay her until the police arrived.

"I wanted to ask you something."

"Ask away," said Natalie, picking up an emery board and smoothing out a jagged nail.

"Those two photographs of you, over there." Megan pointed to the table in the corner of the room.

"What about them?"

"You've had some cosmetic surgery?"

"Yeah. So what?"

"The one of you outside the cinema at the premiere of *Pride and Prejudice* was taken in 2005? Is that right?"

Natalie shrugged. "If you say so. I can't remember. I used to go to lots of film premieres. You meet lots of rich men there, you know."

"The amount of surgery you had doesn't come cheap."

"No, you're right, it doesn't. That's why Adrian paid for it."

"Ah, right," said Megan. "Thing is, you hadn't met him in 2005 and you told me you were virtually broke before you got together."

Natalie's face clouded with confusion. "What are you talking about? Of course I'd met him."

Megan shook her head. "No, you hadn't. You didn't meet him until 2006. You told me when I first met you in Petal's flower shop. If you need reminding, though, just look it up. It's on every internet site about Adrian – and there are a lot of them."

Natalie's cheeks flushed. "Oh, that's right, silly me. I meant Adrian paid for some surgery *after* we got together, and I paid for some myself before I met him with some money I won on a scratch card." She barely missed a beat as the words spilled from her lips, although her glare was steely. "Look, I don't know what you're getting at, but I've never made any secret of the fact that I've had surgery. Why are you so interested, anyway?"

As Megan opened her mouth to answer, the doorbell rang.

A minute later, Natalie came back into the living room with Sam Cambridge and Fred Denby in tow. "The police are looking for you, Megan," she said, smugly. "I do hope you're not in trouble."

Sam acknowledged Megan with a nod and two raised eyebrows. "Miss Fallon. I was hoping to find you here. Are we interrupting?"

"Not at all," said Megan. "I was just talking to Natalie about her cosmetic surgery." She pointed to the photographs on the table. "It's amazing, isn't it?"

Sam and Fred examined the photos. "It certainly is. Never fails to amaze me what a difference a few nips and tucks can make," said Sam.

"The photograph of you and those women," said Megan. "I thought they were nurse's uniforms you're wearing but they're not, are they? They're carer's uniforms. The uniforms the carers from the Heathside Care Home wear."

Natalie shifted in her seat. "What is this? Why have you been checking up on me? So, I used to be a carer before I met Adrian. What's the big deal?"

Fred Denby, who had said nothing so far, chimed in. "The big deal is that when you worked for the care home, one of your clients was a Mrs Curtis, isn't that right? The DI and I both worked on the case, by the way, if you're wondering how we know about it."

Natalie opened her mouth, then shut it again. "Yes, she was one of my clients, but not for long. I left the company and someone else took over. And she was the one I was most glad to see the back of. Silly old bat and that cat of hers."

"Yes, we know you left three months before Mrs Curtis's cat was stolen. That put you well out of the picture when we were investigating his disappearance," said Sam. "You weren't even mentioned as a person of interest for questioning."

"Why would I have been?" said Natalie. "I wouldn't have stolen her cat. I can't *stand* cats. Ask Megan. When I went round to her place, Tabastion almost took my eye out when he attacked me for no reason. I was lucky not to be scarred for life."

Megan, Sam, and Fred traded glances. "How did you know the cat was called Tabastion?" said Sam.

"What? Well, Megan must have told me, obviously."

Megan shook her head. "I didn't. I didn't know that was his name until *after* you came round. I didn't know what his name was until the day someone broke into my house and tried to take his collar. And, for the record, Tab didn't attack you for no reason. He lashed out at you because you leaned over him to check his collar still had the bell on it that you hid the sapphire inside. You startled him. *And* he remembered you, I'm sure of it."

Natalie shot her another furious glare. "You need to be very careful who you start accusing, Megan. You have no idea what you're talking about. Slander is a very serious offence, as I'm sure DI Cambridge will confirm. If you didn't tell me your crazy cat's name, I must have heard it from someone else. And I don't know anything about a sapphire."

Megan nodded. "I see. So these aren't the trousers you were wearing when you broke into my parents' home?" She pulled them from the bag. "Because I expect they've got your DNA all over them, as well as Tabastion's where he lashed out and ripped them. It didn't occur to me until yesterday that it must have been his claws that tore this fabric. Four, thin tears, just like the four, thin scratches on your wrist that Tab gave you when you first came to my parents' cottage."

Natalie sat perfectly still, an impassive expression on her face. Then she jumped up from her seat. "You don't understand! How could you *possibly* understand with your perfect life, and your perfect family, and your perfect everything? I saw a chance to make something of myself and I took it. What's wrong with that?

"After I left my job at the care home, I went back and took Tabastion before moving to Bliss Bay. No one got hurt, did they? Mrs Curtis had more money than she knew what to do with, so she didn't miss those sapphires. I used most of them to pay for my surgery and to pay for six month's rent on a flat, but I kept the big one. I knew no one would think to look for it in the bell, so hanging from Tabastion's collar was the safest place for it. I couldn't let him out of my sight, though, so I had to keep him in a cage outside.

"I'd had my eye on Adrian for a while, so I wanted to be close to where he lived. Until I got together with him, that sapphire was my rainy-day fund but that damn cat got out one day and ran away. I looked for him everywhere but I couldn't find him. It killed me to think that he was mooching around somewhere with that sapphire hanging round his neck. I couldn't believe it when I saw him again at your place, Megan. As soon as I saw his manky ear, and that bell, I *knew* it was him. I had to get the sapphire back – I'd been kicking myself ever since he ran away with it. I'd already heard you and Petal talking about the stray cat that had made itself at home at your parents' place and slept halfway up the stairs, but I didn't know it was Tabastion until I saw him that day.

"That's why I broke in. If your alarm had gone off, I would have legged it, but it didn't. I never meant to hurt anyone, or steal anything of yours. I just had to get that sapphire. I thought I'd be able to take it off Tabastion's collar but he had other ideas. He went crazy.

"Ever since that day, I've been trying to think of how I could get close enough to rip the collar from his neck. I promised myself I was going to get it, if it was the last thing I did. I've been watching him, see, so I know he comes out at least once during the day to sun himself on your garden wall. Even if I had to wait outside all day for him, it would have been worth it."

"You kept him in a cage?" It took all Megan's self-control not to fly at the spoiled footballer's wife. "No wonder he freaked out when you went near him. I thought it was just a coincidence, but he really *is* a good judge of character."

"I *had* to keep him in a cage," whined Natalie. "I couldn't risk him running away, could I? I don't know why you're getting so uptight – I gave him food and water, so what's the problem?"

Megan clenched her fists and turned away, shaking her head.

"Didn't your husband ever wonder how you'd managed to pay for your cosmetic surgery before you met him?" asked Fred.

Natalie hung her head and sobbed until her false eyelashes dropped off. "I told him what I told Megan earlier – that I'd won some money on a scratch card. People do it all the time, so there was no reason for him to be suspicious." She reached for her phone. "I need to call him – he'll sort this out – he'll pay whoever, whatever needs paying to make this go away."

Sam shot her an incredulous look. "I'm afraid this is one problem that money won't solve, Mrs Castle."

As he read Natalie her rights, and Megan went on her way, it warmed her heart to know that justice had at last been served, and that Tabastion – having found his forever home at Kismet Cottage – would never have to feel threatened again.

CHAPTER TWENTY-FIVE
Four weeks later

At the village hall, the residents' meeting to object to the construction of the hypermarket was full to the rafters.

"Wow! It's standing room only – there must be three hundred people here. What a fantastic turnout! If this many people feel so strongly about it, I'm sure we must have a chance of getting the planning application overturned," Petal shouted above the chatter, as she and Megan edged through the crowds.

"I hope so." Megan blew a kiss to Des and Sylvie who'd got to the meeting early to get front row seats. "Look, there's Olivia and Rob. Let's go and stand with them."

"I think the meeting's going to be starting late," said Olivia, nodding to the po-faced woman at the front of the hall who'd just answered a call on her mobile phone.

"Who's she?" asked Megan.

"Thora Bland. She works for a couple of the parish councillors, but I don't think either of them are here yet." Olivia craned her neck to see to the back of the hall. "Nope, can't see them anywhere. Sometimes they have a chat with some of the residents before the meeting starts but they must be running late."

"I hope they're not going to be no-shows," said Petal, fanning her face.

"Well, if they think we'll all go home and forget about it because they don't turn up to a meeting, they're sadly mistaken." Rob held up his homemade placard proclaiming that there was, *No Home for a Hypermarket Here.*

"Ooh, look, I think we're going to start without them." Megan pointed to Thora Bland, who was on the stage, attempting to switch on the microphone.

"Hello. Can everyone hear me? I have an announcement to make." She cleared her throat. "I'm sorry, but the residents meeting for this evening has been postponed indefinitely." Her monotone voice relayed the information with as much animation as a recorded announcement for a delayed train. She waited for the uproar to die down.

"And I've been asked to pass on the news that the sale of the old Bliss Bay secondary school site was completed at four-thirty this afternoon. You can protest all you want, I doubt it'll do any good. The new owner is meeting with surveyors at the site tomorrow morning, and work is due to commence at the end of the month."

ooooooo

The following morning, Megan, Petal, Daisy, and Blossom made their way to the site of the old school to meet the group of residents who were assembling outside for one last time before it was razed to the ground.

Now that the deal had gone through, there was nothing they could do to stop the bulldozers from moving in, but they'd all agreed to gather in solidarity and protest their opposition to the hypermarket plans until the last brick was knocked from the school's foundations.

At the top of the small hill, Megan's faithful mini chugged into a parking space beside the school, rattled, and let out what sounded like a sigh of relief when she turned the engine off.

"Well, that was an experience," said Daisy, her eyebrows raised as she gently tipped Tabastion off her lap and shuffled out of her seat. "You must remind me to introduce you to an old friend of mine, Megan – he's called third gear. I thought we were going to start rolling back down the hill at one point."

"Yeah, I thought you were joking when you asked us all to rock backwards and forwards to make it to the top," said Blossom.

"Vinnie's old, that's all," said Megan, indignantly, as Petal giggled behind her hand. "And he's not used to carrying so many people. He does his best."

"It's a car, Megan, not a donkey," said Blossom, bending to stroke Tabastion.

"Yes, I know that. I just feel a bit protective when people criticise him. I know it's ridiculous but it's the way I am."

The Montgomery women gave her an identical eye-roll.

"Come on, Miss Oversensitive," said Petal, linking an arm through Megan's. "Let's go and find Lionel." She chuckled. "And I'm sorry to laugh, but did you see the look on his face when he overtook us on his bike and we were all rocking backwards and forwards? You've got to admit, it was pretty priceless."

Before long, her chuckle had turned into raucous laughter and all four of them were clutching their sides, tears rolling down their cheeks.

"Oh my," said Megan, wiping her eyes. "We'd better make a move. Keep up, Tabastion. We've got a protest to get to."

oooooo

Surrounded by members of the Bliss Bay Women's Association and their husbands, Des and Sylvie stood at the head of the crowd, holding up placards bearing inhospitable slogans.

"You'll never believe it, but Sylv wanted to chain herself to the school gates, suffragette style," said Des, raising his eyes.

"Yes, and I would have done, too, if you hadn't been such a fuddy-duddy," snapped Sylvie.

Petal kicked at a tuft of dry grass. "I can't believe the deal went ahead, despite all our objections. How could they ignore us like that?"

Des rubbed the pads of his thumb and fingers together in front of her face. "Money. That's what it's all about. It's a damn disgrace."

"Listen," said Megan. "Why don't we try to look on the bright side? You never know, a hypermarket might end up being an asset to Bliss Bay. It'll bring a load of jobs to the area, won't it? And people coming to shop there will probably stop and walk around the rest of the village, won't they?"

"Doubtful," said Blossom, with a doleful expression. "They'll have already bought everything they need in the hypermarket, *and* had something to eat and drink in the fancy-schmancy cafés and restaurants. Why would they want to walk around boring old Bliss Bay village afterwards?"

Megan smacked her forehead. "Because it's *not* boring! It's charming. And people love nosying around quaint villages, that's why." She raised her hands in exasperation. "Don't underestimate the value of what you have here in Bliss Bay. It's better than what some hypermarket has to offer any day."

"I doubt our shop will survive, though," said a subdued Olivia. "I mean, I'm sure people will still come to us for convenience when they run out of milk or cereal at eight o' clock in the morning, but we won't be able to survive if we become a convenience store, and nothing more."

"She's right," said Rob. "We've always been at the heart of the village. People come to us for everything from a loaf of bread to their weekly shop, but they won't once that hypermarket's built."

"And I'll tell you something else," said Lionel. "Petal and I closed the shop this morning so we could be here, but when all those new cafés and swanky florists are open, we might as well close the doors permanently. We won't be able to compete. And I don't think it'll be long before other businesses follow suit."

"Oh, come on!" said Megan. "What's happened to all of you?" She strode back and forth, gesticulating wildly. "Where's that Bliss Bay optimism? That drive and sense of purpose you all used to have? When I first came back here, you wouldn't have let *anything* get you down. Where's that fighting spirit gone? That—"

Her rallying cry was stopped in its tracks by the familiar purr of a car engine. As she strained to listen, her heart beat a little faster.

No. It can't be. Can it? Can it really be?

She couldn't keep the smile from her face as Jack Windsor's Mercedes appeared over the brow of the hill and drove into the car park.

He pulled in beside Vinnie and strolled towards them, eyes hidden behind his favourite sunglasses, hands in pockets, and whistling softly.

"Mornin' y'all. Hey! You brought Tab along." He bent and stroked Tabastion under the chin and was rewarded with an eardrum-bursting purr.

"Well, he's as much a part of this community as anyone," said Megan, a grin reaching from ear to ear at the sight of the friend she thought she'd never see again. "We couldn't *not* bring him with us. You were the last person I expected to see, though. When did you get back?"

"A couple days ago. Did you miss me?"

"Actually, I did," said Megan, catching him in a hug. "I'd just started getting used to having you around, and you upped and left. I'm really glad to see you."

"And you couldn't have picked a better time to show up," said Sylvie. "We could do with a bit of brawn to stand up to those developers. They may have won the battle but if they think we're going to let them flatten this place without a fight, they don't know us very well."

Jack chuckled and stuck his sunglasses on top of his head. "No, they sure don't."

He strode over to the wooden signpost hammered into a barren flowerbed, and which now bore a red and white flash across it announcing that the property had been 'SOLD'. Leaning forward, he grasped it and rocked it back and forth before pulling it from the ground.

"Heehee!" Sylvie chortled. "That'll show 'em." She mimicked a boxer taking down an opponent with a swift one-two.

"Er, I think we were planning a peaceful protest, Jack – you know, to state our case," said Megan. "We weren't intending to rip the place up." Her anxiety level crept up a little and she sucked in a gulp of air.

"Glad to hear it," said Jack. "I wouldn't like to fall out with anyone."

Megan's eyebrows dipped. "What are you talking about? Why would *you* fall out with anyone?"

Jack stared at her for a while. "Because this is my property. I bought it yesterday."

One hundred and ninety-seven jaws dropped open in perfect synchronisation.

"What are you talking about?"

"Well, I've been looking for somewhere to renovate for a while, so when Uncle Bill told me about the plans that a developer had to buy the school and put a hypermarket in its place, I got on the phone to the agent managing the sale. He started playing me off against the developer, though, so I knew I needed to come down and negotiate in person. Anyways, it was looking touch and go for a while but I finally signed the contract yesterday afternoon. Turns out the developer's funding hadn't come from entirely ethical sources, which gave me the advantage."

"So that's why you came back to Bliss Bay in the first place?" said Olivia. "Because you wanted to buy the school?"

Jack nodded. "And that's why I had to go away again. I didn't want to tell anyone what was going on, and I wasn't sure I'd be able to keep it a secret, so I thought it was best if I disappeared for a while. If my offer hadn't been accepted, I might not have come back, but," his lips parted in an amiable grin, "seeing as it was, I'm your new neighbour."

Des's voice broke the silence. "So you're the good-for-nothing who's going to rip the heart from the community?" His jaw squared and his fingers bunched into fists. "And I thought you were a decent man. Let's go, Sylv," he said, shaking his head, "before I do something I'll regret."

"Des, wait." Jack stepped forward but Des put up his hand and turned away.

"Save the sweet-talk for someone who's interested. Come on, Sylv."

"Ah, don't be so stupid, Des!" Bill pushed through the crowd. "Anyone'd think yeh'd lost yer senses. Fer the love o' God, man, come back an' listen t'what Jack has t'say."

"I've heard enough, thank you very much," said Des. "I'm not interested in anything *he's* got to say. And you! You can stay away from me too, Bill. You knew about this, didn't you? You didn't tell *us*, though, did you? Huh, I expect *you're* going to be alright. Once Jack's sold the site on to someone for mega bucks, you and Rita will get a cut and you'll all be laughing, I expect? You make me sick to my stomach, the lot of you."

The crowd voiced its dissent, becoming louder as indignation grew.

"Whoa, whoa, hold on a minute." Jack's calm voice spoke over the protestors. "First of all, I didn't want to ask Uncle Bill to keep any secrets from anyone, so I didn't tell him about the deal until yesterday afternoon. He didn't know anything about it before then, so you can stop blaming him right now. And second of all, I'm not knocking the school down." He leaned against the trunk of a gnarled willow tree and folded his arms. "In case anyone's interested in listening."

"I *said*, I'm not interested in anything you've got to say. And—" Des stopped wagging his finger and fiddled with his hearing aid, cupping a hand behind his ear to make sure he'd heard right. "What did you say?"

"I *said*, I'm not knocking the school down."

"But you just said you've bought it," said Des. "What else are you going to do with it? It doesn't meet with safety regulations. That's why they moved the kids out in the first place."

"Yes, I know. That's why I'm renovating it and updating everything before I move in." said Jack. "And I'll be keeping as many of the original features as I can – clock tower and bell included. It's even going to be called The Old School House. I'll be making some changes on the inside, for sure, but on the outside, I'd like to keep it looking pretty much the same as it does now. I hope you'll be happy to know I have no intention of turning it into a concrete box. It's going to be my new home."

Megan's jaw dropped again and Sylvie pushed it up with her finger.

"Why didn't you tell me?"

Jack's eyes met hers, an amused expression on his face. "Because I didn't want to say anything until it was definite. And it wasn't definite until yesterday, so I had nothing to tell. I would have—"

"So there isn't going to be a hypermarket?" said Des, interrupting and cocking an eyebrow.

"Not a hypermarket to be seen," replied Jack.

"No queues of traffic gumming up the roads and polluting the air with their fumes?" said Blossom, a smile curling her lips.

"None of that either," said Jack, with a grin.

"And no fancy-schmancy cafés or florists?" said Petal, her eyes glistening with tears of relief.

"Nope."

"So our businesses are safe?" said Olivia, her voice quivering.

Jack grinned. "Well, they are from ruthless developers and hypermarkets."

"Wahooooo!" Rob pulled him into a hug and Olivia burst into tears and flung her arms around his waist.

"Oh, Jack, I could kiss you. I can't tell you what a worry this is off my mind."

"Is that why the residents meeting was postponed yesterday?" said Megan. "Because the deal was going through?"

Jack nodded. "But like I said, I didn't want to say anything until it was certain."

"But where in the world did you get that kind of money from?" Megan wouldn't normally have dreamed of asking such a personal question but it was out of her mouth before she could check herself. Her cheeks flushed. "Sorry, it's none of my business. You don't have to answer that. It was rude of me."

"Don't worry about it." Jack smiled. "Didn't I ever tell you what a high powered executive I am?" He flexed a bicep and laughed his easy laugh. "Seriously, though, I'm actually quite successful back home. Hard work and lots of luck. Have you heard of the advertising agency, Windsor McQueen? Well, whether you have or haven't, we sold it earlier this year."

Megan gawped for the third time that morning. "Are you kidding? *You're* the Windsor in Windsor McQueen?"

"Who's Windsor McQueen?" asked Sylvie.

"Only one of the most successful advertising agencies in the world," said Megan. "It's got offices in every major city." She smacked her hands to her cheeks. "I can't believe it. I've organised team-building events for you, *and* your company Christmas party in London a couple of years ago."

Jack nodded appreciatively. "Good job. I was in London for that one – it was fabulous. I had no idea you'd organised it."

"I dealt with your assistant, Tess."

"Ah, yeah, most likely. She used to deal with stuff like that."

Megan looked him up and down. In his worn jeans with the frayed hems, his tee-shirt that had seen better days, his tousled hair and his easy manner, it occurred to her that she'd never seen a less likely high powered executive.

"But home will be here now, won't it?" said Megan.

He frowned. "I don't follow."

"You just said, "I'm actually quite successful *back home*", but if you've bought the old school, Bliss Bay will be your home now, won't it?""

"Oh, I see what you mean. Yeah, now the company's been sold, I'm selling my house in Berkshire and moving in with Uncle Bill and Aunt Rita. Then I'll oversee the renovation until it gets to a stage where I can move in." Jack fixed his eyes on Megan. "Why are you so interested, though? You're only here until you find another job, aren't you? And then I'll be losing my new best buddy. Won't I?" He didn't drop his gaze as he waited for an answer.

Megan looked around at the small crowd of people who had become so special to her over the past weeks. She'd thought a lot about extending her stay in Bliss Bay. She had a little money behind her, a roof over her head, and she was happier than she'd been in years. To cap it all, there was the prospect of working again at a job she loved, albeit on a much smaller scale. She couldn't have asked for more.

When Evie came back from New Zealand, she'd be working in Cambridge so it would make little difference to her where Megan decided to put down roots, and the fact that Laurence also lived in Bliss Bay would be a bonus for Evie; she'd have both her parents in the same village, so visiting would be easier.

Why *wouldn't* she stay?

Even the thought of her ex-husband and his awful wife weren't enough of a deterrent to dissuade her. True, they were blots on an otherwise-perfect landscape, but with the support of her family and friends, she felt she could deal with anything. Of course, ongoing, she'd have to deal with Kelly, but even that didn't seem quite as scary as it once had.

A contented purr made her look down. Tabastion was curled up at her feet and blinking his sleepy, amber eyes.

"Looks like someone wants you to hang around," said Jack, a grin on his lips.

"Oh, come on Megan. What d'you say?" Des looked hopeful. "You've got to admit, we make a cracking team. Bliss Bay could do with a pair of amateur sleuths like us. We'd give old dopey Denby and Co. a real run for their money."

Sylvie nudged him in the ribs. "Des Harper, if Megan makes the move to Bliss Bay a permanent one, the last thing she's going to want is you hanging around like a verruca." She shook her head and mouthed an apology to Megan. "Although your mum and dad would be over the moon. Not that you should do it for them, of course."

"Come on, love. Put us out of our misery," said Des. "What's it to be?"

Megan chewed her lip and put any thoughts of Laurence and Kelly from her mind. *Stuff him, and stuff her, too. I'm not running away this time. It's time I started standing up for myself.*

"Well, I want to speak to Evie and Mum and Dad first, and I'll need to go back to my place to sort out a few things but... I think I'd like to stay."

As Petal, Olivia, and Sylvie jumped on her, Des and Bill took out their harmonicas and played a little jig, and Rob pranced around in celebration. The news even coaxed another smile onto Blossom's face as Daisy crushed her in a hug.

Jack lifted Megan off the ground and swung her around. "Thank God. I thought you were going to leave me friendless and alone with all these crazy people." He winked at Aunt Sylvie who punched him on the arm.

Megan hugged him again when he put her down. "Not a chance."

She felt a jab on her shoulder, the joy draining out of her when she turned and realised that her nemesis had returned from caring for her mother and was back in the village.

She shuddered when she saw Kelly's expression. It was the same dark, hateful one that had looked back at her when she'd been crowned Carnival Queen. Laurence, on the other hand, looked positively charmed by the prospect of his ex-wife returning to Bliss Bay.

"So sorry to interrupt your fan club convention," spat Kelly, as she towered above Megan in four inch stiletto-heeled boots, her blonde hair standing up in angry spikes. "I've just got back from two very stressful months looking after my mum, so to come home and find you're moving back to the village doesn't do anything to improve my mood.

"I'm sure you'll understand why I'm not quite feeling the joy about you staying on in Bliss Bay but in case you're in any doubt about my feelings on the subject, let's get one thing clear. *I'm* Mrs Ford now, so you'd better not get any ideas about sniffing around Laurence." She waved her diamond-encrusted wedding band in front of Megan's face. "And he told me how you've been flirting with him ever since you got here, so I've got my eye on you. If you even *dream* about getting your grubby little mitts on him, you'll have me to deal with. Got it?"

Megan glanced at Laurence who was smirking over at her. "He told you *I've* been flirting with *him*?"

Kelly took a step closer, a sneer on her fluorescent-pink upper lip. "That's right. And Laurence doesn't lie."

Megan would normally have backed down but, surrounded by goodwill, she felt a rush of bravado and held her ground. "Listen, Kelly, let me put your mind at rest, once and for all. I've seen Laurence once since I've been here, and that was one time too many. If he was the last man on earth, I'd avoid him like a dose of the plague." She tried to swallow, to find her mouth was completely dry.

Kelly's eyes flashed with anger. "You'd better. I'll be watching you. It takes a lot to keep a man like Laurence happy and now I'm back, I'll be making sure he is."

From nowhere, Aunt Sylvie and Petal appeared, one at each side, like Megan's guardian angels.

"Told you. Bedroom tricks," Sylvie whispered loudly behind her hand.

"Everything alright?" asked Petal, throwing Kelly a look of sheer disdain.

"Fine, thanks. Everything's fine."

"Megan, love, we were just saying that this calls for a celebration," said Sylvie. "Petal and Lionel are going to keep the café open for a private party this evening, Des is going to whip up some goodies for eats, and I'm going to invite some of the villagers." She cast Kelly a disparaging glare. "Obviously, that invitation doesn't extend to you or that hubby of yours."

As Kelly flounced off, Sylvie beamed up at her niece and held out an arm. "You've been away from Bliss Bay for far too long, lovie. That's a lot of parties you've missed out on. How about we start making up for lost time right now? Now come on, we don't want to waste a minute more."

As Megan's shoulders relaxed, she gave a sigh and linked her arm through Sylvie's.

She was among family, and the best friends she could wish for.

She was home.

The End

I hope you enjoyed the story.

If you'd like to receive a notification of my new releases, please join my Readers' Group at https://sherribryan.com

Details of all my books can be found on page 413, but as a preview of what's to come, here's the beginning of the next book in the series.

Secrets, Lies, and Puppy Dog Eyes – Book 2
PROLOGUE

In the staff room at Bliss Bay School, Dawn Hillier opened another exercise book and sighed at the sight of the illegible handwriting on the page.

Three times a week, she spent an hour every afternoon after school, giving extra tuition to the students who struggled with their reading and writing, but for those who'd gone for years having barely held a pen, let alone written with one, she had her work cut out.

She picked up her marking pen and put right the errors, writing encouraging comments in the margins until the white pages were hardly visible for red corrections.

They were only a week into the new school term and Dawn had already had to deal with a detention for a disobedient student, and a visit from anxious parents following their daughter's return home with a black eye after a playground game had turned a little too boisterous.

All she wanted to do was get home and curl up on the couch with her husband, and a big bowl of the stew that was bubbling away in her slow cooker.

The door creaked open and a head poked around it, its auburn hair cut in the popular pageboy style of the day.

"Oh, Sandra. You startled me," said Dawn. "I thought I was here on my own."

"I had some work to do, but I'm off home now. Will you be long?"

"I'll be leaving for the bus in about an hour, I should think, but I must finish marking these books. I'll see you tomorrow."

"I don't suppose you get to give many of these out, do you?" said Sandra, sidling over and picking up a small bag of gold stars that was on the table.

"Not as many as I'd like to, but some of the students really do try, so I always give one for a good effort."

Sandra nodded and perched on the arm of Dawn's chair. "I suppose you're off home to see that lovely husband of yours? Lucky you to have someone to go home to."

Dawn shifted uncomfortably, but managed a smile. "Yes, I am lucky." For a moment, she almost felt as though she should apologise, she felt so guilty about the awful tragedy Sandra had suffered not so long ago. Instead, she said, "Anyway, I don't mean to be rude, but I must get on with these books, or I'll still be here at midnight."

Sandra smiled, despite the rebuff. "Yes, of course. Sorry. I'll be seeing you."

The door closed with a click, leaving Dawn alone in the staff room once more. She pinched the bridge of her nose and blinked hard. Her eyes ached after poring over all those exercise books and the students' scrawl.

Forty minutes later, she finished the last book and closed it with a breath of relief.

Checking her watch, she calculated that if she caught the quarter-past seven bus, she'd be home in five minutes. She could walk, but the wind would be blowing in her face all the way and, besides, she didn't want to risk getting a blister on her heel from her new shoes.

It had been a while since she and Edmund had spent an entire, uninterrupted evening together. Since his promotion from Senior Clerk to Assistant Manager, he'd taken his job at the bank even more seriously than usual. Every day, he worked much later than he needed to make sure everything was shipshape and accounted for before he left for home.

Today, though, was one of the rare occasions he'd promised to leave work on time. Usually, Teresa and Barnaby – Edmund's children from a previous marriage – would be home at this time of the evening but tonight, Teresa was out at the cinema with some friends, and Barnaby was at a Scouts' meeting. Dawn was thrilled that she and Edmund would have the house completely to themselves for a few hours.

She'd been feeling a little low recently. Sometimes, she couldn't help it. She wanted to forget all her troubles tonight, though, and make the most of the evening.

Belting her new suede coat, and slinging her handbag over her shoulder, Dawn flicked off the staff room light and called out to the caretaker who was doing his rounds, checking that the school was empty before he locked the doors.

"Goodnight, Walter, see you in the morning."

He smiled and touched the tip of his flat cap, his russet curls poking out from underneath it. "G'night, Mrs Hillier. See you then." He stared after her as she walked off down the corridor, her handbag swinging jauntily from her shoulder.

The chunky heels of her purple suede platform shoes clunked against the pavement as she walked briskly to the bus stop. They were a little higher than she usually wore, but when she'd seen them in the shoe shop, she hadn't been able to resist them. She couldn't believe her luck when, a couple of days later, she'd seen a card in the village shop window with a Polaroid photo, advertising a nearly-new suede coat for sale, in almost the same colour. She'd called the number right away and nabbed a real bargain.

She took a tube of peppermints from her pocket as she waited for the bus, popping one into her mouth and pushing it against her cheek where it could dissolve slowly.

As she pulled up the collar of her coat against the stiff breeze, the sound of approaching footsteps made her turn.

"Hello," said Dawn, her smile dimmed by the puzzled furrow at her brow. "What are you doing here?"

Those were the last words Dawn Hillier ever spoke.

A sharp jab on the forehead, followed by another on her shoulder, pushed her off balance and she fell backwards with a scream. Her arms flailed wildly, grabbing at nothing, as she tumbled down the incline beside the road, landing with a sickening thud, and leaving a solitary shoe behind on the pavement.

"Bloody hell, Red! What did you do that for? What's wrong with you?"

"Shut up, Curly! I wasn't expecting her to fall down the hill, was I?"

They stumbled down the incline, panting and shuddering at the sight of Dawn's motionless, twisted body, its leg sticking out at a strange angle, and blood seeping from a head wound caused by the impact against a tree trunk.

"Do you think she's dead?" said Red, in a trembling voice.

"She can't be," said Curly, trying to keep calm. "She only fell a few feet. Why don't you feel for a pulse?"

Red hesitated. "Can't you do it?"

"No, I can't." Curly took a step back. "Sorry, but I'm not touching a dead body."

Red took a deep breath and leaned forward, moving Dawn's handbag out of the way and placing two fingers against the inside of her wrist. "There's nothing."

"Well, try the pulse at the side of her neck."

"Nothing there, either." Red stood up and took stock of the situation. "We'd better get out of here. If the bus comes and anyone sees us down here, they'll think we had something to do with it."

Curly's eyes opened wide. "We did have something to do with it. Well, you did, anyway."

"Yes, but what's going to happen if the police find out I pushed her? They have ways of finding out things like that, you know. I've seen it on TV. And, in any case, you'd be implicated, too, so it wouldn't just be me who'd be in the frame."

Curly gulped. "It doesn't seem right to leave her here and do nothing. She's a nice woman. We should at least tell someone."

"A nice woman?" repeated Red, with scorn. "That might be your opinion, but it certainly isn't mine. Anyway, what's the point in telling anyone? There's nothing they can do for her now, is there? I think we should just get out of here before someone sees us."

Curly's beady eyes surveyed the scene, darting this way and that as the shock began to turn to fear. "You touched her handbag when you felt her pulse, didn't you? You'd better take it and get rid of it somewhere in case you've left any fingerprints on it."

Red tugged the bag from Dawn's lifeless body, struggling against the literal dead weight. "Look, we don't tell anyone about this, okay? Not a word."

"Don't you think we... we should call an ambulance?" Curly's voice faltered.

"I just said there's no point, didn't I?" snapped Red. "She's already dead, so what would they do for her. Anyway, did you hear what I just said about keeping quiet?"

Curly nodded and took great gulps of air. Red was not a good person to get on the wrong side of. "I won't say anything, I promise, but what are we going to do now?"

"Nothing – that's what we're going to do. We're going to get out of here, find somewhere to get rid of this handbag, act normal and keep our mouths shut. Got it?" Red threw Curly a threatening glare. "We won't go back up the bank, though, in case the bus comes and someone sees us. We'll go along the low road and no one will ever know we were here."

As they ran from the scene, the sleeve of Red's jumper caught against a branch on a nearby bush, leaving behind a strand of wool, which fluttered, unnoticed, from a twig.

When they had run until they thought their lungs would burst, they stopped to get their breath.

"Oww, I've got a stitch," said Red, bending forward and breathing heavily.

Curly pointed to the snag in the jumper. "You mean you *need* a stitch to fix that hole. You must have done it when you caught your sleeve on that branch."

Red peered closely at the snag. "Damn it! Now I'll have to get rid of the handbag *and* this jumper. We can't risk going back now to check, but if I left any wool on a thorn, and someone sees this snag in my sleeve and puts two and two together, I don't want to think what might happen."

"Well, I doubt that's likely," said Curly, "but it'll probably be for the best. You don't want to take any chances, do you? Now, come on, let's find somewhere to dump that bag before someone sees us with it."

ooooooo

Dawn Hillier's body was found later that evening,

When she didn't come home, her husband, Edmund, had driven to the school to find it closed. He'd driven back home again and called all their friends, before driving to the Scouts' hall to collect Barnaby, and the cinema to find Teresa to ask if either of them knew where Dawn might be.

His children hadn't been happy to see him. Barnaby, because he lived for the time he could be away from his dad and his constant criticism, and Teresa, because she didn't appreciate being embarrassed in front of her friends: even in the gloom of the cinema, her cheeks glowed like beacons.

When they'd seen how troubled their dad was, though, Barnaby had left his Scout meeting and Teresa had left the screening of the film she'd waited so long to see, both promising to help search for their stepmother.

"How was she at school today, Teresa?" said Barnaby who, at almost eighteen, was in a different class to his sister.

"She was fine." Teresa squeezed Edmund's hand. "Don't worry, Dad, she's bound to be somewhere not far away. She's too sensible to have run off, or done anything adventurous. Like I just said, she was fine today at school. You know how she gets sometimes – she's probably gone off somewhere to be on her own for a while."

Edmund acknowledged her with a distracted smile. "I hope so, but she's never been gone so long before, and she's always found a phone box to call from to let me know she's okay. This time feels different. Don't ask me why, but—"

They were all thrown forward in their seats as he braked hard, bringing the car to a sudden, sliding stop.

"Flippin heck, Dad! I almost broke my nose on the dashboard," grumbled Barnaby. "What did you do that for?"

Edmund pointed with a shaky finger and opened the car door. "Look."

Teresa and Barnaby's eyes followed his finger, coming to rest on a solitary shoe – purple suede with a platform sole – next to the bus stop at the side of the road.

oooooooo

Dawn's death was eventually ruled as suspicious.

Originally, the police had suspected it was accidental. Based on the information given to them by her husband and stepchildren, it came to light that Dawn was unused to her new high heels, and had probably stumbled and fallen down the incline.

However, when her handbag was found to be missing, a bag snatch which had caught her off guard and pushed her off-balance was thought to be the reason for the fall.

The case took a turn, though, when the post-mortem revealed a fresh bruise just below her shoulder, indicating she'd received a significant push before she'd fallen, and the police finally changed the status of the case to suspicious.

A small strand of wool on a branch, a gold star which was stuck to Dawn's forehead, her coat, and shoes were the only potential items of evidence in the vicinity of her body.

In the absence of any suspects, the evidence was bagged, referenced, and put away in an unsolved case file.

ooooooo

The funeral was well-attended.

Dawn had been a popular member of the community and highly thought of by the majority of her students, along with every teacher in the small Bliss Bay School.

All through the service, Sandra Grayling's sniffing and wailing rose above the sermon as she leaned against her brother, Walter, for support. This was a devastating event for them both. So soon after their own family tragedy, Dawn's death was almost too much to bear.

As the coffin was lowered into the ground, Edmund Hillier stood beside the grave, his mouth set in a thin line, and the muscles in his jaw tensed as he fought not to break down. Next to him stood his son, Barnaby, his eyes puffy and bloodshot, and his daughter, Teresa, clinging to his arm, her face red and her cheeks wet with tears.

Edmund stepped forward and threw a single white rose into the grave. "I'm sorry,

Dawn," he said, before stepping back, turning on his heel and taking his children with him.

oooooooo

Three weeks after Dawn's death, a lone figure lurked by the row of lockers that lined the entire length of the wall outside the school assembly hall.

Looking around to make sure no one was watching, Curly shoved a textbook into the narrow gap behind the lockers with a gloved hand, and breathed a sigh of relief.

The note inside it was short, but it told the true events of what had happened to Dawn Hillier on the evening of her death.

Curly knew that going to the police with a full confession would have been the proper thing to do but Red would have found out and gone berserk, and Red wasn't a good person to have as an enemy.

Leaving the note was just a small gesture but it made Curly feel better. At least, this way, the truth may become known at some point in the future, and the identity of Dawn Hillier's killer would finally be revealed...

BOOKS BY SHERRI BRYAN

<u>The Charlotte Denver Cozy Mystery Series</u>

Tapas, Carrot Cake and a Corpse - Book 1
Fudge Cake, Felony and a Funeral - Book 2
Spare Ribs, Secrets and a Scandal - Book 3
Pumpkins, Peril and a Paella - Book 4
Hamburgers, Homicide and a Honeymoon -
Book 5
Crab Cakes, Killers and a Kaftan - Book 6
Mince Pies, Mistletoe and Murder - Book 7
Doughnuts, Diamonds and Dead Men - Book 8
Bread, Dead and Wed - Book 9

<u>The Bliss Bay Village Mystery Series</u>

Bodies, Baddies and a Crabby Tabby - Book - 1
Secrets, Lies and Puppy Dog Eyes - Book 2
Malice, Remorse and a Rocking Horse - Book 3
Dormice, Schemers and Misdemeanours -
Book 4
Last Words and Ladybirds – Book 5 (Coming
in 2021)

ACKNOWLEDGEMENTS

Thank you to Steve Sadler, the winner of my Name the Cat competition who suggested the name, Tabastion, for my feline character. It's a great name and one that I, and the other judges, thought best fitted the feisty, silver tabby, formerly known as Cat!

A MESSAGE FROM SHERRI

Thanks so much for showing an interest in my book. I can't tell you how much I appreciate the support.

Whilst I have tried to be accurate throughout, for dramatic purposes, my imagination may have called for actual facts and procedures to be slightly 'skewed' from time to time, and I hope this will not detract from your enjoyment of the story.

As I always say at the end of my stories, this one has been proofread and edited multiple times but, even so, there may still be the odd mistake that has slipped through. If you should come across one, my apologies. I'd be grateful if you could let me know so I can correct it.

You can get in touch by email at sherri@sherribryan.com, or contact me on my Facebook page at https://www.facebook.com/sherribryanauthor Even if you'd just like to say hello, I'd love to hear from you but please bear with me for a reply – I get quite a few emails and it may take a while for me to answer.

If you enjoy my books, please consider telling your friends or posting a short review. Word of mouth is an indie author's best friend and always very much appreciated.

With gratitude, and best wishes,
Sherri.

ABOUT SHERRI BRYAN

Sherri is also the author of The Charlotte Denver Cozy Mystery Series.

More books are on the way, as she needs a place to put all the ideas she is constantly filling notebooks with.

She lives in Spain and spends most of her time thinking up new mystery plots, and what to cook for dinner, and can most often be found writing, reading, walking, or creating something experimental in the kitchen.

Sherri Bryan

Printed in Great Britain
by Amazon

31879614R00235